THE HEARTLESS DIVINE

VARSHA RAVI

This is a work of fiction. Names, characters, places, and incidents either are the product of the author's imagination or are used fictitiously. Any resemblance to actual persons, living or dead, events, or locales is entirely coincidental.

www.varsharavi.com

ISBN 978-1-70349-390-0

November 2019
First Edition

But your anger touched them,

Brought them terror,

Left their beauty in ruins,

bodies consumed by Death.

— Patirruppattu 13,
(Translated by A.K. Ramanujan)

1
LYNE

Suri opened the door to a boy bleeding out on the pockmarked concrete, her dollar-store welcome mat crushed under him. He turned his face up—gold eyes glowing in the darkness—and shifted, struggling to find purchase on the blood-slick floor.

She had never believed in gods, even when she probably should've, and yet, faced with this, she thought, *Maybe this is a sign. Maybe—for once—I'm on the right track.*

There was a soft sound of contempt from below, and then the boy drew himself upward, swaying. A black coat, damp with rainwater, was draped loosely over his shoulders. He was bare underneath, flashes of warm brown skin visible under the blood. It streaked him from collarbone to ankle; drops touched the edges of his jaw and danced through the ends of his hair.

Abruptly, he stilled. The blood continued to splash against the floor, but the rhythm of the drops had become at once dissonant and hard-edged. One arm reached out for support and found it on the very edge of the stairwell.

He glanced up, and she knew people like him were the reason why her grandmother painted runes on the outside of her shop in wood ash, the reason why she had installed three locks on Suri's front door when she had moved out.

The boy's irises were the color of gold coins, molten and overwarm. His face was fine-boned and lovely, though oddly austere in the way of sepia photographs. In the dead of night, he looked to Suri like a bloody shred of some unfinished fairy tale.

Distantly, she could sense the fear and confusion she should've felt, the winding, plaintive urge to shut the door in his face and dial Miya. And yet, she also felt a whispering sense of truth—the kind that makes itself known only when everything else has gone to sleep.

Suri fidgeted with her sweatshirt and thought about how to arrange her words. *I don't know if you've noticed, but you're bleeding. Am I supposed to know you? Do you know what happened to my family?* Finally, she managed, "Are you okay?"

He held her gaze with the kind of careful blankness that warned of well-hidden venom, a cottonmouth that had stretched into something human-shaped. Though she was sure there was more to him than just clear, amber-eyed disregard, it was impossible to discern the depth of what lay beyond—the identity of it.

The boy stared, swaying again before stumbling forward and into her arms. Soft, labored breaths warmed the side of her neck as his arms hung loosely around hers.

Blood wet her skin—there was so *much* of it, nearly unbearable in the awe-damp silence.

Outside, a police siren wailed. She looked down at the form in her arms—bloody, warm, and slight. Slight in the way of a thin, sharp knife; slight in the way of a blossom in the first days of spring.

You could just leave him in the street, a voice whispered, still haunted by the empty glow of his eyes. But it was late, and he was bleeding to death, and she had not been raised to be malicious, only wary. It wasn't as if his venom was pointed at *her*.

And, there was always a chance he knew something about what had happened that night—a night like this one, born of blood and death and fire. He certainly held enough impossibility in his bones for the notion to be worth considering.

Suri heaved another sigh and retreated into the cramped apartment with him in tow. She pulled an arm free and dragged a throw blanket from the couch and toward the puddle in the hallway. Pinpricks of red shone through, turning the faded gray fabric a deep crimson.

The boy shuddered when she laid him down on the sofa; a brief, contained spasm. He curled into himself, fists pressed into his blood-slicked chest. He had been so still when conscious. A ragged sound escaped the corner of his mouth as she pulled his hands from his skin.

The first aid box, she thought, staring at the lukewarm blood on her hands. Then the boy exhaled brokenly, and she left to find bandages and rubbing alcohol.

Suri wasn't entirely sure what she expected to see when she peeled off the black coat he wore. More blood. A deep, gushing cut to his abdomen—a bullet wound, perhaps.

There was nothing.

Nothing visible, at the very least. She wiped off the blood; even through the terry cloth, she could feel the thick, blistering warmth of his skin. It was a miracle he hadn't died from fever alone.

The blood came away, revealing a thin, warped scar over his heart. Beneath it were the vestiges of another set of interlocking cuts, slotting together to create a star.

Tight around the scars, locked in thick, concentric bands, were three dark circles. They looked like tattoos, each one constructed out of a different set of tangled runes. They shone under the blood, glossy and uninterrupted save for flashes of brown skin in between the rune lines.

Still, there was no entry wound in sight. The blood had stopped coming, and for a moment, she wondered if it had ever really come from *him.* Nausea hollowed her. Had the young girl known she was tending to a wolf? Had she cared?

Suri shut her eyes and scolded herself. It didn't matter whether he was a boy or a wolf or a ghost. Even if he wasn't bleeding, he was still feverish. She brushed her hand against his forehead as she set a damp towel on it and winced from the abrupt, angry heat.

His breaths had begun to even out. The area around the faded scar was an angry orange gold; it held a soft, burnished glow where she'd expected to see the warmth of a fading bruise.

She sat back on her heels and stared at him. The boy clearly wasn't from here, but what defined *here* was still debatable. The smart choice would've been to go to the police and drop him on the steps like a bag of potatoes, even though she had never trusted the Lyne Police Department and probably never would. The smarter choice would've been to go to her grandmother, but it had been only a week since the academic year had started and Suri wasn't sure if she wanted to be subjected to a set of disappointed lectures this early on into her newfound freedom. It certainly wasn't life or death, not anymore. She comforted herself with the knowledge that the boy was no longer dying.

The kitchen clock flashed a fluorescent reminder that it was nearing four. She dragged herself to her feet, wiping bloodstained hands on her pajama pants. *You should've left him,* she thought sullenly. Even if he ended up proving useful, she couldn't help but think that he would likely be more trouble than he was worth.

Suri tilted her head up to the ceiling and scanned the cracking plaster. *If any of the gods are listening,* she thought, *please add this to my cosmic karma credit.*

She tossed the soiled throw in the trash and cleaned the hallway, falling asleep a little before dawn. Curled on the carpet at the foot of the sofa, she was so close to the boy that she could hear his rough, ragged breathing between nightmares. Above, the gods listened, and they mourned.

Kiran woke with a knife to his neck, held with enough pressure that it had begun to draw blood. It trembled against his skin, the edge shifting from side to side. He thought absentmindedly that whoever was holding it had very little experience with knives.

Pain yawned through his body as feeling came back into his limbs. Thin, searing blood pooled at the crook of his throat but nowhere else—he'd been cleaned. And tied up. He snapped his wrists in their bonds once briefly, to test the integrity of them. His heart sank. He'd have to get the knife away from his throat before he could wriggle out of these. Perhaps if he were stronger, it would have been a simple matter of pressure and flame. But he wasn't—he reckoned that was how he'd gotten restrained in the first place.

He shifted, and felt the knife digging into his skin as his captor made a sharp sound of surprise.

"Could you take off the blindfold now?" he asked evenly, voice catching on the last word.

"What?" It was a girl, maybe his age. Fear had cut away at her consonants and pressed her vowels up against them.

"The blindfold," he repeated, a rasp more than anything. He didn't see why she'd taken the time to clean off all his blood if she'd meant to cut him again.

"Oh," she said. The pressure of the knife eased, the cotton falling to his collarbone. Blood began to dampen it.

"Thanks," he exhaled, and flicked his eyes up. The room was dimly lit, strewn with haphazard piles of dog-eared novels and cleanly highlighted papers. To his right was a compact table and a kitchenette, neatly slid between the door and a hallway that led away into darkness. To his left lay a sliding glass door, and the city beyond.

His captor was seated on the couch in front of him, hands folded anxiously in her lap. Dark circles ringed light brown eyes, and dried blood spattered her sweatshirt and pajama pants. They had cartoon clouds on them, bright white with curved black mouths.

When she spoke, it took a few seconds for him to realize her words were directed toward *him.*

"Who are you?"

He drew in a long breath, but before he could respond, she'd clenched her hands into fists and added, "Where are you from? Why are you here? Did you know my parents? Do you know what happened to them? Why was there so much blood?"

The last word hung in the air, echoing. The questions held an imperative edge to them, him the genie, this odd, foreign world his lamp. He coughed a laugh and tilted his head down, indicating his neck. "I'm not sure the past tense is necessary."

The girl scowled and grudgingly slid off the couch. Her hair was cut in a choppy, dark bob, and strands fell away from her face when she stood. In the faint lamplight, her features were barely discernible but achingly familiar. A thoughtless, painful familiarity, recognition written into every line of his heart.

I know you, he thought. But his memory was a simple blackness, and he wasn't hopeful about what he'd find if he tried to look in.

She bent toward him hesitantly, unknotting the blindfold and dabbing it against the shallow cut on his throat before tossing it on the table. His coat was neatly folded beside it; he saw it and felt cold with relief. Glancing down at himself, he found a loose T-shirt, with the words *Splashy Splashy Water Park!* lettered across it in bright blue.

A human, taking the time to tend to him. Even if they somehow knew each other—unlikely in this lifetime, considering her questions—it was unsettling. It had been a very long time since someone had thought to take care of him.

The girl was back on the couch, tilted forward with a trembling kind of anticipation, all fear and daring and mortal curiosity. Her kitchen knife lay abandoned beside her. It was ichor-slick, but she hadn't seemed to notice the blood's pallor. Shock had most likely rendered that irrelevant.

"So," she started, clearing her throat. A faint ache rolled through him, flames reigniting in his veins. Slowly, though. Too slowly for it to be natural. "Who are you?"

Who are you? he thought. Someone old, someone sad. His memory was a gaping chasm, negative space nudged into something that held form. He remembered *what* he was, but he doubted she would believe him. Kiran lifted his shoulders in a shrug. "I don't know."

She narrowed her eyes. "You don't *know*?"

Kiran nodded. "I don't remember anything, besides my name. Nor how I ended up in your apartment, so I apologize if I did anything untoward."

The girl's mouth twisted in something that resembled scorn. "Were you drunk?"

"I don't drink," he informed her. *At least not mortal liquor.* "And I haven't touched alcohol in years. You would have smelled it when you cleaned me up." It was an odd kind of lie—he had not touched alcohol in years because he had not been *here* in years.

Her expression softened imperceptibly. "Then you must have amnesia." She hesitated a moment, and then asked, "You don't remember *anything*?"

"Just my name," he said. "Not much else. Why?"

"Nothing," she said, faintly miserable in a way that betrayed that it was, in fact, something. Despite himself, he felt a pang of remorse. She turned away, hair shadowing her face. "Why me, though? Why this apartment? It's up five flights of stairs."

"If I remember, I'll be sure to let you know," he replied. Already, details were beginning to return—dry, useless things, like his age and the color of the sky the day he'd last died. "May I leave now?"

She snorted in derision. "You were bleeding out in my hallway last night with what *should* have been a fatal fever, and now you're saying you have amnesia. I'm taking you to the hospital to see a doctor."

"What?" he said, mildly alarmed. "No. No need for a hospital. Wouldn't mind getting out of the ropes, though."

She ignored him. "Give me one good reason why I shouldn't take you to the hospital right now."

My blood is the color and consistency of champagne. I have been running a fever for the past seventeen hundred years. He opened his eyes; she was still staring at him, inexorable. He nodded at the coat. "I don't have money on me. I won't be able to pay for it."

"Family?"

Kiran shook his head, and she pursed her lips.

"I'll pay for you, then."

Nausea was thick and heavy in his stomach. *Some people,* he thought, *were just too nice.* Kindness got you nowhere in life—at the end of the day, everyone ended up in the earth all the same, whether it was a knife to the front or a knife to the back. And out of all those in the world, mortal and immortal and everything in between, it was ironic that she was being kind to him. *Wrong god,* he wanted to tell her. Instead, he leaned back against the chair. The grain was rough against his skin where the shirt slipped down. "What's your name?"

Her brows drew together. "Suri."

Once again, he felt that odd clench in his heart, phantom pains that traced fault lines. "Suri, I'm thankful that you didn't just let me die in your corridor last night. I really am. And I'm sorry that I can't be of more help. But I won't go to the hospital—I can't pay, and I don't want you to." He forced a smile, but he wasn't good at those, so he could not be entirely sure of its strength. "Besides, I'm sure my memory will return soon enough. And then you would have wasted your money for nothing."

Instead of answering, she rose. As she began to undo the knots tying his wrists together, she said, "Then you can stay here. I can take the couch, and you can take the bed."

The rope fell from his fingers, and he turned around in the chair to meet her gaze. This close, she smelled like blood and citrus blossoms. Her expression was pinched in a way he recognized from people he could not remember—there was no winning this conversation. He'd just have to stay for a few days, and leave when she wasn't around to notice.

Kiran pointed at himself and said, "Sofa."

The skin around her eyes creased in a way that belied the hard set of her mouth. "Fine. It smells like blood, anyway."

Suri crossed to stand on the other side of the couch. She hung a patchwork blanket over the edge, and turned to him, patting it. "You should get some rest. Give your brain time to restart."

"What time is it?" he asked, yawning. Sleep sounded like the best idea he'd heard since he'd been reborn—already, his limbs were leaden, his eyelids heavy. And yet, a faint sense of discomfort followed.

"Two in the afternoon," she said, switching off a lamp beside the kitchenette. "Sleep well."

Kiran stayed in Suri's apartment for two days and two nights. On the third morning, he woke up with the memories of his mortal life. And then, he left.

The boy was a ghost in the house. For the most part, he seemed content to sleep through the days, his coat draped over him on the couch. If Suri put food in front of him, he ate it—if not, he never asked. It had been two days since he'd first woken, and she still didn't know his name.

Two days, and she was still no closer to understanding him.

Part of her wanted to just chalk his appearance up to coincidence—say he was just some hedonistic foreigner who'd lost himself on a trip and his memory in the process. Everything about that strange, unsettling night was explainable if she took it apart for long enough—he could've gotten in a fight, he could've been wearing contacts, he could've hit his head. He could've been a fugitive, for all of his discomfort with hospitals, but she suspected he was just a runaway.

But, for the most part, she didn't have time to think about him. Her grandmother had allowed her to move out on the sole condition that she continued to help out with the shop. Running errands didn't mean she forgot about him, though—her gaze would catch on the golden statuettes of gods that the Enesmati grocery mart's employees lined up along the edge of the counter, and her thoughts would inevitably flit back to those feverish eyes.

Suri considered asking a couple of the shop owners for advice about the boy—he certainly looked Enesmati—but figured the information would get back to her grandmother soon enough, and then it would be an interrogation and a lecture on letting bloody strangers in after dark.

In the afternoons, she had classes at the university. It had been her mother's alma mater, and sometimes she would find herself tracing foreign buildings and worn footpaths, wondering if her mother had walked the same ones. Recently, though, all that warmth and pain had faded, and she found herself tuning out lecture after lecture, caught in the memory of that night. Meanwhile, Dai doodled small black blossoms on her wrist, and Aza scrawled song lyrics in the back of her notebook, both of them bickering over which twin was oldest, and who would pay for dinner.

After classes, she either went straight home—uneventful, as the boy usually only woke up for small intervals that consisted of making the necessary preparations to go back to sleep later on—or walked over to Beanzz, the coffee shop where she worked, a small, hooded place that always smelled of potpourri and cigarette smoke.

Suri was at Beanzzz when she started feeling the chest pains. At first, they didn't really bother her—they were sharp, shooting pains that faded for moments at a time. She was taking a pair of cappuccinos over to a couple beside the window when the pain swelled jaggedly. She lurched to the side, managing to put down the coffee on a nearby table before forcing herself down into a seat. Agony ripped through her, taking away her capacity to breathe, to speak. She distantly registered her coworker handing off the platter to the couple staring over at her.

Tarak knelt beside her and placed his hand over hers. Concern twisted his expression. "Should I call your grandmother? The police?"

She almost said yes, if only to stop the pain—to give it a reason. But something told her that neither choice would do those things, so she simply shook her head, tried to even her breathing. "It's fine. I'm fine now. I think I'll just have to leave early."

He nodded. "Yeah, of course. I'll let Rick know what happened."

Outside, cold, icy rain had begun to come down. It could only be described as sleet in early September. Another abnormality in a week of strange terror.

Suri hadn't even brought a coat—the forecast had assured a clear, sunny day, and she'd had no reason to assume it would be anything otherwise—so she hunched her shoulders and set off in the direction of the sharp, dragging pain.

By the time she found him, the pain had evened out to a faded, sleet-numb ache. Tolson Park was on the residential outskirts of Lyne, where the apartments met old shopfronts and houses built decades ago. It was a small enough park, dotted with oak trees and centered around a limp artificial lake, but the empty horizon made it look larger than life. It was damp and cold, and right now it looked decidedly pathetic. It was empty of all the usual dogwalkers and small children, empty save for a few families of ducks and the boy.

He was crouched beside the ring of trees that surrounded the lake, leaning unsteadily against the bark of an old oak.

When Suri finally spoke, her voice was pitched high, a little hysterical from anger. "What are you doing?"

The boy glanced up, unsurprised to see her. Rain streaked his cheeks like tears, tracing the curve of his faint smile. He held up his fist, revealing cupped breadcrumbs. "Feeding the ducks."

She gestured wildly at the sleet, at the cold. She couldn't fully parse her own anger, but figured it had to do with his absolute lack of it, his flippant amusement in the face of inevitable hypothermia. "You could *die.*"

"Really can't," he said blithely, but he was more rainwater than flesh at this point, so his words didn't hold much weight. Suri tilted her head up, partly in exasperation and partly to look away—he was holding her gaze with an odd, inscrutable intensity.

Finally, she exhaled. "Why are you even out here? And *don't* say you came to feed the ducks."

He cocked his head, the amusement dissipating from his expression. "Suri, you came because of the pain. Right?" When she nodded hesitantly, he tossed the handful of breadcrumbs to the side—the ducks leapt toward them—and cleanly ripped his shirt off, revealing rain-damp skin and blood leaking from cuts like broken glass.

She knelt beside him, drawn by the strange magic of the blood. The boy simply continued to watch her, still as she lifted a hand and traced the three black marks on his skin. A single cut ringed every tattoo, dripping thin, clear, golden liquid down his chest.

This close, he was still fever-warm, the cold sleet sliding down his skin uselessly. His voice was low and quick, nearly secretive. "I meant to leave today. Don't ask why, it's no longer important. I'm thankful for your help, but I could not stay forever. Regardless, I started walking around in this city of yours—" he nodded toward the gray skies, the metal and rain. "And I only made it as far as here, the edge of this tree. Then the pain started, and the cuts began to bleed, and it did not cease nor slow, not until you got here."

She looked up at him, but there was no trace of humor in his expression. Beside them, the ducks had finished eating the breadcrumbs, and then they had gone, leaving them alone in this glittering rain-soaked world, where blood ran gold and escape was impossible without agony.

Suri sat back on her heels. "I'm taking you to see my grandmother."

Surprisingly, he didn't immediately protest. Then his mouth twisted, a ghost of irony flickering on his face. "Is she a doctor?"

"No," she said, pulling herself to her feet and extending a hand. "She's a seer. And she's probably the only person in the city who knows how to get your memories back."

The boy pulled the dress shirt back on and followed Suri silently through the streets. They made an odd pair, her shivering and pulling her soggy sweater closer to her chest, and him soaked yet untouched by the cold.

The few times she did look over, he was still studying her face, examining it with a strange intensity. As if questioning why, out of everyone in the city, *they'd* gotten stuck together. She couldn't help but feel the same, and yet—a small part of her didn't mind, still wondering if this was a sign he *was* connected to their deaths in some strange way.

By the time they made it to the shop, it was already nearly seven, and the sign hanging on the door had been turned around, the colorful, crooked letters of an eight-year-old spelling out *CLOSED.* Suri peered through the rain-streaked glass and saw a flicker of light in the corner. Halfway through the knock, a series of five rhythmic sequences she'd worked out with her grandmother when she was eleven, the door swung open.

Rana Gayathri was old as stone, and built just as sturdily. She was a few inches shorter than Suri, with a coil of silver-gray hair tied up in a braided bun and almond-brown skin lined with age and warmth. Usually. Right now, she was glaring up at Suri, her arms folded over her embroidered tunic. Then her gaze slid sideways to the boy. He'd been catching raindrops in the palm of his hand, observing the splash and the mist of them, but at the movement, he glanced up and waved cheerily at her grandmother. Her expression darkened, and she glared at Suri again before nodding toward the shop. "You'd better come in."

They followed her in, dripping on the wet hardwood as she painstakingly lit the candles that sat on every surface. After lighting the last one—a carved, black candle Suri had gotten her for her seventy-fifth birthday a few months prior—she blew out the match and left it on the table next to the shadowed, bead-strung archway that led into the back room. She then turned the full force of her disapproval on both of them, which meant she was turning it on Suri—the boy wasn't paying attention as he sat fingering the soft, serrated leaves of a holy basil sapling beside the sleet-frosted window.

"You," she said, jerking her head toward him. The boy glanced up, pointing delicately at himself. She scowled. "Yes, you. Why are you around my granddaughter?"

"You know each other?" Suri asked uneasily.

The boy spoke before she could, gently stroking the plant. "I'd reckon she can tell *what* I am, judging from the runes on the walls."

What he was, as if it was something strange. As if he wasn't human.

Her grandmother refused to look away, but her mouth twitched in a frown. "What do you go by, down here?"

A crooked smile split his face. "Call me Kiran."

"He showed up at my door the other night," Suri cut in, spreading her hands in explanation. She suspected the two of them would either get along rather well or loathe each other, and things weren't looking good so far. "Bloody. Half-dead, burning up with fever."

"And you let him *in*?"

"He was *dying, anda,*" she emphasized. "I couldn't just leave him."

"You should've," she said, sharp with horror. She glared over at him. "You should've told her to leave you."

"I lost consciousness," he said. "Also, I've lost my memory, so I'm unsure why I was at her door in the first place. And on top of that—" he pulled the lapel of his shirt to the side, and even in the dim firelight, the three bleeding tattoos stood out in stark relief. "There are these."

Her grandmother didn't speak for a moment, and when Suri glanced back at her, her expression was set with an odd, foreign dread. Outside, sleet lashed against the windows, a thudding, arrhythmic beat. Finally, she shook her head in an exasperated kind of resignation and then jerked her head toward the back room. "Come with me." Suri stepped forward, but her grandmother shook her head. "Not you, him. The godling."

The boy—Kiran—raised his eyebrows, but followed her nonetheless. The beaded curtain shimmered and shook behind them, leaving Suri in the shop alone. *Godling,* she'd said, and he hadn't flinched, hadn't looked surprised. Suri felt a little sick to her stomach; she'd asked the gods for a sign, and they'd left one on her doorstep, gift-wrapped in ichor and foreign blood.

They returned a good half-hour later, after Suri had gotten antsy and swept the entire place clean and reorganized the bookshelf alphabetically. She'd changed into old pajamas, and straightened the blanket around her shoulders when she saw her grandmother's expression. She fixed Suri with a sharp glance, but she didn't look angry. Mostly, she still looked a little discomfited, a little unsteadied.

"What is it?" Suri asked. The god had wandered back to the holy basil plant. "Is he okay?"

Her grandmother heaved a faintly frustrated sigh, and joined her at the table where she did the majority of her readings. The tablecloth was dark blue, dotted with silvery-white constellations that shone in the firelight. "Long story short, no. You really should not have let him in, *muru.*"

Suri bristled. "He wouldn't have been okay either way. At least he's no longer bleeding outside of someone's apartment. What happened to him?"

Kiran turned from the plant, the shirt open on his shoulders. He pointed first to the outer circle on his skin, then to the middle one, then finally to the center ring. "Your *anda* recognizes them."

"*Sankhili,*" she said distastefully. "Chains, seals. It's dark magic, bad magic. Someone must have marked him a while ago. The first one binds his memory, the second his power, the third his soul. It's meant to tether him to you."

Suri frowned. "I don't have them, though."

She shook her head. "You don't need to. Your friend here, only with that kind of magic could they fully restrain him. Since you are human, his tether works to bind you, as well. They will fade, but it will take time. Until then, he will have to stay."

Only with that kind of magic. Not only did magic exist, it existed in slender, scarred boys who looked to be her age. She glanced back at him, disbelieving. "So he's a god? Of what?"

"Oh, don't tell her, Rana," he said pleasantly, smiling over at her. Since when was he on a first name basis with her *grandmother?* "I want to hear what she guesses."

"Cruel," she scolded, but she didn't look too angry with him. Suri felt a little like her life was imploding around her—she had tied up a god and held him at knifepoint and now her grandmother was seconds from *adopting* him, and no one would tell her what he was a god of, and gods were *real* and *magic was real,* and—

"Suri," her grandmother said steadily. "Since he's tethered to you, he'll have to stay with you for the time being, no matter how much I dislike it. Is that okay with you? If it isn't, I'm fully prepared to let you two move back into the attic back here—"

Except the attic was the size of a cupboard, and Suri's old room had been renovated into a meditation room, and no matter how much Suri's head felt like a watermelon, this was reality. And reality meant that, practically, he had to stay with her. She drew in a long breath. "No, no, it's fine. He can stay with me. For how long?"

"As long as it takes for the innermost *sankhili* to fully break," Kiran cut in, nearly apologetic. "The rest I can do without, but that one will take the longest, I think. The bright side is that as it fades, we'll be able to go further and further from one another without as much pain." He offered them both a grin, candlelight lining the sharp planes of his face. "Don't worry too much, Rana. I'll play by the rules, keep an eye on her."

"You'd better," she said firmly, but it was more out of habit than out of true threat. In the firelight, she looked aged beyond words, concerned in a way Suri had never seen her.

"I'll be fine," Suri repeated, reaching out a hand and putting it over hers. She looked unconvinced, but simply sighed and looked away.

"Your friend will be working at the shop to pay for his board," she added, nodding around her. "Even soul-bound, he'll be able to help out with a few of the chores you usually do."

They worked out the logistics of the agreement for a little bit longer, and as the sun went down outside, the sleet left with it. Before they left, Suri's grandmother reached out and picked up the holy basil sapling Kiran had been examining and handed it to him. He raised his eyebrows but said nothing.

"For good luck," she explained. "You seem to like it, and it seems to like you, too. Take care of it for me."

They made their way back to her apartment in the damp fluorescent night, his arms wrapped around the sapling and his shirt still inexplicably open. Still, he didn't seem cold.

"You're really a god," she said, but it came out like a question.

He glanced sideways at her, golden eyes glittering in the dark. It was eerier when the sun went down, the jagged glow of them so starkly inhuman. His easy warmth in the shop had disappeared, leaving his expression utterly unreadable. Eventually, he simply said, "Yes."

"Like the statues in the temples," she continued, unable to stop. "Like the drawings on the talismans. An Enesmati god."

He nodded, surprisingly indulgent, and her breath caught. "Which one are you?"

Suri had never bothered to learn her gods—even growing up with a seer, she hadn't found it relevant. She was a born atheist, a cynic from the moment of her family's death. The notion of gods, of immortal, kindly beings meant to guide and protect them, hadn't ever sat well with her. But now that she was confronted with one, she tried to scrounge up what little knowledge she could recall.

There was a goddess of the sky, and one of the earth, and one of the ocean, and beyond that she could remember nothing. Kiran didn't look interested in answering, either, but finally, he said lightly, "The hot one."

She made a rude gesture, a kneejerk reaction that she immediately regretted. What if he *smote* her? Did gods still smite people?

Instead, his mouth curved in a faint smile, and he held out his free hand. "I truly feel bad for inconveniencing you and your grandmother, so I will give you a hint—it does not define me, but it may lend a little bit of context."

A ball of fire sparked to life in his palm, trembling and gold. She leaned close enough that it was warm against her cheeks, unbearably bright, and watched it burn, watched it breathe. It was real, true fire, borne from oxygen and divinity. It was impossible. It *should* have been impossible.

"God of fire," she said, when she'd meant to say, *what the hell?*

He shook his head, curling his fingers and extinguishing the flame. "Close, but not quite. Fire is something I have control over, but it is not who I am. Call me cruel, but I'd still like to see you guess."

Without the fire, without the sunlight, he seemed carved from shadow and smoke. It made a little sense that he was a god—he was beautiful and young, but he did not look *youthful.* There was a sense of divinity in his gaze, a faint chill.

They turned onto another street and walked down the pavement to the front of Suri's apartment complex. "Who would want to hurt you?"

"Pardon?"

"Why would someone bind you?" she asked, following him up the stairs. "The *sankhili,* I mean. Who would want to get rid of your power?" *And why would they bind you to me?*

Kiran tapped his temple. "An old enemy, I'd suppose. Clearly, I can't remember who, but they must have marked me before my last death."

"Your last death?" she asked, struggling to hold his gaze as she pulled her keys out of her soaked book bag. "I thought gods didn't die."

"We do, same as humans," he affirmed, waiting for her to unlock the door and then ducking into the warm, dry apartment. "It's a little harder to kill us, though. And you all have a little more freedom in when and how often and whether you want to reincarnate; for us, it's usually more about how long we have until we're needed in the mortal world. Currently," he said, nodding down at himself, "I'm probably on sick leave."

The phrasing made her smile a little, and so did the sentiment, the idea that one day her family would return and have a chance at a kinder, more peaceful life than the one they'd left. She looked away, then jerked her head toward the sliding doors. "Come with me. You can put the plant out there."

So he followed her out onto the balcony, the waning moon casting the piteous garden in a milky glow. His expression was oddly grave, drawn and pale. He knelt beside the jasmine flowers and set the sapling down beside him before taking a blossom between his index finger and thumb. He held it with an odd gentleness, enraptured, before glancing up at her. As if by explanation, he said, "I used to have a garden a little like this. Is this yours?"

She lowered herself to the cement and sat beside him, crossing her legs. "Yeah, my grandmother helped me plant it when I moved out. The jasmine is my favorite, too."

He shook his head slightly, in disbelief or dissuasion. Dropping the blossom, he took the sapling into his hands again. "I used to know someone who loved jasmine."

"I thought you had amnesia," she said, raising her eyebrows.

Kiran ran the pad of his thumb against the edge of the sharp, sweet leaves. "I've remembered my mortal life. I assume the memories of what came after pose more of a danger to whoever bound me."

"You were human?" she couldn't keep the surprise out of her voice. He glanced up, amusement and something sharper mingling in his gaze.

"I was, for a bit," he replied, oddly remote. "I'll tell you the story, one day. For now, we should get this planted. I'm not entirely sure I remember how."

And yet, strangely, he did remember. Every single movement came to him with such swift, unwavering precision; Suri was reminded of what her grandmother had said when she had given him the plant, about it taking a liking to him.

"God of tulasi?" she ventured hopefully when he'd finished and leaned back on his heels. "God of plants? Planting? Agriculture?"

"You're insulting several different gods right now," he said, reaching his hands up to scrub at his face. They left streaks of dark soil on his cheeks, and it made him look a little more human. After a moment, he spoke, his eyes still fluttered shut. "You should sleep, Suri."

"Is this because you told my grandmother you'd take care of me?" she asked without heat, already beginning to straighten up. A contradictory part of her wanted to stay to spite him, but she *was* tired, and she had an exam the following day.

"It has nothing to do with what I told Rana," he reassured her. "It's late, and you're tired. Wouldn't want you to faceplant into the soil, now would we?"

Suri made a rude gesture at him, and he smiled without opening his eyes. She moved to return to the apartment, then glanced back. For a single, oddly indulgent moment, she watched him trace the night sky above with closed eyes, and then she shut the screen door behind her.

Judging from how little Kiran knew about pop culture and modern history, Suri estimated that he hadn't been in the mortal world for a while, at least a century or two. But he picked it all up quickly enough.

Even though he knew functionally how most of the machines in the apartment worked, that didn't stop him from sticking his head in her room late at night and informing her he'd broken the "hot box gadget" again. It got to the point where—after breaking the microwave, dishwasher, and communal washing machine—she forbade him from touching any of them if she wasn't in the apartment. The mere thought of the damage he'd unleash in a department store served as endless nightmare fodder.

Fortunately, Kiran seemed disinterested in the outside world. Apart from spending the mornings at her grandmother's shop, dressed in lurid, clashing outfits from her closet, he was content to burn through her collection of old books: classics she'd inherited from her grandmother, dry nonfiction that had belonged to her parents, and worn nursery tales her brothers had read before they'd gotten their brains splattered on asphalt eighteen years prior.

Oddly enough, he had a morbid fascination with reality television. Most days, she came home to him curled up on the couch with a bowl of stale popcorn watching one of those elimination shows, where people fall in love and promptly fall out of love and it's all tallied and held out for the world to judge.

She'd dared to ask him why he found them so interesting once, and he'd ripped a piece of popcorn apart until it was butter and shreds. "Why do they make the shows? Because they're entertaining."

And she knew he found them entertaining for an entirely different set of reasons than the rest of the world did, saw it in the line of his smile, tilted sideways like humanity itself was a joke only he was privy to. But she hadn't said it, hadn't needed to.

Part of her inherently resented him. Even if he hadn't been alive when her family had died, he represented everyone who had, all the gods who had cast their gazes upon slowing hearts and bloody skin and deemed them insignificant.

Another smaller, crueler part of her simply sought to understand him, a mortal ascended. She wondered if his heart was painted in shades of gold and sable, whether she could open him up and find blood that had once run red crystallized into glittering jewels of divinity.

But she never asked, and he never explained the miracle of his soul. They fell into a kind of routine that way—rain-soaked early autumn days went by and life passed, untouched and viscous around them. And then he stopped sleeping, and the stories began.

The first time, she'd thought she'd been lost in a nightmare of her own, that something horrible had happened and once again, she hadn't noticed until it was too late. But she was laying on her bed, heartbeat rapid and lips pressed tight.

When she padded into the living room, he was leaned absently against the side of the television stand. There was a careful neutrality in his expression, and yet it had been hastily made—even from this far, she could see the worn, jagged edges of it. An old, familiar mask breathed into new life.

"I forgot," he whispered, the timbre of his voice low and rough. He stared at the empty, mussed couch as if it held nightmares.

"Forgot what?" she asked warily, stepping forward until she was beside the table.

Kiran turned dark gold eyes on her, haunted and heedless and not quite human. "That I don't sleep."

She waited for him to explain, but he didn't. He just exhaled and tilted his head back, languorous and trembling. The silence stretched and tangled between them, and then he said, "I apologize for waking you, Suri. You can go back to bed now."

"And what will you do?" she pressed, pushing herself onto the table and letting her legs dangle over the side. "Try to go back to sleep? Watch reruns of old sitcoms?"

He spoke without looking at her, soft and amused. "I suppose so. Maybe I'll watch old seasons of *Heartbreak Hotel*."

But he wouldn't, she knew—he'd watch television, and the words would go straight through him and the nightmares would stay, would echo through bone and blood. They never left, even if she was too afraid to close her eyes. She'd seen it all, felt it all, and even if he didn't remember who he was supposed to be, she knew he remembered this, too. It was muscle memory, knowledge that seared and scarred.

So she just slid off the table and padded over to the couch, creased where he'd screamed awake. It smelled a little like him, smoke and soil. She curled into the abandoned blankets. "Tell me a story."

The corner of his mouth quirked to the side, but he joined her, leaning back against the opposite arm of the couch. In superhero pajama pants and a hand-me-down sweatshirt, he looked boyish and kind, ironic when you considered he was neither. "Why?"

"You owe me one," she said simply, tugging the fleece around herself. "And I like stories. You must know a lot, having lived as long as you have."

He grinned crookedly. "Are you calling me old?"

"Maybe," she replied, returning the grin despite herself.

Kiran wrapped his arms around his knees, brows drawn together in concentration. After a few minutes, he tilted his head up, faintly triumphant. "I think you'll like this one. It's a bit long, though."

"Really?" she challenged, the word already a little fuzzy with sleep.

"Yes," he said. That odd, bright spark had not left his expression, though now Suri couldn't help but wonder at it, how it looked less and less like triumph with every passing moment. "It's about princes and princesses and love and death, like all the best stories are."

"Promise I'll like it?" she asked, head dipping forward with fatigue even as she struggled to stay awake.

"Swear on Idhrishti's grave," he said softly, amused even though the phrase meant nothing to her. And then he leaned forward and brushed the hair away from her face, close enough that when he began to speak, she could feel the warm breath on her cheeks. "A long time ago, in a faraway land, there was a princess, and she was afraid of blood."

2
ENESMAT

It didn't take long before the nausea set in.

Suri accepted a glass of palm wine from the waiter, offering an amiable smile. Without meeting her gaze, they slid away to accommodate the next guest. *Hehyava.* The word followed her like a ghost even here, to the edges of the empire.

It was a cruel sort of name for a princess, but one that held a certain sort of awe to it, a certain measure of respect. Strange, considering she knew the people saw her with neither.

This was a lesser state function, some celebration of a new conquest or a new marriage, and she usually would not have been expected to attend. She was exempted from most functions, even ones in the capital; she knew the glances the other guests were surreptitiously throwing toward her were less about parsing her demeanor and more curiosity. *Who will die here tonight?*

The doors swung open, and the servants beside the door announced the newcomer's formal title to a room of people who cared little and offered nothing but mild applause. She took a sip of her wine, acrid and too sharp, and left it on the imported oak table beside her, leaning forward to consider her mark.

The deputy governor was a young man in his mid-twenties, ideal for his position—he had been born into a noble family and followed directions without curiosity or defiance. It had made him arrogant and careless, and after the applause faded, he strode into the room with the self-assured insolence that ignorance bred and bloomed.

Hehyava. Reaper.

Suri pushed off the edge of the table and snagged two more glasses of wine off a passing tray. She handed one to the man and took one for herself, smiling coyly. He glanced around, wary—this late, he must have heard the rumors of her presence, the empire's illustrious blade—but whatever he'd thought to look for, he had not found it. There were no tall, shadowed figures cut in imposing shades of gold and blue, smelling of blood and iron. There were no scythes to fear, no scarred faces and cut lips to run from.

There was only her. Hesitantly, he smiled back.

A soft life had so clearly rotted the wisdom from his mind, if it had been there to begin with. She plied him with a few more drinks and he accepted them, and when she suggested they leave for some fresh air, he agreed laconically, eyes glinting dark.

As she'd expected, he didn't take her home, to the grand, sprawling house the deputy governor shared with the viceroy of the border province. He led her out toward the outskirts of the city, toward the ports and the sea and the festivals. The air smelled of spices and brine, and for a moment, she felt faintly homesick. The moment passed, and she followed him down uneven, dimly lit streets toward an inn set on the water.

Sahet was a border city; it skirted the northern edges of the empire, where the lowlands of occupied Eryan land—the kingdom had been cut down to half its old size in the previous war—met the jungles that separated the Najan Empire from the southeast parts of the continent. The empire stretched from the Sahen border across toward Dauri, and then swung down toward the rest of the peninsula. There were a few kingdoms that hadn't yet fully surrendered, giving up slices of land with every new war, but the rest of the world recognized their grip on the peninsula.

Here in the provinces, they worshipped the old gods, built towering, beautiful temples out of marble and crushed pigments, and celebrated their exploits with blossoms and spilt holy water. It was one of those celebrations tonight, and the streets were full of peasants wrapped in dyed cotton and garlands of tied flowers. The procession continued down the avenue, incense-soaked and incense-sweet, as they sang hymns and held up a jewel-encrusted palanquin, carrying a marble statuette decorated in silks.

"The birth of Kazha," the deputy governor explained, as they skirted around the procession, his soft hands encircling her wrists. Her skirts, beaded and reflective in the faint light, sagged with the weight as they stepped from stone to stone. There was a distasteful edge to his voice when he spoke, harsh and derisive. He was Ashanth-born and Ashanth-raised, and the coarse rituals of peasants must have seemed barbaric to him. "They have been celebrating it for the greater part of the day, but this is only the beginning."

She feigned surprise, even though she'd already attended. Her parents often sent her on jobs during the festival week, if only because the fervor and joy adeptly hid the shock that followed death. "Kazha?"

His features softened at her ignorance—how childlike she must seem to him, a girl of seventeen years swaddled in the patterned silks of the capital. She toyed with the edge of her sash, flightless birds embroidered in gold thread across the edges. "The Enesmati mother goddess, patron of Erya. You should not worry too much. Even though she serves savages, she is a kind goddess, and so the revels are gentle, too. The southerners of Athri serve Avya, and I've heard he bids them to bleed."

Suri let her breath catch in shock and horror, and he laughed at that show of vulnerability. His humor shielded him completely from the truth, just as clouds thickened and smoothed across the glow of the moon until the night sky above them was black as pitch. He led her toward the inn, greeting the innkeeper and then taking her up the stairs toward his room. This was done in flagrant disregard of the rules of Najan courting, and if anyone had seen them, they'd have turned up their noses, revolted by the wild, heedless love of youths. But the innkeeper had spared them little more than a cursory glance, and the deputy governor was drunk to the point of uselessness, fingers dipped in the Lethe, and so no one saw them, and no one would remember.

The room was sparsely decorated, nothing more than a basin of water, a coarse mast-wood trunk, and a cot beside the window. This was where he took all his lady loves, she guessed, after nights in taverns and those so-called barbaric festivals. To snag a pretty, flushed noble girl from the capital—it was an added bonus, but it would be no change from the routine, not for him.

Even before the door slammed shut behind her, he pushed her up against it, presumptuous in the way men of his kind often were. Hungry, desirous, indolent, like young gods who believed the world twisted and bent to their whims.

His fingers caught on the edges of her beaded bodice, on rhinestones and glittering golden thread. It was tight against her skin, made in the Najan fashion so it cut off above her midriff, allowing her silk sash to wrap around her waist. His other hand traced down her side toward the knot of her sash.

She counted the beats of silence before the celebration in the streets below came to a crescendo, and the hymns shattered the night-dark quiet. His fingers worked diligently to undo the knot, and she slid her hands down the slits in her skirts, pockets cut for her work, and pulled out her two knives. She pressed one to the inside of his wrist and the other to his neck, and twisted soundlessly so their positions were switched and he was pressed against the door.

He was drunk enough that it took some time for the reality of the situation to set in, but not so gone that he could not understand the cold, sweet blade at his throat. Suri's blood sang with the promise of this bargain, her nausea sloughed off like snakeskin, like a phoenix throwing off old ashes.

"What is this?" he rasped, trapped by the truth of the knife, eyes bright and bemused. He looked at her as a man might look upon a child with blood on its hands, with pity and a sliver of terror.

And perhaps she was a bloody child, but it had been a long time since she had warranted pity. Languid, she pressed her knife in closer to the hollow of his throat. Solitude etched lines into the smooth, untested skin. "You have been stealing from royal coffers."

He flinched, either at the cold of the knife, or at the lilting knowledge of her voice. He tipped his chin up, proud and quavering, and said, "I have not."

"Oh, but you have," she whispered, dipping closer so her voice brushed the shell of his ear as the steel slid, sickly sweet, against clean skin. "Did you think the crown would not notice?"

He was trembling, now. "Why are you here?"

Her lips curled in a smile. It was the only question to ask, after all, but they both already knew the answer. She told him, "To clean up."

And then she crooked Solitude to one side and slit his throat.

The blood came first, as it always did—rushing from the wound, soaking her fingers and her flesh, as if she were meant to carry it all. The smell—rotted, soiled metal, warm with life—assaulted her next, and she swayed for a few moments, pressing his dying body against the door. She felt paralyzed by this revulsion, by this weakness she could never leave behind.

Then she recovered herself and pulled back, before carrying his body carefully to the low cot beside the window.

Already, the air in the room was heavy with iron, and she longed to open the window and let the smell of the incense smoke and blossoms wash away the acrid odor. But it was simply a wish, a dream of a world where she could visit faraway cities and open the windows without fear.

She pulled a creamy white cloth out of her pocket, marked with the icon of the ring of braided flowers and the crown within, and slid it under the interlaced fingers resting on his chest.

Suri bent beside the deputy governor's basin. She washed her hands until the blood had gone, until the smell had gone, until all that remained was pain—the sensation of her nails on her own palms, scrubbing against reddened, raw skin. She dried her hands with a cotton towel beside the basin, and then set the towel on fire with trembling hands, and watched the fabric disappear into flames and ash on the wood floor.

Outside, the hymn swelled as the people of the city prayed to their benevolent goddess. How she wished that such a goddess truly existed, that this was a world where gods granted wishes and created beautiful things out of ash and cracked, dry ground. But it was not, and though Anyu chided her for those wishes, he could not truly scorn her for them, not when he told her stories of those worlds every night.

The deputy governor's blood slipped off the blades and into the muddled water, red swirling through it like ink. The sight sickened her even now. After the knives were clean and dried with the inside of the sash, she replaced them and retied the fabric. She glanced toward the dead man sleeping on his cot, embroidered flowers under his curled fingers, and finally opened the window and crept out, climbing up and onto the roof above. The revels had not yet finished, and the air was still sweet with faith and song.

Her hands felt heavy with the heft of her knives even though she had put them away. If she was in Ashanth, this would be when Anyu found her, and took her to the edges of the cliffs and told her fairy tales of distant lands. But Sahet was alive with entirely different stories, of foreign gods and lovely monsters and hope that her family could not kill even with a hundred wars.

She tucked her loneliness into her sash, the way a *hehyava* might tuck away a finger bone or a severed heartstring, and swung her legs over the edge of the inn's roof, watching the moon fall toward the horizon.

Anyu met her at the docks, brows arched expectantly. There was nothing harsh about the planes of his face, though, not like the imperious slant to Rohit's features when they passed one another in the corridor, as if blood bonds were so easily washed off. Not like their parents' cold dispassion.

"You smell like incense," he told her, taking her trunks and helping her off the barge. His eyes glittered. Those were their father's eyes, hard and inexorable. "Did you join the revels?"

"Should I have?" she retorted, pulling her mantle closer around herself and following him down the quay and toward the edges of the city. She hadn't participated in the revels, but Sahet had been thick with the smell, the festival heavy in the air even in the morning. It had not been something she could simply wash off with water and amber soap.

His lips twisted sharply as he hefted the trunks over his shoulder. "You should have, so you could return and tell me all the strange stories you heard. I tire of weaving new ones night after night."

It was a lie, of course. He never tired of those tales, not after twenty-one years of breathing them and seventeen of pouring them into words. She knew that well enough. When they had been young enough that neither of them could reach the tops of bookshelves without stools and magic, he had told her that sometimes he felt like dreams split him from the inside out, dreams that bloomed into tales of faraway worlds. He had told her that he gave those stories to her in the hopes that one day they would grow into life, buds opening like blades and catching on the edges of reality. He had told her, quietly so their parents could not hear, of a world he had dreamed up—a kind world, where war was a thing of days past and life was not something they crushed in calloused hands.

That was the world he wanted to create, and he had whispered tales of it to her. And she hadn't believed him, not really—back then. his blood disqualified him from the throne even though he was the oldest, his skin smooth and dark as cadamba bark; his mother's skin. There would be no bastard king, no crown given to a child of southern blood. But he was strong and skilled and clever enough that the Najan crown—which prized power over everything else—had lent itself to him, as he was the most powerful of the king's three children. He was born for the crown, as Suri saw it, and so she endured the blood because there would come a day when she would not have to kill anymore. And he would bring it.

Ashanth was carved into the sides of cliffs. The city walls were tall as gods, battlements and parapets carved into them all the way around. It was a warlike capital for a warlike people, and even when the guards stepped aside and allowed them into the inner city, they looked ahead to the heavy defenses of the castle. Moats were obsolete now, but her parents had dug one rumored to go a hundred feet deep, rumored to be filled with sea snakes and poison.

The people let them pass in silence. This was not deference, she knew. It was fear, and it was respect. They did their work so the people could do theirs, and so Naja worked, a careful, diligent ecosystem built on the bones of stolen land and stolen blood.

When they arrived in the throne room, her parents were already seated on their thrones of iron and gold. They nodded to the servants beside the door, and they came forward. Isa tried in vain to catch her eye, but Suri looked away, handing over her trunks wordlessly. She left to put them in her rooms, and the doors shut behind them, leaving her and Anyu behind with the king and queen.

She kept her gaze on the rug below, a deep crimson wound through with gold and navy where it showed stars against the night sky. It was a scene of victory, though, like all the other decorations in the palace, and so it was mostly red, the red of glory and of blood.

"You have new work," her father said, his voice a low rumble. There would be no pleasantries exchanged, she thought bitterly, no asking whether the journey had treated her well. This was business, nothing more.

The queen tilted her head down toward them. "We've arranged for you to marry the Virasankan of Athri. The wedding is set for the autumn equinox of the coming year. Your assignment will be to leave for Athri once summer comes and undergo the necessary preparations to marry him. Once you have wedded and you are recognized as a queen, you must kill him, and take their lands for us. After this is done, if you wish, we will release you from your work."

Suri looked up sharply. It was a foolish thing to do—it betrayed her eagerness with clean, obvious intensity. But she could not fathom this, not wholly. The hope of it rattled around inside her, broken glass or perhaps the disassembled pieces of children's toys. "Released?"

Her mother was clever and ruthless, and she looked down at her daughter as if they did not share blood, her eyes smooth, pale. "Yes. Released. We know you've wished for it many times—" Now Suri turned to look at Anyu, accusing and shocked, but her brother would not meet her gaze. "—and you have served well. So this shall be rewarded. If you desire freedom, you will have it. Once this work is done, you may leave the capital behind. We will supply you with the required funds and supplies to build a new life for yourself."

Released. The word set a fire inside her, her heart beating to some new, lovely song, lilting and sharp like the hymns from Sahet. She folded her arms, unwilling to fully bind herself to her hope, to this fool's gold. "The Athrians marry for love, do they not? Has he agreed to this?"

Suri conjured up what she could recall of the Athrian boy king. His entire family had died in the war nine years ago, his parents and sister slaughtered along with many of the chiefs and their ministers. He had ascended with no prince regent, no backbone of support beyond a handful of other survivors in the city. She had seen him last at a ball a few summers ago, celebrating the Eryan queen's birthday. He firmly refused to attend Najan state functions.

He had reminded her a little of Anyu, if only because she thought he suited his crown of obsidian and gold quite well. But that was where their similarities ended. Anyu was cut from a cloth of dreams and nascent blossoms, and the boy king had been crudely carved from the mountains that had bore him, cut from thorns and cold rage.

The Athrians married for love, and she knew, without a doubt, that there was no world in which he could learn to love her. If given the choice, he might sink his fingers into her chest, rip out her heart, and set it on fire, as though he could burn down her crown, her family, with those same flames.

The queen regarded her with familiar disdain. "He has. In an odd turn of fate, he has set his pride aside and done the politically intelligent thing for his nation." She didn't comment on the irony of this, on the tragedy of it. Such sadnesses were of little importance to her mother and father. "Do you accept?"

It was amusing that they would turn to formalities now. This had never been a choice, or a request. It was an order—*go to the deep south, marry the king and kill him.* There had never been any chance of her refusing it.

And yet, she wondered. About the boy king, and the land he ruled, and the way she would ruin what remained of it, turning it over to her parents without a care. It was not often that she thought of things like this with sympathy and hesitation, but this was to be the last of her work and she could not forget the way the word had rang when her mother had spoken it. *Freedom,* honey-sweet and wound through with glimpses of faraway lands she had never allowed herself to love. It might sting, of course, to know she built this freedom off the corpse of another kingdom, but her life had always been built off of corpses, off of ash and bone. If she had refused her first assignment, she would've been killed at age six. If she had refused her tenth, she would've been killed at eight. And so on and so forth.

She turned to Anyu, trying in vain to piece together an answer to this senseless question with the lines of his face. His head was bowed, the pin on the collar of his coat glinting in the sunlight. A ring of flowers encircling a crown—the symbol of their army, of their throne.

If she left, she left the empire in his hands. And he would take care of it the way he had taken care of her when they were youths, two unwanted children—a girl and a bastard—in a castle that threatened to swallow them, an empire with sharp teeth.

"I accept," she said, and her parents dipped their heads in acknowledgement as they rose from their thrones. They were carved in the western style; beautiful, blunt sculptures of tigers built into the iron and gold. Across the back of her father's throne, there was an inscription in written Najan, and above it, a depiction of the first prince staking the ground upon Ashanth with a spear. There was a cold beauty in this world, but it was beautiful all the same. And now she would leave it.

She ducked her head in a bow as the king and queen passed her, shutting the door behind them. The sound of it—wood against wood, fading footsteps—unsteadied her, and she leaned to the side, grasping at a loose tapestry to steady herself. Her legs felt soft and malleable underneath her.

"You must send me letters of your exploits once you've left us," Anyu said, and she turned to face him, pressing her back up against the tapestry. The silk and cotton yielded under her fingertips and she sank into them, inhaling the familiar smell of amber and stone.

"Anyu," she said, because she felt like if she said anything else, she might shatter into tiny shards of bone and hardened heart, crystallized into brittle glass. Taking a moment to slow her breaths, she shut her eyes. The tapestry felt like it might swallow her, might fold her into its depths and allow her to disappear completely. "Anyu. Is this your doing?"

"Does it matter?" he asked, and he sounded genuinely curious. She opened her eyes, and saw him passing his fingers over the edges of their father's throne. Not with covetous intent, as Rohit might have performed the same movement, but with a certain pensive thoughtfulness, a starry eyed distance that came over him when he thought of the future that lay in front of them, paved by stones that glittered and shone in the light.

He glanced up and smiled at her, his mother's smile—warm and affectionate. It was an affection that did not exist in her or Rohit—she had wanted it once, thought she might absorb it from Anyu's blood the way she learned his stories and wrote them into her heart. But that affection had never helped him nor his mother—the king had not considered him as an option for succession until after the courtesan had passed away and he had lost those lingering dregs of softness and youth.

Anyu smiled at her, and his smile held untold dreams inside. "Go and marry that king, and kill him, and never return to Ashanth. But you must write me letters, of the stories you hear and the stories you make so I do not run dry, left here alone. Understood?"

The words were wry with the weight of parody, twisting their father's orders into a joke that hid the truth of what she was being offered. Suri leaned into the warmth of the tapestry, and allowed herself a small smile back. "I will."

The world was dying.

Kiran knew this the same way he knew he was dying—the burn of a long-forgotten wound slowly substituted by a lingering chill. Flames whipped across the sky and blood dripped on the stone beside him and he was *dying*, but he couldn't bring himself to care when confronted with the decay of everything he had ever known.

It was a dream, but dreams were little more than specters of a future he knew would come to pass, and so he scraped his gaze across the crumbling world and tried to put it into words he would remember when he opened his eyes.

He was kneeling beside the altar he had grown up with, his hands forming bloody handprints on the uneven stone. Smoke and iron hung heavy in the air, but he was alone. Almost alone. The fire kept him company, even as it left to burn down the remains of the city, and the body did, too. A silhouette was balanced against the far pillar of the temple, slumped against crumbling stone and lit from within.

The body was closer, laid carefully on the dust and ash, and the fire did not touch it. But it was no matter—they were already dead. Kiran squinted. She was. Blood-soaked fabric clung to her skin where it wasn't white with ash, and her mouth was set in a very faint frown, one that spoke of pained regret.

He did not know her, but that held little importance. Prophecies wore a hundred different faces, and catastrophe knew millions of names. Still, he memorized the angles of her face. Viro would want to know, at the very least.

His heart shuddered in his chest, and pain wracked him briefly. It was a lasting kind of anguish, a pain that had lived in him until it had made his heart its own. A heavy, soul-deep agony that drained the light from his flesh. Not the pain drawn out by a knife, and yet the ceremonial dagger was still loosely clenched in his left hand. The blade scraped against the carved stone as the flames whistled through the emptying bones of the city.

Kiran was dying, but he could no longer tell whether it was from the blood staining the stone red; he could no longer tell whether this death had been pulled from his body long before the knife had ever met his skin. The anger had taken that knowledge from him, had blurred the lines between gold and red. His mouth tasted of blood and ash.

Dawn blazed on the horizon, sunlight meeting smoke and the glow of old fires in between emaciated buildings. He had woken to see the sunrise every morning of his life, and yet he had never seen one like this. A heavy, crackling quiet blanketed the ground. Bitterly, he thought, *I always thought death would be louder than this.*

But it wasn't. He felt faintly fatigued, and it was possible that, before this moment, there had been something of substance to push him to this edge. A bang that had elicited a whimper that had resounded through the knotted bones of the earth. *This is not how it is meant to be,* he thought, and it was impossible to know whether that strange discomfort stemmed from the silence in the air or the fire that wrapped around his bloodied body.

He could not feel his heart, and that was wrong. The girl was dead, but she was not burnt, and that was wrong. He was dying, but there was still suffering—there was still death, and harsh barrenness in the dusty, packed earth surrounding the burning temple—and that was wrong in a way that was nearly unfathomable to him.

Why? he thought. He pressed his raw, red fingertips into the stone, pressed against the growing numbness in his chest and prayed for what was most likely the last time.

It was a useless endeavor, of course, to ask the gods for what they would not give. Prophecy did not work like that. When he woke, it was likely he wouldn't remember this. If he was lucky, he would remember the shadows of it. The smoke in the air. The blood on the floor of the temple. The frown on the girl's face, and the ash that colored her hair.

The fire lingered on his skin even now, casting the remnants of his home in golden light and the premonition of catastrophe.

His hands slipped from the stone, and he fell to the ground prostrate. His pulse thudded in his ears, but even the rhythmic sound was far away. He was untouched by this fire, and he was untouched by the blood, and he was untouched even by the death that was ripping him apart in his heart of hearts, holy and broken.

When he had asked Kita how she thought he would die, she had reprimanded him for being morbid. And then he had asked again, and she had given him a death that seemed both too beautiful and too terrible for him. She had said she suspected the divinity in his blood and the earth in his skin would pull apart, and that he would fall to dust and watch himself fall to dust.

Where does the divinity go, then? he had asked her.

She had shrugged. *To the sky. That is where all divinity goes after it is dead.*

But the sky was too far away, and there was not enough left of him, divine or not, to guarantee safe passage on a trip so long. But he could feel himself drawing away from the pain around him, even now. The warmth of the fire was the only thing left. His anger wrapped around it and kept it safe, even as his heart fell to dust.

3
LYNE

Living with the reincarnation of someone who he'd once loved wasn't too painful for Kiran, except for when it felt like he was smashing his body against a car door, which was a good majority of the time.

But it was a familiar pain, like this had happened a hundred times before and would happen a hundred times more before the gods finally released him. It burned like memory, like joy, like loss. The singular positive to the entire situation was that as long as she continued to stare at him like he was chopped liver, he'd probably be able to last through it all without doing something foolish, like falling in love again.

"Somebody's trying to break into the house!" he shouted in the direction of the other bathroom, where Suri was currently attacking the issue of the stuck pipes.

"Tell them to fuck off!" she screamed back.

Kiran ran a hand through his wet hair, which was dripping all over the carpet—that would be yet *another* stern lecture to look forward to—and tied a towel around his waist, unlocking the splintering door in the midst of one of the knocks. Four teenagers froze, hands hanging in the air as they stared at him.

He regarded them with cool amusement. "Are you Suri's friends?"

Deafening silence. One of them, a lanky dark-skinned boy in a band T-shirt, muttered, "Jesus."

"Not quite," he said cheerfully. He couldn't truthfully say he wasn't enjoying the ego boost, but he figured Suri wouldn't appreciate it if he left her guests out in the hallway. "Are you Suri's friends?"

"Yeah," said a tall girl in blocky black heels and a floral print dress. Her dark eyes were wide, as if she was faintly shell-shocked. The other two, likely related, with the same dark, hooded eyes, messy, black hair, and lightly tanned skin, were completely silent. "We're her, uh, friends."

"Suri," he yelled, turning toward the bedroom. "Your friends are here!"

"I'll be right out," she screamed back. Shortly after, there was a shrill noise and the sound of spraying water, quickly followed by a long stream of expletives.

He turned back to them, gesturing toward the empty couch. "She might be gone for a bit. Would any of you like refreshments? I'm quite good at making tea."

By the time Suri finished, the sun had gone down completely, and her entire body felt like someone had run it over with a tractor.

After taking a quick shower, she padded out toward the living room. Kiran's voice rose up before she turned the corner. She lingered in the hallway for a moment. It wasn't really eavesdropping if it was your own house, she reasoned.

"So how do you know Suri?" Ellis asked. "This is really good tea."

"One of my only real talents." The god sounded pleased by the praise. "Her mother and mine were close friends. I'm staying with her while I do a gap year."

"Her mother's dead, though," Aza cut in, faintly suspicious.

"So's mine," he said easily, and Suri figured that, in a roundabout way, he was telling the truth. Except that his mother had died a long, long time ago, long before hers had even been born. "They were old college friends."

"What are you planning to study?" Dai asked.

"Oh, I don't know," he replied, and there was an odd, mischievous edge to his voice that was meant for her, only her. "A little bit of everything. Might do a focus on Enesmati history. Always fun to splash around in the past."

Thinking she'd probably heard enough, she ducked out into the living room, raising a weary hand in greeting to her friends. She froze, blood draining from her skin. "You've got to be kidding me."

"What?" Kiran asked innocently, looking up from where he was leaned against the side of the coffee table, sitting cross-legged. His towel was slung low around his waist, slow rivulets of water dripping down his—*Jesus. God. What the hell?*

"You," she said, voice so strained she could barely recognize it as her own. "What is *wrong* with you? Couldn't you have—" She made a complicated, hectic motion with her hands. "*Changed?*"

"Into what?" he asked, arching an eyebrow imperiously. "According to *you,* my sense of style is atrocious. Plus, it's not like I could've left your lovely guests to, what? Make tea for themselves?"

"Out of my sight," she managed, oddly shrill. She snapped her fingers at him. "Go! Go put actual clothes on! I don't care what they are as long as they're made of fabric!"

He waved goodbye to her friends on the way out, who all watched him leave with the faintly shocked sense of disbelief that Suri felt in every single cell of her body.

She woodenly walked around to the couch and took a seat on the edge of it, sagging back against the worn upholstery. After a few moments of silence, she lifted her head and said, "I don't want to talk about that. Don't make me talk about that."

Miya's eyes were alive with light. "I can't imagine why."

"Oh, stop bullying her," Dai said mildly, blowing on his tea. "It's probably weird, seeing a childhood friend after all this time. Speaking of, where *is* he from? That accent doesn't sound Enesmati."

There was no easy way for her to say that she had absolutely no idea. He was right, though—Suri had grown up around Enesmati immigrants, and she couldn't place his accent among any of the old languages. *Maybe gods have their own language,* she thought. "A dialect, maybe? He's never bothered to explain."

Her gaze drifted, then fell on the old poster board slotted between the armchair and the sofa. From here, she could see the glint of glitter glue, the yellowing edges of the newspaper clippings. Her heart was something strange and sunken in her chest.

"Suri," Kiran said, dropping a hand on her shoulder. The dry, searing heat drew her out of her reverie; she glanced up at him, vacant, and he stared back steadily.

Finally, she said, "Did you cut that off with craft scissors?"

The old camp T-shirt been cropped, a few loose threads and the ragged, scalloped edge betraying the hasty job. He tilted his head, offering a faint smile, which was answer enough. Nudging her slightly, he squeezed in between her and Miya, pulling his knees up. "So what did I miss?"

"Nothing," she exhaled, scrubbing at dry eyes. "Nothing."

Instead of trying to hold his gaze, intense and overwarm, she dug around for the television remote. And then the conversation shifted organically to a discussion on the week's shows, and season finales and eliminations and events that had once seemed interesting and now seemed horribly, painfully mundane.

Suri nudged Kiran, interrupting him in the middle of a long tirade he'd been delivering on the merits and pitfalls of the current elimination system in *Heartbreak Hotel.* He cut himself off, raising his eyebrows at her. She whispered, "Kitchen. Now."

He dipped his head in a satirical bow and followed her into the kitchenette. In the distance, Suri could hear Ellis playing with the remote control. The voices on the television fluctuated, swelling and falling in comical tempo.

"What did you want to talk about?" Kiran asked, taking a seat on the edge of the countertop. The fluorescent light cast him in sickly shades of white, washing him out into a ghost of himself. He tapped his fingernails on the laminate. "It's not like talking in here will provide much privacy, but to each their own, I suppose."

Suri rubbed at the back of her neck, hesitant. She wasn't entirely sure how to broach this issue, how one even tried to segue into it. The only option was just to—wade into the dark, thick mess of it all. "You have to—you have to be understanding of them."

He cocked his head, an oddly feral movement. "What do you mean by that?"

"It's just—" She trailed off, making a noise of frustration at her own ineptitude, her own inability to articulate what she meant to say. "They're human. They're young, they're stupid. I don't know, if they ever screw up and say something stupid to you, or, I don't know, disrespect you? You'll have to be understanding. You can't just—" She waved a hand. "Do something to them."

Kiran was silent for long enough that, finally, she forced herself to look up and hold his gaze. There was something unrecognizable about him just then, carved with the beauty of a blade balanced on thin skin. This was what a fire looked like right before it burned, before it seared.

He slid off the countertop and crossed the distance between them, soundless. He reached out a hand and tilted her chin up to meet his gaze, his touch oddly gentle, fingertips rough and calloused. The planes of his face were fairytale-sweet and just as sharp. "Are you afraid of me, Suri?"

Her breath caught—from fear. Even with her senses dulled and singed by flame, she understood she was supposed to fear him. Wonder was a low roar in her blood.

"Do you fear me?" he continued, watching her with that same intensity. It was impossible to say he resembled a boy now—his divinity marked him in distinct ways. In the glow of his eyes, the warmth of his skin when he stood so close. "Are you afraid that I will punish them if they step out of line? For the sake of punishment, for pure, power-drunk sadism?"

Step back, she thought vaguely. He was too much up close, too strange and alive with divinity. There was a reason stars existed too far away to touch.

"You should be," he said softly, but a little distantly. "I won't harm any of you, regardless. Not only because you are doing me the prodigious favor of housing me, but because I tire of senseless violence. I have already drunk my fill of that, been satiated and saturated with it. But you should be afraid of me, Suri. Gods are not kind. They have never been kind, and they never will be. Humanity would do well to remember that."

A scream of laughter came from the living room, and the overhead lights flickered. He inclined his head toward them, all youth-borne joy. "Go join your friends, Suri."

She turned to leave, too quickly for it to go unnoticed. But even after she returned to the couch, pulled her knees up, and settled into watching episode after episode of a show she wouldn't be able to recall the next day, she couldn't help but think of the god's warning, of the unfamiliar sadness in his eyes.

4
ENESMAT

Suri watched the flat, cracked soil of the borderlands begin to fade into vetiver grass and shrubbery. Athri was a clever country, wrapped by the arid wastelands in the way it was. Her family had stolen land that was dry and salted—the heart of the kingdom's crown still lay within the ring of mountains.

The carriage followed a trade route—one of only a handful—that led between southern Naja and northwestern Athri. Their western border was arid; thin soil stained red as blood, dotted by grasses and neem trees. There were settlements, of course, a handful of villages and cities that spread across the expanse of the wastelands, some on occupied land and some not. But they were few and far between, and in this world of dusty heat and dead air, they cared little for the crown that marked itself upon the land. A native Najan wouldn't last a day here and the Athrians knew it, glancing at the passing carriage with the faint, haughty disdain that came from pride and loss.

Suri traced the line of the tattoo below her collarbone—a dark, sharp design of thorns and flowers that she had been given as a child—and tried to focus not on the scenery but on the component parts of the assignment in front of her. Yet her mind continued to wander. Anyu had bid her farewell at the capital; the king and queen hadn't allowed him to accompany her to the border. She had wanted to hug him, but hadn't wanted it to come off too stilted, and so she had just stood there for a while until he had stepped forward, a little wry, and hugged her.

Never return, he'd repeated. It was the kind of order, the kind of promise, that made her think she was in a fairy tale of her own, that this was an inexplicable gift the fates had offered.

Outside, the grasslands became flushed with blossoms until they dipped and rose into low foothills. From this vantage point, she couldn't see where they cut off, but she knew it well enough—she'd studied Athri's geography intensely in the days before their departure.

It was humiliating that she hadn't made note of it prior to this engagement—she knew the rest of the peninsula like the back of her hand, from mountain to mountain and sea to sea. But she had never spent as much time in the southern kingdom as she had in the others. Out of the remaining free lands, it held the least Najan influence, stony and aloof.

The soft hills grew into dark stone, the Niravu Mountains clawing out of the ground. Suri remembered what Isa had murmured, watching her poring over the atlases of the mountain nation. *It was beautiful,* she had said wistfully. *I had family in the capital when I was younger, before the war. I cannot say if it will be the same, but it was beautiful.*

The war. They called it the Athrian War, not because Athri had won, but because Naja had fought far too many wars for every one to hold their name. She remembered it vaguely; nine years ago, she had been busy with insurrection in the northeast. But the boy king had lost his family to that war she barely remembered. He would hate her, surely.

The carriage rattled to a brief stop, a respite before the drop. Suri glanced out the window and stilled. *It was beautiful,* Isa had said, past tense hanging heavy in her voice, but war didn't break places like this. Time didn't touch them—it skirted around them, and left the edges worn and sepia-toned.

On one side, the ragged rock of the mountains fell away into the hills they'd just passed. On the other, they curved inward, creating jagged spires like teeth that flattened out into shorter cliffs before giving way to a wide valley that reached across to the other side. In the morning sun, it was a black crown, shining against the light.

Isa was silent beside her, but she could not be sure whether it was from awe or sadness.

The capital, Marai, was barely visible from here, but Suri could make out the edges. A crowded, tangled city pressed up against the base of the mountains, and a palace curled into the stone of the lower hills. A thin line wrapped around the capital—a gate, perhaps. Other settlements dotted the rest of the land, connected by roads as wild and decayed as the one they'd just traveled.

As they descended back onto flat ground, the shining stone of the mountains gave way to endless paddy fields, villages built around palm trees that bunched and crooked upward. The causeway toward the city was beaten and worn, and she felt the hatred of every staring farmhand and every young child on the outskirts of the fields as they passed them all by.

Before long, the spiderweb of villages gave way to the city gates. They were made of the same dark rock as the mountains, reinforced by iron and topped by towers and watchmen. It would've been daunting if the structures hadn't been so obviously worn from age.

They met the envoy on the other side, after the guards finished gruffly reviewing their papers. It was a strange duo—a pair of pale-skinned *yavanas*, one a little older than Suri and the other around her father's age. They looked identical, but not in the way of a father and son—they had the same plain cloak, the same boots, the same brooch on their collar, and the same mannerisms. The boy narrowed his eyes at her in appraisal, crossing his arms. "You're the bride?"

Suri winced, and the older man set a heavy hand on the boy's shoulders, glaring down at him. Then he offered them a warm smile, nodding toward their bags. "Hush, Lucius. We can take those, your Highness; the crown sent us to escort you to the palace. You can call me Galen."

She exchanged a glance with Isa, but handed over the trunks. She felt oddly jittery in this foreign world, cut so clearly from a different cloth than all the cities she'd known before.

The tenements ran unevenly in a half circle against the base of the mountains, and the incline toward the palace held another set, glittering in the morning light. It was hard to understand the mechanics of the city from the very bottom; Suri could only discern details through the banners that crisscrossed the streets, the bright-eyed vendors, the pungent odor of spices in the air.

The central market held an empty square at the center, the beat stone edges cluttered with the edges of stalls and baskets. Spice vendors, hands streaked with seeds of dried chilis, handed bundles of bound spices to servants wrapped in dyed cotton and dull metal bracelets. Sacks of millet and rice were heaped on the stalls on the edges of the markets, and stray grains scattered the ground like dust.

Isa tightened her shawl around herself. They'd been steadily receiving curious looks—from small children and the parents that steered them away, from vendors and buyers and beggars alike. The looks had quickly turned probing—Suri was a few shades light for the southern tip, and Isa's servant's tattoo was visible through her shawl.

"How long until we arrive?" Suri asked Lucius, and he looked at her askance, surprised.

"A few minutes, perhaps," he said. "There is a shortcut through the upper city that may spare you two the scrutiny of the citizens."

He gestured up a set of steps cut into the stone of the mountain before starting up them cheerfully. Galen followed, glancing down at them with concern, but Suri gestured for him to go on.

"What did you expect?" Isa asked, so low that her voice was nearly inaudible in the din of the *angadi.*

"I don't know," she said truthfully, glancing around. The air here was perfumed with flowers and spices, and she was reminded strangely of Sahet. "Perhaps I thought we might be granted a certain measure of anonymity. Though I suppose that isn't the purpose of this assignment."

Isa regarded her with warmth, but it read somewhat like dry pity. "I'm sure you will learn to disappear into the city quickly enough."

Suri raised her eyebrows—it was the closest to a proper compliment the other girl had ever given her, but she was already climbing up the steps toward the upper city.

After finding Lucius beside the gates, Suri introduced herself and Isa to a guard, explaining why they had arrived. The words sat strangely in her mouth—*Suriyalekha Adityan, here to visit the king.* She'd never referred to him that way before, and it weighed on her heavily. He was cut from a different cloth than every king she'd met and killed before, even her father. Especially her father. There was something sharp and youthful and feral about the boy king that did not usually live in crowns, no matter how dark or strong they happened to be.

The guard watched for a moment, uneasy, before nodding to another, who peeled apart from the rest and left for the palace. The guard returned with a young woman dressed in servant's clothes—a thin, muslin skirt and a dun-colored, cotton tunic layered on top. A pattern of flowers was embroidered along the edge of the tunic, done in uneven, painstaking patches. She was unadorned apart from the pin on her collar, made out of the same dark metal as the gate, and her black hair hung in a thick braid down her back.

The girl paused before bowing deeply to Suri. She suppressed a frown—it reminded her a little too much of home, of how marks might look at her before she slit their throats. Resignation mixed with fear.

Suri hesitated before putting a hand on her shoulder, signaling her to rise. She smiled, and the other girl smiled in kind. Her features were soft, but her eyes were bright and alert. She glanced around at the party—recognition toward Galen, warm neutrality toward Isa, and a kind of dragging appraisal directed toward Lucius.

"I've never seen you," Lucius said, and it was just as much for his own sake as it was for Suri's. "You must be new."

"I've helped out as a scullery maid for years." She glanced at Suri, a frown flickering on her lips. "My name is Mohini, my lady, but—"

"Then I'll call you that," Suri said, attempting a reassuring smile. It felt foreign and rigid on her face. Galen tapped his protege on the shoulder, and he tore his gaze away from Mohini.

"I'll see you all around, I'm sure," Lucius said, dipping his head before turning to follow Galen as he disappeared through the far doors. He shot Suri a quick smile. "Hopefully, the *nakshi* will take a break to show you around."

Mohini stiffened at the word—*nakshi*—but said nothing, and Suri waved as the other boy left for the doors.

"What… does *nakshi* mean?" Suri managed in broken Athrian. She hadn't studied the language in a long time, and a few weeks of poring over scripts hadn't helped much. She'd managed to get by speaking Najan with Lucius and the guards, but it was to be expected that Mohini wouldn't know the language. Or that she might hate it.

But Mohini just gave her a warm smile. "You can speak Najan with me if you wish, my lady." Her expression darkened a little, but she looked away before Suri could understand it. She nodded at the guard and he opened the door, letting them into the palace. "*Nakshi*… it means war dog. It's a nickname for the king."

Before she could ask more, Mohini turned away and started down the halls. The foyer of the palace was beautiful, with vaulted ceilings and iron fixtures hanging from above. Corridors were cut through either side, but the back held a panel of doors. Behind them, Suri could see the beginnings of a huge courtyard.

Mohini led her down one of the corridors on the left and up a flight of stairs. It would take her a few days to understand the inner workings, and even then she was unsure if she'd be able to wrap her head around all of them. There was something fluid and impenetrable about the palace, thin but strong. A stone heart dipped in glass.

Mohini stopped in front of a gold-inlaid door. The walls that led up to it displayed paintings of previous monarchs.

"The king takes part in the morning and evening guard," Mohini said, with no small amount of pride. She gestured toward the door. "He won't return until night, but I will take you to see him then." Nodding toward a set of adjoining rooms, she added, "I'll be a moment—I need to bring my belongings from the maids' quarters."

They were smaller than Suri's rooms at home, but not by much. A canopied bed lay in the center, flanked by a nightstand that held precious sculptures in gold and silver. Three windows, panes pressed against one another, were cut into the wall opposite the door. From one, she could see the city below and the rolling farmlands beyond. From the next, she could see the barracks on the edges of the city, and the mountains beginning to ascend. The last one showed the curve of the peaks, showed the stone thin out into spires that sharpened to points under the sun.

After returning, Mohini offered to give them a tour of the city. Already, Suri felt consumed by homesickness, by the strangeness of streets soaked in revulsion and blossoms, but something about the earnestness of the other girl's smile made her agree.

Suri glanced down at the set of stairs leading to the throne room as they passed it. She wondered if the boy king loved his throne the way her parents loved their carved thrones of iron and gold. The thought brought a faint smile to her face. *War dog.* It was a wonder he hadn't splintered the mountains yet, that he hadn't shattered the ground.

Mohini pointed out the noble houses of stone and marble, the servants' quarters, and the barracks before descending into the lower city. Navigating the *angadi* was trickier than it had been before. Suri considered herself adept at learning the tangled streets of the cities she visited, but there was something more frantic, more alive about Marai, as if its king's furious energy had soaked into the very ground.

But Mohini folded into the city easily, despite her nervous warnings at every junction. By the time they reached the streets that lined the base of the main temple, Suri's sash had unwound and hung loose around her waist. She pulled it tight before peering up the looming building, the heights of the towers rivaling the spires of the palace.

The entrance was painted in bright, almost garish, colors, barely dried from the preparation for the monthly festivals. In Enesmati fashion, the doors were carved with tales of gods and monsters and magic.

The high priestess stood by the entrance, dressed in the traditional white wrap of *sirai maravuri,* the dress gathering loosely above her ankles. She was young—she couldn't have been more than nineteen, perhaps a year older than Isa—but she stood with a steady self-assurance and the other priests deferred to her absolutely. A straw-colored cord was wrapped around her right bicep, marking her class.

She smiled when she saw them approaching, inclining her head forward to indicate Suri. "We've been expecting you."

It should not have been a surprising statement. Her engagement to the boy king had become public months ago, and it was far from unlikely that the king had told the temple to prepare for her arrival. But something about the way the girl said it made Suri think she was speaking of something else entirely.

She smiled again, a secret between them Suri hadn't quite unraveled, and gestured toward the temple. From here, she could see the doorways that led past the entrance and into the central area. Sunlight spilled out onto the stone and glittered on a shallow pool. "I'm assuming you've come for a tour."

The priestess led them through the foyer first, immune to the glory of it. Painted carvings of gods slaying demons covered the walls, and the ceilings were streaked in an intricate looping pattern that made Suri's head spin.

As they walked, she offered her name with a faint, rueful laugh, as if she had forgotten. *Kita.* Like the jewels that grew in the stone of the mountains. It was a fitting name. Isa trailed behind Kita, an unfamiliar expression on her face. It was a little like awe, a little like pain.

She led them out of the darkness of the foyer and into the main colonnades, four stone walkways bordered with walls and *yali* pillars. Intricately carved doors cut into the walls, one for every corridor. Beside the columns, steep, painted steps led down to the edges of the pool. In the midday sun, the water glinted pale blue, clear all the way through.

Braziers flanked the pool at all four corners, flames licking against the air. Kita turned at the corner and gestured for them to follow down a matching stone corridor. Suri traced the painted carvings on the walls as they passed. Each one held a different battle, a different divine memory traced out into stone.

There was a service set to begin in less than half an hour, and the high priestess bid them farewell at the north entrance. Kita leaned against the stone base of the north tower, rubbing her thumb against the carvings as though each was an old friend. "You are welcome to stay, of course. But I thought Your Highness might want to return to the palace before the heat becomes unbearable."

The high priestess nodded to her right, where a nondescript door lay, nearly hidden by wooden boxes. "Enter through there, and take the beaten path through the trees at the base of the hills. It isn't glamorous, but it should be adequately shaded, and it's the shortest path to the palace that I know of. It leads to the northern gardens."

Mohini nodded in understanding. "Thank you for all of your help, High Priestess." Suri could see her waiting in her periphery, but she leaned forward and traced the carving at the base of the tower. It depicted a figure kneeling beside a dark lake, hands awash with dark red. The maiden had her head turned upward to the sky, as if seeking something. But her eyes were closed.

"My lady." Isa's voice was insistent, but pitched low. She turned to follow the other girls out through the corridor, glancing back at the priestess with the expectation of seeing her back, white fabric dancing around her ankles in the faint breeze.

But Kita had her eyes on her, and only smiled when Suri turned to look at her. There was something knowing in her gaze, a kind of wry thoughtfulness that surprised Suri. But she simply held her hand up in farewell before disappearing down another hooded corridor, the fires of distant braziers blurring her figure.

On the other side, Mohini was leaning against the dried grass walls. At first glance, it was difficult to tell that it led to the temple—it resembled a supply shed, or a small cottage. Just as Kita had told them, a soft dirt path led out from the door and snaked through a copse of kino trees beside the base of the mountains.

Unwilling to meet Isa's gaze, she tilted her head up to drink in the view. The grass of the northern side quickly faded out into black stone, and the small incline that the path gave them allowed Suri to look out on the city, clustered and chaotic.

Mohini continued to elaborate on the capital, detailing the rooms of the palace. The three towers—tall, crooked spires of black stone that twisted into the sky—divided the palace into the eastern and western wing, separated by two courtyards and the ballroom, throne room, and court down the center. She gestured at the dark soil that crept up into stone. "In any case, these mountains are our best defense. They are as close to adamantine as anything natural can come. No human being would be able to stand the terrain for long."

Beyond the curve of her face, something glittered in the distance. Suri tilted her head, squinting against the faint glare of sunlight filtering through the leaves above. "What is that?"

"My lady?"

"You said no one can survive in the mountains," she said, words slow as she darted around the maid to get a better look. "So who lives there?"

It was a premature surmise, to call it a home. Even from a better vantage point, Suri could only intuit that another beaten path led up to it, although at a much steeper incline. There were four pillars with no roof above them, and a smaller alcove tucked into the sanctum, barely distinct from the edges of the mountain. Another path led out to the side, along the edge of the slowly narrowing cliff.

It was just as much a home as the clump of trees was a forest. But it held the notion of holding something, of simple significance.

When Mohini said nothing, she glanced back to find her mildly uncomfortable. It was an expression Suri was surprised to see on the girl's face, rather like how a young child might look at a butcher, too young to know of the context and old enough to shrink back from blood.

"Mohini?" Isa probed, placing her hand on the other girl's shoulder. She blinked in response but didn't say anything, just narrowed her eyes at the building above them.

Finally, she dropped her gaze, rubbing her hands together and moving past them. "You would do well not to venture there, Your Highness."

Suri blinked, shocked at the rebuff. "But… someone does live up there?"

"Yes."

"And?" Despite everything, she found herself impatient at the dragging, discomfited pace of the girl's responses.

"And you should stay away. From him and the temple," Mohini said. "Ask anyone in this city—in this kingdom—and they will say the same."

Isa raised her eyebrows, not at Mohini's foreboding silence but at what Suri was sure was something righteous and ugly beginning to bloom on her face. "Why? Is he a criminal in exile? Why would he live in a temple? And so close to the palace?"

Mohini waved her hand. "He is not a criminal. But he is dangerous all the same. And one day, very soon from my knowledge, he will die anyway. So there is really no reason for Your Highness to get involved with him. And, to answer your question, he lives up there because the gods favor him. Far more than they favor the rest of us."

"Is he cruel?"

The other girl's eyes widened, surprise flitting across her face. But she took her time to respond, scrutinizing Suri's face before she did. "He might as well be."

Isa laid a hand on Suri's arm and leaned in. "Restrain your anger on behalf of the people. You have enough enemies here already. Seeking out another one will get you killed."

Suri shook her off and made a face. "I won't seek him out. I will just… quietly reflect on my displeasure."

"Quietly, in the safety of your rooms."

"Of course."

Isa looked unconvinced but she smiled at Mohini, and the other girl shook her head, the discomfort on her face quickly replaced by blithe cheer. "There is no saying you will even have to meet with him, Your Highness. I've only seen him in the city a handful of times."

With that, she led them out of the copse of trees. But Suri looked back, gaze drawn back to the temple. It looked more like ruins than a place for prayer, and yet, without the trees impeding her vision, she could see a single stream of smoke rising from a brazier at its heart.

It was a little like this job, the volatility of that smoke. Suri could see the faint outline of her freedom on the other side of it, and it held true form. But then it flickered and blurred, a mirage after all.

"This is a terrible idea," Viro told Tarak's back. The other boy didn't move, but after a moment, he spoke.

"You've been saying that ever since we returned," he said, running his hands over the edge of the gilded throne in front of him. It was a formality, really, to use the throne room at all, but Viro supposed speaking with the Najan princess required it. Tarak turned to watch him, brown eyes glinting in the lamplight. "You should sit. There's no point in being here if you're going to perch on the windowsill like a bird."

Viro raised his eyebrows, and the other boy's mouth quirked to the side in a smile. He slid off the windowsill, but leaned back against it. His mouth felt odd, cotton-soft and choked. "I don't use the throne. You know that. If that offends her gentle Najan sensibilities, so be it."

Tarak sighed, heavy with resignation, leaning forward so he could card a hand through his hair. "Promise me you will at least make an effort. Any kind of effort." His mouth twisted in a faint grin. "Turn on that charm of yours."

"What charm?" he muttered, looking away and out the window. This late, Kiran was likely still at the main temple. He'd left early that morning—Viro had only been able to see the blaze of the first fire before he'd left the upper city.

Something was bothering him, something he didn't want to reveal right now. If there was anything that the past seventeen years had taught him, it was that Kiran's unease was without a doubt more dangerous than whatever threat the foreign princess posed. Even if she meant to take the rest of Athri for her family.

"My king," Tarak said, leaning forward and taking his hand where it rested on the edge of the windowsill. The cuffs of his uniform were worn from all the years he'd served the kingdom, patched and darned by Kiran in his spare time. The sight of them felt like a knife in his sternum, another reminder of all they'd lost.

He pulled away. "I told you not to call me that."

"Worrying about him isn't any better than worrying about the princess," he replied, ignoring him. His fingers ghosted over Viro's, but he didn't take his hand again. "Kiran can take care of himself."

Viro snorted. "Perhaps. I can never read him, and he tells us little."

Tarak arched his eyebrows. "If you asked, perhaps he might."

There was a knock at the doors, bullet wood swept with intricate carvings older than the war. The princess, then. Tarak returned to his place behind the throne and, after a moment of hesitation, Viro leaned against the side of it. It was all bravado and illusion, but if the effort would sate him, Viro could at least try.

"Come in," Viro called, and the door swung open. The guards stepped aside, and three young women filed into the room. One was a palace maid wearing a black pin and a gaze that refused to meet his. The second was likely the princess's handmaiden; she wore a hard smile and plain clothes meant to hide her identity. Her proof of service was covered up, too. A sloppy job—he could see the lines of the banded tattoo under her shawl, and it hung awkwardly on her shoulders, too purposeful to be convincing. She might've passed for an Athrian otherwise.

Even if the guard's eyes hadn't lingered on her, faintly revolted, he would have been able to distinguish the princess from the others. The north clung to her, in her strong brow and upturned eyes, in the mild brown of her skin, the color of sandalwood. It had been years since he'd last seen her, but her features had changed little; the old, deceptive softness of her face had disappeared, and she was sharp as a knife.

He relaxed his grip on the side of the throne and straightened. "It's a pleasure to see you again, Your Highness."

The princess smiled, but it was brittle, as if she could feel the artifice in his words. "If we are to be wedded, you should call me by name." She hesitated, a momentary misstep, then nodded toward Tarak. "Won't you introduce me, Your Majesty?"

This was a terrible idea. Already, he longed to write back to her parents, to that nest of vipers, and call this entire engagement off. He slid his eyes away and forced his lips to curve unconvincingly. "Please, call me Viro. And… Tarak is the captain of the city guard. We were just discussing security."

Her eyes were chips of spun burnt sugar. "My handmaiden told me you served shifts on the city guard, but I didn't believe her. How do you find the time?"

Viro shifted away from the throne, closer to those glossy windows, their shadows cast in firelight against them. The words were innocent enough, but bitterness seared through him in eulogies. "I make the time, Princess. The safety of this city is a priority of mine."

Unsaid words threatened to rip him cleanly in two, but he turned to meet the girl's gaze. She was a few months older than him, and yet she felt so foreign. As if, beside her, he was both an old man and a wailing infant. He wondered if she was struck by it too; the seas that divided them, the wars that had set wastelands to ash.

But her expression was marble smooth and inscrutable. He thought petulantly of how she and Kiran might enjoy one another's company, fruitlessly trying to crack layers of stone and polish until one finally hit upon a core of candor. "How admirable. Will I be able to see you, then?"

"I'm sure we'll find time for each other," he said warmly. His fingers were clenched in fists so tight he feared his nails might draw blood. "There's no need to rush, regardless."

She dipped her head in acquiescence, but it was forced. "Are you free for dinner tomorrow?"

He nodded. "I'll see you then, Suri." The name was bitter and unfamiliar on his lips. He had only known her last name, had only known it as a curse.

The other two girls left the room. She raised a hand in farewell and gave a brief, knowing smile before following them out.

The door shut with a faint thud. Tarak's footsteps shadowed the sound, and his hand brushed Viro's shoulder before he stopped to lean against the jeweled table in front of the throne. His eyes danced with amusement, but his mouth was set in a sharp line. "You won't like what I have to say."

Viro raised his eyebrows. "What is it?"

"She reminds me a lot of you," he said, turning to survey the darkened city outside, milky with lamplight and the empty shine of the new moon.

"How so?" Viro pushed off from the throne, turning toward the windows. It had been years since it had been cleaned, years since it had last bled, but his fingers still felt tacky. It was not his throne to touch, he knew.

Tarak lifted his shoulders in a shrug, bringing his index finger and thumb together in a quick snap. "The same spark, like flint and moonstone. Who knows? Perhaps you'll learn to get along, fall in love." He rose from where he had knelt beside the table, ragged nails tracing lines of pearl and garnet, and offered him a small, weary smile. "I have night watch."

He let his hand fall from the carved windowsill, but it lingered, the pads of his fingers pressed to uneven stone like a handful of broken kisses. *I do not want to fall in love.* "So you do. Promise you will take care of yourself."

It was a well-worn routine of theirs, vows softened by age and sorrow, and so, when Tarak spoke, Viro could hear the faintest hint of a smile in his voice. "I always do."

5
ENESMAT

Marai was pleasant enough, all things considered. Suri hadn't expected a warm welcome, and the city had responded in kind, lukewarm enough to be tolerable but cool to the touch. And those brief, rare, moments when Athrians could not hide their bitterness, their disgust—she didn't begrudge them for it. She was slowly distancing herself from the apprehension regarding the job, the dread of looking at places and people and wondering what they would look like once dead.

It had been over a week since she had arrived, and she still had only stolen glimpses of the boy king. She had taken to calling him that in her head, reluctant to recognize his name. It would become harder that way, would draw her mental outline of him further from a target and closer to a human.

"Are you awake, Princess?"

Though it was already difficult enough to imagine him as something with blood, with a beating heart.

Suri flicked her gaze up from where she had been studying the tablecloth. The boy king sat across from her at the other end of the long dining table. He raised his eyebrows, amused. "Have you not been getting enough sleep?"

"No," she said, dropping the cloth. "Simply lost in thought."

The corner of his mouth twitched, but he said nothing. They had dined together every night of the past week, a perfect opportunity to lower his defenses if there was one, and yet every single meal began and ended in silence. Suri hadn't thought there was anyone in all the seas more paranoid than her father, and yet she had been so cleanly proven wrong.

"Your Majesty—" she began.

"As I said, you're welcome to call me by name," he said, cutting his curried chicken into small pieces and bringing one to his mouth. "As we are betrothed."

It took all Suri had not to flinch, but the king was watching her far too closely for her to make a misstep and have it not be fatal. She took a bite of rice, just enough to feign an appetite. "I never see you around the palace."

"A nation doesn't run itself."

Even one as small and pitiful this one. The words sprung to her mind, casual and thoughtless and true. She hid a frown behind her hand as she reached for her glass of water.

"I can ask Tarak to show you around, if you're listless. He's busy enough, but you'd be safe with him."

"Tarak?" she questioned before recognizing the name, muttered low under the king's breath nearly every time they met. The captain of the guard was inseparable from the boy king, an appendage just as natural as a limb. "I couldn't impose on him like that. My maids already accompany me. It is just that…"

The king tilted his head in a question. It was a youthful gesture, and it looked odd on him somehow. "What?"

"I barely ever see *you.* As you said, we betrothed," she said, willing the words to come out as interested and genuine-sounding as she could. "I feel like we should know each other better."

He lifted his shoulders in a shrug. "We have time for that, Princess. Not everything is like the stories, where heroes bewitch their lovers in seven days and slay the demons in eight."

His tone was faintly abrasive, as if it took effort to hold his scorn back. But she supposed she had walked into that, naive as she was meant to present herself.

The captain of the guard, Tarak, had been a little less unpleasant in conversation, but he was nearly as busy. The one time they did cross paths, it was the other boy that found her.

"Do you like flowers?" The question came so abruptly that Suri nearly slid a knife out of the makeshift pockets she'd cut into her skirts. She dropped it and wiped her sweaty hand on the fabric before bringing it up to tuck a piece of hair behind her ears. The captain held his hands up, a gesture of peace. "I didn't mean to startle you. Your Highness. Apologies, I'm unused to honorifics."

Suri bit back a snort. "You're very close with the king."

The captain beamed, warm brown eyes bright against his dark skin. "We've been friends since childhood, actually. All three of us. Though Viro can be a bit prickly at times, which I'm sure you've learned."

Prickly doesn't come close to covering it, she thought. "How did you know I like flowers?"

"You come here every day," he said, nodding at the rosebush in front of her. The palace had four gardens—one in the east courtyard, a simple one adorning the main entrance, a terrace on the roof of the western spire, and the northern gardens. The northern gardens were the largest and most elaborate, and despite her best interests and Mohini's warnings, Suri found herself drawn there day after day.

Suri wasn't precisely sure whether the recluse in the mountains could hurt her from this distance—sometimes she still doubted his existence—but she limited nighttime visits, for Isa's peace of mind if nothing else.

Tarak took a rose in his hands, rubbed a thumb over the unopened bud. "My mother was a gardener."

Suri blinked. "Pardon?"

He dropped his hand from the bush. "My mother loved to garden. She taught us—or tried to. Viro didn't have the patience—still doesn't—and I, unfortunately, don't have the hand for it. Flowers wither in my hands. But they are beautiful."

"They are," she said. A silence followed, thick enough to cut with a knife, even though the other boy hadn't looked up from the rosebush. "What happened to your mother?"

"She died. In the attacks on Marai, later in the war." Tarak smiled and straightened up. "You're wondering why I don't hate you."

Suri had been wondering that, and on any other occasion she would've worried at being so easily read. But his expression was calm and surprisingly friendly, and so she forgot to be afraid.

"War is war," he said simply. "People aren't nations, even though they may wish it. No matter what happens, war will continue, and people will die. But where I stand now, I can try to limit the latter as best I can." Tarak turned his attention back to the rosebush and plucked a fully bloomed flower before handing it to Suri. "I can't bring her back, and so I have no reason to resent you for what you haven't done."

Suri played with the stem of the flower to avoid looking up. "That's a very unique point of view, Captain."

"Unfortunately," he agreed. He opened his mouth to say something else, but a shout arose from far away, mildly resembling his name. He shook his head and offered another small smile before raising his hand in farewell. "I'll see you around, Your Highness."

Wandering around the palace alone was still too suspicious to be safe, and so Suri made it a point to take Isa or Mohini with her whenever she made to "explore." But even that was an unexpectedly difficult task, considering how infrequently she found them where they were meant to be.

Isa, at least, tried to be clandestine about it, stealing away from her room adjacent to Suri's early in the morning and late at night. Suri applauded the effort—if not for the fact that stealth was her profession, she might not have noticed her on some occasions.

It wasn't as if Suri didn't have her suspicions. She was often awake far before Isa returned, and the girl often returned through the northern gardens, and occasionally the eastern gate. On walks around the city, she would subconsciously take a more circuitous path, passing by the entrance to the temple instead of cutting through the heart of the markets like Suri was wont to do. Any attempts at subtlety on Isa's part had gone horribly and undeniably wrong, though Suri was willing to wait until the other girl wanted to talk about it.

Mohini made no attempts to hide her distraction. Many mornings would pass with her completely absent from the entire west wing of the palace, only to return long after the sun had risen, dressed in her clothes from the previous night. Oftentimes Mohini would go missing, eventually tracked down in some dusty alcove of the library sorting through correspondence for Galen and his apprentice. But there were just as many times when Suri would open her door in the early morning to find Lucius on the other side, a strangely strained expression on his face.

"Is there anything I can get for you?" she asked dryly. "Laxative herbs?"

He gave her a dirty look before pulling a sheaf of bound parchment slips out of the leather bag by his side. "These are… Well, when I was going through maps with Gal and Mohini yesterday, she seemed interested in western history… And I just thought she would appreciate them more than dusty old cataloguers… I was planning to give them to her myself, but I can't find her—"

"She's washing up."

"Ah," Lucius said, face blotchy. "That explains it. Give them to her, will you, Princess?"

And then he had shut the door in her face and run loudly down the corridor.

A sheaf of letters was just as often a pastry from the bakery down the street, or a flower that had fallen from a bush, or a note written in truly unintelligible handwriting and folded until it became little more than a ball.

Despite it all, Suri found that, surprisingly, it took little time to learn the city, and even more surprisingly that she actually enjoyed Mohini's company, her wide smile and mischievous take on the littlest of things. The palace still eluded her, though, full of locked doors and dusty, unlit hallways that always ended in dead ends.

And, no matter how hard she looked or how long she waited, she never saw the boy from the hill.

It was not a loss in the strictest sense of the word. Suri liked the upper city well enough, but it wasn't alive in the same way as the *angadi* and the buildings borne from it. To walk a few meters in the lower city was to hear five people's life stories and a hundred vendors calling out into the humid midday air. To walk an entire street's length was to hear more than a few whispered rumors, heavy with wild fear.

If the boy king was the kingdom's smile, harsh and cutting, the boy from the hill was its blood, everywhere and nowhere at all, slick with smoke and secrets.

No one could seem to agree on who he was, what he was. Mohini had made it clear that first day that she disapproved of either his actions or his existence—she had never deigned to clarify which one—and that they were all better off without him. The boy king never spoke of him, but sometimes, Suri could feel him in the air—a dangling pronoun in a conversation that she wasn't supposed to hear, silver ash streaked against the inside of his wrist.

The people of the lower city spoke of him without really daring to, a dance from one thought to another, suspicions grown into something new and frightening. A handful of matronly women hanging out their laundry on a terrace far above the packed dirt street—*I heard he can touch fire, that he can drink it, that he was borne of it, pulled straight from the hearth in the middle of the storm.* Children clad in colorful rags darting out from one alley into another, dipped and danced around Suri, fingers interlocked and mouths stretched open in rictal smiles as they sang a song that must've been new but sounded old as bones—*The orphan of the earth and the ashes, the only hope of the night-struck land, the messiah.* A few older kids, perched on the edge of an arching, elegant fountain on the outskirts of the markets, worn down by decades of use and whitened by the sun—*Which of them? The thyvaayan? The gods whisper in his ears so often, my atha told me he has to go to the apothecary for herbs to stem the bleeding.*

The rumors were so elaborate it was impossible for them to be true, and so specific it was impossible for them to be made up. He was a criminal, a peasant too dangerous to live near others; he was a long-lost prince from Erya that the king's late parents—gods bless them—had taken in out of the goodness of their hearts; he was a god himself, a fallen sort of god that was being disciplined and had been forced to live with humans, and yet he hated their faces so much he couldn't stand to live in the city proper.

An old woman, hemming a dress on the stoop of a low, crumbling tenement building as a thin summer breeze blew through, even suggested, in a thoughtful conversation with the dragonflies beside her, that he was not real at all, just a figment of smoke—an illusion breathed into something near alive that they had all believed because it was simply too difficult to attempt the alternative.

Suri was not entirely sure what to think of him, apart from a bone-deep wariness she had acquired from years of experience, a knowledge that people only left whispers of themselves behind in the minds of so many people if they were foolish or dangerous. And she did not think he was foolish, not yet.

She did not want to visit him, not really. He was not her target, and he was not her ally—it was likely he'd impede her path before he aided her—but it was impossible to let it go. If only because she wanted to knock his teeth out for scaring Mohini so badly.

But he was a ghost and a shadow and more the scent of smoke than the dark, ashy thread of it, and she never saw him, not once.

"Now," Lucius said, tossing an apple core from one hand to another, "Will you finally tell me where you have been?"

Kiran held out his hand, and the other boy dutifully placed the core in it. He placed it in the waste bin and wiped his hands with a washcloth hung on a low ring, speaking without looking back at his friend. "I don't know what you're talking about. I've been here all week."

"Yes," Lucius said, spreading his hands emphatically as he was wont to do when he was feeling particularly melodramatic. "Precisely. You have been here *all week.* You schedule all your meetings with the *nakshi* in the early morning and pop around the city to say hello, and then do a single circuit of the temple before cloistering yourself in here for the rest of the day. This is not typical Kiran behavior."

"You've been gone for over a year," he said, gathering a stack of treatises he was looking over for Viro into a stack and placing them in the corner of the stout wooden table they'd all made together, when they'd been considerably smaller and had much less hand-eye coordination. Scrolls were swept across the rest of the table, and lay covering the floor in precarious stacks. Stories, ledgers, tales of distant lands—Lucius had brought them with him when he'd first visited after a year and a half of being pen pals, and had never stopped since. The gifts were the closest thing Kiran had to a taste of the outside world, apart from brief diplomatic envoys. "For all you know, I may have changed. And don't call him that."

"Call him what? *Nakshi?* He is what he is," Lucius said, shifting to lie down on the uneven, overused settee. "And, at the very least, allow me this—I *know* you, and I don't need to see you to know you, never have. So why are you hiding? Or rather, who are you hiding from?"

"I'm not going to play along with this, Lucius."

"You don't have to say anything," he said, holding up his hands. There was an irritating, familiar gleam in his eyes. Kiran wondered if Tarak would be terribly upset if he dumped the mess of dealing with him on the royal guard for the day. "All your answers will be in your expressions. Your left eyelid twitches when you're upset, you know."

He looked up from where he was scrubbing the tiled floor and jerked his head at the bucket of water beside him. "I will pour this all over you."

Lucius grinned. "You'd have to catch me first. Is it… that baker who thinks you're a revenant from Dhaasthur?" Kiran kept scrubbing. "Or is it the chief from Maíneli, the one who thinks you asked the gods to ruin their crops?"

"How does Galen put up with you?" he murmured under his breath.

The other boy heard it, as he was supposed to, and his smile only widened. "He doesn't, really. He just throws me out to become someone else's problem after a while. It's quite effective, I think." He shook his head in a laugh and continued, "Don't distract me! Anyway, come Avyakanth, you won't be able to hide in here. The festival's for you and your ilk, after all. And in two moons, the *nakshi* and his bride are set to bring—what was it that they called the match? A union of peace and prosperity? Or was it bountiful riches? At any rate, you won't be allowed to rot away up here. Won't you be expected to give a speech?"

Kiran didn't answer. Sometimes things like these slipped Lucius's mind, little details that he didn't hold onto. Whether it was out of true forgetfulness or out of some kind of denial of the fact itself, he wasn't sure. There was no way to bring it up now without ruining the conversation, anyway.

"Oh. I'm a fool," Lucius said, gaze sober for a single second before transitioning into wry amusement. "It's the bride, isn't it? The Najan princess. Suri."

Kiran had not previously known her name, had not known anything but her face—which he had seen passing by the temple the day she arrived—and her title, which he had put together with convoluted inductive reasoning. And he knew the way her dead body looked, he supposed. Ash and death under a red sky, like the blood had become fire and then crimson-slick smoke and covered the sky in sheets so thick that the clouds faded away altogether. He knew that.

He came back to himself—Lucius was knelt in front of him, a single hand raised above Kiran's shoulder, as if he had almost shaken him out of his thoughts but thought better of it at the last moment. His eyes were narrowed with concern. "Was it—a vision?"

"Not a new one," he said truthfully. "It's a memory of one, and I do not know if that makes it a vision at all. What about the princess?"

Lucius relaxed, a subtle movement. "You're avoiding her. That's why you've been hiding."

He shook his head wryly, despite the fact that he still felt shaken. "Why would I be avoiding her?"

Because she is dead, or will be dead, or has been dead, and you're afraid of it—afraid of what seeing what death looks like on a person up close, even after you have seen it before so many times. Because you think if you stay away long enough, you might be able to save her.

Kiran turned his head away so he could continue to scrub at the floor, heart pulsing with the remnants of fear from the vision, praying Lucius would not think to look too closely at him. He didn't, instead leaning back against the stubby legs of the table and folding his own. "I do not know. You've never been one for prejudice. But it has to be her. I'm sure she wishes I had a reason to avoid her."

"You're close friends, then?" he asked, raising an eyebrow. "Do I mean so little to you after all?"

"Oh, hush," he said crossly. "I *have* spoken to her, and she's nice, if a little sharp around the edges. It's in her blood, I'm sure, the call of war, and all that. *Nakshi* calls to *nakshi*—"

"I told you not to call him that."

"You're no fun, has anyone ever told you that? And anyway, I'm sure she hates me, I am clearly *besotted* with her maid, and it's becoming a problem," he finished, turning wide, puppy eyes on him.

Kiran rolled his eyes and wrung out the rag before returning it to the bucket. "Kazha should have claimed me, considering how often you come to me with problems of your love life. What counsel may I provide this time?"

"I don't know what to *do,*" he said in agony, stretching out his arms above him. "She's beautiful, and kind, and is better at mapmaking than I am—Galen keeps threatening to take her back to the capital in place of me—and I don't know how to deal with it. And sometimes we take walks around the city while she's supposed to be accompanying me on errands, and I know she's pointing out landmarks—not that I need a tour of this damn city considering how many times you've dragged me into it—but all her words go in one ear and straight out the other. It's like I've lost all sense of language and communication."

Kiran blinked at him. "So this isn't the usual?"

"What? Of course it's not the usual. What do you even mean by that, 'the usual'?"

He pulled himself up, shaking out the stiffness in his legs before going to wash his hands with the remainders of a bar of rosemary soap Lucius had brought him the last time he'd passed through. He counted off his points on his fingers as he spoke. "She's pretty, you're bored, you think love is beautiful and poetic so you decide to give it a try, both of you give up on it after a week, and you move onto the next one."

Lucius glared at him. "That is not—I don't do that. And even if I did do that, that isn't what is happening here."

"Really?" he asked, rinsing his hands. "Have you told her about me?" At the responding silence, he tilted his head with amusement, drying his hands with the washcloth. "That should be your real marker of what to do when you feel oh-so-strongly about someone, instead of coming to me with your woes."

He was quiet for a moment more before he said quietly, "I don't think she likes you very much."

"That's not an uncommon response," Kiran said, raising his eyebrows. "And you know that. Do you truly plan to interact with us separately for the rest of my gods-given life? I would not call it a bad plan, it has merit—"

"You always talk like that," Lucius said, a familiar, weary anger in his voice. "Are you so resigned to the thought of it?"

Kita had often asked him the same thing, with less anger and more familial sternness, and he had never answered it, not seriously. He uncrossed his arms and came to sit on the edge of the settee, close enough to Lucius that he could see the boy's hands shaking. "If I wasn't, I would've gone mad by now."

His mouth flattened out into a grimace. Finally, he said, "Sometimes… sometimes I wish we had met under different circumstances."

His mouth quirked to the side. "It's unlikely we would've met at all if I had not grown up like this."

"I know," Lucius said, a glimmer of sad humor lifting his expression. "I know, but it would've been nice. Do you ever wonder what your life would've been like, if it hadn't been this way?"

"This is the only life I've ever lived," Kiran said, and though it was true, a traitorous whisper thrummed under the words, a voice he had never allowed to speak. *All the time.*

Suri had never worked with a kagha before. She had seen one once, as a young girl, reached out a soft, small hand to touch the black bird—it had been fully grown, scaling the length of her torso in height—and pulled back when it had snapped its beak. They were volatile, coarse animals, but beautiful all the same. And nearly impossible to tame by anyone without Athrian blood.

Anyu had informed her that they had already trained one for her and left it in the aviary months ago, assuring her in his pleasant way that it was perfectly safe to interact with as long as she didn't put her fingers near its mouth.

She wasn't planning to, but the entire operation of communication was rendered useless by the simple fact that she could not find the aviary.

Her maids were unsure; Tarak would know, she knew, and so would the boy king, but she could never find the former, and knew the latter would be too suspicious of her motives to give her a straight answer. After a week and a half of fruitless searching, and the first report date already past, it was apparent that if she didn't shake the answer from the palace itself, she wouldn't find it handed to her.

After leaving Isa in her rooms— Mohini had been gone the entire evening, presumably to moon over Lucius while he made idle conversation and pretended he wasn't mooning back—Suri went to find the two of them, inseparable as they always were.

Suri leaned back against the chilled stone walls of the colonnade and looked out on the west courtyard, pillars of stone cutting her view into chunks. The fountain gurgled in the center, the water colored silver-white by the rising moon, but apart from that it was silent.

What had Lucius called him? *Nakshi.* War dog; Suri couldn't judge him for it when her own nickname still ghosted over her shoulders. *Hehyava,* an antiquated word for assassins. *Hehya,* from the sacred wellspring of blood, and *ava,* for girl. They were cut from the same cloth, from scar tissue and iron. *And where would a war dog feel most comfortable?*

She caught the door to the war room as it swung open, ducking out of the way of someone already leaving. She turned to look behind her and see who it was, but Tarak was leaning forward, tapping her on the shoulder, and she pulled her attention away. There was something faintly apologetic in his gaze, a kind of weary irritation, as if he meant to say, *Sorry for all this, but it is to be expected.* She raised her eyebrows, but followed him into the room.

It was empty, save for him and the boy king, who was pacing across its length. With every stride, he seemed to get even angrier, a strange, jagged energy animating his movements. There was a desk in the back, flanked by rows and rows of cluttered bookcases. A grand, needlessly intricate painting of Athrian fields framed the single, high-backed seat, studded with gold.

There was also a table in the center, nearly two-thirds the size of the long dining table Suri had familiarized herself with. There were maps strewn across it, and small metal figurines holding down the edges, paperweights carved into life. The pawns were worn down, glistening with overuse.

The boy king swore, and it was almost surprising—not because it sounded uncharacteristic, but because it had felt like, up until this moment, he had taken pains to *not* swear in front of her, to construct some kind of barely civil façade that wavered on a shaky foundation. And now, it seemed, the foundation was cracking.

He swore again, and Tarak dropped his hand from Suri's shoulder, shot her another apologetic smile, and went to calm him. The boy king lifted his gaze, glanced once at Suri before turning to the captain, and said, "I hate him."

"No, you don't," the other boy returned calmly, the words practiced and smooth on his tongue as if this was a daily occurrence. "You're angry that he's right."

He laughed, unamused. It was a jagged, unpleasant sound, pottery shattering on stone. "Perhaps. Perhaps I am angry that he is incapable of being wrong. I suppose that human error seems like a faraway concept to him. Like most human things do." Tarak's mouth tightened, but the king didn't notice, lowering his gaze to the mess of a table. "This is going to be a bitch to move around in time, if he's right. *And* to get rations to the northern border in less than three days—does he think we can just fly them there, on wings?"

"If he's *right,* then they will starve without them, and you know that," the captain said, reaching out a hand and resting it on his shoulder. Some of the tension dissipated away at the touch, but Suri could still feel his anger from where she leaned against the door.

"I know that," he said petulantly, lips faintly parted as if to add something else before he pressed them together and looked away. He glanced over at Suri, that incendiary anger flattening out to something thin and brittle. "Princess. I thought tonight's dinner was canceled. Something about already eating in the upper city?"

"Yes," she said, the word sharp and unfamiliar on her mouth—her presence in itself felt like an intrusion of sorts, and it had unsettled her greatly. Even though her job, in crude terms, was to intrude upon every single part of the king's life until he no longer had one. "Yes, I was just wondering if—if I could speak with the captain for a moment."

"With Tarak?" he asked, surprise softening the planes of his face. He looked strangely youthful for a moment, like a seventeen-year-old boy who had come by a crown by some trick of fate and was playing dress-up. "Why?"

"A civet ruined my room while I was out," she said smoothly. The king's expression had already begun to harden, but disinterest substituted his usual suspicion, and he waved his hand in dismissal.

Tarak offered her a small smile and followed her out into the corridor. The moon had fully risen, and it shone into the shadowed stone between the pillars, casting them both in milky off-white light. "I'm assuming your room is fine, and that was an elaborate lie meant to draw me away from Viro."

She exhaled a small, sharp laugh. "How observant you are."

"He might have noticed," the captain said, nodding toward the door, "If he had not been so distracted. A friend of ours came by, gave us some bad news. The timing could have been better."

"A friend?" The words came out a little strangled, but Tarak didn't notice. *You have more important things to worry about,* she reprimanded herself crossly, but still, she waited with bated breath for the other boy to explain. It was the curiosity of stories and fairy tales, the desire to blow away dust and find something glittering and night-black and magical.

He nodded and pointed at the hills. This late, the contours of the dark stone and tangled shrubbery had faded into an eerie splash of black below the night sky, the jagged peaks reaching up to touch the stars and then dipping back down to the earth. From here, Suri could just barely make out the outline of the temple, four pillars of charcoal-gray stone and no roof above it all. "He lives up there, so you might not have seen him. Though usually he's around the palace quite a lot."

Not recently, she thought sourly. It was a bitter pill to swallow, the knowledge that she had just *barely* missed him. Even now, she couldn't remember anything about the figure she had sidestepped—the memory slipped away from her, mutable. She shook her head to clear it of the puerile frustration and forced a smile. "Actually, I was wondering whether you knew where the aviary was."

"The aviary?" he asked, cocking his head to the side. "It should be at the top of the northern tower. Why?"

She shrugged, letting her mouth quirk to the side in a melancholy-tinged smile. *This* came easily, the deception and the pretenses. "I'm feeling rather homesick, so I wish to send a letter home to my brothers."

The ghost of suspicion on his face softened, and for a moment, she regretted exploiting him like this. "It is always open to you, then. Though I think the trainer has retired for the night. If you want, I'll send someone to accompany you tomorrow."

"Thank you," she said, forcing another smile and inclining her head in acknowledgement. Tarak returned it before waving and slipping back into the war room. Suri waited until she could once again hear soft voices from within, and then continued down the colonnade.

The north tower was closest to the mountains, and as far as Suri knew, the most secluded of the three spires. A spiral staircase led up to the second floor and above to what she now knew was the aviary, silver metal shining darkly in the shadows. Moonlight streamed in through windows cut into the stone of the outer tower, rendering the entire edifice in shades of ash. Past the second landing—splitting into stoas exposing the east and west wing—the staircase led upward to a comparatively small wooden door. Though it was already locked, a quick search revealed that the key ring was hidden in the shadows of the doorway, under a loose brick.

The door ached as she pushed it open gently, and she shut it with care. It was stuffier in here, the air thick with secrets and silage. At her entrance, a resounding shriek filled the air, the sound of hundreds of kaghas screeching one after another, a harsh, dissonant symphony. Suri braced herself, pressing one ear to the door, but could hear no footsteps. She supposed it was common enough for the birds to rile themselves up over nothing.

Anyu had given detailed instructions with regards to locating the kagha—seventh row, fifth from the right, scar two inches above the third talon of its left foot—and it didn't take long for her to find it. She slipped the letter out of her skirts where she'd hidden it between layers; Athrian finery made it difficult to conceal things, with its tight swathes of fabric and intricately engraved accessories. The heavy embroidery and layers of Najan dresses—though they often cost her respect in the city—were made for simple deception.

Suri examined the letter. It looked innocuous; the contents revealed little, if one did not know how to decipher them. She glanced up again and saw the kagha—it caught her eyes, perched strangely still, as if waiting for her to call it down.

She raised her hand, clicked her tongue, and it swooped down and landed on her wrist. Its talons dug into her skin, drawing blood without any sort of malicious intent, simply out of a sense of instinct and natural brutality. It stared at her, black eyes shining with a preternatural intelligence.

Suri pulled the thread loose from where it lay coiled around the kagha's left foot, then folded the cloth carefully so it was the size of her thumb before wrapping the twine around it and tying it back onto the kagha. She held it at arm's length, scrutinizing it for a moment. Aloud, she said, "You know where you are meant to fly to?"

The kagha simply stared back at her, gaze faintly disdainful. Scorning her doubt. She shook her head and climbed the steps up to the aviary window. They led out onto a thick but small platform a few feet in width, surrounded by wrought-iron bars. From here, the top of the tallest tower, Suri could see the entirety of Marai—this late, the lights glittered and danced, the city a night-dark jewel. It was beautiful, and it was to die.

By your hands, a voice in her head whispered, but she dismissed it. She held the kagha up, turning it to the northwest, and let go. It disappeared almost instantly, a smudgy blot dissolving in the oily blackness of the night.

Her gaze dropped from it, wandering across to where the hills sloped into the mountains. The temple was only visible from the other side of the north tower, but the black stone and faint smell of smoke drew her back to the memory. What she felt—she didn't know what she felt. It was some strange amalgam of childlike offense and curiosity and righteousness, and despite it all, an unfamiliar kind of resonance.

A different voice in her head, far more reminiscent of Rohit, scolded her. *That is not why you are here.* But it was clear that she was capable of doing what she was here for and taking on sundry pursuits in the meantime. And, really, if the boy king and his captain relied so strongly on who—*what*—laid in those hills and the stone that swallowed them, it was part of her work to seek him out. To understand what kind of threat he posed to her work, and how best to accommodate it.

If he would not come to her, then she would just have to go find him.

6
LYNE

In between the story of the princess and priest, and classes and work and brief flashes of sleep, Suri and Kiran made routines of their own.

There was a pleasant irreverence to the rhythm of Kiran's actions. He spent afternoons reading at Beanzzz, knees hooked over the edge of the windowsill, marathoned *Heartbreak Hotel* with Miya whenever she happened to come over, and competed against Aza over which one could fit the most marshmallows in their mouth—a competition no one really won after they started laughing and spit out the sugary, globby mess on Suri's carpet.

Friday nights were always movie nights, often at Aza and Dai's place. It hadn't taken long for the rest of them to realize that Kiran—who hadn't even known what a movie *was* until Suri had explained how the technology had been developed—had never seen any of the 'classics' they'd grown up with. So they'd taken it upon themselves, Dai and Miya especially, to educate him. He bore it all with the blithe complacency of someone with little idea of what they were getting themselves into.

It was a new routine, but it already had its own sense of comfort to it. The opening sequence began; Suri hadn't seen the movie in years, but she vaguely remembered the premise—two people met as children, and then fell in love as adults after years apart. And then one of them died, and the other mourned them. It was all very cliché and depressing and fun to pick apart with other people, but easy to cry to alone.

She glanced over her shoulder during the final scene, unable to suppress her curiosity. Kiran was stretched along the floor, head at an odd angle and propped up by a slowly slipping arm. Aza and Dai's corgi mix nosed endlessly at his side; strangely enough, dogs went crazy for Kiran. He didn't look sleepy, but he didn't look interested, either.

He glanced up and caught her gaze, arching an eyebrow and nodding slightly at the screen, as if to say, *Can you believe this shit?*

"How is this movie so bad?" Dai murmured under his breath, all awestruck horror.

"I thought it was cute when I first saw it," Miya said defensively as the credits began to roll.

"When?" Aza drawled. "When you were, like, six? Back when all we knew about romance was fairy tales?"

"Not like you've gained any experience since then," Ellis quipped, and dodged the pillow she hurled at him.

"Well?" Miya asked, glancing down toward where Kiran was still curled up against the edge of the couch. A bowl of popcorn was securely tucked between his shoulder and the side of the coffee table, and every few seconds, he darted out a hand to pop a piece into his mouth. "What's your verdict?"

"Bad," he said eloquently. "You lot might not have any experience in the world of *love*—" He paused to say this, stretching out his arms in a gesture. "—But *I* do, and that is not how it goes. Less tears, usually."

"Even when death's on the horizon?" Aza cut in, raising her eyebrows.

"Oh, especially then," he replied, eyes bright and glittering. There was an unsaid joke in his words, hidden where none of them could access it, but they were laughing all the same.

"I don't believe you," Suri said, pushing herself up from where she'd slipped down into the alcove of the arm chair. Her hair hung over her face in a staticky cloud, and she blew it away. "About the love thing."

"Really," he said, mildly amused. He didn't bother to elaborate, but then again, he rarely did.

After the movie, Aza pulled out her lifetime collection of board games, and Miya tugged out plastic bags filled with liquor bottles, and they forgot about old love movies. Kiran didn't drink, like he'd said when they'd first met—*she'd held a god at knifepoint*—content to move around game pieces and watch them play. Eventually, though, the games slurred to a stop, tilting them back against the closest horizontal surface as time ticked on.

A little after midnight, the apartment alive with the soft buzz of the radiator, Miya asked, "What would you guys do if you found out you died tomorrow?"

Suri strained herself slightly to push up on her elbows. Across from her, Kiran was silent and coiled, all languid energy. But his eyes were open, sharp with curiosity. Suri felt a faint stab of bitterness at that; it made sense, in a crude way, that immortals would find humanity's perception of its own mortality entertaining. Like they were lab rats, ivory-white and scrubbed clean, set to run the same predetermined races, run into the same predetermined walls, and die the same predetermined deaths. He glanced over, and she looked away.

Dai made a small noise of confusion. "Like, what? A note shows up on my doorstep? Or is it just a hunch?"

Miya shook her head, and her hair tickled Suri's arm. "Doesn't matter. You just know. What would you do?"

"Go skydiving," Aza said mirthlessly. Dai shuddered beside her—his fear of heights was why she hadn't gone skydiving yet. She refused to go unless she dragged him down with her.

"Maybe…" he made a thoughtful sound. "Go through old favorites, with family and friends. Like a quick recap of my entire life based on things I love. Miya?"

"Get banned from as many places as I possibly can," she said cheerfully, though the words came out distinctly slurred. "It won't affect me, anyway, right? Go big or go home, and all that. Suri?"

If she died tomorrow. She prided herself on living a content life, but now it felt a little bit like it was simply boring. Suri didn't dare look over, didn't dare catch his gaze, but she knew he would be looking at her. "There's a story I want to hear finished."

"That's it?" Dai asked in disbelief.

"That's it," she repeated, face splotchy. Quickly, she turned her face up. "Ellis?"

"Spend the day with my family," he said quietly. His family was chaotic and lovely, and from what she knew, never really in the same place at the same time. "Kiran?"

Suri opened her eyes. His head was tilted back, brows faintly arched as if he was surprised he'd been called on in the first place. Then his mouth twisted, and he said, "Step in front of oncoming traffic."

"Dude," Dai groaned, nauseated. A chorus of what-the-hells swelled around him. "I did not need that visual right now."

"Why?" Ellis asked, genuinely curious.

He lifted his shoulders in a shrug. There was something oddly disingenuous about the movement, as if he was playacting himself. "Autonomy. At least that way, I have the final say in how I leave this world."

Aza shuddered. "Too dark. Too philosophical. Who wants more drinks?"

Unsurprisingly, they all did. They had more drinks, and more after that, and Suri lost track of the drinks and the minutes and the words, even as she tossed them up in the air. Like juggling. She'd tried to learn juggling in the third grade, but then she'd dropped an apple on her foot and it had hurt *so much,* so she'd given up. She figured Kiran could probably juggle.

And then he was kneeling beside her, hands light on her shoulders. As if he was afraid he'd hurt her. She wanted to laugh at the thought of it, but she had no laughs left—she'd been drained of them all. *You won't hurt me,* she wanted to say. *You promised, so you won't. So you shouldn't be afraid.*

Aloud, she said, "What time is it?"

She heard the smile in his voice. "Late. Your friends are cleaning up. It might take them a while to get to it all."

Suri shoved at him blindly. "Go… help them."

"I did," he said, oddly soft. "I cleaned everything up, but they're drunk, so they think I did it wrong. Maybe they're right? I don't truly know where things are supposed to go, anyway. I put a bottle of wine in the oven."

She groaned at him, because she was too tired to scold him and knew he'd understand either way. In the distance, she heard rustling, bare feet on carpet. And then, in a profoundly drunk voice: "Suri's wasted."

"Yeah," Kiran said simply. "I'm going to take her back to the apartment. Will you be alright without supervision?"

"Fuck," said her very drunk friend who she could not name but really truly loved all the same, "You. Fuck you."

Then there was something like a laugh—but a little too soft to truly qualify, a little bit uneven—and his arms were back on her shoulders. "Suri."

"Mm?"

"Do you think you can get up?"

"Maybe. I could *try?*" she pushed herself to her feet, immediately listing to the side. Arms went around her, steadying, and for a moment, she thought she could probably spend the rest of her life like this. Even if it was short.

I want to change my answer, she thought. *Finish the story, but like this.*

"What?" Kiran asked, shifting her in his arms to get a better look at her expression.

"Nothing," she mumbled, and then tugged him toward the door. She just wanted to go home and listen to him tell that story, even though she wouldn't remember anything in the morning, and he'd have to repeat it all later. She just wanted to listen.

After a few seconds of futile tugging, Kiran wrapped his arms around her shoulders and she gratefully sagged against him. They hobbled to the door in an odd medley of god and human and boy and girl, and it was horribly inefficient, but warm.

He called something back, and someone responded, and the door shut behind them. Stairs led down into darkness and out into the city. Suri stared down into the dark from the security of his arms, and then untangled herself.

Kiran made a sound of surprise, but didn't try to hold her back. Leaning back against the opposite wall, she tilted her chin up, defiant despite the fuzzy feeling in her head. "Explain."

"Explain what?"

"In there," she said, jerking her head. Words slipped through her fingers; she struggled to organize them, grasping at dissolving thoughts. "You were… weird. Like—" she cut off, waving her hands in a gesture that clarified absolutely nothing. "When we were talking about what we'd do if we died the next day. You were weird."

"Weird how?" he asked, tilting his head so hair fell into his face. In the shadowed corridor, he looked incandescent and young. All the right components of a boy slotted into all the right places, but not quite a boy. *Build-a-Boy's singular business failure,* she thought hysterically, and then rubbed at her eyes until the smile passed.

"Weird," she repeated, dropping her hands to her sides. "It was like you were pretending to be yourself."

He was silent for a moment, gaze resting on the cobweb-misted ceiling above. Without looking down, he said, "I wasn't lying."

"Yeah," she said, pushing off from the wall. She had greatly overestimated her motor control; she staggered forward, teetering on the edge of the staircase. And then his hands were on her elbows, a ghost of a touch, and she held his stare for so long she felt like perhaps she could swallow this moment. She could put it to paper, fold it up, and keep it forever in gaps of skin and bone.

But she wouldn't remember this, she knew. She wouldn't remember how strange he'd acted, and how bad the movie had been, and she certainly wouldn't remember this—the slant of gold in low light, the unsteadying fondness in the uneven line of his smile.

She forced herself to speak. "I know you weren't. Lying, that is. But it wasn't you. I'm asking why."

"That's a secret."

"Even from me?"

His smile was faintly strained, the way it had been when she'd introduced him to Tarak. Smooth as sea glass, incongruity sanded down at the edges. "Especially you."

She frowned at him with the transient irritation of the utterly wasted, then took a step back and held her arms out. "Take me home, then."

So he did, scooping her up with the ease of someone who could likely lift cars and buildings and trees. He carried her all the way home, and Suri kept her gaze on the darkness above, the autumn chill insubstantial around her.

He paused on the threshold, and she gingerly climbed out of his arms. She collapsed on the couch, rolling to one side to make more room. He regarded her with bemusement. "Where am I meant to sleep, then?"

She raised an eyebrow. "Were you planning to?"

He shrugged, then obligingly took a seat on the opposite side, knees sprawled across her legs. A smile pulled at the corners of his mouth. "There's a story you want to hear finished, hm?"

Suri flushed. "I'm invested now. It's your fault for telling it to me."

"You asked for one," he returned.

"Could've said no," she shot back. Suri watched him through slit eyes, all shadows and smoke. She yawned, and then said, "Tell me a story."

"Any story?" he asked. His voice sounded distant, but she hung onto the lilting cadence of it. "You won't remember in the morning."

"I know," she said, tucking her head in between the couch cushions. "I don't care, though."

And he laughed, bright and consonant like temple bells, but he still spoke, still spun out stories like candied pieces of a world he'd long since left behind.

7
ENESMAT

In the quiet of the early morning, the capital looked as if it were simply another appendage of the mountains, all glittering black rooftops and cold shadows. The sun had not yet risen when Suri climbed out of her window, the sky thick with charcoal clouds. This early, the ceaseless din of the city—which she had only recently accustomed herself to—softened into an eerie near-silence, broken intermittently by the screaming of the kaghas, or a faint breeze whistling through the distant tree line at the base of the hills.

Suri wound around the north gardens, tracing the path down from the temple to a flat, sandy area near a small grove of kino trees a few-hundred meters away. It looked like any other abandoned trail, with no proper gate or plaque to distinguish it from the surrounding brush, save for an engraved metallic square at the base. Suri knelt and blew away the soil that obscured it, squinting to examine it in the near darkness. But it gave away nothing—it was simply an old etching on bronze, depicting a thin line encircling a flame. A marker for the temple, she supposed, when people had actually used it.

She pulled herself to her feet and dusted her skirts off, retying her sash and blowing a loose strand of hair away from where it hung in her face. She had dressed in what she referred to as Athrian colors, the blouse and skirts done in black and the sash in a desaturated, heady red. They were the colors that covered the kingdom's war banners when they were flown. The cloak, though, she'd borrowed off an unsuspecting guard, and it was soft but thin, and still smelled of spices and arrack.

As she climbed up the trail, dodging tree branches as they snapped into her face, the world began to lighten around her. The shadows faded and twined with tremulous streams of light. The sun hadn't yet appeared, but by the time she reached the top, the sky had turned a deep, wine-red color, the smoky clouds dissolving into ash-gray wisps.

It bore no resemblance to the grand, awe-inspiring temple it led away from. A water pump dripped onto soil, a gully draining away the excess. Beside it, a handful of worn stone steps led up to the age-smoothed floor of the temple.

As a consequence of her work, Suri had seen the entire expanse of the peninsula. Enesmati temples varied in design by many factors: climate, architectural styles, different cultural predispositions with regards to patterns and favored gods. But she had never seen a temple without a roof.

This temple—if it truly could be called that—was small, a little larger than the boy king's war room. At each of the four corners stood a slim stone pillar, several heads taller than Suri and unadorned by the colorful images that characterized those of the main temple. They were carved with intricate, tangled designs, less concerned with telling a story to devotees and more with a raw display of divinity.

The altar in the center was also oddly simple—a stone slab that came to her waist, resting on a thick base, differentiable only by the carved ash-gray bird at its head and two indents. One held oil and a yellowing wick that ran the length of it, while a second indent lay empty, incised into the surface so that—if one wished—they could fill it with a thin film of liquid. A symbol was carved into the center of this second recess, the same one that had been on the metal plaque at the base of the hill—a slender circle, and in its center, a single flame.

The sanctum was shadowed, but the metal grate had been hauled up. Two stone steps separated the *karuvarai* from the floor of the temple, and the faint morning light revealed a granite statue, glossy but untouched save for a streak of ash across its temple. A few untouched baskets lay beside the base of the statue, holding clusters of jasmine and kino flowers. Below, on the sanctum floor, a clay *unthi* pot and a camphor lamp shone in the murky light. But there was no sign of a flame.

Though the temple was simple, it had obviously been cared for. There was no dust, no cobwebs, and the air smelled sweetly—of holy water and fresh incense smoke.

"Is there anything I can help you with?"

Despite everything, Suri flinched badly. It had something to do with how quiet it had become, as if she had slipped into a new world up here, bare feet on soft stone belonging to a different life. She hadn't noticed the presence of another until the words cut through the air, and it was a strange thing; she could not remember the last time she had not been aware of the heartbeat of every living thing around her, as if even the molten core of her had grown accustomed to snuffing out such sounds.

The voice had come from behind her, she realized, slowly coming back to herself. She heaved a breath and turned to find a figure standing at the entrance, one foot braced on the first step. The sun had still not come up, but the crimson sky had lightened into an eerie, brighter red, and the combination of that faint light and the shadows around the figure limned them in a stark, unearthly contrast. They took a step forward, shadows falling away.

It was a boy—her age, if she had to hazard a guess. A wicker basket was tucked under his arm, identical to the ones lain at the base of the statue—*a priest, perhaps*, she thought, *responsible for taking care of the temple*—and a jagged piece of flint was curled in his other hand. He had not said anything apart from that initial question, and had simply stood on the threshold of the temple, waiting for her response.

"I—" she cleared her throat and continued, as steady as she could, "I'm looking for the high priest of the temple. The one who lives here."

The corner of his mouth twitched, but there was no other change in his expression. The boy ascended the steps—an old, ingrained routine—and slipped past her to place the basket and flint on the steps leading into the inner sanctum. He turned and smiled, humorless but not as cutting as the boy king's. Wry, perhaps. "That would be me. Is there anything you need?"

Another misstep, worse because of all the practice that had gone into avoiding such things, but Suri knew she did not conceal the majority of her shock. Perhaps it was the rumors, or the boy king's frustration, or Mohini's fearful discomfort, but she had expected someone—someone different. Taller, at the very least. The boy had, at most, an inch of height on her.

Yet, despite his height and ascetic frame, he appeared cherubic and stretched thin, a phantasm. There was a faint sense of otherness to him, discernible now that he had come closer. As if he could thrust his hand into the smooth stone of the altar and pull out a beating heart, blood running down his—

"Princess?"

His voice pulled her out of her reverie and she blinked, unconsciously taking a step back. The soft flesh of her wrist hit one of the talons of the carved bird. "My apologies, I—" she cut off, narrowing her eyes. "How do you know who I am?"

The boy raised an eyebrow, moving to stand in front of her. He raised his hand, indicating her dress, her necklace, then the small black tattoo under her collarbone. It had gone unnoticed since she had arrived. "Athrians are too hardened to the morning's chill to wear anything with more than a few layers, if that. Your necklace is made with enough gold that only a noble could afford it, but I've never seen you, *and* your pendant is the old Najan symbol of the broken star. And that tattoo is a luxury, offered only to Najan royalty as children."

Her voice was unrecognizable even to herself when she spoke; a stony rasp. "You know an awful lot about the world for a recluse."

The skin around his eyes crinkled, but he didn't smile. "I wouldn't consider myself a recluse, despite my recent absence. Why are you here, Princess?"

Suri tipped her chin up, curling her fingers into the carved stone. The nickname, the boy king's favorite, struck a familiar chord of old, bitter resolve, even though it sounded different coming from the priest, the inflections distinct and lilting. "I thought I might pay you a visit. I've heard a lot."

The boy took a step back, leaning back against the archway of the sanctum. Even now, he was inscrutable, nearly identical to the stone statue he cared for. "You have? And what have you learned from it, about me?"

She opened her mouth to speak, yet nothing of what she could remember seemed to hold any substance. It was all true—none of it was true. *He drinks fire and dances with gods and can split stone with a single touch and—*

Suri exhaled, shaking her head slightly. "Nothing. That is why I came."

"Really?" he said, voice soft but dry. "And here I thought you simply desired a place to pray."

Instinctively, she glared at him, mouth twisting with dismay immediately after. But instead of fury, his eyes glinted with surprise and amusement. He held his hands up in a placating gesture, one of faux surrender. "I will make you a deal—I won't tell Viro about that letter as long as you do not send another. Fair?"

Her heart dropped somewhere into the pit of her stomach. Out of instinct more than anything else, she slipped a knife—Solitude, bright and fair—out of her skirts and crossed the distance between them in two long strides, pressing it to his throat. The silver metal glinted against his neck. At the very least, he wasn't any long-lost Eryan prince with skin that dark, the color of burnt cinnamon bark.

The sky was no longer red, but the milky early morning glow did little to soften the planes of his face. He held her gaze calmly, coal-black eyes smooth and unreadable.

When she spoke, her voice was low but steady, thankfully. "How do you know about the letter?"

The boy tilted his head and a lock of hair fell into his face, cutting his gaze into pieces. "I am not the sort of person you want to kill."

She snorted, pressing the knife into his skin. It reddened, but did not bleed. "Why, because the gods favor you? Spare me your ego. How do you know about the letter?"

Instead of answering, he raised a hand and covered hers where it clutched the knife. The raised flesh of a scar on his palm brushed the back of her hand. He was strangely overwarm in the cool summer morning, and she would've thought him feverish had she not seen with her eyes the clean lack of expression on his face. "The aviary is dear to me. Ask the captain of the guard if you distrust me. And, as it is clear that no one has taken the time to inform you, the gods favor no one."

"Then what are you?"

He smiled, lovely but hard. "An accident."

Once again, she felt that strange sensation, pressing fingers to a mirror only to find the reflection fluid and slick under her skin. An alloy of sacrilege and an unfamiliar, jagged ache.

But she dropped the knife from his throat, retreating back to the edge of the altar. The boy reached up a hand and rubbed at the reddening bruise that cut across the base of his throat, pensive. His eyes flicked up to hers, but before he could speak, Suri said, "Why? Why is it such a bad idea for me to send a letter back to my family?"

"Apart from the natural suspicion that your presence here is an ill portent for the safety of my nation," he said, drawing himself back up, "Anything that you send—regardless of whether you truly mean to betray us—is bound to implicate you in suspicion and paranoia this early on."

"Nobody saw me."

"I did," he said, but there was no triumph in his gaze. "And if—when—the next time someone catches you, it is unlikely they will be as understanding as I am. Especially if you choose to carry on with this business late at night."

Suri bristled at his tone, the faint distaste that carried with every syllable. "And why do you care so much about me and my safety? If I'm a *danger* to the *safety of your nation?*"

Instead of taking the bait, he glanced away. Away and out, to the outline of the city below them. It had begun to wake up, slowly stretching out its arms and reluctantly getting ready for the day. Without looking back at her, he said, "On the off chance that you aren't, I would prefer you not get yourself killed by sheer stupidity. And if you are, then I consider it within the bounds of my responsibility to keep you from endangering the king."

"How virtuous of you," she said, not bothering to keep the bite out of her voice.

"I try," he said, and the cool, detached quiet of before had disappeared, replaced with that wry amusement. He tore his gaze away from the city, where it had begun to settle on the east spire of the palace, and looked back at her. "Have you acquired a formal translator yet?"

"What?"

"I am going to assume that means no," he said, pushing himself away from the wall. He picked up the piece of flint from where it lay at the entrance of the sanctum and rubbed a thumb over it, thoughtful, before walking past her to the second indent in the altar. He lit the wick and she watched, mesmerized despite herself, as the oil caught fire. The boy looked up, flames dancing across the surface of the oil and heat blurring his expression, and braced himself on the edge of the altar, fingers brushing against the fire. "I'll translate for you, *and* I won't tell Viro about your first letter. All for the rather small price of not damning us all. Deal?"

She could taste the words on her tongue, everything she was supposed to say—everything she had been taught to do in this situation. But they were saccharine-sweet with decay, rotted by helplessness and the slow knowledge that she could not precisely reject his offer. She swallowed hard, met his gaze with cautious indifference. "I don't even know your name."

He raised his eyebrows. "All those things you heard about me, all those things the people of the city presume to know, and not a single one offered my name? That's unfortunate."

"Perhaps they thought saying your name would summon you."

The boy grinned, a strangely youthful gesture on him. The fire turned the slick black of his eyes into something wilder, darker. "Like a wraith. Perhaps." He walked around the fire, now burning sedately, back to the entrance to the sanctum. He smelled of camphor, and faintly, of earth. He held out his hand to her, and after a moment's pause, she reluctantly took it. It was calloused and faintly scarred, slender, thin cuts crisscrossing the back of his hand. He grasped hers tightly, the formality a parody of sorts. "Kiravelan. That is the name my parents gave me But you may call me Kiran."

She narrowed her eyes, but replied, "My name is Suri. Though I suppose you already knew that."

"I did, but the reciprocation is nice. Makes a transaction of it."

In the distance, the bells began to toll, five chimes in total. Kiran's gaze flicked toward where the bell tower stood on the outskirts of the city. He smiled at her, gesturing back at the palace. "You had better return to your rooms, before they realize you've disappeared and raise a city-wide alarm."

Her mouth flattened into a thin line. Even as she turned to leave, avoiding the fire as she returned to the entrance of the temple, she kept her eyes on him. "I'll be back."

"I've no doubt about that," he said softly, but not without amusement. He raised a hand in farewell. "Until next time, Suri."

There was something strange about the way he pronounced her name—the vowels soft and clipped, the end drawn out—but she didn't have time to consider it deeply. She tore her gaze away from him and the temple, slipping her shoes on before returning down the beaten path to the empty gardens below.

By the time she made it back to the room—just barely dodging a patrol of guards circling around the west wing—the temple looked empty, as abandoned as it had always looked save for a single stream of ash-gray smoke rising into the mild, blue sky.

In spite of her last promise, she didn't see him for the rest of the day, though not out of a lack of effort. Avyakanth was in less than a month, and Suri had nothing to wear, save for Najan dresses. They were formal enough, surely, but the festival was an expression of the kingdom's culture as much as its religion, and they would look more favorably on a princess who had deigned to wear their finery. This meant they were constantly flitting from shop to shop, giving Suri enough time to properly contemplate her plight. It would be simple enough to let her family know she was compromised, but that would hurt her pride too much, not to speak of the loss of her reward—*freedom*. The job was likely doomed, but it was faraway, distant danger, easy to disregard.

The next day brought the same laundry list of errands to run, possibly even more. There had been a time, when they had first arrived, when Suri had been allured by the thought of exploring the city, a liberty she wasn't often afforded in between jobs. But little exploration had truly taken place in between the long hours spent in humid, cramped shops and dinners at the palace.

Suri's eyes ached at the thought of the long hours ahead, and she heard the knocking on the door a little too late, once it had escalated from a mild, short sound to a steadier, constant banging.

She rolled her eyes and opened the door, expecting to see Lucius, holding a basket of freshly picked tulips. Kiran's hand was raised in the air, poised to strike the door again. For a brief second, she did not recognize him, and her hand wandered lazily toward Death, the knife she always kept by her waist. It was a quick, cursory movement, but his eyes tracked it, and she dropped her hands.

Suri opened her mouth to say something, but found, bemused and faintly frustrated, that she couldn't. She huffed a laugh and spread her hands in a question.

He smiled amiably, and it fit surprisingly well. He pointed a finger at himself and then said, simply, "Translator."

"I already have my maids."

"They can take the day off."

She narrowed her eyes, fully aware that the withering look in her eyes was sure to raise suspicions if anyone happened to walk by. Taking a step closer, she hissed, "Are you this worried about me killing your king?"

Never mind that he was right to worry. Never mind that she had not slept the entire night, had spent it staring out into the moonlit dark and wondering what his blood would feel like on her palms, whether it would be as warm and bitter as the blood of the others she had killed.

Kiran simply held her gaze, irritatingly calm. "I thought you might visit."

She didn't know if there was a trace of something mocking in the words, or whether it was residual paranoia from having to guess around the meaning of everything the boy king said. She ground out, "I was busy. I am *still* busy."

He didn't look surprised. He didn't look like *anything.* She wondered what it would take to knock that clean, pleasant disinterest right off his face. "I'll help. In place of your maids. Can we leave now?"

"Suri?" A voice sounded from within the room. She swore under her breath, ignoring the amused expression on the boy's face and retreating back to find Isa scrubbing at her face. Her hair hung around her head in a cloud. "I thought we were leaving at seven."

"It is seven," she said, wincing. "I'll wait for you to get ready—"

"No need," Kiran cut in smoothly, leaning against the doorjamb so he would be visible to Isa. The other girl straightened up immediately, though sleep still clouded her eyes. He'd pulled up the hood of his cloak so that—from Isa's vantage point—she couldn't discern the details of his face, and he'd traded in the traditional white wrap and robes for thin cotton clothes. "The king wants to discuss something with Her Highness, and I can aid her for the rest of the day."

Suri lifted her shoulders in a half-shrug, and Isa nodded, sated, before dipping her head in acknowledgement and returning back through to her adjoined room. Kiran was waiting for her in the corridor, and he pushed off from the windowsill when she returned. They walked in relative silence until she finally asked, "Where did you get those clothes?"

The corner of his mouth twitched up, as if intuiting that this was only the first of many questions. "Walking around dressed as a priest attracts unwanted attention. Small changes like this lend me a measure of anonymity. I would expect you to understand."

She did, but that wasn't the point. "Won't they recognize you regardless?"

The boy king could walk around in rags, and it would not change a single thing about who he was. Inbred wealth shone through grime and shadows. But the priest just shook his head, led her down the steps. "Sometimes, sometimes not. Usually they don't recognize my voice, so I keep my hood up. Where do you need to go first?"

It was a clean, enviable segue, one that marked the end of that conversation, at least for the time being. He managed to evade the majority of her questions, regardless of how innocuously she tried to phrase them, guiding her around the city with the practiced ease of someone accustomed to hiding himself from others. The most information she got out of him was that he served as the high priest of Avya, the Athrian patron god of fire. He didn't deign to elaborate on how he carried out all his duties without anyone's help, or how he had been chosen. He did add, though, that he advised the king on affairs when it was relevant. It didn't particularly explain why he spoke of him with such a familiar, exasperated protectiveness, or how he knew Tarak, but he refused to give on those details.

He was true to his word in that he translated better than both Isa and Mohini had, though it was a mystery where he'd learned Najan with such fluency. The seamstress responsible for Suri's dress for the festival raised an eyebrow and jerked her head toward him when she thought he wasn't looking. "Where are your usual maids, my lady?"

It was refreshing to be able to work with someone who did not treat her like she had crawled here out of a sewer, and the days that had gone by had ingratiated her with the woman. "He's… my manservant."

She glanced over at where he was leaned against the walls of the cramped room, examining a finished wrap with too much focus. He was far too observant to have ignored her comment, but his expression was unchanged.

"Really," the seamstress replied, amused. "I cannot speak for how that will affect your reputation. I hope he's competent."

Suri wondered how the seamstress would respond if she knew who he was, but just smiled. "Barely."

Kiran peeled himself off the wall and followed her out into the street. He dodged a wagon rattling down the street with fluid ease, leading her down an alley toward the jeweler's. She didn't have to look over to know what kind of expression he was wearing. "Manservant?"

She turned away, hiding her smile. "That is essentially what you're doing for me. Don't you have more important things to do than follow around a single noble?"

He adjusted his cloak, pulling the hood closer around his head. "I can handle my responsibilities. And besides, you are to be the next queen. If Tarak and Viro meet with you, I should too. Though I am offended that you consider me barely competent."

"You're surprisingly competent," she allowed. "Especially considering I'm not compensating you for this. You must want something in return."

"I'm a man of faith," he said, mild and unreadable, the smooth blue reflection of a depthless lake. "I'm doing this out of the goodness of my heart, nothing more."

"I'm sure."

"You wound me," he said, prompting her to roll her eyes before nudging her into the jewelry shop beside them. Inside, the air smelled of metal and polish, and Suri wrinkled her nose. The jeweler, eyes shining with barely restrained impatience, led her through an assortment of necklaces. She absorbed none of it.

Spending every afternoon he could spare with the princess was surprisingly pleasant, when it wasn't painful.

She bore little resemblance to her dead body, certainly—the tilt of her mouth all wrong, the defiant glint in her eyes dulled to a glossy shine. It was easy enough, at times, to pretend he was just accompanying her for simple reasons—fears of treason, a vested interest in his queen, et cetera. She stiffened enough when he mentioned the former for it to hold weight and pull his actions away from the vague area of suspicion that would come naturally to anyone who knew how uncharacteristic they were.

The vision still haunted him, in daylight and in shadows. He had meant to tell Viro of it, but that had been before the princess had arrived, before it had become clear the other boy would seize upon any opportunity to break the engagement.

The boldness of what Kiran meant to do—evade death, evade fate, save the princess and the city *somehow*—made itself clear to him until it was nearly impossible to think of anything else. *You cannot really mean to do this,* a voice whispered in brief, rare moments of silence, when he was too tired to force it out. It sounded too much like Viro for it to be easy to stomach.

As if turning their backs on him and his reckless, doomed attempt at steering the princess away from death, the gods had gone silent. And by that Kiran meant that Avya had gone silent. The others spoke to him rarely, if at all. A connection of formality, out of respect for a sham prophet borne from error. Avya had always been there, even when Kiran had not wanted him around. But he had left, too. The altar had burned silently for fifteen days and sixteen nights.

Nearly sixteen nights. He had knelt on the smooth stone of the temple since dusk, cupping the flames with hands that trembled from exhaustion more than reverence, and still his chest felt empty. The sun would come up in less than an hour, if that. And then he would have to perform a simple service to the empty mountainside and early morning breeze.

Kiran let the fire fall from his hands, into the golden bowl in the center of the altar, and turned to look at the shadowed city. Even the moon had disappeared, Nila hidden where Kiran could not beg to even her.

It was odd, going into the city with Suri. An old, half-decayed sensation twinged in his chest every time he saw its streets; unrequited love that had bloomed into existence the very first moment he had been brought here, a silent child in a world that never quieted. It was not what he would call pleasant, but it couldn't have been truly horrible, not if he sought it again and again, as if it were a poorly made cure to a heartache that never ceased.

The princess had never asked about it, but he thought maybe she noticed. She was not as easy to read as he would have assumed—then again, his only taste of nobility, apart from fleeting functions in distant lands, had always been Viro, and he had never been able to hide anything. Kiran wasn't sure if Suri's carefully constructed indifference sat comfortably at the baseline, or if it might be a clue he was dangerously ignoring.

Of course, he thought bitterly, *her true intentions matter even less than your excuses to keep an eye on her.* Short of escaping and returning with the full force of the Najan armies at Athrian borders in retaliation for his contrived suspicions, there was little she would be able to do in the long run. Unless he pulled this off; something apparently even his subconscious doubted the possibility of.

It had been so much easier to think of death when it was something that only touched him, a door that led out to a place he had seen so many times before. A half-burned field, his faceless parents standing on the steps of a cottage with no roof. Aswathi sitting on the edge of the pool at the center of the main temple, leaned forward so her fingers brushed the silver-blue water. An empty, glittering temple, and a rudimentary clay pot standing where a carved stone bird was meant to stand.

A palace drenched in blood; a city shattered by it.

And yet it wasn't, not anymore. Kiran traced the scar over his heart absentmindedly. *Is this why you've left me?* he thought, less a prayer and more a question, a request presented to an empty room that smelled of smoke. *Because you know how this will end?*

Kiran knew better, but he could not help the faint stab of disappointment he felt at the ensuing silence.

It shouldn't have been a surprise. The only truly surprising part about it all, really, was that Suri had held out for so long. Against the burn in her chest, the slowly constricting bonds around her heart.

Kiran's presence didn't help in the slightest. There were moments, brief ones, when she would forget her responsibility—and how he played into keeping her from fulfilling it. Pleasant moments. But they always gave way. She felt like something large and formless in her own skin.

Isa had asked her once why she never refused a single mission her parents gave her. Suri couldn't remember what she had said in response—something about how even if she did refuse, it wasn't as if they would accept it. And that was true enough—she was locked into this, with only a vague suggestion of free will to satiate her. But she had been weaned on this—late nights in foreign cities, the tang of metal against rain-stained air, the stomach-drop sensation that came with human contact. It was a kind of hunger in itself, an appetite for something far cruder than victuals. Fist to face, repeat.

The bruises Suri gained from the fighting house were of little importance. She was skilled enough that they were small, easily hidden with makeup or explained away by excuses of clumsiness. The money, however, was a bigger problem.

She was good—she knew that. Distantly, she had been aware of the fact that being in the fights would give her a reasonable amount of money and a dangerous amount of infamy prior to ever entering the building. Back then, it had seemed unimportant in the face of the gnawing hunger. But now the money was piling up, and once it outgrew the space under the loose floorboards in her closet, she was going to have to explain it. Short of kleptomania or bartering her belongings away, there was little reasoning that could feasibly do the job.

But Suri had learned avoidance early, from the silence of her family and the harsh, uncaring world of mercenary work. She had learned to push away issues until it was impossible to hold them off anymore, and so she pulled up another floorboard, and kept fighting, and did not tell anyone.

Isa would have suspected—might have—but even she was silent. Sometimes Suri caught her watching, as if examining Suri's expression would loosen her secrets from where they lay, tight and coiled, in the space below her sternum. She pretended not to notice, if only because confronting it might cause Isa to question her—and if she did, then Suri knew she wouldn't be able to stop herself from telling her everything.

Kiran was too distracted to notice—not the bruises, not the smudges on her cloak, not the circles under her eyes. He looked worse every time he showed up to take her into the city, if he even came at all. His skin had become pallid and drawn, the fine bones of his face jutting out eerily. Dark circles ringed his black eyes, his skin bruised mauve. Even his hair was a mess, the tangled, dark curls tied up in a stubby knot with odd pieces of string and bent metal.

Suri was hesitant to ask if anything was wrong—it was true enough that she was afraid of him questioning her own late-night adventures, but more than that, she didn't want to push him too far. When he spoke, if at all, his voice was distant, brittle. Only once did she give in; she had asked tentatively, "Is there anything wrong in the temple? You look tired."

His expression had sharpened immediately, detached thoughtfulness resolving into something shrewd and heavy. He had reminded her, faintly, of the boy king. "Nothing," he'd said, gaze scraping across her face. "Nothing at all."

At any rate, the risks never came close to dissuading Suri from returning. There was something of muscle memory in it, of addiction. It itched at her skin, unsteadied her in jagged, obvious ways. Every morning, she returned to her rooms sated and ashamed. She'd taken advantage of Kiran's distraction and sent her last letter, dense and useless—she hadn't been able to recover any good information on military movements. But now she could think only of the next.

The ghosts of her past never left her, save for the few moments of aching relief she had in the ring. And soon enough, the ring would be gone—the city itself would be gone, the citizens nothing but ink smudged numbers in a ledger and an addition to the accusatory voices in the back of her head.

Frustration hollowed her out. Someone called her name, one she had invented for the lower city—*Kazha*, the mother goddess of the earth. It was not uncommon, but she knew it didn't suit her, nor her fire. She tugged her cloth mask over the lower half of her face and pulled herself up and into the ring, replacing the flap of fabric that wrapped around the perimeter behind her. She pulled off her hood, and the crowd roared once they caught sight of her familiar braided hair, messy but pulled away from her features. Her opponent's name was announced and the shouts intensified in response, but it felt distant.

All that mattered was this; her wrapped fists and the heavyset young man on the other side of the ring. He smiled unkindly, but Suri didn't recognize him. She bit back a smile—he probably thought her underprepared, some unsteady maiden tossed into the ring on a dare with her face masked to save her dignity.

She was good at that, being underestimated.

Suri dodged his first hit, a clumsy thing, and caught his arm, twisting it back and pushing him to the floor. Her blood thudded in her ears, hot and electric. He kicked back, catching her in the leg, and she stumbled away as he pushed to his feet. This time, she didn't give him a moment to breathe, catching him across the face and holding him in place against the wire supports of the ring. He caught her fist after the third hit, pushing her back and flipping her against the ring. She rolled with the movement, backing away to the other side. Her hip was sore, but she could feel no pain, not now. It all faded away in the face of this euphoric buzz.

The young man's cheek was red with blood, breaths coming heavy. He glanced up at her, confidence dissipating away, replaced with a surprised wariness. She smiled under her mask, for herself and herself only.

Only then, she caught a glimpse of something gold and glittering in the crowds surrounding them.

A bird, she thought at first, bemused in the heat of the fight. But it was not a bird, or a person. It was a pin, slender and golden, bright against the base of the hood of a thin, black cloak. It was rare to find something golden in this part of Marai—gold was something saved up for and treasured. The wealthy soaked in it and the poor indulged in it, kept it safe and locked away.

The figure was moving through the crowds too quickly to track, the only constant that pin against their hood. But even from this distance, Suri knew what it was. A circle of gold, with a flame within.

The young man came at her again after a few moments and she evaded him, let the momentum knock him into the edge of the ring. He swore in pain, glancing over at her with a red-hot anger, an anger she knew better than she knew herself. But it made him too predictable, and she punched him once more across the face before drawing up her knee against his groin. He groaned and leaned back against the edge, glaring back at her through hooded eyes.

But Suri was not looking at him. In the crowd, the figure stilled, looking up at her. The hood cast his face in shadow, but Suri had seen it far too many times—in dreams, in nightmares—for that to be important. The cloth of the hood creased as he cocked his head, a silent question.

She jerked her head toward the door, or what passed for it. *Leave. This isn't any of your business.*

Suri knew what he would say, how he would say it. All dry amusement and faint scorn. *Isn't it?*

He straightened up and disappeared into the crowd, leaving Suri just enough time to dodge a hit. It still caught her on the side of her face, knuckles against the edge of her jaw. The young man's expression tightened, and he lunged forward to hit her again. She twisted out of his reach and delivered a kick to his side, dancing back out of his reach the first moment she could. He howled low with anger and drew his fist back to hit her face.

It never made it there.

He'd climbed up and ducked under the ring—quickly enough that she hadn't noticed, that not even the referee had. The blow had knocked off his hood, and he swayed in front of her, close enough that she could smell wood ash and vetiver incense. But he did not stumble.

From here, she could not see his expression, only his hair, dark and tangled and stained with ash. Yet, past him, the blood had drained from the young man's face. His fist hung loosely in the air until he pulled it down sharply, trembling.

The shouts had all quieted, silenced in a matter of seconds. The room was empty of sound; this was the hush of a crowd bowing before execution, the choked quiet of the silent river of souls that knotted through the earth.

The young man had become so pale, so afraid, that Suri could see his fingers individually shaking. He ducked his head in a quick bow, tentative, before foregoing the moderate show of fealty and dropping to his knees. He pressed his face to the sweaty, blood-stained canvas mats, trembling still.

Kiran had not moved since the blow had hit, carefully still in front of her. But there was nothing calm, nothing gentle, about his stance. Suri remembered what Mohini had told her when she had first noticed the temple. *He is not a criminal. But he is dangerous all the same.*

When she had seen him tending to the shrine, there had been a brief bite of surprise, not because of his youth and size, but more so because of his demeanor, surprising in a servant of a fire god. Level-headed and calm, if a little distant. Even when he had begun to smile at her, and crack small, rare jokes, she had never seen a fire in him. Not the way she saw it in the boy king; not the way she saw it in herself.

He glanced back at her, for just a moment. His gaze burned. Her breath caught, but he didn't notice it, turning back to deal with the young man folded on the floor.

"Rise," he said softly. A rustling sound came, and as the boy rose from the floor, so did the crowd. Suri had not noticed it in the midst of her confusion, but every person in the room had knelt, a wave of motion and fear and awe.

Even though the young man had stood, his head was still bowed, gaze focused on the ground below them. Like eye contact was akin to signing his own death warrant—like it would offend Kiran, and that was dangerous.

"Speak," he said, and—as if by magic—the young man did.

"*T-Thyvasi,*" he started, but the honorific came out strangled, choked with terror. "I wouldn't have—If I had known—If I had known she was—"

If you had known I was what? she thought bitterly. If being under Kiran's protection was enough to result in this, she wondered how they'd react if they knew who she really was.

She wondered if Kiran would tell them.

Suri could not know the lengths he would go to. He had not looked back at her since that first, cursory glance, simple and scorching.

Kiran cocked his head, and when he spoke, his voice was death-soft. "You couldn't have. My friend here… is far too good at hiding for that."

There was a faint bite to his last words. The young man paled further, though Suri hadn't thought it possible. "I will pull out of the fight—"

"There is no need for that," he said airily. He turned back to look at Suri, stepping out of the way so they could fully take each other in. His smile was humorless and barbed. "Isn't that right, Kazha?"

Her heart throbbed in her chest. *He didn't reveal my identity.* She held his gaze, searching for some shred of an explanation. His expression gave away nothing, still carefully neutral save for the mock-pleasant, disdainful tilt of his mouth. She exhaled into the dead air. "Right."

"Then," Kiran said, holding out his hand, "We'll take our leave. Collect your winnings as you see fit."

Suri did not entirely want to take it—a vague, juvenile part of her shied away from what was sure to be punishment. But his tone brooked no argument, and she was not in a position to disagree with him, at least not in full view of the fighters. She laced her fingers through his, startling briefly at the heat of them, and followed him out of the ring.

The crowd parted for him, silent apart from the rustling of fabric as people pressed against each other in their hurry to clear a path. Kiran didn't look at the crowd, though it seemed less out of superiority than out of the effort of keeping a hold over himself. He did not speak, did not look at her—their only point of contact was the tight, bruising grip he had on her hand.

They ducked out of the boarded-up building and Suri faltered for a moment, wondering if he would stop. He glanced back for a moment, that same harsh and searing look, and then led her down a hidden side street. It was exhilarating, to know she still knew so little of the city, that it still held untold wonders.

After slipping down another narrow road, they found themselves near the edge of the markets. The night market had not yet opened, but in the distance, Suri could see the bottom of the steps that led up to the upper city.

Kiran let go of her hand and twisted back to face her. In the wan lamplight, Suri could properly take him in. There were the beginnings of a purpling bruise on the side of his cheek, and his lip was split and swollen. But beyond that, there was his expression.

"What were you thinking?" he asked sharply.

She exhaled. There would be no easing into it, then.

When he spoke, his voice held not the coal-black acerbity of the boy king's, nor the heavy disappointment that underlaid Anyu's when Suri stepped out of line. It was fire, clean and destructive. "Do I even want to know how you're going to attempt to justify this?"

"Why are you so angry?" she asked, less out of provocation and more out of curiosity. Nonetheless, it was not the correct question to ask—he gave a small, hard laugh.

"How do you think it would reflect on Viro," he asked, "If his bride were found fighting, for money—and in Praghama, no less?"

"I wasn't going to get caught," she said, but it came out small. She looked up and caught his gaze, defiant. "I wasn't."

The words were a drop of water on a sea of fire. His mouth twisted, voice serrated. "No, you *didn't* get caught. That does not mean you could not have gotten caught tomorrow, or the night after, or the night after that. And what of safety? You could've gotten hurt. Killed. Do you think they care what state you end the fight in? It only matters that it ends. That is the only condition required for a payout."

Now it was her turn to sneer. "Do you really think I can't take care of myself? I was *winning*, before you showed up."

He shook his head, incredulous. He had not tied his hair back, and in the faint summer breeze, it whipped around his face. Coupled with the shadows of the alley around them, it rendered him something of shadow and ash, less boy and more boy-*shaped.* "You could not have won forever. You are not a god."

"You would know," she snapped. Remorse rushed through her, immediate and nauseating. But the remark had not struck him—his expression was calculating, the fire from before dissipated save for a low heat in his gaze.

"Why were you there, Suri?" he asked. He rarely said her name, if only to avoid drawing attention to them in public. The lilt of it unsteadied her.

Suri exhaled. What was there left to say? *The truth.* But that had never been an option. She tore her gaze away, looking into the flickering candlelight that wound around the edges of the night market. Her mouth twisted bitterly. "I suppose I got lost."

"You won't say?" It was barely a question, his voice soft, bone-dry.

She crossed her arms, faintly defensive. The truth would expose her absolutely, she knew. And even if she had been foolish, she was allowed her secrets. He had his own, after all. "Why should I?"

After a long pause, Kiran smiled, a flash of white in the darkness. "I suppose you're right. But try not to get killed, or caught. The effort would put me at ease." The smile sharpened a little as he turned back into the shadows. "And, a little bit of parting advice—pick a name that suits you next time. The rumors spread slower that way."

It was sound advice, and she might've taken it. But the next day, she pulled up the bundles of money from under her floorboards, rewrapped them for delivery, and didn't return to the fighting house—not that night, nor any that followed.

Initially, he'd thought it was an execution.

Viro had never witnessed an execution before, but he'd heard stories from the scullery maids. They told him in hushed tones of the bloodied stone block, the way the axe glittered against the midday sun before it fell, the silence that swallowed the square at the center of the *angadi* for entire minutes afterward.

Too young to fully understand yet wholly awed by the spectacle of it, he'd waited until the following night to ask Radha what 'entrails' referred to. She'd shut the story book she'd been reading from and pulled him by his ear over to the water basin, cleaning his mouth out with neem soap.

They were something of a bygone era—public executions had gone out of fashion in the years since his father, a civilized man if not a kind one, had taken power. But peering out the window of his tutor's cramped suite in the upper city, he was reminded of those old stories. The streets were choked with quiet, the skies shining coldly even in the late spring heat.

He watched the covered cart trundle down the packed dirt streets as the city stood silently aside and let it pass. If it hadn't been for the cart, he would've assumed the passenger was a noble—the harsh quiet was a little overblown, but it wasn't uncommon for foreign highborn to demand extravagant respect from the citizens of the capital. But the palmyra wood was crudely carved and etched with the scars of time, and a canvas covering had been hastily drawn over the top of the cart to hide the driver and passenger from sight—even from the window, Viro could see wooden poles jutting out unevenly from the sides, causing the canvas to slope awkwardly over their heads.

And so, inevitably, he came to the conclusion that the passenger was a criminal, the dangerous sort who might lash out if someone dared to pull up the veil of the canvas without permission. But his tutor just shook his head a little sadly, the corner of his mouth crooked sharply down. He watched the cart disappear from sight, then sighed and shook his head again before shutting embroidered curtains and returning to his desk.

“Such a pity,” he murmured, shuffling the *olai chuvadi* with funereal solemnity. He raised his eyebrows at Viro, nodding at the armchair beside him. “The procession is no excuse for distraction, Your Highness.”

That evening, his parents sent for him and Radha, and they gathered in the sitting room with Tarak and threw out childish guesses about why they were there. Tarak passed around a loaf of sweet bread, and they tore off little pieces and nibbled at them while they came up with catastrophes, each one more extravagant than the last. Wars, natural disasters, gods rattling the land, divine quests for them to undertake. When the door to the northern gardens eventually swung open, the bread was finished, and they watched his parents escort the high priestess and two children inside.

One, he knew, was the daughter of the temple, a year or two older than him. He stared at the slightly younger one with undisguised curiosity. A soft-eyed peasant boy with soot streaked across his cheekbones haphazardly, as if he’d slept in a brazier.

Viro noted with delight that the boy did not look away—his black gaze held no defensive fierceness, only a mild appraisal, but even at the tender age of five, he was already used to most kids looking away awkwardly when he made eye contact. He was not sure whether it was brazen disrespect or a distinct lack of awareness that motivated the other boy, but he was pleased by the outcome regardless.

Without waiting for formalities to pass, he twisted around the back of the settee and stuck out his hand, in an informal western gesture he’d observed at the markets one day. “My name’s Viro. Who are you?”

The boy glanced hesitantly at the high priestess, but at her amused nod, he tentatively took a few of Viro’s fingers in his own and squeezed them in a rural greeting. His voice, accented by the dialects of the far side of the mountains, was oddly quiet. “My name is Kiran. I am…” he broke off, looking to the high priestess first, and then to the king and queen, as if he was not entirely sure *who* he was.

Fortunately, Viro's father finished smoothly, "Kiran is going to be living at the palace. He is under the tutelage of the main temple, but I expect all three of you to treat him with the same respect as you would any of your peers. Is that clear?"

They all nodded in solemn unison, but continued to scrutinize the strange boy with the artless inquisitiveness of the young and gullible.

He was difficult to pin down—at times, he took lessons with them, while other times he went to the temple. His bedroom was slotted between Viro's and Tarak's, but often he would steal away to the aviary and sleep on the stone floor, cushioned by bushels of vetiver grass. He approached every conversation that Viro started with earnest inexperience, with a hesitant kind of warmth that endeared the prince to him at once.

Viro knew there was a reason why he'd been brought to the palace, but he'd never explained, and after a while, he assumed it was some kind of diplomatic reason—he was a distant relative or an orphan given into the care of the crown, nothing to properly worry about. But the maids and manservants—the same ones who had told him of the old executions, the cutting inflection that came with the Athrian word for terror—shared new stories with each other, and, this time, those stories were about Kiran.

They said that the king and queen had taken him in because he'd killed every other foster family he'd ever had. Because his parents were dead and burned, ashes spread in an endless field, because he crawled out of his crib and slept in dry grass and in paddy fields, because snakes slithered away from him, because he was fire and he was a weapon and Athri was a kingdom on the cusp of war.

He had no idea of knowing which of the stories were true and which were not, and so he sought out Kiran after one of their lessons in the upper city. At the very beginning, he would flinch away from the gazes of nobles and curious citizens, curling in on himself with timid reserve. Quickly, though, he learned to hide himself away in the shadows, and on more than one occasion, Viro lost track of him on their walk from the palace to the houses of the tutors, and again on the walk back. After the young prince found the north gardens deserted, he left Tarak behind with a promise to return quickly and climbed up the twisting staircase to the aviary. The other boy was sitting on the edge of the open platform, legs dangling between the bars of the iron balustrade.

Kiran regarded Viro without guile. "Your Highness."

"Hello," Viro said, taking a seat beside him before cuffing him on the back of his head. "Do not call me that, ever. Are your parents dead?"

He blinked at him, startled. Then he said, "Yes."

"Are you afraid of snakes?" he asked next. "Have you ever killed someone?"

"A little," the other boy answered, pulling his legs up through the columns so he could hug them to his chest. Even in the chill of the mid-autumn afternoon, he looked flushed, sable eyes shining in the faint light. "And I do not think I have."

Viro made a *hmm* sound that he had heard his mother use in contemplation. "I have one last question. Do you have any family left?"

He held his gaze, unsettlingly old, a child god aged beyond his years. Finally, Kiran simply shook his head, the corner of his mouth twisting sharply. "No."

For a moment, Viro considered the repercussions of such actions—these sorts of vows were not to be taken lightly, after all. But the temporary reluctance passed, and he held out his hand palm up, in the beginnings of an old ritual. "I have always wanted a brother. I have a sister, instead, and I love her very much, but I also wanted a brother. Have you ever felt like that?" At the other boy's resounding, bemused silence, he continued, "Do you want to be brothers, then? We can be family."

Silently, he watched Kiran. Shock traced the lines of his face in subtle, strange ways that Viro had learned after months of living with him—brows raised and furrowed slightly, the line of his mouth uneven and sharp, chin tipped a little toward the sky as if in supplication, in remembrance of Nila. After a while, an uncertain smile flickered on his face, faint enough to be illusory, and he held out his hand, palm up.

Viro found a piece of jagged rock on the railing, and in an act of puerile recklessness that would infuriate his parents and the healers after the wound went septic, he cut his palm open with the rock before handing it to Kiran. He did the same, setting the stone aside and clasping Viro's hand tightly. The contact stung, though Viro could not be sure whether that was from the burn of the cut or the warmth of the other boy's skin.

But it was a pleasant kind of pain, and he wrapped it up in grass and gold as he would a proper gift, and held it close to his chest, tucking it between soft, unmarked heartstrings.

8
LYNE

Autumn thickened, decorations of falling leaves transitioning into smiling pumpkins and dancing skeletons. Every day, Dai walked over to Beanzzz with Suri and drew out the next day's special drinks in orange and white chalk. Sometimes, he dragged along Aza, and Aza dragged along Miya, who ended up dragging along Ellis, who had become oddly reticent as of late.

He'd always been quiet, but recently there was a pensive agitation to it. When Suri worked up the courage to ask him if he was feeling okay, he simply explained it away with sleep deprivation or a bad lunch.

The latest season of *Heartbreak Hotel* had finished in early October, so Kiran had turned his attention to Halloween. Everything about it intrigued and repulsed him in equal measure, a reasonable depiction of his feelings toward humanity. He called it All Hallows' Eve with his faded, shifting accent, and binge-watched spooky old movies and read thick, musty books on the history of the holiday. From the beginning, he nagged Suri about getting a pumpkin to carve.

"I don't trust you with a knife," she had said flatly. "And if we forget to throw it out, it'll rot and attract flies. It's gross. And unnecessary."

"First of all," he had said, genuinely affronted. "I am exceedingly good with a knife. Far better than *you* were, mind you. Second of all, I'll throw it out."

She had given him one of his own looks—mild, faintly incredulous. He had recognized it, ears paling with blood, but hadn't budged.

She turned him down that day, but finally relented under the sole condition that he handle everything from the carving to the disposal, and bought him one roughly the size of his head. He'd spent an entire day carving it, detailing a faintly sinister expression with shocking care. He really was quite good with knives.

On Halloween, he placed it beside the welcome mat he'd bled on, along with a decorated bowl of mini chocolate bars. He inclined his head toward her as she pulled on a pair of plastic white wings. "A bird?"

"An *angel,*" she corrected. "It's low maintenance, and easy to run with."

Aza had first come up with the idea when they were sixteen, years after they'd stopped trick or treating in the residential sector. When Kiran had asked why—his research had led him to believe adults turned to alcohol instead of candy—Miya had shrugged and said, "We don't do it for the *candy.* We do it for the chaos. It's a matter of principle."

Kiran, carved from chaos and blade-sharp all the same, had immediately been delighted by the idea. Suri had been in favor when they'd first started, allured by the prospect of tangible rebellion. Now, it was more that the rhythm of the routine soothed her, the familiarity of sour candy and smoke.

Suri's phone buzzed, letting her know that Aza and Dai were on their way over. She folded her arms and narrowed her eyes at Kiran. "Are you not dressing up? I thought you were excited."

"I am," he said, gesturing toward his T-shirt with a flourish. Strangely, she missed his old clothes, his leather jackets and blouses and pajama pants. "I'm dressed as a human."

She arched her eyebrows. "Just last night, you went off on a tirade about how all Halloween costumes must invoke some kind of fear, or they're not 'real'."

"Oh, I know," he replied, eyes glittering. "But humans are the most terrifying creatures of all, don't you think?"

Suri held his gaze for a moment, unamused, before dropping into the armchair. Her eyes fell on the small garden on the balcony. In the fading light of dusk, the white jasmine flowers shone. "Why do you hate us so much? You were human once, too, right?"

"Yes," he said, with no inflection; the shift in his voice was startling, caustic and barren. "And I was a fool. A terrible, cruel fool."

She tilted her head up, but there was a sharp knock at the door, and he turned away to open it. Miya stood silhouetted against the darkness in front of them, Ellis standing behind her with his hands shoved in his pockets. Miya was wearing a black dress and a cheap, shiny, black cloak, a drop of blood painted on her tawny skin. Plastic fangs shone in the dim light when she opened her mouth to grin at them, holding up a plastic bag filled with bottles. "Happy Halloween!"

"All Hallows' Eve," Kiran corrected insufferably, but smiled and stepped to the side to let her in.

Ellis, wearing a sheet with a cutout for his head, followed her in. The skin under his eyes was faintly bruised, and his glasses were smudged, but he made an attempt at a smile and said, "Boo."

"You're not wearing a costume," Miya said, horrified, and Suri turned to find her staring at Kiran.

He glanced over at Suri, an amused tilt to his mouth, but there was no way for him to explain it to Miya, and so he simply said, "I suppose I'm not."

"Well," she said, holding up her plastic bag; a red headband stuck out of the corner. "You're lucky I brought extras."

And then she was dragging him into the bathroom, and Suri and Ellis were getting out glasses and and mugs from the dishwasher in silence. She risked a glance at him. There was a sickly cast to his dark skin, and he seemed withdrawn, faraway.

Aza and Dai showed up a few minutes later. Aza was dressed as a witch, with a black headband and a lace dress that came up to her knees. Dai had dressed regularly, with only slight rips in his clothes, but would be exempt from Miya's wrath—he'd painted gaping wounds across his forehead and cheekbone, droplets of blood doodled across the inside of his wrist.

Aza threw another venomous glance at the crowded city below, swollen with the holiday, and tucked herself into the couch, tilting one of Miya's bottles directly into her mouth.

Miya whistled low as she reentered the room, and Aza's cheeks colored from chagrin. She held up her hands. "Oh, don't stop on my account, Hayashi."

"I hate you," Aza said, pulling back from the bottle. She wiped her mouth with a ferocious intensity.

"Do you?" she returned, arching an eyebrow. Kiran ducked out of the hallway behind her, the light from the kitchenette streaming in through gaps in the drywall and casting him in shadows.

He was wearing a red headband with devil horns on it and a pointed wireframe tail pinned onto the back of his jeans, curled upward. Miya had dusted his cheeks with red glitter. He smiled at her, mouthing *we match* in the midst of Aza's tipsy rant.

Suri glared at Miya. She smiled sweetly back.

After a few drinks, Dai pulled out the annotated map, and they reviewed the places they'd hit up and the order of it.

They all had another round of shots, for good measure, then locked the door behind them and filed down the stairs.

They always started at the far side of the city, close to the western edge. A good chunk of the people over there were a little surprised to see teenagers trick or treating, but for the most part, were encouraging of them "going out and having a good time." It was where they got the majority of the candy.

Then they went down into the south city, and received dramatic door slams and the occasional pack of batteries. By the time they got to the east, they were tired and tipsy, and candy was less of a priority. They took photos with the statues in front of city hall, the building reflecting the night above.

Kiran took photos of Miya posed with the statues, though each one was a struggle against technology. He switched apps three times in succession, accidentally took multiple photos of himself in front-facing camera, and still thought the volume buttons were responsible for most functions on the phone. Even after he finally got the hang of it, Miya spent several minutes striking the most dramatic poses possible.

"Wait a second," she called down from where she was wrapping her ankles around the mayor's bicep. She leaned forward and made as if she were pressing a kiss to his silvery cheek. "Now take it."

Kiran squinted up at her. "Lighting's bad."

"Turn on the flash," she suggested.

He tapped at the phone for a moment, with the mild concern of a man lost in a widening desert. Then he glanced back up. "The screen says *New Game or Resume* on it. There are mushrooms in the background."

"Suri," Miya said, voice faintly strangled.

"I got it," she said, taking the phone from Kiran and snapping the photo. She kept her eyes on the device, but in her periphery, she could see the glitter smeared on his cheeks, his dark hair tousled by the wind, gold eyes held in stark relief against the night. It took her five tries to get the shot right.

Miya heaved a sigh of relief and began to clamber down from the statue, a little too quickly for Suri's liking. She landed on the ground safely, though, wearing a smug smile.

"Am I a badass or what?" she asked, words slightly slurred, tipping half her body weight onto Aza's diminutive frame.

"You're a pain in the ass," Aza shot back, shoving her onto Ellis, who held out his arms to steady her.

Dai sighed wearily, but he was smiling. "Let's get back, before these two send us to jail."

They walked back in relative silence, until a patrolling cruiser recognized them from the Silly String incident earlier in the night and they had to sprint the rest of the way, tugging each other along when someone got too tired to run. They collapsed at the base of the door to Suri's apartment. The bowl of chocolate was empty, the jack-o-lantern still burning merrily along. Suri watched the flame inside sway, enchanted.

Ellis nudged her, and she unlocked the door with shaking hands. They flooded in, taking up their regular spots—on the couch, armchair, and floor—with practiced, worn ease. Aza reached for a bottle of whisky and an empty cup, and Dai surreptitiously moved it out of her reach. She glared at him, but he shook his head firmly, cheeks flushed from the run.

"God," Miya said, moaning into the throw pillow. "I can feel my teeth. I'm so drunk. I'm so *tired*. Why do we even do this?"

"'Chaos,'" Ellis quoted drily, but the word was muffled by the carpet directly below his face, so it lost a great deal of its weight.

Kiran was perched on the side of the armchair, listing to one side periodically. He was close enough that Suri could feel the dry heat of him; the run had not winded him at all, and he regarded them all with crudely hewn fondness.

"Can we stay here tonight?" Dai called after a moment, leaned back against the couch.

Suri waved a hand in acquiescence. "Yeah, sure. Who wants my bed?"

Aza and Miya both raised their hands, then glared at each other.

"You'll vomit in it," Aza told her, listing forward.

"So'll you," Miya retorted.

"Both of you, then," Suri said cheerfully. Miya's eyes snapped to her, round and pleading, but she was far beyond caring. "Dai, Ellis, you two take the couch and the armchair."

"Mm," Ellis said, words muffled against the carpet. He turned his head to the side and repeated, "Where are you and Kiran going to sleep?"

Suri nodded out at the terrace. "There's a chair out there. I think. I'll just bring out a blanket. Kiran can, uh—" They exchanged a glance, him amused and her uncertain about how she could explain his insomnia without sounding insensitive. "I don't know. He can bring his own chair."

Miya snorted at an unsaid joke, then turned her head back into the couch. It became very clear to Suri that she was going to have to carry all of them to bed.

Kiran did most of the carrying, but they were thankfully too drunk to question how he was strong enough to carry Miya and Aza over either shoulder. He dragged Ellis off the floor and propped him in a loose-limbed pile on the armchair, straightening Dai out on the couch before stepping aside and letting Suri slide pillows under their heads. She gave each one a fleece blanket from the storage closet.

By the time she'd retrieved her own—dark blue with yellow stars, like her baby blanket—it was near four in the morning. She nudged the glass doors open, breathing deeply. The night air was crisp and cold, sweet with autumn.

Wrapping the edges of the blanket around her, she tucked herself into the old wicker chair and pulled her knees up, leaning her head against a propped-up fist. The tipsiness of the early night had long since worn off, and now all that remained was the bright, distant memory.

Kiran followed her out silently. He took a seat on the cement across from her, supporting himself against the balcony rails. Tilting his blanket from side to side, he examined the soft blue pattern embroidered with pink flowers. The incongruity of it against his glitter-soaked skin was ridiculous and wonderful.

He pulled the headband off his head. "Your mortal delights are as alluring as you've all claimed them to be, I will give you that."

It irked her for some reason; it was not so much the words themselves, but the way he said them, with practiced remoteness. He glanced up, and she forced herself to hold his gaze, even as her stomach dropped at the glint of his eyes. There was nothing human about those eyes, nothing kind. They were god-borne, through and through.

"I'm not afraid of you," she said, and the words came out surprisingly steady. His eyebrows arched, slightly, in a silent question. She hesitated, reaching for the words, and continued, "I know you said I should be afraid of you. Because the gods aren't kind." She tilted her head, and her headband unsteadied in her hair. "Can't you be the exception?"

"You misunderstood me." His voice was low, empty; mountains carved into shells. "I'm not unkind *because* the gods are unkind. It is true enough that they are not kind, not a single one of them, but you must understand that I am the worst of them all."

Suri watched him for a moment, traced the hard, jewel-sharp lines of his face. When he had first appeared, she'd often stolen occasional glances, not out of some kind of adoration, but out of simple curiosity. Even then, he was so clearly a relic of another world, something wrenched out of the viscous, saccharine flow of time. But now his face was something familiar, and the truth of it chilled her through.

She shifted in the chair, pulling the blanket tighter around her. She felt smudged and incorporeal in the night. Heaving a breath, she said, "I don't believe you."

"Two for two," he said softly, voice lilting. "You didn't believe I'd ever loved. Why do you not believe me this time?"

"That's a secret," she replied, echoing him, and his mouth slid upward in something that nearly resembled a smile. But it was too sharp, saturated with heat.

"How can you presume to know me so well when we have only lived together for a few months?" he mused. His blanket fluttered around his shoulders, like wings. "You don't know my past, all the things I've done and lost."

"Neither do you," she said, earning an amused glance from him. "So, technically, we're on even ground."

"Technically," he agreed. His gaze was faraway, lost in some other time, some other world. He regarded her with wry thoughtfulness. "I suppose you want to hear the story."

"No," she said, curling against the arm of the chair. It was an uncomfortable position, all rough wicker and soft fleece and the distant smell of jasmine and smoke. "Leave the past behind for tonight. Stay here."

For a moment, he was silent, and Suri wondered whether he would leave—whether he would step off the railing and disappear into the night, swallowed by darkness that smiled as if it had birthed him, bright-eyed and hard as a star. But he simply exhaled, leaning back against the wrought-iron bars.

"Okay," he said, steady as flame, steady as blood. "I'll stay."

The next day, the second *sankhili* loosened.

9
ENESMAT

Suri took the money up to the temple a couple evenings later—he would be able to distribute money to the city's poor far more efficiently than her. With Kiran, there would be no suspicions of an ulterior motive, no uncomfortable grimaces when accepting the money. He was a saint in their eyes, after all. However afraid they were, a boon was a boon.

If it meant she could make sure he was still alive, then that was simply an added bonus.

But the temple was empty. The alcove at the head of the altar was alight, casting the decorated statue of Avya in shades of orange and gold, but Kiran was nowhere to be seen. The only sign that he'd been by recently was the fire and the scent of burning incense.

She tied the cloth straps of the bag in a knot and laid it down at the base of the inner sanctum. Hopefully he would come back before someone else arrived. But she had never seen anybody come up here, not even other priests.

He didn't return that night—at least not until Suri had left—but the next morning, there was a knock at her door.

Suri had gotten into the habit of waking up long after sunrise; Mohini and Isa needed the extra sleep after spending nights out and were never ready until after the city had fully awoken. So she answered the door half-asleep, hair tied in a messy knot and strands framing her face in a staticky mess. She yawned. "Hello?"

Kiran was leaning against a column in the hallway, looking out over the city. He glanced up at the sound of her voice and raised his eyebrows. "Did I wake you?"

She nodded hazily. "What is it?"

His mouth twitched, as if to say something, but eventually he simply jerked his head downward. "Council meeting in fifteen minutes. I would not have expected Viro to involve you, though I suspect Tarak had something to do with it. He's hopeful about you."

The words pained and sickened her in equal amounts, immediately throwing off the remaining dregs of fatigue. She scrubbed a hand over her face, pushing her hair behind her ears. "I'll be out in a few minutes, then."

After freshening up, she slipped out of the room, mindful of her sleeping maids. Kiran had resumed looking out over the darkened city, gaze critical—troubled. Suri touched his shoulder probingly, and he blinked before offering a mild, contrived smile. "Sorry."

"Do you have something on your mind?" Suri asked tentatively as they descended the stairs of the west tower. The watery lamplight that filtered in from the windows did little to reveal his expression, but even in the dimness, it was clear he had not been spending the few days away catching up on lost sleep.

"Nothing in particular," he said, a blatant lie. He fiddled with the sleeve of his robes—he was dressed in formal clothes, a high priest's wrap and loose robes draped over it. Unlike Kita's all-white ensemble, his wrap was black, the robes a deep maroon. The golden pin glittered beside his neck. "These meetings can get… messy, that's all."

Suri remembered walking into the war room, seeing the boy king's incendiary anger directed at someone who was no longer there. It seemed so distant, though it had happened only weeks ago.

They walked down the colonnade in silence before Kiran said, "You brought the money."

She lifted her shoulders in a vague shrug. "You'll have more use of it. The citizens will listen if you give it to them."

He laughed, uncharacteristically bitter, examining his bitten fingernails. "You overestimate their opinions of me."

"Perhaps," she said. "But I do not think I do."

Kiran glanced over at her, gaze heavy and considering, lips parted as if he meant to say something more. But he just turned to the side and held the door to the war room open for her. She obligingly ducked into the room, finding it already full. Ministers dressed in black and gold and ambassadors marked with brassy pins sat around the long table in the center of the room. A handful of war chiefs in red and black sat with Tarak beside the head of the table, the seat of which lay empty. At the other side of the table lay two mirroring empty seats.

Upon seeing Suri, Tarak slipped out of his chair and moved to greet her. "You're late."

"Overslept," she explained, unable to meet his gaze. *He's hopeful about you.*

He smiled, warm. "Apologies for waking you up so early, then. Viro prefers meetings in the morning, for some odd reason."

As if the mere mention of his name acted as a summons, the door swung open one last time. The boy king had dressed simply, save for his carved gold armband. He ignored Suri entirely and took his seat at the head of the table, affecting a neutral, vaguely pleasant expression she knew was completely contrived.

Tarak gave a brief mock salute before taking a seat beside him, and Suri reluctantly left to take the seat beside where Kiran sat at the other side of the table. Despite his position across from the king, he seemed more interested in the wood grain.

"Let's begin," the king said, before launching into a dry list of civil affairs. Suri struggled to pay attention, knowing if she ended up missing anything relevant, her next letter would be all the more useless.

Kiran was uncharacteristically silent throughout the meeting. It was nothing of discomfort—he was reclined comfortably in the high-backed chair, cheek leaned against one of his propped-up fists. He watched the proceedings with a hawk-eyed focus, but didn't bother to volunteer his own thoughts. A young priest representing the main temple, perhaps a few years younger than Suri, sat a few places down the table from them. He glanced nervously at Kiran, before saying, "Avyakanth is in three weeks."

The king turned coffee-dark eyes on the priest before flicking them over at Kiran. "And?"

"Preparations are underway," he said, tracing whorls in the wood. "You know they do not change from year to year."

"Without help?" The king's features were narrowed with disdain.

Kiran caught his gaze for a moment. "Yes. Alone."

The nobles and chiefs had gone still in their seats. The other priest had interlaced his fingers, examining them with an agitation Suri could *feel* from across the table. Only Tarak seemed unsurprised, if a little weary.

The tension dissipated quickly after, as Tarak began to discuss military matters—relevant information, finally. Suri mentally noted everything they covered, from army movements to locations of skirmishes.

"Bandits have been repeating pillaging a village on the other side of the mountains," Tarak said, reading off one of the missives stacked in front of him. "Right off the western peaks, near the wastelands. We have no troops stationed there currently, since it's far enough away from the border that the chance of attack from other troops is relatively low. I would suggest moving a unit from the troops at the border, since an invasion is unlikely at this point in time."

He tilted his head thoughtfully. "How frequently has this been occurring?"

“Once or twice a moon,” Tarak said. “According to the reports, they’ve become more frequent recently. It started a little over six moons ago.”

The boy king didn’t answer right away. Suri could feel the room warm, a subtle change noticeable only because she was so close to him. “Leave it for now.”

“For now,” Kiran echoed, after a few moments had passed. The words rang out in the near silence—Suri could have sworn she saw a few of the chiefs flinch. Kiran straightened in the chair, leaning forward across the table so his forearms were flat on the wood. His eyes were pools of dark oil, seconds from going up in flames. “And how long will you leave it?”

The king stared down the table, his mouth twisted in a brittle smile. “What?”

Tarak leaned forward to interfere, but Kiran spoke before he could. “Six moons. How much longer will they suffer before you decide your people are worth fighting for?”

The serrated, acrid fury of his words, and the familiarity with which he wielded them, were more surprising than the words themselves. There was an uncharacteristic volatility to both of them, as dangerous as flame. The king turned to look at him through slit eyes. “You speak of my people. The ones the troops at the borders fight to protect. That *I* fight to protect, while you pass judgment on us from above.”

Suri would not have caught it if she hadn’t been sitting beside him, closer from the anticipation of observing the argument, but Kiran flinched. It was a slight tremor, one that never resurfaced and didn’t show in his gaze or words, but she saw it—felt it—all the same. Softly, he said, “The villagers will die, by blade or famine, without help. There is no need for so many troops at the border. The war is over.”

The tenuous control the boy king had been exerting over his own anger fractured and snapped. His cheeks flushed crimson, and he pressed his palms flat against the table in a last-ditch effort to keep himself still. When he spoke, the words came slowly, as if each one stung. "The war will never be over. We cannot risk it, even now."

"It has been nine years."

"Even *now,* Kiran," he repeated, his fingers pale and clenched on the wood.

A brief, dragging silence followed, as the other occupants of the table held themselves still and prayed for the meeting to end as quickly as possible. Despite their anger, Suri felt as though she was seeing an argument between siblings. It was something of the petulant, bitter timbre in their voices, the familiar tension.

Kiran spoke first, flat and unyielding. "Then move the troops north of Marai."

Suri did not understand the meaning of his words, not at first, but the king's mouth thinned. His voice could've melted iron. "And then who will guard the northern entrance to the city? Who will guard the mountains?"

"Who else?" It was a touch self-deprecating, but his expression was smooth. Only his eyes burned. "Was it not you who said I do not fight for our people?"

The boy king shook his head, a caustic incredulity animating him. His gaze was bright with scorn. "You already have a purpose. Fulfill it." Kiran narrowed his eyes, but before he could respond, the king nodded at Tarak and stood. "This meeting is adjourned."

But even the blessed and the powerful could not bend fate to their wills. The door swung open and smacked against the other wall, revealing a winded messenger. She clutched a scroll in her fingers, the cloth torn and wrinkled from the tightness of her grip. The king's gaze had zeroed in on it nearly immediately, and he crooked his hand in silent request.

She crossed the room, managing a faint, "It's Naja. There's been an attack on a village along the borderlands. They hit not a day after the troops had moved out."

The king scanned the scroll carefully, his previous anger smoothed out to something stony and dark. A storm in flux. He dipped his head in acknowledgement. "Let the chief know I've received his message immediately."

The messenger nodded and bowed deeply before shutting the door behind herself. The sound seemed to snap the others out of the shocked trance the news had dropped over the room, and the ministers and chiefs began to murmur—worry and fear coloring their words. The boy king placed the flattened scroll on the table, taking a second to smooth it out while the chatter around him grew and grew.

Suri heard none of it. White noise had become something hungry, and it consumed her from the inside out—fear slid over her heart, oil slick and darker still. It was fear for herself, to be sure—but she was distantly aware of the fact that it was also fear for others, those of the city. For Tarak, and Isa, and Kita, and Mohini, and Lucius, and Kiran.

Suri knew she was the immediate suspect, though she had been—publicly—privy to the inner workings of the nation for a little less than an hour. She thought to look at the king, to parse and dissect the ramifications of the anger and doubt she knew would have already colored his expression. But instead, she turned to look at Kiran, an ingrained response.

He was already looking at her. *Because he suspects you,* a voice in her head whispered. She swallowed hard, leaned forward to whisper something, but he shook his head slightly. *Later,* he mouthed. Despite everything, he did not look angry—the fury had melted from his expression, replaced with a pensive grimness.

"The movement of troops from Karur to Sakal was not publicized," the king said, once it was clear enough that the room would not calm naturally. His voice cut through the noise, soft but venomous. "There is no natural way that information could have spread."

"A mole?" a chief suggested. Suri ignored the sharp glance he pointedly sent her way.

The boy king did as well, which was far more of a surprise. He turned to Tarak and said something inaudible, to which the captain nodded and rose. Directing his attention back to the table, he said, "As I said before, this meeting is adjourned. Further measures to address the attacks will be discussed privately. Until the mole is found and punished, we will have to convene irregularly."

The silence in the air dissipated as the king got to his feet and left the room. Tarak stayed for a bit longer, addressing instructions to specific people before following him out. His words were unintelligible to Suri—her grip on the table was too tight, tight enough that she could see her veins. The strain was faraway, unimportant.

"Suri," Kiran said quietly, wearily. She looked up, and he looked back. Guilt sparked through her heart—that was not the first time he had called her name, only the first time she had heard it. "Princess. Are you ready to leave?"

She nodded, her voice something jagged and fearful curled up in the hollow of her throat. He held out his hand, and she took it. It was overwarm to the touch, a strange kind of familiarity in the midst of the tumult.

Kiran exhaled slowly as they reentered the west stoa. The sun was rising, washing the horizon in shades of fuchsia and gold. The air was crisp, sweet, but Suri was still far away, trapped in her own mind. The beauty of the sight in front of her was a jewel that dangled a hundred feet away, and she was chained and staked to dry, hard soil.

They stood in silence for a moment, and then Kiran turned to her. Her lips were a forest, a graveyard, of everything she wished to say and everything she could not. He tugged on her hand, a startling reminder that he had not let it go, and nodded toward the north tower. "Come with me."

Though it had been hours since she'd awoken, since the meeting had begun, the corridors of the palace were still mostly empty, and their steps echoed as they ascended the stairwell. Suri caught a glimpse of the temple from one of the staggered windows, a stream of hazy smoke floating up from the brazier and disappearing into the sky. Kiran saw her looking and gave her a strange, pinched look. "What are you thinking about?"

"Do you live there?"

He didn't answer at first, unlocking the aviary door with a key he'd procured from the folds of his robes. The kaghas began to cry at the mere sound, a shrill, piercing cacophony that ceased the moment that Kiran himself entered the room. Without looking at her, he said, "Close. I used to, but there are a few household responsibilities that cannot be fulfilled without a roof."

"A few?"

He grinned, a garish, youthful tilt to his mouth that dislodged the knot of anxiety in her chest. "The rest can be accomplished. With a little creativity." He turned fully, dropping her hand as well as the smile. "Princess—"

"I didn't do it," she said, and the hysteric edge to her words shocked even her. If he believed she had betrayed them, he would tell the king, and she would die—and so it was a matter of common sense, but somehow she knew that this strange, chaotic fear belonged to another world of thought entirely. "It wasn't me—I swear, on Idhrishti's grave—"

Kiran took her hands again, held them tight. Her fingers shook in his grip, bloodless and fear-worn as he unclenched them slowly, rolling each digit out. He cupped her palms, his thumbs pressed against her lifelines. "Suri."

She exhaled, felt it like a crackling shift in the stone below.

"I know it wasn't you," he said steadily. His expression caught, shifted, and he squeezed her hands before letting them go. "You forget I've been beside you this past month. I would have noticed if you had sent word to your family."

There was a spark of something strange and hollowing in her chest at the simple logic of his words, even if they were wrong. She recalled all the letters she'd sent without his knowledge, and looked away. "Then who was it?"

He carded a hand through his hair, blowing out a sigh of frustration. "That is the question I suppose we will have to answer. For his sake, if nothing else." He looked back at her and raised his eyebrows. "What is it?"

"What?"

A crooked smile played on his lips. "I can tell you are holding yourself back from a question."

Suri frowned. "What are you to the king?"

He held out a hand, and one of the kaghas flew out and landed on his wrist silently. Gently, he stroked its neck. "An advisor of sorts, like I said. I see things, and thus, my counsel is valuable. He rarely heeds it, but that's little concern of mine."

She disagreed—she'd seen the sharp, real anger burning between them, the disappointment. But when she opened her mouth, she found herself saying, "He hates you."

The smile twisted with derision. "He can afford to. I will keep him alive, whether he cares to stay that way or not."

"You think he's going to look for the spy," she guessed.

Kiran nodded, murmuring something to the bird that made it fly away, up into the rafters. "Viro won't forget this. The possibility of a spy, of an attack—it will consume him. It is not something I want to see upon this city again either, nor does Tarak, but it will wreck him worst. We must find them first. If he does… it will not end well."

His use of the collective 'we' unsettled and emboldened her; it was the sharp, biting knowledge that she would kill the king in the end paired with the unmooring feeling of purpose. She had only ever known duty when it meant a knife pressed into her hands.

I see things, he'd said. "Is that a prophecy?"

"It's inevitable, Suri," he said, tracing the groove in his wrist where the kagha had landed. His eyes still glittered with old vitriol. "I suppose you could call it fate."

After the missive arrived, Kiran disappeared again. It wasn't particularly surprising—the festival was approaching, and there was always work to be done. But she could not forget the strained, too-sharp angles of his face, anger that simmered and sunk. The third morning after, she woke up a little after dawn and traced the well-worn path up to the temple.

The brazier was lit, incense burning—her misplaced anxiety faded a little, unraveling. Then she noticed a slender path leading away from the far end of the temple, hugging the edges of the mountain. It was wide enough that she could follow it comfortably, but narrow enough that small bits of the cliff would intermittently crumble away and fall to the earth below.

Eventually the path fanned out, widening into a small clearing that hung off the edge of the mountain. It was a little higher than the temple had been, and already Suri could feel the air beginning to thin. A fence made of old, worn lumber, most likely from the forest below, delineated the borders of a small garden. Another path led out from the edge of the garden, snaking around a few empty wicker baskets and a water pump to feed into a small cottage.

Kiran knelt with his back to her, his hands and face streaked with dark soil. Even before she spoke, he turned to look at her, brows furrowed in bemusement. "Suri? Why are you here?"

She might've been annoyed if she hadn't been so relieved. He was paler than usual, but the circles around his eyes had faded slightly. Pulling her cloak tighter around her shoulders, she slipped through the open gates, indicating the garden with her free hand. "This is yours."

He held her gaze for a moment, inscrutable, before nodding and patting the soft grass beside him. Carefully, she knelt, examining the sloping land around her. It was not as grand as any of the palace gardens—little more than a square plot of land split into different regions by plant type. But there was something intensely personal about this garden, something tender and loved.

Her eyes settled on the clumps of flowers on the far side. Kiran followed the line of her gaze and drew himself up, walking around to the flowers. He'd planted peonies and wild jasmine, and the air was sugar-sweet. She crouched beside the jasmine, admiring the bright white buds.

"I've never learned how to garden," she said. It came out hushed, even though there was no one else there to hear her.

"I could teach you." His gaze was fixed on the small white blooms. "If you want. I've been doing this for some time."

Suri glanced up at him, but there was no hint of humor in his expression. He was serious. She pulled her hands back, curling them into the fabric of the cloak. "I would like that."

He smiled faintly, his coal-black eyes shining with the reflection of the white flowers. "I would've expected you to refuse. On the grounds of my overworking myself."

She laughed, pulling herself to her feet. "I know better now. You will overwork yourself regardless. I have no say in the matter."

He looked as if he wanted to protest, but he simply shook his head. "Wait here for a moment."

Kiran returned with a small jasmine sapling in a clay pot, which he then held out to her. "I meant to plant it today. Would you like to do the honors?"

She felt dazed, upset for some distant, abstruse reason. But she took the pot and sat down on the grass. It was faintly damp under her dress, but she couldn't bring herself to care. He knelt beside her, placing a small tub of dark material next to the flowers, as well as a metal spade.

She did most of the planting herself, but he guided her through it. Mostly through instructions, but he would often reach over and place his fingers on her own, showing her where to plant the sapling, how to cover the base with soil so that it stood straight. The instructions themselves were airy and impermanent in her mind, her conscious knowledge of the situation paling in comparison to the simple peace of it.

She patted the soil down, clapping her hands together to get rid of the excess. Her fingernails were dark, moons of dirt hidden under them. Kiran pulled out a flask of water and took her hands gently, washing out the soil from under her nails. The drops fell on the black dirt below, disappearing into the ground. "Will it take a long time to bloom?

There was a smudge of dirt on his cheek, and she raised a hand to wipe it off before deciding against it. "You are always welcome to check on it."

"Perhaps I will," she said, smiling despite it all. It was a very foolish thing, she knew, to smile in a world so quiet and so loved, and even more foolish to admire the sweetness of that love. Adoration was a foreign language to her; she spoke it clumsily, childlike and earnest. "It's a beautiful garden."

She said it because she knew it would please him, and it did. His mouth curved in a small, boyish smile. He gestured toward the city, the smile flickering and fading. "I've taken up enough of your time. I'm sure you have more important things to do."

Suri hesitated, but then rose. She looked back only once, after she'd descended the foothills and crossed the path to the north gardens, but from there, she could not see the cottage—could not see the garden and the boy it had birthed. Only the thin path that led through the mountains and the smoke of the morning's fire, ash-gray as it disappeared into the sky above.

The winter sun shone, all frosted warmth and a pale semblance of light. Athri never got cold enough to warrant true snow, not even in the peaks of the mountains, but it had been a cold year, and the edges of the grass bordering the gardens were tipped white.

It was Viro's turn to look for them—he hated it, always had. There was something eerie and lonely about searching for them in the early morning chill, knowing they could see him but unaware of where they were hidden. But it was Kiran's favorite game—gods knew why—and the preparations for the solstice festival had fatigued of late.

"You owe me," Viro muttered under his breath, nearly inaudible. A small shriek of laughter sounded in the air and he spun on his heel. *Found you.*

He followed the sound of laughter—though it had long since dissipated—to a fallen kino at the edge of the tree line. Viro toed the tree tentatively, ducking under the branches of another. But he could not see their shadows in the forest, no matter how hard he looked.

A branch snapped in the distance, and he looked up. He navigated the frosted forest floor as nimbly as he could—though he had never been as good as Kiran at keeping himself quiet—until he got to the broken branch. He crouched beside it, but as far as he could see, it was deserted. A chill ran down his neck. He wasn't supposed to be out here, technically—even in the game, there was an unspoken promise never to hide in the forest. But calling for help would likely land him in trouble with his sister, or worse, his mother.

Viro pulled himself to his feet, steadying himself against a nearby tree. The bark was cold and dry, rough under his fingers.

He heard it before he saw it.

It was the crackle of ice under calloused hands, a hiss too far away to matter and suddenly too close for comfort. He looked down and found a coiled black snake slowly It was the crackle of ice under calloused hands, a hiss too far away to matter and suddenly too close for comfort. He looked down and found a coiled black snake slowly ambling toward him. It flicked out its tongue, tasting the air, and then continued on, languorous.

Viro did not move.

The snake slithered over the branch, winding around Viro's feet. Its gaze, clear and unblinking, did not falter. It had not bitten him yet, but he felt paralyzed somehow, electric with fear.

He watched it open his mouth. Distantly, he was lost in a sea of emotions, roiling and hopeless. But it was too far away to matter. Faintly, he thought, *I'm only eight.*

Its fangs glittered white. Viro counted his last breaths as they puffed out into the air. Its head reared back, and then fell.

Viro looked up. Tarak was kneeling in front of him, panting. A wooden mallet was clutched in his small, calloused hands. His gaze was focused on the head of the fallen snake, as if waiting for it to rise again. It twitched once, twice, and then its grip on Viro's ankle loosened and it fell away.

Kiran stood beside him. It was impossible to know how long he had been there, how much he had seen. He did not spare a glance for the dead snake, choosing to keep his gaze on Viro instead.

"It's dead," he said softly. Strangely, the words were what finally loosened the tightness in his chest, unwound the dread that had wrapped around his heart.

"I thought I heard you," Viro whispered, a half-hearted explanation.

"You could have died," he said, brows furrowing. He was prone to saying things like this, worrying over the value of life. As if he wouldn't give his away. Viro did not understand how these things weren't interchangeable to him, but he didn't like to argue.

"We should get back," Tarak said, rising. He had dug out a small, shallow grave and buried the snake. His fingernails were dark with soil and he trembled faintly, though his expression was resolute. He tucked the wooden hammer into his satchel and turned to Viro, visibly upset. "You can't put yourself in danger like that."

Viro stuck his tongue out. "Kiran has already lectured me. I am *fine,* because *you* were here to protect me."

Tarak frowned and opened his mouth—likely to scold him further—but he went quiet as Viro pulled him close and linked their arms together. He was still trembling, but it faded considerably. "This entire experience has made me so tired… if only there was some place in the palace where they served warm tea…"

He rolled his eyes, but Kiran straightened up. "I can go ahead and get us tea. Wait in the sitting room."

Viro narrowed her eyes. "No, Kiran, you're still weak from the bloodletting—"

But the other boy just waved his hand in dismissal and set out toward the outline of the palace in the distance. Viro frowned and leaned into Tarak's arms. The boy reluctantly let him in. His gaze was on the silhouette of Kiran in the distance, bracketed between the trees.

"He never cares enough about himself," he said, unable to keep the note of frustration from his voice.

Tarak twisted down to glare at him. "You are *not* allowed to judge him, not now."

He shook his head, insistent. "I'm a fool. Air-headed, absentminded—you two have scolded me enough for it. If the gods told him to, he would walk straight into the brazier."

"He would survive."

"Even if he wouldn't," Viro said, disentangling himself from the other boy. Tarak had stopped shaking, the fear drained from his expression. The cold immediately set in, and he longed to go back, but he'd indulged enough. "Even if it hurt, he would let himself burn."

“Then I suppose he’s fortunate to have us to keep him safe,” Tarak said. He held him at arm’s length, fingers light on the sleeves of his winter cloak. “There’s no point in concerning ourselves with this. Let’s go in and warm up.”

Viro followed him out of the forest, frosted ground crackling under their boots. He exhaled, purposeful, as they traced the well-worn path back to the gardens, and watched the breath cloud in the air. White, like mist. Like smoke.

10
LYNE

It was the smoke that woke her. Suri shifted in the chair, peeling back the blanket with sleepy languor. She squinted at the brightness of the late morning, all sunlight and smoke and glints of white and green.

Smoke. She drew back in alarm; the fallen headband dug into the side of her neck, and she untangled it from her hair with shaking fingers before glancing back.

Kiran's eyes were fluttered shut, chest heaving unevenly. She had never seen him asleep, and she sincerely doubted this qualified. He looked faintly pained, strained in a clear, discomfiting way. The T-shirt he wore was burning in several places, small, controlled fires that loosed thin streams of dark smoke into the sky.

She crawled out of the chair and moved closer, wincing at the heat. Glancing inside, she found the rest of her friends still asleep. They couldn't find him like this. She pulled the blanket from her shoulders and threw it on top of him, temporarily staunching the fires.

Ducking back into the apartment, she got out a pair of pans from the kitchen and began to bang them together. Dai woke up immediately, sitting up so quickly he cracked his neck. Ellis moaned, slowly pulling himself into an upright position. He looked ill.

"What," he asked. "What is going on. Suri."

"Out," she said, trying to fake a mild, sadistic cheer, as if she were throwing them out for the sake of it. Not because Kiran was on the verge of spontaneously combusting where they could all see it. "All of you, out. Now."

"Now?" Dai echoed muzzily. "Why now? My head hurts."

"Because," she said. She tried to keep her voice pleasant, but she could feel the strain in it. "I need to clean up."

They both stared at her intently, neither sober enough to place why she was acting strange. They exchanged a look of resignation, and Suri could've cried from relief. Once they were gone, she could throw Kiran into the shower and call her grandmother, because they did not make emergency hotlines for flaming gods.

Aza and Miya padded out of the hallway. Aza's witch hat headband was hanging around her neck. She peered over at Suri with blank confusion. "Why are you holding pans?"

"Wakey, wakey," she said nonsensically. "Get out of my house."

Miya raised her eyebrows and glanced over at the boys. They shrugged, and she yawned, running a hand through her hair. "Can we shower first?"

"Um," Suri thought fast. She felt like she could smell smoke, but maybe she was just being paranoid. She fought the urge to glance over at the balcony and check if he was on fire again. "No. Pipes broke again."

"Really?" Aza asked, rubbing at her eyes. "I washed my face last night and everything seemed fine."

"Well, they're broken now," she explained, distantly registering the fact that her hands were shaking. She put down the pans. "Before you all woke up. They broke."

"Again," Ellis supplied.

"Yeah," she said. "Again. So you guys need to go."

They all looked at each other, as if weighing the merits of banding together and annoying Suri into letting them stay. Finally, Aza nodded. "Yeah, okay."

"Great," Suri said, her voice pitched unnaturally high. She tossed them their coats and belongings, tucking them into their arms when they didn't bother to catch them, and nudged them toward the door. She cracked it nearly closed so they could still see her face and smiled. "Nice seeing you. Fun night. Have a nice day."

"Suri—" Ellis started, but she'd already shut the door. She slid back against it, her head stinging where it hit the wood. The movement was strangely steadying, affording her a brief moment of peace. Which was fortunate, because moments later, she realized she *had* been smelling smoke.

She returned to the balcony to find that Kiran had not only burned through her blanket, he had *also* burned through the rest of his shirt. His devil tail had also caught on fire and was now flickering behind him. The irony of it did not escape her.

Suri waded through the balmy heat, brushing a hand against his forehead and regretting it immensely. Her fingertips felt scorched. Somehow, his fire had grown, distorted into something guileless and apocalyptic.

She crossed the balcony to the watering can, shaking as she untwisted the top and poured it out on him. There was a faint hiss as steam rose into the sky; momentarily, his warmth faded. From a bonfire to something kinder, like a candle.

She attempted to scoop him up but it was impossible, especially in the face of the heat. Finally, she pulled a discarded cardigan off the rail, dampening it with the dregs of the watering can before twisting it around his arm and dragging him into the apartment.

He made no noise, even as she dragged him over cement and carpet and tile. She collapsed by the side of the tub, breathless, reaching up to twist the handle so that it sprayed out ice-cold water.

The hiss of steam was louder now, and it cut through the silence. Suri let the water fall, let it bounce off his skin and hit her, wetting her face and hair. She felt a little like she might fall back asleep on the bathroom floor.

No, she scolded herself. *You're not done yet.*

She reached into the shower, untangling the cardigan where it had wrapped across his arm and part of his chest. Her breath caught when she saw the marks over his heart—the outer one, the one of memory, was still nearly untouched save for a single faded area. And the innermost one was dark as coal, dark as pitch. But the central one, the one that bound his power, was fading—some chunks had turned a sickly ash-gray and some had faded entirely to reveal the brown skin underneath.

When he had summoned that fire, months ago, she had been awestruck. *So this is the power of a god,* she had thought, a little unsteady, a little fearful. If that was him fully bound—if even a slight release in the *sankhili* meant he burned like the sun—then she could not fathom what he would be like once unbound.

If you lock away a god's power, she thought, *do they become human?*

Kiran opened his eyes.

Gold as honey, gold as gods. He stared at her, gaze fathomless and deep as seas. His chest heaved, and he leaned back against the tile of the far wall. His lips parted, as if to speak, but he simply glanced away, down toward the drain carrying away ash and fire.

He examined the changes in the middle *sankhili* with a surprising disinterest. Then he looked up, saw her still knelt beside the bathtub. She knew she looked like a mess. She just didn't care. He was alive and her home wasn't ashes and for now, that counted as a victory.

"Thank you," he said, the rasp of metal on stone. He sniffed with distaste at himself. "I can promise you this will not happen again."

Suri sat back on her heels. Now that the immediate terror of getting him back to normal had fully faded, she was once again aware he was shirtless in the shower. She watched the water speckle the mat below. "Do you feel stronger?"

She saw him tilt his head in her periphery. Finally, he said, "Perhaps. I cannot tell, not yet."

The memory of fire, of blurring, consuming heat came back to her. She leaned forward despite herself. "Your old enemy, why would they let the middle one weaken first? Wouldn't it be best to save your power for last?"

Kiran shook his head slowly, damp hair twisting with the movement. "Actually, it's quite smart. They clearly thought this out." At her questioning look, he continued, "Power is nothing without purpose. Memory grants purpose. And even purpose is meaningless in the face of ideals, in the face of a moral code. They know I won't act rashly in such a large city. And I cannot leave, not without you. Even then, we would always have to contend with the possibility of my power severing itself with malice and hurting you. So, effectively, I am still useless."

She glared at him, unamused by the phrasing, and he looked faintly chastened. "I may be able to communicate with a few of the gods now. I'm unsure. Before, I couldn't even sense them."

"Communicate?" she asked uneasily. "What does that mean?"

In her head, she imagined him inviting them into the apartment, a reheated dinner shared with ten-foot-tall giants. She imagined him setting up a video call with an ancient, divine being. She was beginning to feel a little sick.

"Nothing extravagant," he said hurriedly, spreading his hands. The water splashed off them and onto her arms. "It won't interfere with your life. You will have to trust me."

He said it casually, but she knew he meant it. Swollen with the knowledge that she did trust him, she looked away, offering a wordless shrug. Despite everything, some of the tension melted from his stance.

True to his word, he ensured that his attempts at communication never interfered with their daily routines. The first time she interrupted him, he was perched on the edge of the bathtub, speaking in low, urgent tones. He glanced up when she entered, a toilet scrubber held loosely in one hand.

"What are you doing?" she asked, blowing a piece of hair out of her face.

"Talking to a friend," he said easily, nodding toward the toilet. From the doorway, she could just barely hear the soft swirl of rushing water.

She raised her eyebrows. "You're friends with the god of plumbing?"

Kiran threw his head back and laughed, a rare, youthful sound. After regaining his composure, he wiped his eyes, grinning over at her. "She's going to love that one. Thanks, Suri."

"*What* is that supposed to mean?" she said, stepping forward. Was his friend easily offended? She had just barely escaped her fears of being smote by *him*—she couldn't return to that terror again. She peered into the toilet bowl, but it flushed before she could make anything out. When the spray dissipated, the water was steady. No sign of a vengeful goddess. She glared over at him. "Is she angry at me?"

"Unlikely," he said, mouth still creased in a smile. "Even if she was, you're under my protection, so there is little she could do."

"Your protection," she echoed grumpily before pointing the scrubbing brush at him, a weapon. "Like *you* need to protect *me*."

"I'm well aware you're capable of taking care of yourself," he replied cheerfully, pulling his knees up so she couldn't bat at his hanging legs with the toilet brush. "I'm just here for… oh, I don't know. Spontaneous bursts of toilet water."

She folded her arms, but the scrubbing brush reduced the intimidation factor greatly. "You're a freeloader. Get out of my bathroom."

He hopped off the edge of the bathtub and left, probably to resume his conversation in the kitchen sink.

The only other time she caught him, he was peering at the wrought-iron railing of the balcony, shining and ash-gray in the early night. His brows were drawn together, mouth open in the outline of a word, before he noticed her heading for the watering can and wisely paused.

She pointed the can toward the railing. "Were you speaking to the god of railings? Infrastructure? All your friends are so sensibly named." She pressed a hand to her mouth in mock shock. "Wait, let me guess. You're the god of furniture."

"Fire and furniture," he said wryly. "Not such a good combination. You're lucky, you know. If you offered such crude names to any other gods, they might get upset. They have very fragile egos."

"I can tell," she deadpanned, and he mimed being struck in pain.

To say he was drawing further away from humanity was a simplification, and wrong in many ways. He felt a little bit more present, more alive. The weakening seal had given back some of his vitality, outlining him in bright, broad strokes shaped like sunlight.

When he'd first arrived, there had been moments where he had seemed like something entirely *other*. Removed from both divinity and humanity, he'd been raw and strange, jagged with muted memory. But now he was oddly settled, even inclined to answer occasional questions Suri asked.

Seventeen-hundred years old, she thought, still unable to fully process the notion. She couldn't fathom what he must have seen, lifetime after lifetime after lifetime. But he remembered nothing of it, not yet, and so in a way, he was still a little human. Close enough to touch, close enough to know.

Suri opened the door to smoke and fire.

For a moment, terror seized her. She glanced around the apartment, convinced it had gone up in flames—it was burning as the car had burned, and it was still burning, and she could do nothing but watch. But it hadn't yet caught flame; it was much like everything else in her life, gasoline-soaked and nearly undone, a match pressed to one corner as if in a kiss.

Kiran was sitting in front of the coffee table, head tipped forward. Candles were carefully arranged around him—dozens, hundreds of them, neatly lined up on every available surface. The room swayed under the weight of fire.

"Where did you get these?" she asked, voice oddly hushed.

He tilted his head up in a slow, feral movement. The flames limned his face, blades dancing in the smooth surface of his irises. "Rana gave them to me."

Suri navigated the peaks of wax and fire and carefully lowered herself beside the coffee table. Across from her, Kiran knelt before the wood, palms face up and marked in ash. She recognized the movement from the temples of her youth. They used sacred ash to mark the cheekbones and forehead of worshippers, but priests, in service, always marked their palms, held them up in supplication before the altar.

The god was still as an idol, save for the faint heave of his chest. His lips moved without sound, the movements smooth and practiced.

"How long have you done this?" Her words slipped out without warning and he paused, cheeks pale from blood.

"I don't know," he said, faintly strained. "A very long time. I would have begun when I arrived, but I could only light a few candles at a time then. Even now, it is difficult to hold so much fire at one time."

Her breath caught. He had lit the candles with power. The flames swayed by his words, by his breath. "Is it difficult to keep them burning?"

"No," he said, slow, measured. "It is difficult to keep them *from* burning. Fire is not a stationary element—even now, I can feel every individual flame, longing to spill out of wax and turn this building to ash." He drew in a rattling breath. "Part of me wants to let it. It is not a part I know very well, but I feel as though I once did."

Memories coming loose, she thought, and felt her stomach twist. His gaze returned to the ash on his hands, dipping into the lines of his palms. She watched the movement, entranced.

"Who do gods pray to?" she asked aloud, a dream with open eyes.

The line of his mouth was sharp enough to draw blood. But when he spoke, his voice was snow-soft, death-soft. "This is not prayer, Suri. It is atonement."

On the morning of the dawn festival, Suri awoke to her phone buzzing beside her.

"Hello?" she asked, muffling a yawn with the side of her pillow.

"Why are you still asleep?" her grandmother scolded her, with the sprightly irritation of someone who regularly woke up at five in the morning.

She shifted the phone against her ear, twisting in the blankets. "It's only eight, *anda.* What is it?"

"Today's Theyni," she said, sighing. People were chattering in the background, an endless stream of white noise. "I attend the temple service every year, but I'm out of town on a delivery."

"What does that have to do with me?" Despite her efforts, Suri could hear a plaintive note creeping into her voice.

"Don't whine, *muru,*" she reprimanded. "I didn't think this trip would go so long. There are a few packages you must give to the priests tonight before the service—hymns, auspicious times. It is not that far from your apartment, you know. It won't take long."

She remembered the temple in flashes, nothing distinct enough to form impressions of its distance and grandeur. She shut her eyes, and said, "Okay, but you better bring back souvenirs."

Suri could hear the smile in her grandmother's voice when she spoke. "Anything for my favorite granddaughter." Then there was a murmur of noise, and the call cut. Suri exhaled, and placed her phone on the pillow.

She wondered what the temple would look like, now that she'd seen gods and felt them. The thought of returning nauseated her; even now, she recalled staring up at cold stone gods as a child and thinking of grave soil and the charred rubber of her infant brother's pacifier. In her addled, malleable youth, she had smelled carnations and thought they were cut from kerosene.

In the early evening, she dragged herself out toward the living room. Kiran was curled into the couch, painting his toenails bright orange. The sight of it nearly made her smile.

He arched an eyebrow. "Where are you going?"

She fingered the edges of her canvas tote, hesitant. "My grandmother needs me to deliver something to the temple for Theyni tonight. Listen, do you mind coming along?"

"To the temple?" he tilted his head, genuinely confused. "Why?"

"I don't know," she said, faking a too-quick shrug. Her mouth was sour with bile. "I don't want to walk back through the city after it's dark. And it'll be more fun to see the festival with someone else."

Kiran considered it for a moment before twisting the cap back onto the nail polish and quickly blowing on the rest of his toes. He reached for his black coat, offering her a small smile. "Well, I would be a terrible guest if I denied a request for company."

They walked through the city alone, the late autumn chill piercing through till it struck bone. Suri shivered, and he pulled off his coat as they crossed the street, tucking it loosely around her shoulders. It smelled faintly of tulasi and incense.

She glanced over at him as the light turned green and the cars rushed behind them. "Take it back."

He snorted, an uncharacteristically inelegant gesture on him. "Do you think I need to be warmed, Suri?"

She resigned herself and pulled the coat closer around her shoulders. It still held a hint of that dry, searing warmth.

Her grandmother's shop was shadowed, dusty from disuse. Kiran leaned against a rustic, scarred cabinet as she rifled through a stack of packages, looking for the one labeled with the temple's formal name in her grandmother's spidery, thin handwriting. She squinted at a similar package, then said, "What do you even do for her, morning after morning? She won't tell me anything when I ask."

"Errands, usually," he said, examining an open book in the dim light. "All of your old chores. Sometimes she will ask for my counsel on auguries, or we will have tea. She's a wise woman, your grandmother."

Suri slid three packages out of the stack, double-checking the labels before hugging them to her chest. She glanced over, narrowing her eyes. "Why would she ask you for counsel on auguries? Are you god of prophecy? Have I finally gotten it right?"

The line of his mouth tightened, and for a moment, she thought he wouldn't respond. Then he said quietly, "I had the gift of prophecy, when I was mortal. I still understand it to a certain degree. That is why."

The packages nearly slid from her hands. Though sometimes he would make offhand, enigmatic comments, he rarely ever spoke about his life as a human, apart from the stories. And there was always a chance that those were entirely fiction, that she was reading too far into them. She was prone to wishing things into reality in that way, hoping and hoping until, in her own head, there was no doubt she was entirely right.

Kiran closed the book and held out a hand. She belatedly handed over the packages, and he stubbed out the candle with his thumb as they went back out into the twilight.

The soaring, brightly lit buildings of the city slowly fell away, revealing the outline of the hills strewn along the southern edge of the city. A thin, winding footpath twisted out from asphalt and led around the hill.

Distantly, Suri could see the glittering highway, the patchwork knots of suburbs below. But they were so far away they hardly existed, glinting in the waning glow of dusk.

The temple lay at the base of the hill. It had been built quite recently—a little over thirty years ago—but with the help of donations from Enesmati immigrants, they'd built it in traditional stone and marble, and the carved faces of the outer entrance shone. Families adorned in their festival best were crowding around the doors. Even from far away, Suri could hear the laughter and the hymns, smell camphor and blossoms. It attracted and sickened her in equal amounts.

Kiran stood by her on the tar-streaked asphalt, packages tucked into the crook of his arm. His brows were drawn together, just slightly, but otherwise his expression hadn't changed. He nudged her when he saw her staring. "Let's go, before it gets crowded."

"It's already crowded," she muttered under her breath as they passed the temple-goers; they were dressed in gold-etched silks, in muslin and glittering jewelry, chattering endlessly to each other as they carried plastic bags filled with cartons of milk and juice.

Carved wooden doors opened into an expansive room, tiled with shining white marble. Small shrines dotted the temple, in each corner and on both sides, wound through with worshippers shuffling through the lines. At the center of the temple, four sanctums stood tall. Each one had an archway flanked by two pillars, carved with intricate designs that varied for each god. Small golden plaques were affixed below the curve of the archways, names written in English, then in archaic Enesmati.

Though the shrines to all four gods were crowded, the two central ones were the most congested. From the entrance, Suri couldn't see the gods themselves, but she could make out the figures of priests performing a service for a gathering crowd. One held up a bouquet and began to strip off the flowers, tossing them at the feet of the god.

At the center of the temple, space had been cleared off the floor. Interlocking woven mats covered the cold tile and families sat on the edges, cross-legged and anticipatory.

Kiran looked lost, but when she tugged at his arm, he followed her around the crowds and through them until they ducked around the shrines in the back to find the prayer room. The head priest was a regular customer of her grandmother, and he greeted them with a smile. "It is always nice to see you here, Suri. It must have been years since your last visit."

"Yeah, I think," she agreed, dizzied by the smoke and noise. Her lungs were filled with soil. Kiran handed her the packages and she held them out, forcing a faint smile. "These are from my grandmother. She's out of town, but she wishes she could be here."

"And we miss her dearly," he returned warmly. He inclined his head toward Kiran, gaze faintly scrutinizing. Fear electrified her for a single, painful moment. If there was anyone who would be able to tell god from human, it would be a priest. Finally, he said, "Are you a friend of Rana's?"

Kiran's smile was so thin it was nearly transparent. "Just an errand boy. This is a lovely temple."

"I suppose it is," he said, relaxing slightly. He offered them a grin, gesturing toward the main temple. "Don't let an old man like me take up your night. Go join the festivities."

They returned; the once-empty mats were now alive as two costumed children play-acted the old myth of Theyni, the story of dawn. An older kid sat by the edge of the mat, singing the hymns that accompanied it, and told the story. Transfixed, Suri lingered by the edge of the rightmost of the main sanctums, labeled in gold with the name *Makai.*

The memory returned as if it were a nightmare; her grandmother whispering old myths to her as a child, Suri's fingers fisted in blankets as her eyes shone, dazzled by magic and gods and the promise of divinity to those who were kind and worthy. Faith had felt like a promise then.

As in the old story, Ashri and Athrasakhi brought dawn to the world. Ashri, queen of the heavens, rode in her lustrous chariot, symbolized by a cardboard box they'd spray-painted gold and taped silvery wheels onto. The god of wrath knelt in the chariot beside her, allowing his hands to hang out of the cardboard box as they tugged it across the woven mats. The child's hands were red with finger paints, and he smeared the floor with them, just as the god was said to have stained the sky crimson with blood.

Without thinking, Suri reached up and traced the outline of the pendant on her thin golden necklace, her only relic from her parents. They had bought the pendant for her as an infant, when they had all been alive—the chain they had purchased to go with it no longer fit her, but her grandmother had bought a new one for her when she graduated.

The age-dulled pendant depicted three crossed knives interlocking to create a jagged six-pointed star. Suri had been born in the early morning, just before the sun rose; when she had begun to cry, the sky had been scarlet. Supposedly, that meant she had been born at a sacred time, a sought-after one. Those born under bloody skies were under Athrasakhi's protection—the pendant, his traditional symbol of war, proved it. He was the guardian god of the Enesmati, the fiercest and the bravest, or so the story went.

Suri seldom thought about the pendant, but she never took it off. It was all she had left of her parents. And, she supposed, looking out over the temple as the hymn came to a close, it was all she had of her birth.

She turned to tell Kiran they could leave now, to apologize for getting lost in reverie for so long, but he was no longer beside her. She had not consciously thought of him as a tether, but now, without him, she felt lost in the chaos of the festival. *Asphalt and glass and burnt hair*—

Turning back to the concluding performance, she forced herself to breathe steadily. She catalogued her surroundings. The minor shrines were all as they had been, and the main four remained to orient her—Makai beside her, Ashri and Athrasakhi at the center, most likely, and another god at the far left.

When she found him, he was on the outskirts. His head was bent over the altar at the base of the shrine. A golden plaque informed her that it was the sanctum of Avya. From inside, a granite idol regarded her with sharp eyes painted on with ash and turmeric. Abruptly, Suri realized he was trembling.

"Kiran," she whispered, and, with no small amount of effort, he pulled himself up. In the darkness, he held little to no form. Even the glow of his eyes was dim, thin with fatigue.

As if in explanation, he inclined his head toward the inner sanctum. The movement unsteadied him somewhat, drawn to it as a moth flits toward flame. "I know this. I know I do, from far more than my mortal life. It is just—" he broke off sharply, shaking his head. There was a bite of self-deprecation to his voice when he next spoke. "I told you, Suri. I am useless like this. A shade of a god."

She opened her mouth to speak, then faltered. He was gazing at the inner sanctum, at the darkness and the fire within, with a peculiar kind of ache, misery diluted by wonder.

Suri had brought him with her to soothe old wounds, so she could step lightly over rough gravestones without fear of cutting her feet. But she had never considered how a home like this, built on dreams and prayers, might scorn those who could not reach for either.

Finally, she managed to ask, "Can you remember?"

Kiran was too skilled at simple deceptions for it to be clear when he was in pain. But Suri knew his face well, had studied it in dreams and in nightmares and in the light of day, and so she saw the fracture lines regardless.

"I cannot remember a single thing, and yet I can still feel the outline of what I've lost." He let out a soft laugh, glass against stone, as he turned away into the light. "Thank you for bringing me here. But I think I'd rather like to go home now."

The services had not yet ended—Suri thought they might last the entire night, spilling out into the dawn of the next morning. They retrieved their shoes and carried them in their hands, bare feet on cold, glittering asphalt.

They left the temple behind, but even after they had returned to the city, the festival still lingered—in the heady scent of camphor and blossoms that had wrapped itself into Kiran's coat, and in the too-sharp, humorless corner of his mouth, crooked enough to be a flame.

11
ENESMAT

Suri visited the garden every day. It was a daily routine—she would wake and get dressed and, regardless of whether Kiran came by to take her out, follow the worn path up the foothills and around to the garden. Sometimes Kiran was around, tending to the temple or to the garden, and sometimes he was not. But she had never gotten there earlier than him, never seen the brazier empty.

Those brief, stolen moments in the garden were, on some days, the only time she saw Kiran. It was rare if he was able to take her through the city once in a single week. Not that she needed that as much anymore. She had picked up enough of the language; not enough to be fluent, but enough that she could engage in conversation.

It wasn't until the next letter arrived that Suri realized she hadn't truly planned to continue in correspondence with her family. The kagha swooped out of the darkness, soundless and bright-eyed, and landed on her wrist unbidden, talons digging into her skin. She stared at it for what felt like an eternity, until the claws broke skin and warm blood began to gush from the wound. The iron smell of it cut through her shock and she stumbled back, leaning against the edge of the aviary window for support.

After she finally worked up the courage to open the letter, she found it disappointingly short uncoded.

S—

K & Q asking for updates. R has made a mistake, and now you have an additional assignment. Priority is still the K—if you cannot complete this, we will understand.

A

P.S. Send me a bouquet of those mountain wildflowers. I have heard they're beautiful once dried.

The postscript made Suri pressed bloodied fingers to her lips, sick with suppressed laughter and terrifying guilt. Then she reread the note again, and then once more, and the laughter faded, leaving behind only nausea and fear.

If you cannot complete this, we will understand. She could nearly imagine him writing it, that strange dreamer's smile of his tilting up the corner of his mouth. He would understand, perhaps, but excuses meant little to her mother and father. Failure was failure, whether adorned or not. If she didn't complete the assignment, there would be consequences.

The mark was a foreign tradesman who had connections with some of the war chiefs. According to the attachment, Rohit had mismarked his paperwork and accidentally sent him classified files. She exhaled a small, bitter laugh through gritted teeth and wondered how Naja would've fared if he'd become king.

She cornered the man in his bedroom, clad only in nightclothes. He looked exactly as Anyu had described him—stout, balding, worn with deep furrows of judgment and wrath—but he watched her with terrified shock, as if she was a ghost, an Enesmati demoness. It was not unfamiliar, not to her, but she had spent so much time in this beautiful city she had nearly begun to consider herself something capable of that same beauty, that same wild tenderness.

But she wasn't, and after she slid the obsidian knife between his ribs, her hands filled with blood until it ripped the air from her lungs and threatened to swallow her whole. *Hehyava,* susurrations of old ghosts crowding against the walls of her skull. Even after she scrubbed her hands clean, they were stained rose gold.

After that, the matter of writing another letter—of sending it—felt insignificant. This wasn't her world to love, even if she wanted to. There was no point in dancing around the violence of why she'd been sent here.

She waited until the aviary was empty of trainers and servants and gold-eyed boys, then sent a letter full of banal updates, carefully printed descriptions of correspondences between the boy king and his associates. She pressed jasmine buds and wildflower stems between the pages and folded it tight. She could feel the imprint of talons on her wrist after the kagha disappeared from sight.

On the night Kiran took her to see the stars, the city was screaming. It was a kind of pre-festival celebration, Mohini had told her. Not strictly religious in any capacity, but tied into the culture of the festival anyway. The people set small fires across the city, in braziers tucked into alleys and at the corners of the markets, and colored them with powders and sang.

From inside the dining room, she heard none of it, felt none of that distant warmth. Only echoes, ghosts of sounds. The king, glancing up from the meal of stewed meat and lentils, said, "Keep your wits about you. There was a murder in the upper city just recently."

Suri choked, pressing her napkin to her mouth and turning it into a cough. There was no threat in his words—they felt like a mild warning, a close imitation of genuine warmth. But the memory of it returned; blood on her palms, under her fingernails, in the spaces between her lungs, threatening to take her apart. She twisted her hands in her lap so that he could not see them shake. "I am capable of taking care of myself."

His mouth tightened. "I am sure you are. Still, it cannot hurt to be careful."

Oh, but it can, she thought, chewing through bite after bite of tasteless food, spices turned to ash in her mouth. She had taken pains to be careful ever since she'd arrived, and now that same caution had turned her soft and fragile, shattered by even a single death. She shut her eyes, but still the memory remained—dead eyes shining like a trout's, skin leeched of blood, the faint smell of iron and the fainter one of rot.

She pushed away from the table, only slightly unsteady as she rose to her feet. "I must excuse myself, I feel ill."

Suri could feel his burnt umber eyes studying her, narrowed in thought. Finally, he waved a hand in acquiescence. "I'm sorry to hear that. Seek out the healer if it grows worse."

She bobbed a simple nod of acknowledgement, fisting her hands in the thick fabric of her skirts and leaving the dining room behind. The embroidered silk slipped under her sweat-slick fingers, cool and dry. But she couldn't throw off the viscous drip of blood, the tacky way it threatened to soak into skin and bloom unseen below the surface. She felt like it might harden, sharpen within her, might turn to jagged chips of garnet that would rend tissue like rose petals. Her chest felt tight, as if she had already begun to break apart.

Lost in that reverie, she walked straight into a pillar. It shifted, one of flesh and not stone, and fingers ghosted across her shoulders, drawing back enough that moonlight spilled between them. Kiran peered down at her, the multicolored glow of faraway fires reflected in the oily black of his eyes. "Are you alright?"

She looked away, taking a moment to steady herself. She felt strangely tethered, the world no longer fragmenting into black glass and bloody memories. "Yes. Were you looking for someone?"

He took a step back, tugging at the cuffs of his woven shirt. "You, actually. I was wondering if you've found anything regarding the spy."

The spy. *The things your parents would do to you if they learned of your treachery,* a small voice whispered in the back of her head, steel against stone. *Think of it: the way they might open your neck, your chest, your skull—*

"Suri," Kiran repeated, close enough that the air smelled of him, of camphor and vetiver incense. Earthy and sweet. It cleared the iron from the air, just for a moment, and she met his gaze. His brows were knit with concern, the pads of his fingers pressed to her forehead. "You're cold as ice."

"I'm fine," she said lightly, but didn't step away. "I haven't found anything. Have you?"

He shook his head ruefully. "I was hoping you would've had more luck. The temple does not leave me enough free time to make the search a priority, though I know I should." His fingers slipped from her skin, and he scrubbed at the bruised skin underneath his eyes.

"We can look now," she said, the words stealing out of her as if they had a mind of their own. "For the spy. I have suspicions, at the very least, places to start."

He blinked at her, faintly alarmed. "But you're unwell. You should rest."

"I told you I am fine, and I meant it," she retorted, folding her arms. The tremors had passed, but she recalled the way they had unsteadied her, shifting bones against bones. "If you are free, then we might as well try to find something useful."

The corner of his mouth quirked up. "Lead the way."

Suri took a deep breath, and it was the first one that didn't feel like it might choke her. "The army chief, Head Chief Venkateshwaran. He just returned from Karur, the village that was attacked. He should have past correspondence with the king, which the spy compromised. They might have left hints of their presence behind. It's worth checking for."

The army chief's rooms were in the east wing. Suri fiddled with lockpicks she'd slipped into her skirts, but when they turned the bend of the east tower, they found the doors crooked slightly open. Despite everything, relief slid through her, slow as syrup. Despite everything, she didn't want to show Kiran this side of her, not yet.

Cracking the door open, she scanned the room and found it empty. The air was stale and smelled of cloth and cloves, and when she ducked inside, there were unbound letters scattered across the four-poster bed. Behind her, he gently propped the door open with a wooden block, then came to look over her shoulder. "What are these?"

Suri rifled through the stack, treatises on war and combat. "Nothing of importance. Look through his shelves. I'll check the desk."

The wood was spattered with ink and dust, dried wax clumping in spots that shone matte in the faint candlelight. Imported leather-bound books and thin pages of written correspondence and reports alternated in stacks that listed to either side. The middle of the desk was left bare, save for a single sheet of silk cloth. A salutation had been scrawled, dark ink smudged from haste, but apart from that, it was empty.

"I found something," Kiran said, pitching his voice so low she nearly didn't notice it over the noise of the revels outside. He handed her two letters, creased with old folds. The surface of the first was translucent, writing spidery and neatly printed. It succinctly explained why the chief believed Sakal needed troops more than Karur—a budding insurrection, violence from Najan nationalists who wanted to purge the borderlands of Athrian influence. The second, an approval of the plan, was written on rich cardstock, marked with the seal of the king.

Neither seemed tampered with.

Kiran looked faintly disheartened, and she looked away so he wouldn't see the dissatisfaction reflected in her eyes. It wasn't as if this was the end of the search—there were other places to check, other people to investigate. But a dead end was a dead end, and right then, it would've been awfully nice to find proof they weren't losing time searching for evidence that didn't exist.

Her gaze snagged on a spot of color at the edge of the chief's letter. Plum-colored like dried blood, but with none of the dark brown residue, none of the sweet burn of iron. Kiran squinted at it, cupping the edge of the letter so he could get a better look. "What is that?"

She brought the slip to her nose from instinct more than anything else. Her chest felt empty. "Flowers. Crushed roses."

There were no roses in Sakal, nor in Karur. The wastelands grew grass and grit, nothing more.

It would've been a stretch to call his expression happy, but there was an edge to his features, faintly pleased. Suri forced her gaze away, straightening the letters and replacing them upon the shelf. "This is something we can use. It's somewhere to begin."

He made a choked off sound, strangled and too soft, and she dropped her hands from the shelf, turning in time to keep him from crumpling to the floor. As it was, he leaned against the bannister of the bed, ragged nails curling into the carved wood. His eyes were shut tight, lips parted and heaving.

"Kiran," she said, his name coming out too sharp, dissonant with horror. She wrenched him to the side roughly, scanning for injuries, but there were no entry wounds. It was either poison or illness.

He looked oddly unsurprised, pulling his other hand from the bannister and resting it upon hers, squeezing once. His mouth moved, and though the effort was too weak to produce sound, she could read his lips. *I am fine.*

"How can you be fine?" she asked, as sternly as she could. The timbre of her voice was all wrong, trembling where it should've held steel. His eyes opened, the smooth black of them marred by flecks of gold that swirled through his irises. The whites of his eyes disappeared for a moment, under the weight of black and gold, before reappearing fiercely, rapidly. He pulled away from her grip, pressing his hands to his mouth to stifle a gasping cough. They came away spattered with crimson.

In the distance, footsteps sounded, the familiar clip of heeled sandals against stone. Kiran wiped bloodied hands on his shirt, a practiced movement, before tugging her toward the shadowed alcove at the back of the room. He drew the curtain of rough cotton across until it hid them from view.

It was barely large enough for both of their bodies, and he stood close enough that she could smell the blood on his hands, on his shirt. A thin line of crimson traced the dip of his chin. She nearly reached up to wipe it away, but fever burned through him, blistering and relentless, and she feared searing her fingertips on his skin. Instead, she moved the edge of the curtain aside so they could peer into the chief's rooms.

A servant stood by the doorway, shifting anxiously from side to side. "Head Chief?" At the resounding lack of response, he shrugged toward the now-open door, knocking the wooden doorstop to one side before ducking back out into the night. Distantly, she heard him say, "He said earlier he wanted me to bring some books by, but he hasn't returned. I'll have to give them to him tomorrow. Do you think the revels have finished by now?"

The door swung shut behind him, leaving them alone once again. Suri sagged against the side of the alcove, dragging a hand through her hair and scrubbing at her face. Kiran was leaned against the other side, head tilted back to the stone. When he opened his eyes, they were fully black.

She watched him slide the curtain open, following him out into the empty room, and thought, distantly, of how she had not feared his blood, had not flinched away from it. He turned to watch her, bracing himself on the side of the desk. After a moment, he said, "I'm fine now."

Now. She could not forget that word, cut so carefully to hide the danger of what had just occurred. "Was it—was that poison?"

The line of his mouth thinned, turning sharp. He shook his head, but didn't say anything more, pushing off the desk and holding out his hand in a silent question. There was something altogether foreign about his expression. A cold, tempered fire in the lines of his face, the flames that covered the surface of stars.

She followed him out of the east tower, their feet near silent on the stone halls of the palace below. The screaming, ferocious song of the revels came alive around them, and when he looked back periodically, the uneven fires of distant braziers lit the planes of his face. He looked a little like he had been born from that silver-blue glow, a heart formed from fire.

There was something unsaid and tenuous between them as they climbed the foothills up to the temple. There always had been, she knew. But now it was impossible to ignore, silhouetted against the stars above, against the darkness of the night sky beyond it. So much of this strange, nameless partnership of theirs was borne out of both necessity and distrust, a resonating understanding that stood on brittle foundations. She was not sure what he meant to do by this—to build something stronger, or to let it fall away to debris. Or simply to see how far they could take this—how long it would take before reality snapped those thin, fragile bonds.

If there were gods, she thought, *surely they laughed at them.*

When he paused in front of the jasmine blooms, she felt strangely unsurprised, as if she had somehow expected this. Her plant had finally bloomed, and the creamy white flowers shone against the darkness of the soil. Kiran moved to cut off two flowers with bloodstained nails, then tucked one behind her ear and one behind his. He had not bothered to tie his hair back, and curls blew around his face in the light wind, pulling him further into the shadow of the mountainside.

He didn't linger in the garden, instead following the path along the cliffs back to the temple. He ascended the steps quickly, barefoot, and she toed off her own slippers before joining him in the empty temple, the stone soft and strangely cold under her feet.

The fire in the brazier had been extinguished, and a grate obscured the statuette of Avya from view. Even the scent of fresh blossoms and incense smoke had disappeared, blown away by the wind and the smoke of the city below. If Suri had not known the temple, she would've felt like a voyeur, an intruder on some sacred, abandoned place.

Kiran laid down on the stretch of stone at the entrance to the temple. He patted the floor as if he meant for her to join him. Suri straightened her skirts and laid down beside him. The stone was cool to the touch, and yet this close, she could still smell blood, could still feel the fever in his skin.

Above them, the stars spilled out against the sky, glittering silver-white in the darkness. His voice was soft enough that the shouts of the city below nearly swallowed it up. "There is an old rumor that the gods reside in the stars."

She looked over at him. "Is it true?"

His expression turned strained. "I wanted it to be, when I was younger. But I think I was wrong. They are here with us, in every word and every breath."

He spoke with a glassy distance, and yet he was so clearly youthful, so clearly alive. So clearly mortal. Her hands twitched beside her, bewitched by this notion. Suri nearly raised a hand to his face, if only for the sensation of it, the knowledge that he was flesh and blood and attainable. He had rubbed the blood from his chin, but even in the faint moonlight, it stained his skin, turned it ruddy and warm.

"I never told you who I was," he said, turning to look at her. That cold fire had not yet faded, but now it was softened by a kind of wistfulness, a kind of threadbare yearning.

She wanted to tell him that he did not have to give her his past, even though she longed for it. But she was rendered speechless by the promise of his words. She waited for him to speak, and counted the beats of the shouts below.

Kiran pushed himself up on his elbows and leaned back against the altar, tilting his head back against the edge of the gray stone. The jasmine flower had become crooked behind his ear.

"When I was born," he said, "The sky split open, and the earth filled with fire. It wasn't my fault, nor my parents'—Avya had been spurned, and was punishing Athri. We just had the poor fortune to be hit. They were killed immediately by the blast—I survived, but I was… not the same. Changed, they say. Avya has told me in the time since that the fire saved me, that that was how he found me, after he had finally calmed down. An infant still wrapped in cotton, set down in the center of a fire."

Kiran pulled down the edge of his shirt, revealing the silvery outline of a scar over his heart, a cluster of jagged lines that created something resembling a six-pointed star. "He saved me, gave me life. But… I am unbalanced. An uneven creation of mortal and immortal. One will win out before long, and I doubt it will be my human heart. I'll burn myself out, in the more literal sense, before I reach thirty years of age.

"It does not affect me much. I still breathe, my heart still beats. I'm afflicted with visions of the future that manifest themselves in brief, accurate hunches or in prolonged, recurring nightmares. I can hold fire, though I can't create it. The most important thing I will ever do, I think, is die."

Suri flinched, turning to look at him so sharply that she listed forward. It was a crooked, abrupt movement and he held out a hand to steady her gently. But he did not hold her gaze. "I will die a week after Avyakanth. With my death, Athri will regain its old prosperity, its old strength. My birth has weakened it, made it more volatile and prone to chaos. My death will restore the balance."

He said the words as if he were reading off a script he had been given. Suri felt the shock of it roll through her—it was not a surprise, not truly. It explained the way people deferred to him, the strange worry both Tarak and the king struggled to hide. And yet she couldn't accept it. It was too cruel, to create someone as a tool of peace only for them to die to enact it.

Suri wanted to express the hollowing, barbed outrage that warmed her. And yet she couldn't—not with the same eloquence, not with Kiran still avoiding her gaze as if he was afraid of what he would see. Finally, she said, the words disjointed, "It's unjust. To do this to you. I thought your gods were meant to be virtuous."

He inclined his head. "In a way, they are. Without their interference, I would've died an infant. I am a dead man walking, Suri. At least this way, I can help my people before I join my parents."

Suri knew death the way she knew her own heart, the lifelines of her palms. She could not fathom this, but at the same time, she recognized the truth of it, the fated tragedy of it. "And so your beloved divine virtue is nothing but a farce."

Kiran's mouth curved in a faint grin. But it was too sharp, too bitter. Where it was meant to hold fondness, it held a kind of carefully restrained sorrow. "There is no such thing. The world changes by our own hands, Princess. The gods are with us, but they can only guide us. And even then, there is no knowing what guides them—what will in turn guide us. We can only hope it is something beautiful, something kind."

It was a beautiful concept, the idea that they had power over their own fates. Suri shied away from it as she would've from fire, from poison. There had always been some higher power that had influenced her actions, held an iron grip over her decisions. The notion that she had entangled herself in this prison of duty—that she still had the power to break out—was frightening and intoxicating.

"Do you resent them?" she wasn't sure whether she was referring to the gods, or to the king and the captain, or to the city. Or simply to humans, whether it stung to have simple, inexorable reminders of his shortened life.

He glanced down from the sky. The stars danced in his eyes as he spoke. "I envy them, at times. But I have never resented them."

Something occurred to her, and she turned abruptly, taking bloodstained hands in her own. "What happened in the chief's rooms, then, that was…?"

"My body decaying," he said, lips twisted in a wry smile. "There have been moments like that for as long as I can remember, but as I grow older, they become more frequent. More intense."

A shrill, piercing sound cut through the night, and they both looked back at the city, glowing with colored fire. A crackling rocket flew into the sky and then broke apart, showering the buildings with crimson sparks.

"It's beautiful," she said softly.

"And it will not last," he added, but there was no hint of anger, of mocking humor, in his voice. Only a distant warmth, that of stars and the gods that had left them behind. "In that lies half the beauty."

Looking at him then, Suri could believe he would die within the month. There was something ephemeral about the outline of him, tenebrous against the darkness of his temple, already far removed from the rest of the city. It felt almost as though if she reached out, she would not touch him—as if there was some unnamable, unknowable distance that lay between them, a chasm that held love and sorrow tight, with no intention of ever letting go.

But when they rose to descend the mountain, he took her hand to guide her through the dark. And despite everything, it was warm—it was alive.

Kiran bent close to the altar and splashed fire on his cheeks.

The flames didn't behave like water—they slid against his skin, smooth and dry as stone. His skin tingled where it had met the fire, and he pressed the heels of his hands into his eyes to stave off the fatigue that lingered around the corner.

He couldn't remember the last time he'd slept. The fire washed away the thick lethargy that threatened to weigh him to the cold stone below, but he could feel the effects of it waning. Now, even submerging himself in altar fire only brought the slightest of reprieves.

His throat still stung from where he'd coughed up blood the other night, the fire in his heart searing him through. He recalled the memory as though it belonged to another—the unearthly silhouettes of the fires in the streets, the curl of the jasmine flower behind Suri's ear, the heady, sweet scent of it mixing with the smell of her, amber and iron.

The night was nearly moonless, dark as crushed velvet and just as absolute. Looking over the shadows just then, he felt as though the world had gone silent, as though all the life and all the beauty he had always known had abruptly disappeared, leaving him behind to search through empty graves.

He shook his head slightly at the macabre thought, leaning back and nearly slipping upon the stone. Already, he could feel the effects of the fire dissipating—already, sleep reached out gnarled, sugar-spun claws to hold him close.

Kiran didn't fear sleep. He feared the moment before sleep, the crooked smile of oblivion giving way to weightlessness, gravity shattering souls against stones as though they were auguries, skulls.

But he was still human; even if the flames wrapped him in their warmth and kept him awake, he weakened as any other mortal weakened when kept from sleep. And, eventually, he grew weak enough that the darkness grew closer and closer and the quiet of the city stole into his blood and silenced it entirely.

Sensation crackled through his skin. When he opened his eyes, he was kneeling in a meadow choked with *kantal* blossoms, slender stalks rising to his shoulders. His robes were ripped and dyed red by blood, turning the fabric stiff and salted with iron.

The field was infinite, the robin's egg blue of the sky settling down on the horizon, where the endless flowers flattened into a line of scarlet. Light saturated the air, but the sky was sunless and serene. When he rose to his feet, unopened, stifled buds crumpled under him soundlessly, poison soaking into his skin.

A vision, he thought, and hope spread behind his sternum. It was a naive thought, he knew, but he could not help the warm sting of it, the notion that perhaps he had not been entirely forsaken. That perhaps this fool's quest of his was not doomed, after all.

Suddenly, his chest seared with heat; he hunched over, shoulders trembling with the effort of suppressing the cough. But when he drew his hands away from his mouth, his fingers were flecked with gold. The gold of kino flowers; the gold of ichor. It was cold against his skin, glittering in the glow of this barren world. It left a saccharine aftertaste on his lips, flesh scorched from the weight of divinity.

He went to wipe his hands on the torn robes, but another cough rolled through him, and then another, as if he was something meant to break apart. Flashes of prophecy obscured the meadow momentarily and he saw himself, skin fractured and brittle as mountain stone, splitting apart from flesh of ash and gold until there was only fire underneath.

His throat was raw, the inside of his mouth viscous with blood and fear. Cough after cough, as if he sought to expel something held within, a glittering red heart held in amber-flecked hands, beating muscle left to throb uselessly on pillows of scarlet and gold.

Kiran didn't register falling to his knees, only the sensation of it, bare skin thudding softly against dark soil. His nails bit into his neck, clawing at the raw skin as a drowning child seeks air in a sea of blood and salt. Around him, the tendrils of the flame lilies lengthened and twined, forming cerise lattices spun with hints of gold. The tepals and stamens tangled with one another until the world was bled of all color but crimson, until the dawn was infinite and alive and savage.

The blossoms crushed him; and then there was nothing left to crush, and everything was nectar-sweet ichor and poison.

He woke slumped over the edge of the burning altar, hands wreathed in flame. There was something strange about his blood and bones, as if he had been broken imprecisely with a mallet, reformed with all the right pieces in the wrong places. As if he was not himself at all, but a shadow that wore humanity like it was a birthright and not a gift.

Wracked with nausea, he stumbled over to the brazier and bent over the hot coals, vomiting tepals that shone crimson and gold in the fading firelight.

Two mornings after the revels, the city was silent.

Suri fisted her hands in her blankets, immediately unsettled by the consuming hush. There was no birdsong, no clamor of vendors from the streets. This was a weaponized quiet, the absence of sound between one's last heartbeats.

Later, Kiran would tell her, the lines of his face harsh and cold, that Athrians mourned silently. Unlike Najans, who beat the funeral drums for days and days after deaths, grief was something that Athri handled carefully, with a measure of suppressed emotion. It was a gift of the war, a latent realization that they could not mourn every death with the ceremony it was accorded and still stand on the battlefield.

The adjoining maids' rooms were already empty. By the time Suri had washed and dressed herself in mourning colors, damson and clean pearl white, Isa and Mohini had returned. The latter startled a little at seeing her up and ready, but Isa's mouth merely flattened into a thin line. "Head Chief Venkateshwaran has died."

She delivered the news with the reserved formality she defaulted to when truly rattled. Suri inclined her head in acknowledgement, unwilling to speak lest her own shock show too clearly. Finally, she asked, "What happened?"

"It was an assassin," Mohini cut in, wrapping her arms around herself. In the thin sunlight flooding through the three windows, she looked wan and uneasy. "Killed him in his own room and dragged the body into a ditch. They found the blood under his covers, masked with clove perfume." She shook her head, blinking rapidly. "It could have happened to anyone."

It couldn't have, Suri knew, a cold ache beginning to settle in her bones. The letters she and Kiran had found—how likely was it the spy had found them too, noted the smear of rose and decided not to take any chances? How likely was it the spy had not noticed the rose at all, had simply killed the chief in order to tie up loose ends? How long would it take before the king himself was deemed a loose end?

They had been in the room after the murder had occurred, there was no doubt about that. The air had smelled strongly of cloves, but Suri hadn't known the chief well enough to note the strangeness of it. The room had been thick with foreign blood, and she had not noticed it. The thought chilled her.

Isa nudged her slightly—at some point, she had crossed the room, and now she stood with her back to Mohini, brows furrowed slightly in an expression that held not sympathy but a measure of caution. Suri gave a brief nod and looked away. "When are the funeral proceedings?"

"Soon, my lady," Mohini said. "We returned to wake you."

A small, bitterly amused smile played on Suri's lips. "And I surprised you, I suppose. Let's leave now, then."

When they arrived, the body was already being mounted upon the funeral pyre. They had built it to stand at the eastern border of the temple, on the edge of the city. In the distance, the dry grasslands ceded and the mountains rose up, ripping into the frosty sky above.

In death, the strong-featured, bulky man looked pale and drained. Kita was conducting the formal procedures, but Suri could see the men of the crown—as they were wryly referred to in the lower city—standing by the base of the pyre. Kiran met her gaze, and though he didn't speak, she could see clearly enough the tense horror that lingered in her own heart in the planes of his face. They had always known, from the first mention of the spy, that this was more than a game, that these were the soft whispers of violence that would curl into a scream of war. But thinking of death was different than smelling smoke and fire, watching ashes rise into the air and stain the sky gray.

"Suri," Isa whispered, so close that she could get away with calling her without an honorific. Her voice quavered slightly—it was not something someone else would have noticed, but in seventeen years of knowing her, she had never faltered once. "You *will* take care of yourself, won't you?"

Though the proceedings hadn't yet finished, Suri tore her gaze away from the pyre and met Isa's eyes, hard and fearful. And, just then, she was stricken by the realization that she could tell her. She could tug Isa back to her rooms and explain everything, beg her for help, lay her head in her lap and confess all her fears.

And yet, she couldn't. Again and again, she was struck by the war chief's supine form, rigid from rigor mortis. It was too late for her and Kiran—they were already inexorably tangled in this, and even then, she wondered if she could dissuade him from continuing. But Isa—strict, kind Isakthi, who was difficult to amuse but had the most beautiful laugh when one managed to charm it out of her. She had served her well all these years, and despite that—because of that—Suri could not pull her into this, could not drag her down into the grave along with her.

She forced a faint smile and turned away, unable to meet her handmaiden's gaze. "Of course. Always."

12
LYNE

Suri woke lost in nightmares. It was an old affliction, the way the horror would not leave her even when she opened her eyes to darkness, even when she pressed cold fingers to the skin above her heart just so she could feel the butterfly wing beat, resonant and real. As a child, she would spend hours still in the grasp of the nightmares, terror-spun claws sunk deep into soft gooseflesh.

Tonight, it was the same recurring dream she had grown up with. There were others, but this one never wavered, never changed. It was more reliable than her own heartbeat.

In it, she was hovering on the edge of the freeway, the moonlight shining down on a world of darkness. She would walk along it, bare feet against the damp road, and find a car tilted sideways. The metal was scraped and burning, windows glassy with heat and spattered blood.

The windows were all rolled down, and she would peer into them. A woman in her early thirties was slumped in the passenger seat, her bright brown eyes—Suri's eyes—open with shock and pain. Her breaths came unevenly, and she held out trembling hands to pull herself up. But she was so slow, an insect in amber, dead from the moment of conception.

Even when Suri shouted for her to get up, sobbed and cried and pounded her hands against the side of the car, she would not rise. She was an interloper in this world, a twisted voyeur, and her flesh passed through metal and skin without resistance.

Beside her, hands loosely curled around the wheel, sat her father, his head tipped forward and hair dripping with blood. She often could not make out his face—when she was younger, before her grandmother had shown her photos of her family, their faces had all been blurred, as if she was stuck in a phantasm of her own life. Here, she could only make out the line of his jaw, traced with sweat from the heat and blood from impact against the steering wheel.

And in the backseat—she had to crane her neck to see them—laid two young boys. One, a lanky, blood-streaked child of near four years old, was leaned back against the car seat, neck twisted at a crooked, sickening angle. The younger one, little more than an infant, had not yet died, though Suri had lived through this nightmare frequently enough to know that he would soon, from the smoke and fumes. Until then, he simply cried, wailing and wailing, the thin, tremulous sound cutting through the dark flesh of night like a knife.

It never ended. That was where the agony of the nightmare laid—the screams continued even after she'd heard her fill, even after she felt as though she were drowned in death. And she could do nothing to end it, nothing to help them. There were times when she would arrive at the car, and a few of them would still be alive. And she would pull at them, fingers going through flesh, and whisper and shout and scream and beg, and still they would not hear her.

She knew they were long dead, knew there was no sense in longing for a family she had never known. She had seen the graves, coveted them. Their love was something distant as stars to her, a warmth she would never feel. But still, there was an incorrigible, puerile part of her that wondered if she could bring them back if she tried hard enough. If she tried harder.

Suri laid in bed; she could feel her heartbeat in her skin, in her bones—it was a syncopated, rattling sensation, one that tangled with the numbness in her chest until the fear faded and only fatigue remained.

After an indeterminable amount of time, she pulled herself out of bed. Blinking numbers on the alarm clock on her night table told her it was nearing five in the morning.

She heard a soft noise in the living room and padded out, the carpet plush under her feet—so achingly different from the rain-damp asphalt of the dream. The house was shrouded in darkness save for the lights of the kitchenette, spilling out into the nook and casting it in a muted white glow.

Kiran was sitting at the table, his legs drawn up so he was cross-legged on the straight-backed wooden chair. His black hair was damp, but she could not remember if he had showered. It framed his face in soft, tangled curls, water dripping down and splashing against the surface of the table.

He was eating macaroni and cheese out of unwrapped tinfoil, a plastic spork poised in his slender, scarred fingers. He stabbed at the pasta every few seconds, examining it with distant, alien scrutiny before lifting it to his mouth and chewing. Without looking up, he said, "It is late, Suri."

"I know," she returned, walking around the curve of the kitchenette and taking the seat opposite him. She hunched her shoulders, the worn bed shirt suddenly too thin in the early morning chill. She rubbed her hands together, nails bitten and spattered with chipping polish. "Nightmares."

Kiran inclined his head in understanding, laying his tinfoil bowl down on the table. He toyed with the edge of the spork for a moment before laying that down as well, one prong cutting deep into the foil. He met her gaze; the skin under his eyes was bruised, and there was a pinched, tired gauntness to him, a haunted desolation. His mouth twitched, as if to attempt a smile, a kind of lasting expression, but the effort was fruitless. He had nothing left to give. Finally, he said, "I've been remembering things."

She leaned forward. "Have you remembered who bound you?"

The god blinked in momentary shock at the jagged, vindictive edge to her words, and she shared it, briefly. But her own anger did not surprise her, not truly. After a pause, he simply shook his head, mouth twisted ruefully. "Nothing so grand. I can't recall people, or lives, or the context lent to them. Only…" he drew in a breath, carding a hand through his hair. "Events, sensations. I will see places in flashes, and then they will be taken away in the next breath, but I can still remember the shapes of them, the imprints. Things such as those."

Suri wrapped her arms around herself. Tentatively, she asked, "What was your life like, back then?"

His smile was joyless. "You would not want to hear of it, Suri. Even without the entirety of it, I can understand that. It was not a fairy story like those you favor."

"Promise me you'll tell me," she insisted. Part of her, that same dizzying, impossibly foolish part that thought death was something reversible even when it cut hearts clean in half, wondered if—if she could make him vow, perhaps it would mean he would stay. That even after the innermost seal broke, he would think to return. "Promise you'll tell me, when you remember."

"Suri," he said softly. Only her name, twisted cleanly out of balance, as if he'd been raised saying it a different way. For a moment, he looked like an old man in a youth's body, clothed in soft, scarred skin and too-bright eyes. "My past—it was not kind. It was not beautiful, and it was not pure, and I do not think any of my lives ended well, not a single one."

"I want to hear all your stories," she said, fierce as fire. "Every single one. I don't care whether they have happy endings or not."

Kiran studied her, amber eyes clear and pensive. Then he crumpled up the empty aluminum foil, glistening with rehydrated cheese. He formed it into a ball and then rose, tossing it gently into the wastebasket, cutting a glance at her mid-movement. "I wanted to thank you."

"Me?" she asked, bemused. "What did I do?"

He gave a soft laugh, surprised and humorless and a little fond. He returned to his seat, drawing up his knees once again.

"I have an inkling," he said, tracing the whorls of the wood in the table absently with his free hand, "That being here, with you and those you love, is the happiest I have been in a long while."

Her cheeks warmed. "Then I'm happy I was able to help. Everyone adores you, you know. My grandmother, my friends."

"Is that what we are?" he asked abruptly, glancing up from the table. There was an odd intensity in his voice, overwarm and yet not unfamiliar. "Friends?"

"Yeah," she said, and the word stuck in her throat a little. She smiled, and she was so tired she could feel it in her bones, but she felt a strange, strained joy, too. "We're friends."

Kiran didn't speak of what he remembered of his past. All the same, it was impossible not to see how it ruined him.

He didn't sleep, hadn't since the night Suri had heard him scream himself awake, grasped so tight by horror and fear. But gods didn't need sleep, not the way humans did, and it had never truly affected him—no dark, bruised under-eyes, no bloodshot gazes. He still did not sleep, but now he looked the part. As if all the years he had left behind, all the years he now felt, were draining him slowly, steadily, of that jagged, reliable cheer.

He didn't sleep, and he didn't often speak, not unless spoken to. Sometimes, while reading at the café, he would turn his head and look out the window, and he might shiver just once, a full-body tremor that carried blood and ash and bone. Sometimes, he would lapse into silence, without warning and without reason, and she would turn to prompt him and find him trembling, gold eyes glassy and distant.

And he would not explain, and she would not ask him to, but the questions remained between them.

Suri knew too well how nightmares carved their way into a heart, cut through connections hidden too deep for human hands to touch. They left wounds that never healed, struck bleeding flesh over and over until all that remained was numbness and the memory of pain.

Kiran wandered there, held between agony and apathy, in the deserts of dreamlands, sand ground from jagged black glass. She could not reach him—he was as lost as a ghost, as dead as her family. If she held her hand out, it would go through flesh, like smoke and fire.

After he had regained his power, he had felt nearly tangible—a boy with golden eyes and a smile lit in moonlight who was strange and overwarm and kind. He had integrated into her life with his leisurely, amiable ease—had hung out with her friends, chatted with her grandmother, learned the city and perhaps started to love it.

But now—Suri didn't know. She couldn't know. He was made of flame and dried blood, and she didn't know how to know him, much less save him.

The memories drew him further away from that soft, worn humanity back into shadow and smoke. He felt less and less mortal with every tremor, with every breath. As if one day, she would wake to see him on the balcony, bracketed between wrought-iron rods. He would smile, silhouetted against a bloodred dawn. And then he would fall away into ash and crimson blossoms, swallowed by his own demons.

Her grandmother didn't ask, but Suri could see concern lining her face as clear as daylight, as clear as rage. She had always been a wary woman, sharp-witted and aged by human horror. But she was too kind for her own good—it was why she had begun her business, why every Enesmati immigrant in the city knew her name. And, though she would never say it aloud, Suri suspected she had seen a little of herself in Kiran, and to see him so clearly shattered broke her in kind.

Her friends didn't know what he was—his smooth, depthless silence revealed that they knew much less than they had previously thought—but it was not difficult in the slightest to discern that something was wrong.

It wasn't that he was disinterested in them, or his old hobbies. He would still hold a conversation with Miya over reality television if she prompted him—but he was less inclined to start one, and tired easily. Aza's conversations on modern music went nowhere. Dai's mid-class doodles of Kiran's stories—he would tell them all abstruse, fantastical ones that were compact and meaningless, magic and words but nothing more—drew little more than a faint smile, though she knew he kept them close. Even Tarak's rants about his reckless, naive best friend never cheered him—if anything, his gaze grew darker, all cracked black glass.

Ellis was the only one who had an effect, if anything. On the infrequent occasions Suri lingered, she heard flashes of conversation about things so mundane they seemed like pretense. The weather, flower languages, the color wheel. But he might smile—sometimes, he would laugh.

Fortunately, though, he never drew away from her. He didn't tell stories anymore, but sometimes they would sit together late at night, each avoiding their own nightmares. She would drink in that simple, dangerous warmth, and his breaths would come easier for a while, and they would both be okay. In the darkness, it was easy enough to pretend everything was okay.

One evening, on a long shift at Beanzzz, he was curled up in the corner booth in the shop, knees drawn up. His so-called roly-poly position. From the counter, she could only see the top of his face over the edge of the thick book, dark skin split by gold.

Tarak leaned toward her. "Everything okay at home?"

Suri flipped him off casually, steadying herself on the rail of the counter. Exams would be coming up soon, and though she was doing well enough in her classes and keeping up on the material, she couldn't stop thinking of this, of nightmares half-dead. Finally, she said, "Yeah. I mean, he gets like this sometimes. He just needs time."

It was a bare-faced lie. Suri had no idea what he needed—she had not known him for long enough to fully grasp his highs and his lows. For all she knew, this was what he was really like, pared down and shattered by the darkness he'd lived and loved, and the boy she'd known for the past few months was a phantasm sprung from innocence, from ignorance.

But Tarak nodded as if he understood. He scrubbed a hand over his face, smudging cocoa powder on the line of his cheek. She didn't see him often outside of work, even though she knew he and his friend went to the same university as her. They rarely crossed paths, never enough to make idle conversation. But he was nice enough—he was one of those genuinely altruistic people you met once or twice in a lifetime, endlessly willing to help those around him. After a moment, he said, "If I can help, let me know. He's a bit…" he trailed off, looking for the right word.

"Weird as shit," she supplied.

He exhaled a laugh. "I was going to say quirky, but that works too. But he's always helped us out. He's good company, and he makes you happy. So I'd like to help, if I can."

"I'll let you know." The words stuck in her throat, and she glanced away. Kiran's head was tilted strangely, hanging crookedly over his book. She squinted at him in disbelief. "Is he asleep?"

"Maybe?" Tarak said, reaching to push open the small door that separated the counter from the rest of the café. "Is that weird? I've never seen him sleep here."

She couldn't really explain that this was because he didn't sleep, ever, so she just slipped through the gap and went to him. His breaths came soft, chest heaving slowly. She was almost afraid of reaching out and touching his shoulder, afraid of disturbing this fragile, ephemeral peace that had taken hold of him.

He looked impossibly young asleep. His memories had aged him, drawing lines of grief and loss across soft, unmarked skin. But now, he looked untested, guileless—as though he were simply a nineteen-year-old boy asleep in a café, halfway through a book of poetry. It startled her a little, and she didn't hear Tarak until he had repeated his words multiple times. "Suri. Should we wake him?"

"No," she said, too loud for it to sound natural. She exhaled, rubbing at her eyes, then repeated, "No. He hasn't been, uh, sleeping well recently. I don't want to wake him."

"Then?" He rocked back on his heels. "We close in fifteen minutes."

Beanzzz was far enough away from her apartment that she didn't know if she could carry someone that far, even if he was made of gold and god. She pinched the bridge of her nose. "You asked if you could help, right? Are you free after work? I can't carry him home alone."

Tarak tilted his head in momentary consideration before nodding. "Yeah, I should be. Do you live close?"

"Not really," she said absently, kneeling beside the booth so she could examine Kiran further. His lashes looked like fracture lines, dark and thick, on his cheeks. "But it's not far, either."

They finished closing up; Suri turned off the lights and the room fell into darkness, illuminated only faintly by the rising moon outside. They were close enough to winter that light was a treasured commodity, available only in achingly small quantities.

The moonlight washed across Kiran's face, turning him pallid and insubstantial. Suri was suddenly glad Tarak would carry him. She was afraid that if she touched his skin, her fingers would go straight through.

She pulled the book out of crooked, bent fingers and tucked it into her bag as Tarak crouched and scooped him up in his arms. He made a soft sound, one of fear or discomfort, and shifted away, away. His lips were parted slightly, twisted in some long-forgotten specter of pain.

In late evening, Lyne came alive. Groups of youths ran through the streets, arms interlocked and faces bright with humor. Families traced familiar roads, little children pointing up toward the signs of toy shops and nearby theaters. Office workers, coming off a long day, shoved past them tiredly as they thought invariably of home.

Suri walked silently as Tarak told her about a protest his friend had roped him into attending later that week. She let the words wash over her, dulcet and a little hopeful. Listening to Tarak, it was easy to think of things such as change, such as peace, and not have them be the punch line to some old, forgotten joke.

She unlocked the door to her apartment and led him in. He gently placed Kiran on the couch. He mumbled something unintelligible, curling into the upholstery. It reminded her strangely of when they had first met, when he had been bloody, freshly born. Vulnerability did not come easily to him—he surrendered it only in moments such as these, sleep-soft and sleep-chained.

"I'll see you tomorrow, yeah?" Tarak said quietly, turning toward the door. She smiled and nodded, and he returned it, letting himself out. She locked the door, and sat down between Kiran's feet and the other arm of the couch.

Suri couldn't know how much time passed as she sat there, slotted into a dip in the couch, her knees bent under her. She felt a little like she was nearly asleep herself. But still, even as moonlight began to stream through the glass doors, she kept her eyes open and watched him. She didn't know what for; it was not as if she could protect him, as if she was a goddess herself. But wordlessly, senselessly, she watched him.

To him, she knew, sleep was something to be feared. It held a certain measure of violence, an insidious, jagged pressure. He woke in the midst of a scream, lips parted in horror, a silent cry that twisted inward into a gasp.

For a moment, she saw him laid bare. And he was afraid; so very afraid that briefly, he looked nearly human.

He blinked, and his expression shuttered instinctively, so quickly it could only have been muscle memory. But then he saw her, and though the fear did not return, his shoulders slumped with relief.

"Suri," he rasped, leaning his head back against the other arm of the couch. His chest heaved, and his cheeks were golden and flushed. "I—I fell asleep?"

His voice dripped with astonishment, too truly shocked to hold any of his casual self-deprecating scorn. She nodded, leaning back. "At the café. Tarak helped carry you back."

Strangely, he flinched at the name. His shoulders were still trembling faintly. At last, he said, oddly stilted, "I'm sorry. For inconveniencing you."

If she hadn't been so tired, she might have been angry. She shut her eyes and spoke with a careful force, a calm she couldn't feel. "You're not an inconvenience. You've carried me before. This isn't any different." Opening her eyes, she examined him. But he'd already lost that sudden, sleep-borne terror. His gaze was careworn. "Are you okay?"

He laughed, and the sound carried in the near-silence of the early night. Even when it faded, his mouth was still carved by it. "I'm fine. Thank you."

She raised an eyebrow. "Why did you laugh?"

Kiran tilted his head, hair falling into his eyes. They were champagne yellow and thin, a wavering flame. "It is not often people ask that question. I knew instinctively, but my memories have confirmed it." His lips twisted, faintly. "I am not… I am not the kind of god others worry for."

"I do." The words fell from her lips like a confession, the only holy act she had ever performed. "I worry for you all the time."

He smiled, and it held his old warmth. "Then you will have to be the first."

13
ENESMAT

Suri woke by water.

A cold wind blew through, chilling her bones. It was only then that she realized she was not wearing much—an unfamiliar, thin robe with a chemise underneath.

She was sitting beside a river, strangely still in the night. It glittered an opaque blue, dark enough it could've been mistaken as black. Her legs were folded beneath her, hands clasped together in prayer.

At least, she had assumed that at first glance. Her fingers were intertwined, clenched tightly. It was only now she realized they were shaking, soaked in blood that shone darkly in the moonlight.

The riverbank was empty, quiet in a strange, unnatural way. The only sound was the gentle splash of blood as it trailed down her fingers and fell to the grass below, following the soil as it joined the river. With every droplet, the river grew darker and darker, water turned to midnight-black oil.

It was not her own blood—she knew this, the same way she knew she was alone, the same way she knew this river would never run again. And yet it did not belong to any one person, either. It was old blood, rotten blood, and it had drained from every heart she had ever stopped—and now it had come to drown her, too.

Fear began to surge up inside her, swallowing every breath she tried to take. Her chest felt tight with it, as if blood had subsumed the air in her lungs, iron-sour and warm with stolen life. She pushed herself forward, kneeling beside the river and thrusting her bloodied hands into the water. But no matter how hard she scrubbed, how long she waited, the blood would not wash from her hands—they remained coated in dark red, the liquid viscous and tacky against her skin.

Water splashed up from the river in her frenzy, dampening her dress and her face and her arms. But her hands, though they had fallen out of prayer, refused to clean.

Eventually, she acquiesced to the demands of the river. She rocked back on her heels, held her hands out in front of her, and looked up to the sky.

Until this moment, she had expected it to mirror the skies of her memories—of the world she knew and treasured. A sea of blackness brought to life by glittering white stars. But this sky was something entirely different, a relic of days long past.

It was the color of freshly spilt blood, the way she expected her hands would look if not for the shadows that cast the entire clearing in darkness. A deep crimson, unmarked and uninterrupted save for a smooth white sphere—a moon, different from the one she had known.

Even without looking at her hands, she could feel the blood on them. It had taken her seventeen years to overcome this fear and yet it refused to fade, haunted her from day to day, a specter she could not banish. But she had found solace in the fact that blood would always yield—water would always wash it away. Even if she still felt it underneath—burned into her skin like a brand—she could remove the eerie, suffocating proof of it. She could escape it—she could run.

But she could not run from this. Under this strange, too-bright moon, this wrathful sky, she was trapped.

She wrung her hands out, a futile effort, and then clasped them tight, tilting her head up to the sky. In the silence, the only sound louder than the white noise in her own head was the thud of the blood against the grass—the uneven beat of her breaths.

Suri let her eyes fall closed, and prayed.

Kita had long since gone to sleep.

When they were younger, she would join him on these midnight walks, tracing the hidden paths of the temple over and over. In the darkness, their steps did not echo—the night swallowed them even as they ran through the shadowed corridors, hands clasped tight.

But it wasn't as if Kiran begrudged her for leaving him for sleep. It was true enough that the preparations for Avyakanth left him drained on top of his usual responsibilities. But the ceremonies performed at Avya's smaller temple—though more tiring—were ultimately shorter. Kita was responsible for orchestrating the festival after, a night-long series of rites and performances that required meticulous planning. She slept early and rose early.

And so he walked through the empty temple alone, the silence holding him close. He paused in front of the north tower, tracing the carvings. He had been there when Aswathi had them first painted, still remembered when she had told him and Kita the story of it.

"Her name was Nila," she had said, struggling to steady Kita on her knee. "She was an orphan of a nearby village. This was in the old days, the age of monsters." She had paused to make a scary face at them, and Kita had twisted her face, turning to hide in her mother's arms. Kiran had not reacted, already lost within the story—Aswathi had always been able to bring words to life. He had always thought she should've been the prophet instead of him, a broken, disjointed peasant boy with fire in his heartstrings.

"Nila had grown up in this horrible, frightening world, you see," she had continued, voice softening. "She thought herself used to these monsters, and dreamed of fighting them so she could protect those she loved alongside the warriors of the village. But one day, the closest thing she had to a father, the blacksmith, was killed by a monster with no legs and two hearts."

She had paused here, rubbing her hand soothingly against Kita's back. He'd set his chin on his knees, leaning forward thoughtlessly. "What did she do?"

"What would you have done, Kiran?" she had asked, smiling. But it had held a certain measure of weary sorrow, the same sorrow he caught in her gaze when she thought he wasn't watching, the same sorrow he saw in the eyes of the king and queen, and in the captain's. "She sought to kill the beast. Nila went to the river that encircled the village. It was a sacred river, said to have been blessed by Makai, daughter of the sea."

"She prayed to the goddess, asking her to give her the strength to kill the beast. The goddess appeared to her on the riverbank and warned her that the blessing would not come without a price—if she did not control the strength of the river, it would consume her and everyone around her. But Nila was headstrong and heartbroken—she accepted."

Already Kiran's heart had begun to chill. He had an inkling of how the story would end, and longed to ask her to cease telling it. But he had not been able to speak—curiosity had silenced him, curiosity and a strange, bittersweet ache. Aswathi had rocked Kita on her knee in time with her words, but the lull of them had slipped away, revealing the jagged, ugly truth underneath. "The blessing of the river gave her the strength to transform into a bear twice as large as any ordinary human. But it pulled her heart out of balance, made it difficult to think straight. Yet even in that addled state, Nila held enough self-awareness to keep track of her objective—to kill the beast. And so she returned to the village and tracked down the beast, right before it killed the baker. Her claws lengthened, needles tipped with oil-black poison, and she attacked the beast through the side, piercing it through both hearts. It fell and died before her, but her rage was not satiated. Nila ripped it to shreds, and after it was nothing more than flesh and bone and congealed blood, she attacked the baker—and then the baker's daughter, and the baker's son. It was only after she went after the blacksmith's daughter—her adoptive sibling—that she realized what she had done."

"Nila fell to her knees beside the river, having transformed back to human while traveling through the forest. She wept and wept, but her tears could not wash the blood off, nor could the water of the river. The young girl looked to the sky and prayed for Makai to release her from life, prayed for the goddess to wash away her sins. The goddess could not manage the latter—Nila's mistakes were her own and no divinity could erase them. But she took pity on her, and released her. It is said that Nila floated up to the sky—that the blood on her hands turned it crimson and her tears coalesced and formed a white jewel that held her soul. And every moon, we mourn her—those she lost and those she killed and those she loved."

There had been silence for a moment—and then Kita had asked quietly, "What happened to the river, Mother?"

At that, Aswathi had turned away and smiled softly, as if amused by a personal joke. "They say it runs black, my sweet. They say it runs black."

Looking at the carving now, wrapping around the base of the north tower, Kiran was struck by the expression on the young girl's face. It was one of sorrow, but also one of weariness. As if she had looked into the eyes of death itself and not flinched. As if she knew it. It was a familiar expression to him, but he could not place it. Bitterly, he thought he could've seen that expression on anyone he knew—the war had not spared any of them. That faint, unknowable sorrow he had seen on their parents' faces now lived on in their hearts.

There was a distant sound of panting, ragged and frantic. Normally, he would not have been able to hear it, soft as it was. But the temple was deathly silent in the night; he let his hands fall from the carving and retreated back into the main area.

The moonlight illuminated only the pool in the center, a clear, pale blue color against the silver light. There was a small figure hunched on the last step, kneeling beside the edges of the pool. They were pitched so far forward that for a moment, Kiran feared they would fall into the water. And yet they did not, rocking back and forward to a rhythm he could not parse.

For a single, heart-stopping moment, he thought it was Aswathi—her ghost back to haunt him where he would not be able to run.

But the figure was not dressed in a priest's robes. They were dressed in simple cotton nightclothes, wrapped in a thin, dark cloak. Kiran descended the steep stone steps. They were not damp, and yet he feared falling nonetheless. There was something about the water beneath that paralyzed him, spoke of simple, quick suffocation.

Kiran knelt beside the figure and hesitantly reached out a hand to turn them toward him. His breath caught from surprise. "Suri?"

She flinched, scrambling away from him. Her eyes had snapped open, but there was a feral, jagged terror in them that wiped away all traces of recognition. He reached out again, then thought better of it and dropped his hand. "Princess—"

But she was not listening—she had glanced down at her hands. Kiran inhaled sharply. Her hands were covered in blood, her palms ravaged with small, shallow cuts and a long, uneven one. A cheap kitchen knife lay beside her, drenched in blood.

She made a choked, strangled sound, of abject terror or utter disgust—he could not tell which one—and surged forward to the pool of water. Suri scrubbed at her skin with a ceaseless, intense fervor, washing her hands of the blood long after they had become clean. Her skin was beginning to pink, small scratches showing under her fingernails.

Kiran reached forward and held her hands tight, stilling their motion. She struggled against him for a few moments, writhing in his grip, but eventually she calmed. Sharp, rough sobs ripped out of her; she looked up at him—still distant, still lost, but tired. He let go of her hands and wrapped his arms around her, holding her tight. For a few minutes, the sound of her crying echoed in the empty temple, her tears soaking into his skin.

Eventually, the shuddering sobs faded into trembling. She pulled herself back, and he realized he was still embracing her, his hands light on her arms. He moved to let go, but she raised a hand and placed it on his, leaning into the touch.

"It's the blood," she said, explanatory and nonsensical. He nodded as if he understood, but she tilted her head, as if aware he did not. She exhaled, long and slow, and dropped her hand from his. There was something achingly weary in her expression. "Take me back to the palace, Kiran."

He wanted to ask her why she was here—why she had been crying, how she had cut herself and why it had shaken her—but every question he had felt unimportant in the face of her request. So he rose slowly and took her back to the palace with one hand still on her shoulder, a kind of lifeline. The guards were still awake, and they were too tired to come up with excuses, so they took the long way around—through the hidden shed and along the beaten path. They silently walked through the gardens, following the west colonnade back to the princess's rooms. He could hear faint rustling from inside—the sound of her maids sleeping, no doubt.

Suri's face had regained some of its color, but it was still pale, the color of damp sand. Her expression, too, had receded, an uncharacteristic uncertainty tilting her mouth. She began, "I am sure you are tired—"

"You know I do not sleep," he said, soft where the words were disdainful.

She glared at him and he was glad of it, if only because it drew her further out of that slick, silk-strong fear that had held her. "I could not ask you to go out of your way any longer."

"That is what I have done since you first arrived," he reminded her, a little surprised at his own forcefulness. "I have long since grown used to it. And if I left, who would dress your wounds?"

Suri glanced down at her hands, surprised, as if she had forgotten the cuts. They had not begun to bleed again, but they had grown into an angry red color in the time since they had left the temple. She looked at him grudgingly, as if she were considering the merits of allowing him to stay. Yet there was something habitual and fragile about it, too.

Quietly, she unlatched the door and let them both in. She lit the lamp beside the entrance, casting the entire room in an eerie amber glow that created shadows out of them both. She darted a nervous glance at the two adjoining rooms, but they remained alone.

Padding across the room, she took a reluctant seat on the bed, glancing up at him expectantly. "The bandages are in the night stand."

He obediently pulled open the first drawer of the night stand, rifling through its contents before moving on to the second one. Suri made a faint, nearly inaudible sound in the back of her throat, but did not say anything when he turned to look at her. That drawer was filled with imported books, though he could see the edge of a white slip near the bottom. The third drawer was empty save for a small wooden box, filled with linen cloth and a series of bottles. Kiran pulled it out and laid it beside her on the bed.

He cleaned the wounds in silence, interrupted only by the occasional hiss of pain when a cut was particularly large. It was only when he began to wrap them, trying his best to keep them from constricting her, that she spoke. Her voice was a little ragged, though he was not sure if that was from the pain or from the experience itself. "I am afraid of blood."

It explained part of what he had seen, but not all of it. "For how long?"

She closed her eyes. "I am not sure. Longer than I can remember. It is one of my first memories."

Kiran frowned up at her from where he knelt beside her hands. "One of your first memories is of blood?"

Her hands stiffened within his, her entire body going still and brittle, as if a single touch could crack her. When she spoke, the words were careful, soft, as if she was drawing each one out of herself painfully. "I have always been a tool of blood, of violence. Of death. It is the way of my family."

Suri did not elaborate on her words, but Kiran thought he understood what she meant to say regardless. She was gritted teeth, gravel-studded palms, bloody smiles—a perfumed, crimson rose, every petal cut into a razor blade. She was a storm of a girl with lightning in her blood; and she had been born with it sparking, but she had been taught to turn it outward, into blood and blades.

He had always suspected, right from the beginning—the knives, the suspicion, the cutting, heavy glances. But the visions had hidden the danger of her heart, obscuring it in ash and flame. Besides, if blood on one's hands absolved others of the moral responsibility to care for their life, he would've died a long time ago.

He finished wrapping her hands, removing the excess. Without meeting her gaze, he took them in his own, flattening them so the wounds did not bleed. "I should have known, and I did, in a way, but I didn't act on it. But—if you want—you don't have to help me with the spy. I would never force you; I know you have your reasons. The blood, your family—I cannot ask you to continue."

She squeezed his hands in hers so tightly the last words petered off, falling into silence. He met her gaze reluctantly;

her gaze was hard and bright, cooled embers held up to the light.

"I appreciate it," she said, a touch sardonically. "I appreciate *this.* But I knew what I was involving myself with when the messenger sent the first missive—I knew when I came to this city." Suri gave a little laugh, soft and dry. "It is a little late for me to remove myself from these matters now. I might be so closely enmeshed that to cut me away would stop my heart on its own."

"Don't say that," he said sharply, and she pulled her hands from his. The wounds had begun to bleed again, soft crimson blossoming against the coarse bandages. She watched the blood with a cool distance borne of suppressed discomfort—it was a familiar expression to him; he'd seen it on Viro a thousand times before. He blew out a sigh, but his chest still felt tight with fear. "You cannot speak so blithely of death. The gods are always watching."

The corners of her mouth curled in a crooked smile, a strange display of amusement. "If you say it, it must be so." Abruptly, she turned away, leaning over her bed and rifling through the drawers of her night stand before pulling out two glittering knives with no small amount of satisfaction. She gave them to him the way a mother might show peers her children, flushed with equal parts self-consciousness and pride. Hesitantly, she said, "I wanted to show you these, when I saw your garden. I don't know what that says about my utter lack of self-preservation, but—the garden is something beautiful you've grown and loved, and these are close as I've ever come to that."

Kiran took the knives into his hands. One shone brightly even in the dim candlelight, with a hilt of gaur bone and a glittering steel blade, while the other was dark as night, with a hilt of varnished mast-wood and a blade of obsidian. He knew the ceremonial daggers almost as well as he knew himself, but he had never taken any measure of joy in bloodletting—it left him exhausted and faintly resentful at the best of times. But he could feel Suri's fastidious, careful kind of love in the knives—in the worn hilts, the sharp glint of the blades, the faint warmth in her eyes when she looked down at them. Truthfully, he said, "They're beautiful."

She beamed despite herself, twisting her hands in her lap. The cuts still bled, but the blood seemed to bother her a little less than before. She pointed at them in turn, first at the silver one, then at the black one. "My eldest brother gave them to me before my first assignment, after I wore out the practice ones. This one's Solitude, and this one's Darkness."

He looked up from where he had begun to run the pad of his index finger along the slender edge of the obsidian knife. *Darkness.* His mouth quirked to the side in a wry smile. "What did you name them for?"

"A story book of Isa's," she replied, shoving at him lightly when a brief laugh left him. Her cheeks were flushed, the old pallor beginning to fade. The knowledge that he had warmed her even this small amount—it was heady, dangerous. Dangerous the way the sea was at night, when sailors gone salt-mad would gaze down at the shining black water and step over stone and soil and into darkness.

Suri tilted her head, strands falling away from her loose braid and framing her face. "There was this line, I still remember it—*Death is gracious in that it grants us both darkness and solitude.* I suppose I fancied myself a little like death back then." Her gaze turned dull with bitter self-deprecation. "Easier for a child to bear, of course, the notion of being a tool of some greater power rather than just another assassin. As if my heart was worth anything more than blood and ashes."

"It is," he said, so sharp and quick and certain that she glanced down at him, a little shocked. He was slightly surprised by the conviction in his voice, but not by much. "You are more than what your family deems you. You may be a tool of violence—" her mouth thinned at the phrase, but she did not speak, "—but that is not all you are."

She fell silent at that. After a few moments, he looked up, but her gaze was faraway, set on some distant, un-seeable point through the windows of her room. Then she glanced down at Kiran. "You saw the letter."

He sat back on his heels. "I did."

"Despite your threat, I send them regularly," she said, lips twisted and sharp. "Though the information is often useless. I haven't sent this one yet."

A smile flickered on his face, out of place. "If you had, I doubt I would have seen it."

Her mouth twitched, but she did not smile. When she spoke, it was a kind of confession, bloodied hands holding out something fragile and valuable and aged. "I do not want to send them anymore. You know this, I'm sure, as you know everything—you would not have let me live otherwise. The possibility of my betrayal is too dangerous for your kingdom. But it is the truth."

It was true that her betrayal could have destroyed them all. But it had never truly occurred to Kiran as a possibility. They had first met with the shadow of her death hanging above him, her blood tainting every conversation they had exchanged since. But he knew the part he had to play. "I saw the letter," he said. "And I know you have not sent it, and I know you will not."

"A premonition," she said, a faint, humorless smile hanging from her lips.

He shook his head slightly, letting go of her hands. "I told you before, didn't I? That you are more than a tool of violence. That your own heart guides you. I know you will not send it."

"You would stake the future of your kingdom on this hunch," she said, an attempt at scorn lacing her voice. But it was too soft, too afraid. "You would risk the crown—because you think you know my heart."

Kiran tried at a smile, but it was uneven, tenuous. "I would."

"And if I betray you?"

"Better chances than those that lie in front of us have already passed untouched," he pointed out.

"If I did?" she insisted. "What would you do then?"

"I refuse to consider it."

"You're a fool." She sounded nearly hysterical.

If only you knew, he thought, bitter all over again. *If only you knew how much of a fool I really am.*

"Perhaps," he said, bold in the near darkness of the room. The distant candlelight turned them both to ghosts, to whispers. Kiran was suddenly painfully aware of his own heart, of its warmth and of its mortality. "But I do not think I am."

Suri turned to look at him, gaze red-rimmed and lost. Her lips parted, as if to say something more. But before she could, a door behind them cracked open. Her grip on the bed frame tightened, and she winced at the pressure.

"My lady? Why are you awake so late at night…" the voice trailed off as Kiran glanced back and caught the gaze of a maid. He did not recognize her—her dark hair was braided loosely in a traditional style, and her soft brown eyes were hazy with sleep. But the sight of him had sharpened her gaze, disbelief cutting through her expression. And another emotion, something more familiar to him—fear. Her gaze fell to the knives on the bed, lingering strangely before breaking away.

After a few moments more, the other door opened as well, and another maid entered the room. He recognized her as Suri's Najan handmaiden from the banded tattoo on her arm. But she also seemed faintly familiar, as if he had seen her around the temple before, though he could not recall what for. She did not look as surprised to see him, only vaguely wary. Her gaze flicked from him to Suri, a silent question the other girl refused to answer, her eyes on the floor.

Kiran pulled himself to his feet, shaking out the residual stiffness in his joints before dipping his head in a brief bow to Suri. "Think on my words, Your Highness."

She looked up at him, her expression momentarily pained before she smoothed it out. Quietly, she said, "I will."

When he returned to the temple, the brazier had gone out. It was the first time in the twelve years he had tended it that it had extinguished on its own. He put his fingers on the still-warm coals, bracing for the soft sting of fire and finding nothing.

"A fool," he murmured, closing his eyes. *Is that what you think of me too?*

There was no response, but for a moment, Kiran thought he felt the coals grow cold.

"That was—he was—" Mohini had been speechless since Kiran had left. Her arm was outstretched, finger crooked loosely toward the space he had vacated. "*That was*—"

"That was who?" Isa asked innocently. She pulled her shawl tighter around her when they both glanced toward her, but her eyes were hard. Isa might not have met him, but hanging around the high priestess all the time, Suri had no doubt she would've heard of him.

Mohini was still watching her, a little fearful and a little wary, as if unsure whether the other girl was joking or not. In a low whisper, she said, "That was, you know, the high priest."

Isa crossed her arms. "I thought Kita was the high priestess?"

The other maid's mouth puckered as she slowly caught on to the fact that Isa was toying with her. Still, she continued, "The other high priest. The *thyvaayan.*"

She tore her gaze away from them. Suri still felt a little lightheaded, though she was unsure whether that was from the blood loss or that strange, unsteadying show of faith. She couldn't fathom it—the thought of someone putting that trust in her, the reality of that person being him.

"My lady?" Isa repeated, placing her hand on her shoulder. Her tone was brittle, and Suri knew she had finally seen the bandages. There was an unsaid question in those two words—*Did he hurt you?*

She shook her head, the lies coming easily to her lips. "I was sleepwalking, and I fell and cut my hands. He walked me back and cleaned the wounds."

"But why was he out there this late?" Mohini asked, tone hushed and clipped, as if she had tasted something bitter. She shivered, as if the concept of him wandering the city was something to fear, something that held danger.

Irritation sparked behind her sternum. "He suffers from insomnia, Mohini," she said sharply. The maid flinched with surprise at her tone; her mouth twitched as if to say something in response, but eventually she fell still, gaze trained on the floor.

Isa looked at her curiously, but Suri turned away, pulling her knees up. She spoke without looking back, keeping her eyes on the glittering city outside. "The walk has tired me. I would like to rest."

They left without complaint, but Mohini cornered her the next morning before they left for the day's errands.

"My lady," she began, and then paused, unsure of how to continue. Finally, she said, "It is not that I do not trust you."

It took Suri a few seconds to understand what she was referring to. She exhaled, weary though the sun had only just risen. "It is him you distrust. Is that what you mean to say?"

Mohini glanced around them nervously before saying, "I do not distrust him. After all he has done, who could possibly doubt his loyalty to the crown?"

Suri raised an eyebrow. "Then?"

"It is simply that—" she cut off, sighing. "I have not seen this, only heard of it, but—there is a rumor that—"

"A rumor, Mohini?"

"Please, my lady," she pleaded. "I only say this because I—I worry." Her voice was tense, shoulders bunched together.

Suri pinched the bridge of her nose and waved a hand to show her acquiescence. Mohini mustered a ghost of a relieved smile, but it dropped off her face seconds after. "There is this old rumor, you see. From before the war—when the late high priestess was still alive. She taught her daughter—the current high priestess—and him all that they know, as it goes." She swallowed hard, and then continued, "The temple was newly made for him—Avya had told him how he wanted it built, and he had given the laborers meticulously detailed descriptions. And this, this was his first service he would truly participate in. If I remember correctly, he was less than seven years of age. And… And when he picked up the *unthi* to clean the statue, it is said it cracked and shattered under his fingertips. Simply from the touch—he had not said anything, nor thrown it. He had only touched it."

His scars, she thought. The thin, short white lines that tangled on the backs of his hands. She had assumed he had gotten them in some kind of conflict, and yet it was strangely fitting. A pot, broken by innocence. She pursed her lips to keep her expression neutral. "And what is so frightening about that?"

Mohini looked at her sideways, as if she were the odd one for not immediately understanding. "He is not human, my lady—he is not *normal,* the way you and I are. If he could break a pot with his bare hands as a *child,* with no effort—with no intention—imagine what he is capable of. If one were to anger him…" She shuddered and made a quick gesture of protection. The irony of it sat bitter on Suri's tongue.

"I will keep that in mind," Suri assured her. The way Mohini had described it nauseated her, but a small, wary part of her—the part that had always kept her alive—wondered if she was right. If Kiran had only grown in power since that misstep, if his fingers—his blood—could split open the sky, just like his patron's had.

14
LYNE

She didn't hear him approach. Kiran had always been quiet, but this was a cultivated silence, something taught and learned. He ducked into the living room, dark hair curling and damp against the nape of his neck. His borrowed T-shirt hung off him at an awkward angle, exposing wet, nut-brown skin. He nodded at the board in her hands. "What's that?"

Her hands tightened around it instinctively, and his eyes tracked the movement. Carefully, he perched on the edge of the armchair. "You don't have to tell me. You are allowed your secrets, Suri."

And she was, but part of her still wondered, still dreamt. She had asked the gods for a sign, and they had given her him; for the longest time, she had considered that the divine equivalent of them flipping her off. But she'd been trying to piece together the tangled web of this for years, had gone over all the evidence hundreds of times, thousands. He was something new—logically, she knew it was unlikely he wasn't related, even if he hadn't been behind it.

She gave the board a cursory glance. Her grandmother had bought her a pack of poster boards for a grade school project and she had used all but this one. When night fell, she would take it out and work on it by lamplight, by moonlight. It was so clearly the work of a hopeful, naive child. She handed it to him, only slightly shaking.

He took it, covering her hand with his for just a moment. And then he let go, drawing back and taking in the poster board. After a while, he spoke. "How long have you been working on this?"

She could only manage a bitter, choked-off chuckle. "A long time. Longer than I should have. I don't know why I never stopped, it's just—I don't know. I've thought about it, over and over. And it doesn't make sense."

Kiran cocked his head in a silent question. He rubbed his thumb over the yellowed newsprint picture of the burning car.

"It's the car, you see," she continued; the words refused to be stopped. *Where were they coming from?* There was a gaping, ugly hole in her, taped up with glitter glue and red sunlight. Offering him the board had ripped it open abruptly, and now she was bleeding hope. "They said the car spontaneously combusted. Fuel leak. That was the public statement. But, when I started looking, the police report says the car was completely fine. External fire, apparently."

"Police report?" he asked, raising an eyebrow.

She folded her arms, flushing. "I was curious. Defiant. Probably a little too unbothered by things like the law or my own youth for my own good. It took me a while, but I kept searching, and it doesn't add up. None of it."

"Tell me how it happened," he said, leaning back. The red yarn she'd used to connect evidence together slid under his skin. "How you think it happened, not them."

The words unsteadied her. *How she thought it happened.* All she had were hypotheses, fragmented ideas and thoughts that connected at tangential points. She drew in a breath and said, "I'm not entirely sure. I'm still searching. But… I think they were murdered. I think someone started the fire in that car, and I think they covered it up. I just can't understand why someone would want to kill my parents. They were good people, innocent people."

"Murder is not always an action of wrath," he said softly. His eyes were critical, but thoughtful, too. As if he took her words seriously, trying, in his own way, to help. "People often wield it as a tool. A scythe to carve the world in an image they desire." He glanced up and held her gaze. "You started this years ago. Why haven't you shared it with anyone?"

Her lips twisted bitterly. "I know I can't show my grandmother. She's too cynical; she'd dismiss it immediately. And if she did believe me, if she got her hopes up and then had them dashed—I don't think she would be able to bear it. This is all… speculation. It's not baseless, but there's no empirical proof. No one would believe me. They'd think I was paranoid."

"I don't," he affirmed. His mouth quirked to the side sharply. "Then again, I may be paranoid myself. I've seen a lot of strange things happen in the world, Suri, but this is stranger still, and coincidence is rare. Do you know anything more about the fire set in the car, apart from the police report?"

"No," she said, hesitant. Reaching forward, she pointed at the sigil she'd drawn on the board in black permanent marker. It was dry, matte, but she still felt as though it might peel off the board and grip her tightly. "But when I was seven, my grandmother left me alone in the shop. It was for a short while, and I'd been left alone for longer before. A man came in, pale and cold, dressed in black. I can't remember much about him apart from that. He laid a letter on the front table, said it was for my grandmother. And then he gave me a bag, plastic and bound with a blue tie. Told me it was a gift—sweets. After that, he left."

Kiran had gone still. His skin was dark, bloodless. "What happened?"

"I almost ate them," she said, and the words were cloying on her tongue. She was only alive by fortune, by chance. A ghost in all but form. "But my grandmother came back, saw the bag. Holly berries, dusted in white granules. I'd thought it was powdered sugar, but it was more poison. In case the berries didn't do the job."

In a rare moment of reverence, he made an unfamiliar gesture, an ancient one. She tilted her head in a question, and he said, "A rite of protection, for you."

She forced a weak smile; he looked truly shaken. But the truth of it was that even speaking of that day still unsettled her. She wanted to forget it so badly, wanted to dismiss it as a fluke, an illusion. But it wasn't. "The thing is, though, the letter the man had placed on the table—it had no writing. It was blank, save for this single mark in the middle. A circle and a strike straight through. I didn't understand it back then, but I think it's related. To whoever killed my parents, and why they did it."

"I agree." Eyes shuttered, he rubbed his thumb over the mark. "I don't recognize it, and I'm sorry for that. I know you thought I might know something. I will help you look, though. If you will have me."

There was a strange uncertainty to the offer. She smiled a little, despite herself. He was solemn at times, but never shy, never unsure.

Suri nodded, surprised at her own resolve. "I wouldn't have given you the board if I didn't want your help. I trust you."

He ducked his head, the three words piercing him as though they were knives. She had not meant them to hurt, and he knew that. And yet, they cut. "Then I'll try to earn it."

"I think," Kiran said lightly, "That you all need to take some time to unwind."

"Gee," Aza drawled, the single word dripping with sarcasm. "You think?"

Kiran simply smiled at her faintly. It wasn't one of his old grins, sharp and fever-warm, but it still knew how to shine.

Dai rubbed at his bloodshot eyes. "I appreciate the sentiment, but honestly, I don't even think a massage would help at this point."

"Speak for yourself," Miya mumbled, poring over her textbook. "I would love a massage. Any massage."

Exams were around the corner, and the past few weeks had been hectic. Busy work days, back-to-back projects, and in Suri's case, running around the city doing deliveries for her grandmother. Kiran did the majority of the work, but even he couldn't cover it all. "I'm not talking about massages."

"Then what are you talking about?" Suri said suspiciously, glancing over at him.

His eyes glittered with humor, but they were strangely hard, too. "Have any of you ever learned to fight?"

Ellis sipped his tea and stared through him. "Please don't suggest what I think you're about to suggest."

"And what's that?" he asked pleasantly, goading.

Aza raised her hand. Her legs were thrown across the side of the armchair, and she was peering intently at something on her laptop. "I have. Tried to teach Dai, but he hated it. Refused on principle."

"Principles don't really come into play when somebody's threatening to kill you," Kiran replied. Suri cut a glance at him, but he didn't meet her gaze. His memories made themselves clear in small, sharp gestures such as these. Old bitterness, tempered by pain. "Self-defense, at the very least. And stress relief, for the rest of you."

Miya rolled over on the couch. "I wouldn't mind. It might be fun to punch someone after all the time I've spent fantasizing about punching this professor."

Ellis made a reluctant noise of assent, and Aza turned to convincing Dai. He was pointedly staring at his book, but he hadn't turned a page in a startlingly long time and his expression was strained. He was notoriously avoidant of confrontation.

"Please," she wheedled. It was a ridiculous look on her, like a poodle growling. "Dai, *please.* It'll be fun."

"It won't be fun," he said tonelessly. "Hitting people is not fun."

"It kind of is," Miya said, and he glared at her.

Dai threw his hands up. "Why are you all trying to convince me? Ask Suri. If Suri says yes, I'll come."

All eyes in the room turned to her.

"I'll buy you ice cream for a month," Aza said, solemn.

"It's almost winter," she replied, arching an eyebrow. But she knew they wouldn't relent until she gave an answer.

Suri had never learned to fight, had never really thought about it. Life in her grandmother's shop had always sheltered her. Self-defense hadn't seemed necessary.

But Kiran had proposed it for a reason, something more salient than stress relief. She turned to him; there was a plea in his eyes, dark gold and meant only for her. *Please.*

She lifted her shoulders in a shrug. "Whatever. I vote yes." Dai gave her a wounded look, and she patted his arm. "Sorry. Self-defense is important."

"This is a bad idea," he announced. "I'm just putting it out there. This is going to go horribly."

After they'd all left, she brought it up to him. "Why do you want us to learn how to fight?"

His features were limned by the flickering glow of the game show. A contestant got a question right, and flashing blue and white lights colored his skin. His mouth was a thin, thin line. "A man tried to *kill* you."

"It was twelve years ago."

"And your parents died seven years before the act," he returned, fluid and unrelenting. There was a terrible softness to his voice, and it nearly resembled concern. "Time is irrelevant here, Suri. He tried to kill you, and he could try again, and so could someone else—what of whoever bound us? You need to be able to protect yourself."

She turned to face him, and in the darkness, she struggled to piece together his expression. But it was only ashes and fear, bitter on her tongue and cold on his. Eventually, he said, "You trust me."

It was a question that tried so hard not to be. "I do."

Kiran exhaled, a brittle sound. "Then trust me now, and let me teach you. Please."

Silently, she watched him breathe, traced the heave of his chest and the slant of his jaw, the sharp line of his mouth, twisted with anticipation.

She didn't think knowing how to block a punch would keep her alive, not if someone truly meant to kill her. And she thought maybe Kiran knew that too, and that odd, strained ache in his gaze was because he knew it. And still, he wished for this. She couldn't deny him his hope. "Okay. I'll do it." A contestant got a question wrong; canned laughter filled the air, and he smiled.

Kiran was flippant and fastidious by turns, and he took the matter of teaching them how to fight far more seriously than he'd suggested he would. Ellis suggested a gym on the southwest edges of the city, and they met there after finishing their exams for the month. Finals were coming up soon, but there was little point in taking a test if you couldn't temporarily forget that academia existed for a short period of time afterward.

The gym was nestled within the bare bones of an old warehouse. Suri would've thought it abandoned if not for the scattered signs of life—a few cars parked haphazardly near the city limits, lights flickering from inside, the distant sound of shouts.

They lingered by the entrance while Kiran talked to the owners of the gym, two ladies in their mid-twenties. He said something, and they both laughed before handing him a shining, crooked object and ducking out of the building.

"You can come in now," Kiran called, and they hesitantly shuffled into the building. The warehouse had vaulted ceilings, lanterns hanging from the thick, wooden beams slotted into the roof. High windows lined the walls, letting in the faintest drip of moonlight.

Kiran was leaned against the edge of the ring, a keychain hanging from long, scarred fingers. He gestured for them to join him, and they all exchanged glances with each other—Aza's mouth curved with that sharp, small grin that meant she was excited, Miya arching a single eyebrow, Ellis mildly bemused, and Dai vaguely nauseated.

Suri didn't know how she felt about this yet—every time she thought deeply about it, she remembered Kiran's gaze, soft and pleading. *Please.*

They toed their shoes off, and one by one, pulled themselves up and into the ring. Aza led them through taping, looping it around their wrists and hands. Kiran twirled the keychain around his finger, then slipped it into his pocket. His lips parted to speak, but Aza cut in. "I know we're all thinking this, so I'm just going to come out and say it. Can *you* fight? Like—" she gestured at him, as if it was meant to be an explanation.

In a way, it was. He was not much taller than Suri, slight and lean. She doubted any of them had forgotten what he looked like shirtless, but he didn't *look* strong. Divinity, she was sure, made body building a low priority on his list.

"Are you doubting my abilities?" he asked her.

"Yeah," she said bluntly. She bounced on the balls of her feet—she was more than half a foot shorter than him, but she looked blade-sharp, defiant. "I mean—I'm happy we're here, don't get me wrong. But you're scrawny as shit."

Kiran's mouth curved in a smile, amused. He spread his hands in a question, steadying himself leisurely against the edge of the ring. "How about this? If any of you beat me, I'll buy you dinner after this. You can team up, if you wish."

Aza snorted. "You've got to be kidding me. *Any* of us? And we can team up?"

"Yep," he replied, magnanimous.

"You're broke," Suri called, cupping her hands around her mouth. "I've never seen you carry money in my entire life."

"Exactly," he said amiably. "Who wants to go first?"

They glanced over at each other, silently discussing. Suri knew him well enough that she absolutely refused to step forward. He was planning something. Ellis seemed interested, but in the slapstick way of someone intrigued by coming disaster. Miya held up her hands, silently pulling out. Dai still looked like he was about to vomit.

"You're all assholes," Aza said, even as she stepped forward. "Cowardly assholes. But it's okay, because I'll beat his ass, and then we'll get dinner. You all owe me for this."

Kiran grinned, a brief, jagged slash on his face. He nodded at them, pushing off from the edge of the ring. "One of you will have to referee. Don't worry, it won't take long."

"Cocky bastard," Aza muttered, taking up fighting stance. Her black hair was pinned away from her face with clips, and it made her look a little bit like a thorn bush, dark and sharp.

He took up the same stance, but on him it seemed almost flippant. Miya whistled, high and shrill, and Aza surged forward, compact and agile. Suri didn't see Kiran move at all—the fist cut toward his face, and then Aza was folded on the floor, one arm pinned behind her back. His touch was firm, but not forceful. Aza groaned and tapped the ground beside her and he leaned back, letting her move away.

She crossed her arms, legs sprawled under her. "What the hell was that?"

"Experience." Kiran pulled himself to his feet and extended a hand. He nodded toward the rest. "Any questions?"

They looked slightly shell-shocked, but Suri wasn't surprised in the slightest. Taming a wild animal didn't mean it forgot how to kill.

He split them into two groups based on who wanted to learn how to actually fight—Aza and Miya, the latter still dead-set on the cathartic experience of punching somebody in the face—and those who were interested in self-defense, which was just Ellis and Dai. He insisted Suri learn both, so she darted from group to group as he went through the motions.

Despite the initial shared suspicion that he would be as useful a teacher as the Internet, he clearly knew what he was doing. *Experience,* he'd said when Aza had asked him. Not practice—experience. Suri couldn't help but wonder which of his lives had taught him to move like that, as if violence itself was a dance he'd glutted himself on. But she also knew he wouldn't tell her, even if she asked. Some demons were meant to stay nameless.

Ellis and Miya took to it quickly, and despite Dai's constant complaints, it wasn't long before he managed to reasonably mimic Kiran's movements. Suri was the sole outlier.

Aza, on the other hand, spent most of her time honing her skills, with the aim of fighting him again at the end.

She pointed at him defiantly as he moved around her to correct Miya's stance. "I want a rematch. Several rematches. As many rematches as I need."

"And you can have them," he said, eyes twinkling as he shifted Miya's arms. "The offer for dinner is off, but I don't expect to leave tonight until at least one of you can engage me for thirty seconds."

Thirty seconds. It seemed absurdly short, but Suri found herself wondering if any of them would be able to do it. Her stance faltered, and he patted Miya's shoulder as he came to stand by her. The easy smile had fallen from his expression.

"Afraid I can't be your star pupil," she joked, letting her arms drop.

Kiran shook his head, tense without ire. "I'm making you learn both at the same time. I don't expect it to come easily."

He gestured for her to assume the stance again and then adjusted her arms, gooseflesh prickling where his fingers ghosted on bare skin. Once he was satisfied, he stepped behind her. When he spoke, the words tickled the curl of her ear and she shivered once, despite herself. "Okay, left jab."

She blew out a long breath, but reluctantly threw her arm out in a punch. He inclined his head in disagreement, stepping to the side and repeating the punch. The movement was fluid, cutting.

Suri mimicked it, or tried to. "Like that?"

"Nearly," he said, guiding her arm. His touch was careful, gentle; fine-tuned control over raw fire. "Like this."

She swallowed hard—it wasn't as if he was doing this on purpose, as if he was aware she was finding this difficult to bear—and then threw out another punch, the way he had. He rocked back on his heels, offering a bright grin. "Exactly like that."

He led her through the rest until she could mimic him to a reasonable extent. Then he gathered everyone back up, all in varying states of fatigue.

"Who wants to go first?" Kiran asked, leaning back against the edge of the ring again. His skin was pale, flushed by ichor. "Only one of you needs to make it to thirty seconds. No team-ups, though."

Miya raised her hand tentatively and stepped forward, yielding a grin. Ellis searched up bell noises on the internet. He tapped at his phone and it obliged, letting out a bright screech.

Initially, it looked like she might actually make it—instead of fully pinning Miya like he had with Aza, Kiran stuck mainly to defensive maneuvers, with a few gentle punches. Still, she threw a bad punch at the twenty-second mark, and he sidestepped her and held his hand out in a semblance of a punch, a warning. More a suggestion of what he would have done than the movement itself. Miya groaned good-naturedly, returning to the line.

After a quicker pair of defeats with Dai and Ellis, he turned to Suri. She put her hands up. "No."

"Suri," he sing-songed, drawing out her name in his odd accent. "Why not?'

"Because," she said firmly. "I don't want to humiliate myself."

"Your friends already have." Aza shoved Kiran, and he moved with it, laughing. He turned his attention back to her, holding his hands out, palms up. "I don't bite."

She seriously doubted that. "You look like you do."

"You would know," Miya called, wiggling her eyebrows. Kiran cocked his head, blissfully ignorant, and she shook her head in dismissal.

"Later," she said, waving a hand. "I need more practice. You can teach me more at home."

He frowned at her, but turned back to Aza with a mischievous smile. "Time for that rematch, then."

Lo and behold, Aza lost at a little over thirty-two seconds. More than a little bit of the time was spent in syrup-slow defensive maneuvers that Kiran didn't actually need to affect in order to win. But they were all tired, so they sat on the edge of the ring and unwrapped the tape from their fingers as Dai moaned about never repeating this experience again, ever.

They trekked across the city to get shitty burgers in the near-winter cold, grins white with what could've been snow, on a different day. After they returned, and Suri followed Kiran out onto the balcony, scented with earth and something sharper than smoke.

"Tell me the story," she said, before he could say anything. There was a strange twist to his features just then, and she was less afraid of what he would do and more afraid of how she would react to it.

He considered her words, bracing himself on the wrought-iron railing. Night-borne, blood-riven. She didn't think she could know somebody like him, not wholly, but for the first time, she allowed herself the desire of wanting to. Eventually, he crossed the distance and brought her hands up in the fighting stance, spacing her legs.

"After you practice," he said quietly, close enough that the winter chill was nonexistent.

She shivered from something entirely different, cutting a glare at him. "There was a time when I thought you were kind."

He shook his head, lips wrung out from laughter. "Do you want to know a secret? I try, sometimes. For you. I don't think I'm good at it."

"Then practice," she said, offering a lopsided grin.

"Will you teach me?" he asked.

Without dropping the stance, she twisted to look at him. She remembered his words, quiet and earnest. She was not as good at that as him, but she tried. "If you'll have me."

His hands dropped from her shoulders. "I will."

15
ENESMAT

Kiran was burning. It was an odd feeling, more so because he knew what flames felt like when they wrapped around someone—had grown up gorged on the feeling—and knew instinctively that what he was feeling right now was something fundamentally different. It ripped him apart, tore skin from flesh from bone and seared his blood, turning it to something corrosive and alive. It was different, because he could not see it.

Curled on the floor of the temple, he struggled to raise his hand, stared at it through slit eyes. His skin was untouched by fire—and then he blinked, once, twice, saw it wreathed in blood and wreathed in flames, and then simply his bare skin again.

He knew, logically, that these were just visions—illusions pressed on top of one other so that they tangled into something new and frightening. The fire, too, was not real—at least, real as others would define it. It was not a fire of flint and air; it was one of blood, and it had ignited the moment he had opened his eyes in the flames of his birth, and it would never cease, never die—not until he did.

Kiran was distantly aware of his own screaming. It was a shrill sound, ragged from exhaustion. But he could not truly feel it—not his raw throat, nor the tears wetting his cheeks. He was lying on the floor of the temple, knees shunted to the side and hands curled uselessly against the stone. But there was another version of him that lay aside, a version that wasn't dead because it had never truly been alive, and this dulled, incorporeal Kiran was on fire.

A figure knelt beside him. He felt a watery kind of surprise, as if he were at the bottom of a deep, dark lake and the emotion lay untouched at the surface. He had endured these alone for longer than he could remember—there had been a time, years, nearly decades, ago, when someone had sat beside him. But he could not remember their name, could not remember their face. The longer he thought of it, the less real the memory seemed to be, fading and fading even as he stretched his hands forward to hold it tight.

There was a light pressure on his hands, a touch that broke through the pain of the fever momentarily. For a second, he felt his own body, felt the stone beneath him.

Visions addled him, pulling reality out of focus. Ghosts crowded upon the figure in front of him, tilting them into those he had lost. He murmured their names in a nonsensical string, a prayer he knew would go unanswered. The figure shifted beside him, said something blurry and far away—too far away for him to touch.

Then they pulled their hands away slowly, letting his own drop to the stone. His chest tightened with some abstruse, unknowable ache, and he reached forward again. He could not think, could not form words—at least not in the language of mortals, the one he had learned and loved and had now lost to the flames. When he spoke, it was more out of instinct than anything else, a phrase he could form purely out of muscle memory.

The figure stilled above him, and after a moment dropped to their knees again. They said something in that strange, human language, and he nodded without understanding. There was a soft, amused sigh, and then—that familiar, slight pressure on his hands. It did not ease the pain of the fever, the burn of the flames, but it loosened the knot in his chest, brought him closer to himself.

Kiran held their hands tight, and then allowed himself the one bliss he had not indulged in since he was a child. He let go.

Kiran's eyes fluttered closed, his body going limp on the floor of the temple. His hands still seared her own, but they had gone still, casting off the slight tremors of a few moments prior. Suri's heart beat a terrible, ceaseless rhythm against her ribcage as she turned him to the sky and pressed a hand against his chest.

There was a soft rhythm—a faint heartbeat. She exhaled. So this was what a boy looked like wasting away from within, ruined by bladed flames. *I am a dead man walking, Suri.*

She gingerly brushed away his hair and held a hand against his forehead, wincing at the heat. He would not survive the night, not if she left him out here. She pulled off her own cloak and wrapped him in it, lifting him carefully in her arms as she left the temple.

Suri had only found him out of coincidence—she had left the palace to comb through the north gardens late at night, as if she would find the spy there, admiring the rose bushes innocently. As if this nightmare was something so easily unraveled.

She'd felt the screams before she'd heard them, a rolling, low sting that drew her away from the blossoms and up toward the temples. She had only begun to run after they had first begun to choke off from exhaustion and agony.

She examined him as she walked along the narrow ledge that separated the temple from his cottage. In sleep, he looked at peace, uncharacteristically youthful. But Suri still remembered how he had looked on the floor of the temple, with his eyes slit open. His pupils had disappeared, irises blown out and turned golden with fire. And then there had been the tears, burning down his cheeks and shedding a faint glow on his skin.

He had obviously been delirious with fever—none of what he had said made any intelligent sense. But she could not forget what he had said when she had pulled away, told him—uselessly—that she would return with help, with Tarak and the boy king and the high priestess and everyone else. He had made that choked, raw sound—a sound of prey, of children—and held her hands tight and pleaded, the words intoned as if part of a prayer, "Don't leave me."

And so she had stayed.

It had been as simple as that request, and yet Suri knew it was anything but. Even now, she was struck by how easily she had acquiesced—how little she cared about the danger he posed. In the temple, holding him could have killed her. Carrying him now could easily be lethal, and she wouldn't know it. She suspected she wouldn't care either way.

They passed the garden, glittering and dew-wet in the early morning. She shifted him in her arms as she reached around to unlatch the door. He was surprisingly light, more fire than flesh.

Inside was a cramped room, the lack of space exacerbated by the addition of extraneous decorations and knickknacks—a handful of engraved ceramic pieces on a windowsill, precariously tall stacks of books and scrolls listing dangerously to the side. A short, shoddily made table sat in the center of the room, bordered by a worn settee and a wicker chair. Blankets were sprawled on a wooden cot pushed against the far wall, and a sprig of lavender tied to the frame filled the air with a faded floral odor.

She laid him on the settee and pulled a thin throw over him. He curled into the fabric, lips moving uselessly though she could hear nothing of what he said. He was still burning up, his cheeks flushed with fever.

Suri dampened a towel, the cold water chilling her fingers. She folded it and pressed it against his forehead—he hissed at the contact, clenching his fingers at his sides, but still he stayed unconscious, lost in some odd, foreign world she could not pierce with human hands.

Even as she moved around the cottage, straightening up old, discarded belongings and lighting the candles he had placed on every window, she could not seem to understand that this was his home. It was easy to delude oneself into believing he had somehow been borne of the temple, had sprung from the brazier fully formed and shaped by the fire into something flame-sharp and nearly divine.

And yet he wasn't—he had cried out in fear, in longing and in mourning, and he had a heart that beat and bled, and this soft, achingly warm place had raised and loved him. Mohini had said that he was not human, alien to everyone and everything mortal, and yet Suri could not believe that, not faced with this. She brushed her hand over the top of a sheaf of Eryan fairy tales and wondered whether he had the same dreams as Anyu, wondered whether he had stories of his own.

Rustling came from the settee. Kiran was struggling to support himself, pushing up against the arm of the sofa and slipping, too weak to hold the position for long. After a few fruitless attempts, he relented, letting his head tilt back against the wood. His chest heaved slowly, unfocused eyes trained upon the ceiling.

"You stayed," he said, brows furrowed. As if he could not quite believe it. As if he still did not. He turned to look at her, the effort eliciting a faint grunt of exertion. His eyes were black again, the black of the night sky, of soot. "What happened?"

"I found you on the floor of the temple. You were—in pain, feverish." She paused, unsure whether to add in what he had said. "You… lost consciousness, so I brought you here."

He exhaled low and closed his eyes. The blanket was still tangled between his legs, the towel crooked on his forehead. He did not look like a prophet touched by the gods, like a messiah. He looked weary, lost. Without opening his eyes, he said, "Tell me of Idhrishti."

Suri blinked. "What?"

"Idhrishti," he said softly. "The Najan saint. I have heard retellings, but I want to hear it from you. Tell me his story."

Suri tilted her head in a silent question, but he did not clarify the meaning of his request—the reason for it. Finally, she settled herself on the wicker chair and pulled her knees up. His fever had reduced, but it still burned so bright that sitting this close to him was difficult.

"Idhrishti was a prince of Naja, one of the first," she started, oddly self-conscious. She could not help but think of the rasp in her voice, the strange, arrhythmic cadence of her words. But Kiran said nothing of it—his eyes remained closed, his breaths coming slowly and softly. "When he was a young man, he fell in love with a star. The star had streaked across the night sky, appearing to him on a failed hunting trip. It was not love at first sight—the star scolded him for lighting a bonfire at night, and discarding things in the lake, and all matters of misdemeanors.

"The prince thought the star sensitive and fastidious, and the star thought him callous and careless. But that was not the end of it; the star returned to chastise him on the second hunting trip, and the third, and so on. Eventually, the prince grew used to the star, and looked forward to seeing them." She shifted on the chair, reaching forward to adjust the towel on his forehead. His eyes fluttered open briefly, but he relaxed after realizing what she was doing. "The tragedy of it all, though, was that the star had fallen in love with the prince. They could not have each other—how could they? But for a time, they pushed this out of their minds and danced around each other, courting one another without truly confessing. They sought solace in one another, fully aware that nothing could come of it and yet unable to stop themselves."

"And then the war came," she said, darting a glance at the other boy. He did not say anything, but his hands curled into the blanket, forming loose fists. "The prince's father died in the war, and so he took up his place. He was afraid—he had always preferred diplomacy to violence, and had only ever continued hunting because of the star. He survived throughout, but the star watched from overhead, torn apart by worry and unable to interfere—for that meant they would fall."

"It was the last battle of the war, the final stand. The prince fought bravely, but a well-placed, well timed attack from behind threatened to fell him—and yet he did not die. Without the knowledge of the prince, the troops, or the stars above, the star had fallen and stolen armor to fight in. They took the blow, a fatal one. As the star fell, the prince held their dying body and confessed his love, far too late for it to be of any use. But the star died loved, skin disappearing into sparks and smoke. They died knowing they were loved."

There was a beat of silence, Suri's chest tight from the story and Kiran's breaths coming softly. After a moment, he asked, "What happened to the prince?"

She smiled, brittle. "He wept on the battlefield, Kiran. What do you think happened to him? He was killed."

He shifted on the settee to look at her sideways. His expression was wry, but he was still so hollowed out, and the ghost of emotion felt incorporeal. "And what is the moral of the story? I would not have expected a patron saint of love."

"Lost love," she corrected, throat tight. She remembered asking that same question of Anyu. *Why do we pray for a story of love?* "A saint of sacrifice. The moral, as it goes, is that love is dangerous, blinding."

"Melancholy," he noted.

"But true," she said. He looked over and held her gaze once more, as if by doing so he would be able to understand some strange, hidden part of her.

Outside, the sun was rising—a world awoke, gleaming and beautiful and utterly meaningless. Even as Suri rose from the wicker chair, even as she readjusted the towel on his forehead out of some sense of responsibility, though it had gone lukewarm and dry, she felt as though she were walking through amber. As if she had tethered herself in some inexorable way, heartstrings strained and aching.

Kiran attempted, once again, to pull himself up from the settee. She held out her hands, but still he continued, managing to balance himself against the back. It was an uncomfortable position, but he hung on by sheer willpower, expression faintly listless.

She turned, got as far as the door before he spoke. "Thank you."

Suri knew he had not meant for her to answer, and right then, she did not think she was capable of answering. She drew the latch across and shut the door behind her.

Viro lay back on his bed, absently pinching the corner of his blanket between his index finger and thumb. He so often fell asleep at his desk, or curled at the foot of Tarak's bed. It was an unsteadying, unwanted luxury to sleep here.

The thud of incoming footsteps sounded from the outer corridor. He bit back an amused, fond smile and mused at how long it would take. Perhaps thirty seconds, perhaps less.

The steps faded to a stop, and then: "Step aside."

"His Majesty is resting."

A soft, derisive exhale. "I doubt that. I do not know what he has ordered you to do, but please step aside. I must speak with him."

Then came a pause—the guard weighing the benefits and possible pitfalls of the situation that lay in front of him. As usual, they were skewed upsettingly in his disfavor; the door opened.

Tarak dismissed the guard and then shut the door gently behind him. Viro did not have to look up to know he was examining him, reading his mood. He let go of the blanket and said, "I assume you've seen the missive, then."

"Tell me you won't let it go," he said, the words shaped like a plea. "Tell me you will not ignore this." At the resounding silence, he let out a low, strangled noise. "How is it that you cannot fathom any kind of insult to your nation, and yet the moment you are in danger of harm—is it of no consequence to you whether you live or die?"

"They want me to react," he said, pulling himself up from the plush bed. It truly was incredibly uncomfortable; he had not thought it possible, but there was such a thing as *too soft*. He held up the folded cloth he had found slid under his door in the morning. "What is the nature of a threat? To elicit fear. Ignoring it is all I *can* do."

Tarak's mouth thinned. At times like this, he reminded Viro of his father, the previous captain—brave and thoughtful and worried, always worried. He scrubbed at his eyes. "So what is it that you propose? That we change nothing? That we *do* nothing? What if—if these threats are not empty, then—"

"They are empty," he said, little more than an exhale. "And I do not need more guards. I have you."

Viro could tell that he had truly been shaken by the threats, because he did not make a face as he would've normally. The remark sobered him somewhat; there was a raw, afraid gleam to his gaze that Viro knew well, had seen in the mirror for years. He pushed off from the bed, placing his hands lightly on the other boy's shoulders. He was just tall enough that he had to look up when speaking with him from this close, just tall enough that it was distinctly irritating.

"What if I am not enough?" Tarak asked, the timbre of his voice hollow and dissonant.

He allowed himself a brief laugh at that; the other boy glanced down at him, surprise lighting up the planes of his face. But Viro did not look away. "You have always been enough. You cannot doubt yourself now."

The skin around Tarak's eyes tightened, and his lips parted as if he meant to say something. But he pressed them tight once more, silent in the soft, unshakable peace of the unused bedroom. Finally, he said, "Why do you never sleep here?"

It was an admission cloaked as a question, painstakingly wrapped into something wholly different. But Viro had always dealt in these half-truths, had always loved them in an odd, self-deprecating way.

He turned away, going to stand by the window. A smile curved his lips, but it was faintly bitter. "I think I am a little terrified of tenderness. And this room, shaped like my old heart, demands it."

"And mine doesn't?" Even without looking back, he could imagine his expression, the wry arch of his brows, the amused slant of his mouth.

Viro leaned forward, bracing himself on the windowsill so he could look up into the night sky, gleaming with cold, distant light. "You've never demanded anything of me that I wouldn't offer of my own volition. But you still ask."

16
LYNE

In freshman year, Aza and Dai had started a band with a few of their classmates and named it Cherry Headache by turning to random spots in the dictionary.

Throughout the years, they had expanded their discography, even getting a consistent amount of gigs. There had even been a brief stint, early in their senior year of high school, when Aza had seriously considered giving up on university in favor of pursuing the band. It was the only time Suri had ever heard Dai angry—he'd spit her name out as a curse, *Azami.* Even after, neither of them ever explained the depth of the argument, or how they'd resolved it.

At any rate, Aza's decision had ended up proving fruitful after Imogen, the lead singer, had to leave second semester to take care of her grandmother. After nearly a year of hiatus, though, the band had gotten back together in October. They were already booked through the rest of the winter.

Their first gig was in early December, slotted cleverly in between exams. Suri dragged Kiran to the venue—a shitty, hole-in-the-wall bar in southwest Lyne—a little before six so they could watch the band set up. She had slept through the day; staying up to practice fighting was far more exhausting than simply listening to Kiran tell stories. She could still feel the dregs of fatigue on her skin, cold and drying.

By the time they got there, the band was already arguing on the stage, their voices pitched high over the background noise of one of their recorded songs. Ellis was slumped at a wooden table beside the platform, a glass of ice water drained beside him. Miya was scrolling through her phone; every now and then, she shot an amused glance at the stage when one of the members made a particularly rude comment.

Dai glanced over and saw them, and pure relief washed over his face. He gathered a stack of papers from the corner of the stage and hopped off, jogging over to them.

"I owe you," he said, holding up his papers. A string of doodled baby chicks lined the side of a homework packet. "They haven't stopped arguing since they got here. Do you want anything to drink?"

They exchanged glances, and Kiran shrugged. Suri nodded toward the stage. "Not really. Why are they arguing?"

"First of all, I know you said no, but I'm going to muck around behind the bar to get away from them for longer," he said solemnly. "Second of all, about everything. I'm not kidding. Imogen wants to change the set list, and Az's lost her favorite drumstick and—"

"Fuck you, Chris," Aza said acidly, cutting through the noise.

"And Chris," Dai continued wearily, "Wants to postpone the gig. Which we can't do, obviously." He jerked his head at the empty table beside the stage. "You guys just wait there, I'll go get—something. You don't have to drink it, just look at it like it's appetizing."

Suri tucked herself into the chair beside the stage and Kiran took the opposite one, and for a moment, they let themselves drink in the noise of the bar, the shouting and the music and the far-off sound of Dai dropping ice cubes into glasses. They met each other's gaze, blinked, and then fell into laughter.

"This is a mess," she managed, wiping her eyes. "I promise the music's good, though."

"Ah, I don't mind," he said mildly, leaning back in his chair. He looked tired, but it wasn't quite as bad as usual. "I like messes. It's nice."

"It's a good distraction from everything," she added, and he made a noise of agreement. The usual night at the apartment either involved reality television and takeout, him quizzing her with paper flashcards, working on fighting, or trying to make progress on expanding the poster board. So far, they'd only managed to really succeed at one of those things, and that was because both of them were well versed, in their own ways, in reality television.

Even with the single-minded focus of an actual god, they hadn't been able to find anything relevant about the black sigil. Suri was trying not to give up hope—Kiran certainly hadn't—but sometimes, she felt a little foolish pursuing it after so long. At the end of the day, it was likely she was just a little girl pretending not to be a little girl, obsessed with ideas of revenge and reason, obsessed with explanation.

Kiran leaned forward, tapping his fingers softly against Suri's temple. She blinked, stared over at him. He smiled, faintly. "I can see you overthinking. Get out of your head."

Her skin burned. Before she could respond, Dai came back with a platter and two iced glasses, filled to the brim with neon fruit smoothie. Suri sniffed hers, a deep red color. Pomegranates. Kiran's was pastel orange, with a slice hooked on the edge. They both thanked him for the drinks, and he nodded, gracious, but his gaze was traveling back to the stage circuitously, tinged with fear.

Kiran pulled up a nearby chair and patted it. "Stay for a bit. If they ask, I'll take the blame. Say I made you recite the ingredient list for this or something."

"It's just orange and ice and milk," he said, managing a smile.

"Really?" he asked, examining the drink. "Marvels of modern science, I suppose."

Dai slid out a familiar bound book. On the cover, *THE LOVERS* was stenciled in ink, gray-blue from age. He opened to a half-completed page, the outlines of the panels already defined. Kiran tilted his head. "What's that?"

The other boy gestured toward Suri; she raised her eyebrows, but explained, "Dai's been working on a graphic novel since middle school. It's about, well, lovers. But he named it after one of Cherry Headache's songs, which they named after the tarot card."

"I want to get it published one day," he said absently, pulling out a thin black pen. "I'm not optimistic, though. Dreams are meant to be held, not believed."

"You'd be surprised," Kiran replied, but didn't elaborate. He tapped on the corner of a page in contemplation. "What's it about?"

"Lovers," he repeated, rubbing at old pencil lines with a black eraser. "Star-crossed lovers that can't be together, for reasons they can't change. And they try to defy it because, you know. They're in love, and they'll do whatever they have to do to stay together. But in the end, they always die."

He blew off the eraser dust. "They meet in every lifetime and fall in love, and the reasons why they can't be together change but their fate doesn't. I'm still playing around with how I want the story to end, though. I want them to end up together, but Aza thinks it's too unrealistic. I think I'm a little in love with happy endings, to be honest."

Kiran was quiet for a moment, taken with a still, cold silence that unsettled Suri. Finally, he said, as upbeat as he'd been when the conversation began, "There are worse things to love."

Dai hummed in agreement, and leaned over the paper. After a while, Aza stomped over, mouth set in a straight, smooth line that meant she was still pissed off about what had happened earlier, and informed him that they were setting up. They managed to get through that fine, with minimal shouting, and then before they could launch into an entirely different argument, the evening took a dip for the worse. People showed up.

The dissonant, warm noise of the early evening was nothing compared to the cacophony of the place filled to capacity. And that was on top of the fact that people were getting drinks from the bar—though a few of them actually drank, the majority proceeded to spill them on the floor. The air was sickly sweet with artificial flavoring and the sharp, piercing smell of alcohol.

Where they were sitting, tucked into the alcove beside the stage, they were shielded from the majority of the chaos—but it also meant that every few minutes, someone stumbled into their corner, drunk or worse, and they had to gently spin them outward back into the crowd.

A loud squeal of noise filled the air. They glanced toward the stage. Aza's hair was tied up in an electric blue bandana, and matching highlighter marked her cheeks like war paint. They ran through the setlist for the night and then Aza cracked her drumsticks against each other and the room drowned in sound.

They all sang along with Imogen, cheering at the brief solos. Miya was a creature of fire and fondness, and she danced around their corner in full visibility of Aza, bringing every single lyric to life. Ellis was more reserved, but still he sang along softly, smiling at Miya's antics.

Kiran didn't know the songs so he simply watched, a strange look on his face. It was almost the expression of an interloper, of wanderlust reversed. And there was pain in it, but there was softness too. Nostalgia, cracked and shattered and then pieced back together with longing.

Halfway through the set, Miya peeled away from them to go dance in the crowd. Once in a while, they would see her dark hair pop up, glittering with colorful plastic jewels.

A little while after, Ellis's phone buzzed, light cracking the darkness of the bar. He raised his hand in farewell and they smiled back, and then they were alone. On the stage, one song ended and another began, sharp and sweet.

In the shadows of the bar, they were forgotten to all but each other. And Suri saw the knowledge of it etched on his face, knife into stone. They were alone, but he'd been alone for far longer.

His gaze slid away from the stage, as if he'd sensed her watching him.

For a long time, she would think of this—the rest of the night twisted into a manic blur, but she remembered this moment as she would a brand, a nightmare. Summer-grass eyes fell on hers, and he smiled, boyish and lovely.

It was strange; she had seen his beauty when he'd first arrived, soaked by the blood of men and burned by the blood of gods. She hadn't thought it possible to fall in love with someone like him then—her eyes caught only on the preternatural glow of his blood, the way his toes curled around the edges of roofs, poised to fall. How arrogant she had been, to think herself immune to divinity.

He's going to leave, she thought, braced against the needle-sharp pain of truth. *Don't do this to yourself.*

Impossibly, he was still smiling. She could think of nothing but it. When he spoke, her lungs unfolded, empty with desire. "What time is it?"

"I don't know," she said roughly. She shook her head and dug her hands into the pockets of her jeans, searching. "Late, I'd guess. Where's my phone?"

He held it up with an illusionist's grace, frowning as he turned it on. The bright light washed out his skin, hollowed him. "Quarter to eleven. When are we meant to leave?"

"Midnight," she managed, reaching out for the phone. Kiran shifted it from one hand to the next, holding it out of her reach. It was ridiculous; he didn't have that much height on her. "Give that back."

"No," he said, the line of his mouth crooked and sharp. He rose out of his chair, limned by the lights of the bar. "I'll give it back if you can catch me."

Kiran turned on his heel and slipped through the crowd; it parted for him in brief, uneven gaps, and she ducked through the same gaps, shoving through before they closed entirely. She could hear his laughter in her head like a song, and she followed it all the way out into a side street straddling the bar.

The door fell half-shut behind her, crashing against a wooden crate. The sounds of the bar were distant—low, thrumming alt rock, shouts and chatter. The air smelled like sugar syrup and rainwater as she wound through discarded furniture and crates in the alley.

He glanced back at her, eyes bright like a challenge, and she swore under her breath, reaching forward to wrap her fingers around his wrist. But he slid out of her grip, laughing even as he did it, and despite everything, she found herself smiling too, as if this were a game—as if the night had turned everything dream-slick and mutable and none of it was real, not a single damn thing.

Eventually, she managed to grab a single shoulder and she dug her nails in, holding him still until she could fully catch up. Suri twisted him around, slamming him back into the brick wall of the bar and bringing up her other hand to hold him in position.

His gaze was dark, soft with something like yearning or pain. She loosened her grip on him as awareness flooded through her, but he didn't move. She felt jagged, raw.

Something crackled in the air streets away—even from this far away, she could hear the tinny melody of the band, the useless delight of strangers. The glare of distant streetlights cast them both in a faint glow, just bright enough to see what they were not allowed.

Let go, she thought, the words so quiet, so muffled they seemed of no importance at all. *Let go, and ask for your phone, and then you can leave early.*

But her heart stuttered, unthinking, and she bent toward him, and she felt the precipitous, terrifying movement without the opportunity to draw back. Muscle memory, but abyssal and eternal and old, as if she knew him by heart and the knowledge was carved into her, soul-deep.

His breath caught, hitched as if with fear or anticipation, and her lips met warm skin, knuckle after knuckle after knuckle. She opened her eyes, mouth pressed against the back of his hand, and stared at him. There was nothing more to say; he held her gaze, cheeks flushed and pale, and then removed his hand silently. The night air was cold, sweet, and she drank it in.

Suri pulled away, taking a step back, and then another, until she stood in the center of the alley. She wrapped her arms around herself in the chill and refused to shiver, refused to look away.

"I'm sorry," he said, faintly stricken. "It isn't that I didn't… want to."

She folded her arms, impossibly tired. "I know you wanted to. I saw it. So why?"

Pain flickered across his face, quick and violent. Kiran pushed off from the wall, stepping closer to her before pausing, hesitant.

He held out his hand; her phone laid in it, dull and glittering, and she took it carefully, without touching him. They walked for a bit in silence, back to the side entrance to the bar. When he spoke, his voice was strained. "You remind me of someone I used to know."

"In a good way?" she asked warily, glancing over at him. The planes of his face were opal-smooth, eyes glittering like a prayer flame.

He made a soft noise of amusement, but it held its own measure of sorrow. "In every good way, and in every bad. In every way that matters."

Suri wasn't sure how she felt about that, about her effectively being a cosmic stand-in for someone he'd once loved and lost. She wondered, idly, if it was easy to pretend they were the same. But there was a careful gravity to his voice, one of shallow, deathless graves, and so she discarded the bitter humor and ventured, "What happened to them?"

"She was hurt," he said evenly, after a moment had passed. "I'd rather you weren't."

"How?" she asked, suddenly gripped by an intense, insidious curiosity, the kind that led young children down forgotten forest paths and into the bellies of beasts.

Kiran looked at her oddly, as if surprised she expected him to answer. She poked him, forcing a smile. But it was too sharp, too humorless. "Are you afraid of speaking it into life? Make it into a story, then."

His lips twitched upward, wry and self-deprecating. A car drove by the mouth of the alley, reflecting thin white light onto them, not unlike the sheets pulled over fresh corpses. "All stories have power, Suri. Even dead ones."

17
ENESMAT

"Hold still," Isa scolded, voice muffled by the pin stuck in the corner of her mouth. "I cannot fix your hair properly if you keep shifting from side to side like a child."

Suri relented, bracing her palms on the edge of the vanity in a futile attempt to keep herself still. But it only worked for moments—then she began to fidget with the corner of her wrap, embroidered in gold thread. Isa let out a long-suffering sigh but didn't say anything.

The festival had come quicker than she had expected—it had always been a far-off, unreal marker of time, one that delineated so many different events. The upcoming assassination, the upcoming war, the upcoming destruction. But now, she could only define it in a single way: *I will die a week after Avyakanth.* The words reverberated through her, a lilting, melancholy melody.

In an uncharacteristic moment of daring, she wondered if she could convince him to escape. But the thought disappeared just as quickly as it had appeared. There was nothing that could possibly shake his faith in his nation, his sense of duty. And more than that, he seemed resigned to his own death.

A knock came at the door, and Isa shot it an exasperated look before finishing Suri's hair and going to unlock it. Lucius was leaned against the doorframe, roguish and sheepish as always. He had discarded his old cloak, opting to dress solely in black and deep Athrian red. He grinned when he caught her looking, explaining, "The streets are going to be full of fire. I doubt the city will be anything but warm all night."

She rolled her eyes. "You would bet your comfort on those fires?"

He lifted his shoulders in a shrug. "I have attended for ten years, and the festival has never wavered from my expectations."

The adjoining door cracked open, and Mohini entered the room. She glanced at Suri—quickly, nervously—before offering Lucius a faint smile, which he reciprocated.

They walked through the halls, the lovebirds chattering away endlessly. Suri kept quiet, and yet there was an odd, jagged kind of desire in her chest. It was childish, hopeless and heedless, and it colored the frustration that rose up to meet the reality that no matter what they did, their moves were predetermined, their souls long ago set into the crooked slots of this old tragedy.

The citizens were slowly trickling from the gate at the far edge of the street to the thin, winding path that led over to the foothills and up to the temple. In the night, they were a stream of fire burning through the darkness.

Lucius pulled crimson candles from his satchel, lighting them in a nearby brazier before doling them out. The flames cast them all in an uneven golden glow, and it lit Lucius's face when he smiled. "We should hurry. The temple is small; if we arrive late, we may well be watching the service from the foot of the hills."

Mohini's thin, strained expression betrayed that she truly did not mind watching from so far, but if Lucius noticed he did not let on. They carried the candles as they trekked across the empty expanse of land that wrapped around the city, and Suri futilely tried to keep her mind off what awaited at the top.

By the time they arrived, the clearing around the temple was congested with so many people the ground was invisible. Yet the temple itself was sparsely populated; Suri could only discern the silhouettes of Kita and a few other priests. They were all dressed in the customary white of the main temple, but the high priestess's ivory wrap was embroidered with soft golden flowers and flames, her robes a sheer red.

The captain and king were nowhere to be seen, though there was a small contingent of guards by the far pillars, organized near the inner sanctum. The statue within had already been decorated, kino blossoms and creamy, star-shaped magizham flowers framing the black stone, wrapped in glittering red cloth. Silver ash cut strong, elegant lines across the idol, giving it the illusion of life. Even the stone bird at the head of the altar had been doted upon, wrapped in gold thread and dotted with shining *kita* jewels and flowers.

The temple was nearly unrecognizable, a stark, unsteadying contrast to the warm, empty place Suri knew. There had been a kind of safety in its emptiness, in its loneliness—an untold secret, a hidden adoration. And yet it was beautiful now as well, lovely and immortal and alive with fire and faith.

Lucius weaved through the crowd, flashing the pin on his collar when asked for identification, and paused at the front. Suri frowned at him, but he simply grinned. "A courier's badge gets you into many places. Regardless, I couldn't have allowed the future queen of Athri to watch the service from the edge of the mountain, could I?"

Her stomach roiled at the title, sick with nausea, but she forced a faint smile. The chatter of the crowd shifted and suddenly cut off, a heavy silence falling over the mountain. And in the midst of this soft, expectant hush, as if borne from it, three figures peeled off from the pathway that led to the high priest's cottage. Two figures—distant and blurred in the light of the flames, paused by the contingent of guards, while the last one cut through the crowd without words or commands.

Kiran passed them without pause, but he glanced at Suri out of the corner of his eyes. He was expressionless, a practiced calm, but his eyes glinted, dark and blazing. There was an unspoken challenge in them, and it set her heart on fire.

He ascended the steps quickly, pausing beside the entrance. The priests had taken up rehearsed positions, standing one after another between each of the two sets of columns. They faced the city below, but each held a different object in their hands. Kita stood by the inner sanctum, the only of them to hold Kiran's gaze.

He accepted the objects from each of the priests and then laid them on the edge of the altar. He murmured something soft and unintelligible under his breath before taking a knife and slashing his palm open. He dipped the fingers of his other hand in the blood and then traced something on the altar—it was too far for her to see, but Suri knew it was the carved icon, the single flame.

As the service continued—he wiped his hand clean and then lit a scarlet candle, touching it to the surface of the blood and lighting it aflame—a soft, lilting murmur began to course through the crowd. At first it was nothing more than a faint rustling, but then it swelled into something resonant and melodic, and Suri realized it was a hymn.

The song rose and fell as a heartbeat, and Suri watched as the boy king strode forward from the guards, the captain behind him. They ascended the steps separately, each holding a candle in their hands. Kiran cupped his hands around the flame, lifting it gently away from the wax and letting it fall from his fingers into the small, blood-borne fire of the carved symbol. He marked a line of ash across both of the king's cheeks and the latter dipped his head in a brief show of reverence before descending the steps. And then Tarak stepped forward, and the process began again.

There was a rhythm to it, one that twined in harmony with the hymns. The crowd resolved into a coiled, serpentine line, one that led up to the altar and then led down and twisted around the mountainside.

"Where are they going?" Suri whispered to Lucius.

"The main temple," he replied, words nearly inaudible in the wake of a swell in the hymn. "That is where the majority of the night's festivities will occur. This is simply a tribute to the god."

Mohini nudged her, and she saw that the line in front of them had dissipated—Kiran stood at the altar, waiting. Lucius went first, uncharacteristically deferential, as he held out the candle and ducked his head. There was a wry tilt to Kiran's mouth as he accepted the flame, but he did not speak.

And then it was her turn. Suri focused on the flame so she did not have to meet his gaze, and yet she could feel the heat of it. His fingers closed around the wick and tugged the fire away. He dipped his fingers into the ash and brushed them against her cheekbones, the touch feather-soft but searing.

She was oddly breathless as they descended the mountain, as if she were still lost in that moment, in the heat and the smoke. A lingering, suppressed ache spread through her chest, but she refused to acknowledge it.

The reverence dropped from Lucius the moment they left the temple, and he chattered on endlessly as they returned to the streets of Marai. The braziers were still burning, but the silence of the city had faded; in the distance, Suri could hear the sound of sparks popping in the sky, shouts of joy and of desire.

The entrance to the main temple was, unsurprisingly, flushed with people. By the time they made it through the foyer and to the main area, another hymn had begun, distinct from those they had sung at the mountain. This one was less melancholy, hungrier—there was a wild beauty to it.

Lucius led them down the steep stone steps that ringed the pool, down to the moonlit walkway. Priests rushed by them, shouting orders to one another and carrying baskets that overflowed with supplies. Out of respect and a certain measure of fear, they flattened themselves to the edge of the steps and allowed the priests to pass. Suri glanced over at Lucius. "Am I to assume this is another benefit of your badge?"

His smile cut across his face, bright with mischief. "Yes. Though this particular benefit has less to do with what Galen gave me and more to do with a friend of mine."

Suri expected him to elaborate, but for once, he seemed unwilling, amusement glittering in his eyes.

After a few moments, the boy king and the captain joined them at the edge of the steps. The captain was tugging the king along by his wrist; the latter glared at him spitefully. Tarak smiled sweetly at Suri. "How are you finding the festivities, Your Highness?"

"They're beautiful," she said truthfully. "I've seen little like them."

His eyes crinkled at that, pleased. He elbowed the king unsubtly, who frowned up at him before dipping his head in acknowledgement of her. She reciprocated, silently grateful that all they would have to do was exchange formalities. She thought she understood the king a little more these days, but it changed nothing of his hatred, of the chasms that lay between them.

"How long will it take?" Lucius asked. Suri startled for a moment before realizing he was speaking to Tarak.

The captain tilted his head, considering. "The tributes should be finishing soon. And then he'll have a few moments before the dance."

Once the two boys had left, Suri turned to Lucius. "What dance?" There was nothing of the temple that suggested it could—under any circumstances—be transformed into a ballroom, but still she worried.

He laughed, nodding toward the pool. "You'll see."

Her breath caught. The pool had been drained of water, yet it was not dry; a thin layer of oil glistened against the gray stone. "You cannot be serious."

"But I am," he said. He glanced around, gaze catching on a pair of faraway figures. "Oh, there they are. Princess, I'd like to introduce you to someone."

Suri looked helplessly back at Isa and Mohini but they waved her off. Isa smiled faintly, but it held a hint of inexplicable amusement, an untold joke where only Suri could catch it.

Despite the crushed shadows that lingered beside the entrance to the north tower, it had not taken long for the citizens to realize who they were standing beside. The crowd parted, slow but sure, as Lucius and Suri ascended the steps.

Kiran and Kita were speaking about something, their voices low and hushed. There was ash smeared across both their faces; they glanced up in synchrony when they approached, Kita's eyebrows curving upward.

She patted Kiran's arm before dipping her head toward Suri in a swift bow. "Well, I must begin the preparations for the dance. Try not to take too long." The last part was directed toward Kiran, who—in an odd display of youth—made a rude gesture at her. She laughed and took the steps down to the emptied pool two at a time.

Lucius grinned at both of them. "Your Highness, it is my pleasure to introduce you to the high priest of the temple of Avya. Kiran—"

The other boy was watching him with no small amount of amusement. "We've met, Lucius."

He blinked at him, eyes wide with mock hurt. There was an easy balance to the way that they spoke, a casual warmth Suri could not help but envy. "And you, what? Decided not to deign to inform your loyal old friend? Now I've humiliated myself."

There was a fond exasperation in the line of his smile. "Apologies. Did you enjoy the service?"

He had turned to Suri, and it took a few seconds for her to realize the question was meant for her. She opened her mouth to speak, but for some reason, the words caught in her throat. She recalled the fire of the altar, the cupped flame. The ash on her cheeks burned. "I did."

Kiran smiled, just as lovely and just as wild as the temple he served. "I'm glad to hear it."

Lucius glanced between them and shot his friend a familiar look. Suri had to endure it from Isa constantly. But when he spoke, he only said, "It is poor manners to keep the people waiting, Kiran. They're all here for you."

He glared over at him, but nodded in acquiescence. "I should go." He paused beside Suri, head tilted so Lucius could not see his expression. There was a hint of ferocity in it, beautiful and terrifying. When he spoke, it was soft enough that it was nearly inaudible, delivered in the careful, hushed cadence of a confession. "This is my favorite part."

And then he was descending the steps, the crowd silent for him, only him. His bare feet touched the last step, stone against skin, and the hymn began again, each word filled with a swelling, intense ardor. He disappeared into a small door built into the base of the steps, the flames of the brazier blurring his shadow.

Suri followed Lucius down the steps, avoiding his gaze the entire way. They paused beside Isa and Mohini, but the boy nudged them slightly, nodding toward the crowd above. Suri raised her eyebrows at him. "I thought these were special seats."

He grinned at her, obviously still amused by the conversation with Kiran. "It's best not to be near the dance when it begins." He jerked his head at the king and the captain, who were slowly moving up the stairs until they were halfway up. Even the priests were dissolving into the crowd above, flashes of white in the sea of red and black.

The hymn continued, the only sound in the otherwise quiet temple. Kita, the only remaining priestess beside the pool, finished scattering blossoms around the edge of it, and then lit a match. She chanted something, inaudible in the midst of the hymn, and tossed it into the oil.

Before, it was easy enough to ignore the oil, think of it only as a damp, sticky layer at the bottom of the pool. But now, as it grew into an orange-gold blaze, the heat palpable and searing even from so far away, it was so distinctly, wholly dangerous that for a moment, Suri was afraid. It felt like something that could burn; something that could kill.

The door at the edge of the steps opened, and the crowd fell silent—the hymn dissipated on the edge of a word, and there was that same kind of expectation, for something unfinished to become whole, as Kiran stepped toward the fire.

He had traded in the ceremonial, embroidered black wrap and red robes for something simpler—a maroon half-wrap that tied around both legs and left his torso bare. Ash and sandal paste streaked across his chest in looping, intricate symbols, trailing down his arms and up to the base of his collarbones.

Kiran paused beside the fire, hands palms up, his eyes fluttered closed. The hymn resumed, holding out that single, echoing note, and he walked into the flames.

For a moment, Suri did not breathe. The blaze grew with his presence, fear burning through her heart. *No one could have survived that,* she thought. But the fire was still burning; the people were still singing. And in the midst of the flames, a shadowed, indistinct figure spun and twirled, every step in sync with the melody that rose in the air.

It was just as it had been in the temple on the mountain—the beat of the dance intertwined with the melody, with the heartbeat of the people, and twisted into something strange and new and touched with divinity. And yet it was so much wilder, so much more beautiful for it. It held none of the softness, none of the sadness of the hymn on the mountain—this was something anarchic and deific.

Kiran was a whirl of movement in the flames, somehow both coarse and graceful. To think she had dared to think she knew him—to think she had thought it possible to wholly know someone made of holy fire, multifoliate and jagged-edged. And yet the dance, the foreign, flame-sweet air of it, only made her want him more.

A dry laugh drew her back into the present, and she glanced to the side. Lucius was watching the flames with a sharp, amused smile, the shadows of the fire flickering across his face and giving form to that oddly knowing expression.

"Usually," he mused, "Kiran considers this little more than a formality. Yet, if I did not know any better, I would say he's putting in an undue amount of effort tonight."

Suri shifted uncomfortably. "He said this is his last night."

Lucius's expression sobered for a fraction of a second before he smiled, rueful. "Perhaps that is why. But I rather think he's showing off."

He winked at her, mouth still curved in mirth, before disappearing into the crowd. Mohini had left at some point prior, which surprised Suri even less than Lucius going to look for her. She turned back to the flames and caught Isa watching her. She pursed her lips. "What are you thinking?"

Isa held her gaze. For a while she didn't speak, the hymn in the air substituting the need for speech, and Suri found herself glancing back to the flames.

"He can play in the fire all he wants," she said drily, eyebrows faintly raised at how Suri had to wrench her gaze away from the pool below. "But you will still burn if you touch the flames."

She opened her mouth to protest, and yet she found she could not. Isa had cut straight to the heart of the matter, as she was prone to doing, and now Suri was faced with a simple enough decision, one of self-preservation.

She closed her eyes; the fire turned the inside of her eyelids pink, that same furious, fervid ache from before burning through her. A small, hungry voice in the back of her mind spoke, one she had never paid attention to. It had starved and starved, and now it awoke, carving into her consciousness. *Damn self-preservation.*

The singing had long since become shouting, a blaze of noise to match a blaze of smoke and flame. And as it swelled into a crescendo, so did the fire, roaring in the airless night. And then it fell all at once, a dissonant, uneven exit that tumbled to a stop. The fire moved with it, disappearing into nothing—into smoke and prayers.

Kiran stood in the center of the pool, drenched from either sweat or oil or liquid flame, the ash and sandal paste on his chest blurred into an unreadable mess. He dipped his head forward in a shallow bow, then ducked into the door beside the steps without waiting for the roaring applause of the crowd to fade. It was the only time, Suri realized, they had given him anything but soft, awe-strained silence.

Kiran pressed a damp washcloth to his chest, willing his heart to calm as he scrubbed his skin. He could still hear the crowd's shouts, the swell of the hymn echoing in his ears, could still see Suri on the edge of the steps. The memory of it was intoxicating.

Outside, the festival was only beginning—he could hear the distant melody of another hymn roll in beat with the steady thrum of the drums. But from this point on, he was effectively free. To return to his cottage or to return to the temple, or to wander through the city alone, savoring the emptiness of the shadows.

And yet when he exited the small, cramped room under the steps and rose unseen to the north corridor, he found his feet taking him somewhere else.

The north tower cut through the sky, a glittering, variegated gopuram of stone and paint that had always mesmerized him. The princess was standing beside it, fingers tracing the carving of Nila. He cleared his throat, and she startled, glancing back. Oddly, her expression tightened once she realized it was him, an unrecognizable glossy darkness coloring her gaze.

He paused by the tower. "Do you know the story?"

"Of Nila?" she asked absently, her eyes molten in the night. "I learned of it recently."

"And what do you think?"

She looked up at him, her mouth set in a hard, youthful line. Her cheeks were suffused with crimson from the heat of the fires around them. "I think it is beautiful, and it is cruel. And I think…" she paused here, uncertainty straining her expression. "I think it is life, in a way. It holds the same tragic irony, the same broken idealism."

Kiran shut his eyes, recalling the lilt of the fairy tale, black rivers and red skies. "I agree."

She smiled, but it was mechanical, not quite there. That dark, tangled look had not left her, had only stretched into something far more abstruse.

He held out a hand to gesture toward her clothes, a silent question. Suri picked at the hem of her wrap self-consciously. It had been made into the style of Athrian nobility, sheer crimson fabric that wrapped around her torso tightly, the edge of which dropped away and began to wrap again around her hips. It bunched there before draping loosely against her ankles. The edge of it was embroidered with small golden flames, mirroring the golden cuffs that circled both her biceps. Strands of her dark hair were twisted with amber thread and jewels, while the rest swept across her bare shoulders, unbound. She looked, he realized with a stomach-dropping sense of awe, like a queen.

"Does the fire hurt?" she asked suddenly, so softly it was impossible not to understand that she had held this question in her mind beforehand, that this was simply the act of letting it go.

He shook his head. There was still oil on his skin—he could still feel the fire, the warm glow of it around him and the smoke rising above. Yet it had never hurt, not once. She nodded once, as if processing this, and then asked, equally soft, "What does it feel like?"

Kiran struggled to put it into words. "A warm embrace, but never gentle. At first, it was overwhelming, but now… I cannot explain it, not wholly. It feels like a second home."

Her mouth twitched as if she meant to ask something further, but finally she simply exhaled. Turning from the tower, she looked out toward the city, alive with revelry. The wood ash on her cheek glittered in the moonlight, smeared from where he had held her.

He reached out a hand, and there was something distant about the movement as he it, as if he were watching it all from a different room, from a different world. Suri did not move even as he cupped her cheek, did not look away even as he laid the pad of his thumb against her cheekbone and smudged the silver ash that streaked across it.

And yet there was a silent question in her gaze, and it scraped across him, seared what remained of his rational thinking. *This is the worst mistake you have ever made,* he thought. And then he leaned forward and kissed her.

She made a small, unintelligible noise, not of surprise but of something harder, sharper, and his chest ached with desire. But he forced himself to pull away. Absently, he realized he still held her wrist loosely in his hand. He dropped it, chagrined, and rocked back on his heels.

Without looking at her, he said, "I-I apologize. For overstepping the boundaries, and—"

Suri cut in, her voice a low rasp. "What are you apologizing for?"

He glanced up. She was looking up at him oddly, eyes glazed and dark. Her lips spread in a wild, fierce smile, star-bright against the darkness behind them.

Something cracked and shattered in the heat of his heart, glass abandoned to night-black flame. And then they were kissing again, but it was impossible to know who had moved first—Suri's hands were cupping his face, harshly holding him in place, and he was leaning down into her mouth. There was nowhere to put his hands, so he let them trail everywhere, following the curve of her neck down the golden bands around her arms. He rested them there, ghosting over her elbows simply to hold her against him.

They broke apart after some indeterminable amount of time had passed. In the distance, the shouts of the festival continued. They both glanced toward the entrance to the north corridor, and then back at each other, and Kiran knew they were thinking the same thing—someone, *anyone,* could find them here. It was too much to risk. And yet to leave together was another step into the unknown, into the searing, desire-sharp darkness of what lay between them.

Kiran held out his hand and Suri took it, and they left the temple behind.

Kiran was made of fire tonight, Suri mused as he led her up the mountain, shadowed and incense-sweet in the late night. Then again, so was she. That first touch had set them both aflame, their hearts shot through with kerosene. But she knew it had started long before this; with blossoms and with crimson dawns and with secrets they had held like promises—with gentle hands and trembling breaths.

They ascended the steps of the temple. The blood-borne fire was still burning somehow, curled into the carved symbol like it had found a home. Avya watched them from the decorated statuette, the moonlight cutting across the ash on the stone.

And yet Kiran did not care. There was a reckless, lovely warmth to him as he guided her around the fallen, strewn blossoms, bare feet against fire-warmed stone. She tripped over a crack and fell forward, but his arms caught her, bracing her shoulders against him. He helped her up, a bright laugh in his eyes, in his smile, and Suri could not stop thinking of that smile—of the streaks of oil and soot that littered his body, and the fragrant, heady scent of turmeric and wood ash that enveloped her when she leaned too close. He was a fire, she knew, and it didn't matter that fire was meant to burn—it didn't matter that the flames were coarse and imprecise and destructive, because she would step into them every time. As long as it was him, she would let them burn her.

She let him move her around the petals and lean her against the column of the temple. It still smelled of smoke, of wax; this was something sacrosanct carved out of the stone of the mountain, and all the glory and all the gold of the service paled in comparison to the simple, reverent silence of the temple as Kiran leaned forward and pressed a soft, chaste kiss to her lips.

Suri made a noise in the back of her throat and pulled him closer, and he smiled against her, lips faintly parted as she buried her hands in his curls and steadied herself.

She wanted to stay here forever—she wanted to hold him forever, hands twisted tight and hearts pressed close, like a dream breathed into trembling, delicate life. Yet she knew, logically, that they could not—that this was something born to fall, born to burn.

Kiran pulled away for just a moment, eyes dark and glittering with desire, and yet sad as well. As if he, too, knew the inherent tragedy of this—of all love. To hold someone so tight was to know you would one day let them go; to love was to thrust soft, unmarked hands into a fire and let them catch flame.

But they kissed again, and again, and again, and she let him lift the anger from her chest and kiss it too, nothing more than a soft press of lips and a hint of fondness, and when they were spent, lips numb and bruised, they leaned on each other, fingers intertwined, and held each other so tight she could feel his heartbeat. He walked her to the cottage and she shut the door behind her as he struck a match and lit every individual candle, casting the room in soft firelight.

Suri crossed the room, sat on the edge of the cot in the corner, and rubbed the edge of the single, threadbare blanket with her thumb. It smelled of lavender and incense. He finished lighting the candles and then took a seat beside her, crossing his feet so they faced each other—her leaning against the wall and him with hands braced on the frame behind him, head tilted back in strained thought.

She held out a hand, only half-aware of her own actions, and traced the now-faded lines of ash and *santhanam* on his chest, traced the edges and crooks of them. He held her gaze, an inexplicable, wordless fondness in it. She moved closer, raising her hand until she was tracing the lines of his face. She drew her finger across his lips, and he smiled against it.

Her chest ached with desire and pre-ordained loss. "Let me give you a secret: I do not want to marry your king."

The smile went crooked, and he tilted his head, her finger falling from his lips. "Let me give you one: I do not want to die."

She leaned forward, pressing her forehead to his in a strange, impulsive show of vulnerability. "What fools we are, then, to masquerade as those who we are not. Fools with eyes bound in silk and bark."

"'Love is dangerous, blinding,'" he quoted, voice soft against her cheeks in an empty semblance of amusement. He pulled back slightly, just enough that she could see the gentleness, the raw warmth in his gaze. The clean lack of regret. "And yet, I see you so clearly."

They fell asleep like that, trading soft, careless kisses in the dark until it stole them away. When Suri awoke, it was to the low groan of a shift of the bedframe. She rubbed at her eyes and turned, blearily, to find Kiran pulling himself off the cot. He looked down at her apologetically.

"The sun is coming up," he explained, crouching down to brush a strand of hair away from her forehead. "I did not want to wake you. But I know you must leave."

The realization of what they had done—of how much she ached for it again, even now—cut through the haze of sleep. Suri pulled herself up, crossing her arms over her chest. In the night, the fabric of the wrap had come loose and half-unraveled, and now it lay over her, sheer and uneven, like a glorified blanket. When she spoke, her voice was a thin rasp. "Did we..."

He shook his head. There was a foreign touch of resentment to his voice, a sharp bitterness. "Neither of us could risk that, I know." Kiran looked down at her, an uncertain, reticent gentleness guiding him to sit beside her ankles. He looked as if he meant to say something, as if he meant to hold her still and kiss her again, the way he had in the night. But the thin, watery sunlight that streamed in through the windows had torn them back into something with demarcations, each one deeper than the space between two words, between two hearts. In the morning, she could not know if this was something they were allowed; in the night, she had not cared.

She tore her gaze away, focusing on the cotton of the mattress. Quietly, she said, "Then, I will return to the palace."

"How will you explain your absence?" he tilted his head, considering, and added, "On Avyakanth, the city is chaotic enough they may not have noticed it. But, in case your maids have."

She lifted her shoulders in a shrug. "I can say I got lost in the city, and you brought me back to the temple because the streets around the palace were too crowded."

It wasn't a perfect excuse—even now, still faintly drowsy, she could pick it apart with a half-critical eye. It would barely hold up, but they would have no reason to push further. Isa, she knew, would have already suspected the truth of the matter.

Kiran nodded, looking away, before pushing off from the cot. He extended his hand and Suri took it, and in an odd, painful echo of the previous night, he walked her to the door. He leaned forward, and in a single, indulgent moment of tenderness, he readjusted the wrap, fingers warm against her skin as he tucked the fabric into itself.

And then the hand dropped away, and he stepped backward. Suri forced herself to turn away, to focus on the blossoms of the garden and the smooth, cold warmth of the sun. She began to walk away, and though she felt strained and careworn, she did not look back.

18
LYNE

The next morning, Suri lay in bed, bleary eyed and mortified. Memories swirled in her mind, and, overwhelmed, she turned to the side, curling into a ball. Her alarm clock informed her it was nearing noon—she had lost half the day to this.

She showered and dressed quickly, and hesitated behind her shut bedroom door. Everything about this was unbearable and exaggerated; she felt like a child, cracking open her door and peering out into the hallway. Eventually, she drew in a breath sharply and shut the door behind her, keeping her gaze ahead. *It'll be like ripping off a Band-aid,* she thought. *If you don't focus on the blood, it won't even hurt.*

The living room was heavy with the pungent, smothering scent of jaggery and clarified butter. Kiran stuck his head out of the kitchenette, fingers glistening and loosely interlaced. He'd tied his hair up in a stubby knot, and bright pink barrettes pinned pieces away from his face. He stared at the floor, skin flushed from the heat.

"I'm going to go out," she told him, staring past him at the wall. Her face felt hot for no good reason. "To the library. I have a project. Group project, it's due Monday. We're very far behind."

"Okay," he said softly. There was a streak of gram flour on his cheek, wide and sweeping. He didn't seem to find it important, even though Suri could not stop staring at it.

"Okay," she repeated, steadying her voice, then turned on her heel and left. She tried to focus on the beat of her boots against cement, the clatter of voices in the crowded streets around her, but the sounds slipped through her, fluid and disinterested.

She went to the library. For hours, they worked on the PowerPoint, spoke to each other, wrote things down. When the doors shut behind her, the cold winter air buoying her slightly, she could remember nothing of what they had done. And yet, in a cruel turn of fate, she could still remember his smile.

When she returned to the apartment, it wasn't as humid, but the smell of jaggery and clarified butter hadn't entirely faded. It stuck to the air, sweet and heady and comforting, the scent of afternoons she'd spent in the back-room kitchen, watching her grandmother form sweets with worn palms. Kiran ducked out of the kitchen, brisk until he noticed her. There were plates of sweets balanced in his arms, and he held one in his mouth, stretching his lips out into an *O*.

Carefully, he placed the plates on the coffee table, taking a delicate bite from the sweet in his mouth before drawing it away. For a single, dizzying moment, she thought he might give it to her, but then he took a seat on the edge of the couch—to the side, making room for her—and nodded toward the plates. "If you want one."

She took a seat beside him, reached forward for a thick square, and bit into it tentatively. Almost involuntarily, she let out a low moan and stared over at him in wonder.

"What?" he asked self-consciously, a flush high on his cheeks. "Is it bad?"

"'Is it bad?'" she repeated, incredulous. She felt boneless. "Even my grandmother doesn't make it this well. Are you a wizard?"

"No," he said, faintly smiling. There was a tilt of pride to it; her heart clenched briefly. It was impossible to avoid the foolishness of this game they were dancing through, their crude lack of skill and the way they twirled, blindfolded. And something about him, about his smile and the way he still smelled of flour and fire, made her want to play that game—made her crave the thrill of it, the thought of making fate itself bow at their feet, pressing skin to stone.

Oh, she thought distantly. *This is a problem.*

He was still speaking. "I learned to make it a long time ago. I didn't know if it would come out well, since I'm out of practice."

"It did," she assured him, ducking her head to take another bite and hide her expression. "Why now?"

Kiran turned away, lifting his shoulders in a loose shrug. But it was practiced, and she read through it—read through him—with a simple fluency that left a cloying taste on her tongue. "I suppose I was a little homesick. It doesn't happen often." The words were a little strained, and in a flippant, contrived tone, he added, "And now I have all these extra sweets, and nowhere to put them. It's not like we'll be able to finish them ourselves."

"You severely underestimate my abilities," she said, halfway through her third sweet. He might as well have been the god of sweets, of sugar and milk. But it seemed too mild for him; she figured that golden eyes borne of honey shone different than ones borne of fire. "And this is only two plates."

He pressed his lips together, eyes dancing with suppressed laughter. "There's five containers in the kitchen. Each."

Suri gaped at him. "How long have you been making these?"

"All night," he said, bringing up a hand to rub at the back of his neck. He was staring at the sweet he still held in his hand, golden and round, teeth marks marring the smooth surface just slightly. "And all day. You shouldn't go in the kitchen for the time being."

While she had been sleeping off her regret, he had been cooking it away. She snagged another sweet from the table and popped it in her mouth. After chewing, she said, "We can take some over to my grandmother tomorrow, she can give them to her clients."

Kiran glanced doubtfully at the kitchen, as if thinking of the stacked containers, but simply inclined his head in assent.

Her phone buzzed in her jacket and she slid it out, tilting the screen surreptitiously so he couldn't see it. Miya had texted: *u won't believe what just happened to me.*

Three dots danced on the screen, spoke of message after message of righteous anger. Kiran was watching her, brows raised. "Miya?"

She exhaled a laugh. "Yeah, Miya. I'll be in my room. Do you want these?"

"It's fine," he said, shaking his head. He was nearly expressionless, save for a shade of a grin. "You can have them all. I don't actually like sweets that much."

"Blasphemy," she said, unable to fight the accompanying gasp. She slipped her phone back into her pocket and gathered the plates in her arms, unsteady under the weight.

The sight made him laugh, a sweet, carrying sound she kept with her even as she left the room, even as she shut her bedroom door behind her and leaned back against it. She felt nearly content, hearing that laugh, felt like she could wrap herself around it and fall asleep for years, decades, centuries. Like it was a home, or they could make it one.

Suri lay back on her bed and dialed Miya's number. She picked up immediately.

19
ENESMAT

Viro put his hand on his heart and counted the beats of it. *One, two, one, two, one, two*—a wordless promise of life, an assurance he was different, somehow, than the bodies on the floor.

He could not see them fully; the door of the cabinet was crooked just slightly open, only enough for him to breathe. But the air of the library was just as stale as the air inside the cupboard, perfumed with blood and soiled steel.

From this vantage point, he could only see shreds of death—blood streaked across rapidly paling skin, the ripped cloth surrounding an entry wound. And yet he could hear it all; could feel it all. In the distance, people cried out in pain and death came alive, turned to something agile and vengeful.

Stay here, Radha had said, tucking him into the cupboard as if he were still a small child, easily held in her hands. She was only four years older, and yet she had looked so brave, so aged, even as her hands shook on his shoulders. *I must go find Mother and Father, but you have to stay here. You cannot make a sound.*

Like the game, he had said. The soldiers had been few and far between then, the screams of pain easily equated to squeals of joy. He had not understood; now he did, but it was too late.

But she had smiled down at him, stretched with the attempt to calm him. *Yes, like the game. You must hide and stay quiet, so no one finds you. Promise me you will.*

Okay, he had said. *I promise.*

That had been the last time he had seen her.

He could not know how much time had passed; at some point, the fear had dulled into a buzzing, painful numbness. Hours, perhaps. Days. Time was something fluid and anarchic and useless in the midst of this blood-drenched nightmare.

Finally, the screaming ceased. It did not happen all at once—it was gradual, shouts fading out to soft gasps of pain that fell away to a strained, eerie silence.

Viro knew something was wrong, even as he slowly, quietly shut the door of the cupboard behind him. A sense of injustice, of fundamental error that went further than the bodies on the floor, the blood on the walls. This was something fate-slick and bitter, and he felt it soul-deep.

The halls of the palace were silent, drowned in death. The numbness had not left him; it dragged along behind him with every step, wrapping him further and further into that eerie sense of detachment, grief and apathy walking side by side.

Are they all dead? he thought as he passed another body on the west colonnade. The man lay against the stone crookedly, face pushed into the floor of the corridor but body twisted sickeningly to the right. It was the first dead body Viro had ever seen, the first one he'd fully looked at—he had been too afraid to meet the eyes of the ones in the library, to look into their glassy, distant gazes. It was less that he was afraid of death, and more that he was afraid of what he would see—regret and spite and sorrow. *I wanted to live one day longer. Why couldn't I live one day longer? Why is it you, and not me?*

It was a question he could not answer. His birthright gave him nothing; his heart still beat the same way all of theirs had before life had been wrenched from them. And yet, he was alive.

In a strange way, the attack did not surprise him. The rage, the sadness, the fear—that had all been cleanly washed away by the numbness. All that remained was a pensive dispassion, an oddly clear view of the world around him. And it lent him a certain distance, a clarity of mind that allowed him to remember the previous day, if in flashes.

He recalled Kiran tugging him and Tarak to the war room, tears streaming down his cheeks. He had been shouting for them to hurry, his grip bruising Viro's wrist. He remembered his own surprise, his dismay. Kiran had never shouted before. He had never cried.

And then he had banged on the wooden door until it swung open. The mild irritation on the captain's face had dissipated into something that resembled unease. As if he too could not help but wonder what had reduced *Kiran* to tears.

A voice had sounded from inside—*What is it?*—and the captain had stepped aside, the high priestess appearing beside him. She had crouched beside Kiran, eyes shining with concern as she wiped the tears from his face. But though he had let go of his and Tarak's wrists, he had not answered her questions, opting to pull himself from her embrace—roughly, as if the gesture pained him—and then moving toward the table, to the chair at the head of it.

He had tilted his chin up, defiant despite his tears, full of an unfamiliar, trembling fire. *You have to keep the troops here.*

The king had looked at him with familiar bemusement. It was difficult to truly, honestly believe a child knew of things he had never heard, knew of things that had not yet happened. But Viro and Tarak had grown up with his eerily accurate prophecies—most had not.

And then the king had smiled, warm but disbelieving. *We need the troops at the borderlands. There has been an attack.*

I know, Kiran had replied, still impossibly afraid. *But you cannot move them. You must believe me.*

The high priestess had crossed the room and bent to put a hand on his shoulder. *What is it that you saw?*

Kiran had shuddered, a ragged, ghastly tremor running through his entire body. Like the shadow of it still lingered in his bones, a nightmare given form and intent. Eyes black as night, black as rot, he had looked up. *Please. You must believe me.*

His father had simply shook his head. *To keep the troops here is to condemn those of the borderlands. It is not as if our lives matter more or less than theirs, especially when we do not face such a threat. Why should the troops stay here if they may aid them, protect their lives?*

But the words had fallen on deaf ears. Logic was of little consequence to someone who played with fate, to someone who had been born from fire. He had seen something, Viro knew, and he could not let it happen. For the first time since he had been brought to the palace, Kiran had fallen to his knees, pressing his face into the floor in full supplication. The words muffled by the stone, he had pleaded. *Please. Please.*

But his father had only smiled again, as if amused. *I do not know what you saw, but it does not have to come true.*

Kiran had pulled back, face smudged from dust on the floor. *It doesn't?*

He had shaken his head. *It doesn't.* And then he had knelt beside Kiran, impossibly warm, and held out his hand. *I will not let it pass. I give you my word.*

And yet it *had* passed, Viro knew. Looking around the palace now, shattered in some fundamental, irreversible way, he knew in his bones that this was what Kiran had seen. He could not know what part of it—the silence, or the blood, or the bodies—but he thought, more than any of those things, he had felt this same sense of wrongness; of a crooked bone, a festering wound.

Viro ducked into a shadowed archway, pressing his fingers to his face in shock as he entered the foyer. It was not only the smell—hot blood and bile—that struck him, but the artless carnage of it. The strewn corpses, the discarded weapons still hooked with entrails. Nausea seared through him, sudden and lasting, and he had to clench his teeth to keep from vomiting. The sound would give him away.

He carefully stepped over the eviscerated bodies, taking care to avoid touching the blood with his bare feet. It would leave footprints, signs of life. A soft creaking sounded, and he looked up, found the door to the throne room cracked open slightly, as if by the wind. Light streamed out of it, dull and watery—*life,* he thought, and in a spark of true, hopeful anticipation, he opened it fully and ducked into the room.

Viro's heart beat once, and then paused. It hung in the cavern of his chest, silent, and he could feel his blood still in his veins as desolation turned it all to stone.

He could not speak, and he was glad of it; there were no words for this, no gods left to pray to. They had left him, left all of them, abandoned them to this cold, endless darkness.

His parents lay in the center of the throne room. The *ariyanai* was soaked in red, their bodies strewn over it like trophies. They were intertwined, the king draped loosely over the queen—as if at some point in the now-distant past, he had tried to shield her. It did not matter, of course. They were both dead now, gone to Dhaasthur with the rest.

Radha was crumpled in front of them, another useless shield. She had died on her knees, and had fallen forward in the time since, her wrap torn and stained with blood. She was curled so he could not see her wounds, could only see the eerie shine of her eyes, the stiff tilt of her body.

It was wrong, that she was dead. It was so horribly, irreconcilably *wrong.* She had put him to bed last night, had sung an old lullaby. That had been her voice, sweet and high and *real.* She could not simply be dead.

And yet, she was. All death cared for was the act of taking; of dismantling something that had once breathed and shattering it into a corpse.

Distantly, he registered his own movements; he knelt beside Radha's body, pressed his hand to her heart as he had to his own. But there was no heartbeat, no sound of life, no blood left to lose.

A jagged, mocking laugh sounded in the room. Viro slowly raised his head, shock turning him faded and lethargic. A soldier stood in the doorway. He wore a black leather tunic embroidered with a ring of braided flowers, a crown held within. The symbol of the Najan Army.

Viro held his gaze, but did not remove his hand from her chest. A cold, remote fire flickered to life in his own, burning through what remained of his heart. It was just blood and ragged flesh at this point, as dead as his sister. The fire consumed the pain, the rage, left nothing behind but ash and smoke.

"Suppose we missed the little runt, did we?" The man said, stepping forward. There was a wickedly sharp sword in his hand, already blood red from the lives that had been lost. The sharp, cruel slant of his mouth told him the man did not mourn for those lives—that they were simply numbers on a list, a statistic in progress.

Viro watched him approach, already detached from the thought of his own death. He was thrown into the recesses of another memory, of another day in eternal winter. This man, with his black shining leather and lethal sword, reminded him of the snake. Slow and uncaring and drowned in malice.

The man raised the sword, and just like the snake, he never had the opportunity to bring it down. Instead, he fell to his knees, lips parted faintly in shock. Before he fell, Viro noticed the tip of something red-swathed and glittering emerge from his chest and disappear.

Behind him, Tarak stood, a knife clutched in his clenched, shaking hands, ashen with shock. The sight of him knocked Viro out of his reverie somewhat, brought him closer to his body. He pulled himself to his feet and walked toward him, but Tarak did not look up, gaze fixed on the dead body of the soldier. His eyes were so wide, so bright.

"I killed him," he whispered, voice cracked and barely audible. "It is not that I—I did not mean to. I-It was only that he meant to hurt you. He meant to kill you, and I could not let him, I couldn't, and now he's—"

He cut off, dropped the knife. It hit the marble point down, cracking the stone. Tarak made a strangled, choked noise, of terror—of disgust—and looked up at Viro as if in a plea. "I did not mean to—I just… he would have killed you. I could not let him kill you."

Viro opened his mouth to say something, to reassure him, but found he could not find the words. There was an alarming hollowness in his chest, a concavity that seemed to spread through his body as if it could fully gut him, turn him to dust and shadows. But he kept walking, and then leaned forward, pressing his face into the other boy's chest. *Take it away,* he thought. *Take away the pain, take away the emptiness.*

He did not know to whom he was pleading; the gods had gone silent and the city was razed and dead.

The streets were filled with bodies; a fortunate few watched them pass from their homes. Viro knew there had been people who had survived the massacre in the palace as well, those that had hidden well enough. Marai was not a ghost town, not truly, and yet it was bloated with enough blood that it resembled a corpse, pale and deteriorating.

They found Kiran in the main temple, knelt beside the pool. It had turned crimson from blood, clouds of dark liquid tainting the water. There was somebody with him, another child holding a body in their arms. Viro realized it was the young daughter of the high priestess, hair tied and bound in an intricate bun the way her mother had always braided it. As they approached, sound began to pierce the thick, buzzing silence that surrounded Viro, that suffocating numbness.

The girl was crying, he realized, screaming with pain. She was shaking, holding the body of her mother to her chest with a pained, useless ferocity, as if she could bring her back with sheer willpower.

They walked down the steps and paused beside the pool. Tarak had gone still, the sight of the body an indelible reminder of the dead soldier. Occasionally, a brief, sharp tremor would wrack him, an aftershock of grief, of revulsion.

Kiran looked up at them. His eyes were bloodshot, lips pressed together in a thin line. But there was a weariness to the planes of his face, an old, faded anguish in his gaze.

The sight of him lit a match in Viro's chest. There was nothing left to burn, and so it simply flickered in the darkness, held in the hands of ashes. "Why did you not save them?"

He tilted his head, bemused.

Viro flung his arms out, gesturing toward the high priestess's dead body, toward what remained of the palace. Before, he had thought himself incapable of truly feeling the depth of the rage that lined his blood—now it felt as if that was the only thing he *could* feel, as if the rage had filled in the gaping, corroded chasms in his soul and sharpened him into something new. "What is the use of all your divinity—all your cruel gods—if you cannot *save them?"*

"I tried," Kiran whispered, a small, miserable rasp. "I tried to warn them."

He laughed, humorless and sharp and so, so bitter. "And what was the worth of your warnings? They are still dead. They will never return, and you cannot bring them back."

Each word bit into the other boy, his agony so palpable that for a moment, Viro feared they would cut through skin, through hearts. Out of the corner of his eye, he saw the young priestess lay her mother's body down and rise, but Tarak held her back.

Kiran wrapped his arms around himself, leaning against the edge of the steps and sliding down them so his hands loosely intertwined around his knees. He was still so pale, so shaken.

"Are you not going to say anything?" he demanded, contempt scorching his veins.

He looked up at him then, gaze flat and dark. Where rage had sharpened Viro into a thorn, grief had carved him into something distant and inured, a cold star.

Viro vaguely noticed Tarak tugging at his arm, whispering for him to calm down, to come back. *Let us return to the palace,* he was saying, but Viro did not want to return to the palace, did not want to return to that silent, blood-soaked lake of hell. Even as the other boy pulled him away, grip tight on his upper arm, he refused to turn away from Kiran. The young priestess knelt beside him, shaking his knees lightly, as if to rouse him from that odd trance he'd fallen into.

"This is your fault!" Viro shouted, unaware of the words even as they left him. They were made of an adamantine anger, borne of a fury he himself could not fathom. "Their blood is on your hands!"

And still, Kiran did not look up from where his gaze rested on the crimson pool, hands palm up in hopeless prayer.

When Suri had returned, it had still been early enough that no one had noticed her, and the few that had hadn't cared to make an issue of it. Isa and Mohini were still asleep—or perhaps had never come back at all—and so she had slipped back into bed, pulling the covers over her head as if it could erase the previous night from existence.

But you do not really want that, a small, mocking voice whispered. *You simply wish it to happen again.*

There was nothing left to say, no words that could possibly justify her actions. And yet, where she had expected to find a knot of unease building in her chest, she found nothing. She regretted nothing. It was as the voice said—she only mourned the fact that it would not, could not, happen again.

Suri didn't fully register falling asleep again, but hours later, she woke to the sudden, shuddering feeling of Isa shaking her awake. She scrubbed at her eyes and threw out an arm in a vague, desperate plea to make her stop, then turned to look at her.

Her gaze was strangely somber. "There is someone at the door for you."

She narrowed her eyes, but Isa simply stepped back, unwilling to say more. Suri picked up a dressing robe from a nearby chair and wrapped it around herself, unlatching the door. A hopeful, naive part of her sunk a little when she saw who it was.

Tarak's shoulders were hunched, hands intertwined and fidgeting. He looked up when the door opened, offering something she assumed was meant to be a smile. "Council meeting in fifteen minutes."

She swallowed. "I see."

Another faint smile, and then he disappeared. Isa opened her mouth to say something, but Suri shook her head. *Later.* Suri dressed quickly, darting short, infrequent glances at the other adjoining door, but it never opened, and Mohini never appeared.

It had only been a few hours and yet the palace was fully awake, bustling in an oddly hysterical way, the same kind of horror-struck fatigue she had felt in Tarak's smile. The war room was filled to the brim, dangerous with the spy still on the loose, but perhaps in the midst of the chaos no one had thought to acknowledge their presence. Tarak was not sitting beside the head of the table—he was darting around the room, giving updates, calming people.

The seat at the head was empty, as it always was until the very, very beginning of the meeting. Yet, strangely enough, the seat at the other side of the table was empty, too. Suri took her seat beside it and tried not to let it visibly unsteady her, though she thought that perhaps a bit of a lost cause at this point.

As if the unfamiliar, nightmarish disorder wasn't enough on its own, Suri did not recognize that the king had arrived until he had sat down at the table. It took several seconds for everyone else to notice as well, not until Tarak stilled, struck by fealty and some unreadable alloy of fear, and went to his own seat silently.

A switch flipped, the rest of the room quieted too, slowly but surely, as people took their seats, and those that did not have seats sat on the floor, and when the floor was a sea of skin and cloth, the remainder leaned against the far wall. And still, no one filled Kiran's seat; it sat empty, haunting and mocking.

The boy king did not bother with formalities. He was unrecognizable in the early morning, eyes as black as his brother's. "As of an hour ago, the Najan Army is marching through the borderlands. Within hours, they shall reach the edge of Athri. In days, they will reach Marai."

He did not look at Suri, oddly enough. His gaze was fixed on a distant, invisible point, as if he were only half here, ripped from the past into the present and back again. He shook his head, a slight, imperceptible movement, and then leaned back in the high-backed chair.

"There have already been reports of attacks on preexisting villages and settlements in the borderlands," he said tonelessly. "At least three have been burned to the ground, and two are heavily impacted. I will lead a unit of soldiers to the borderlands to defend the remaining settlements and prevent them from reaching the border."

Tarak looked at him sharply. From this angle, Suri could not quite see his expression, only the unfiltered terror held in the edge of it. He opened his mouth, and then closed it, but there was something strained about the line of his mouth.

The boy king did not look over, but his hands tightened slightly into fists, as if the effort of keeping himself still was something that emptied him entirely.

The door opened without warning. There was no knock, simply the crack of wood against the back of the poor man who had been leaning against it. A rustling ran through the crowd, a murmur of wonder and fear as they pulled the man away and opened the door fully, revealing Kiran.

Suri sucked in a breath; she recognized the pallor, the flecks of gold in his irises. He had seen something, and it had burned through him, uncaring and searing. Exertion and fever gave his cheeks an unhealthy glow, and his chest was heaving slightly. But still, he did not tear his gaze away from the boy king. There was something faintly terrified in that gaze, a touch of true disbelief.

"Don't," he whispered, so softly that if the room had not gone quiet with anticipation she would not have heard him. He shut his eyes, swallowed, and then opened them again. The gold shone against the black. "You can't."

The king's mouth twisted in a sharp, rancorous imitation of a demure smile. "I cannot do what?"

"You can't leave," he said, stepping forward. The people pressed to the side in desperate attempts to get out of his way, as if they could feel the fire in his skin. He took another step, clearing a path to the table, but still he did not sit down, simply leaned forward, palms splayed against the bullet wood. There was something frustratingly abstruse about his words, about the vagueness of them, and a hint of that own frustration flitted across his face. "It is—if you leave, there will be consequences."

"For who?" the king bit out, narrowing his eyes. "This is not the ambush on Marai, Kiran. This is an invasion, a war set to repeat again and again until we are strong enough to stop it. If I do not go, they will push the border back further, and they will do that with the blood of civilians."

"What consequences?" Tarak asked quietly. It was the first time he had spoken since the boy king had entered the room. But now he looked at Kiran with a sobering, washed-out fear in his gaze, an old one.

Kiran hesitated, pulling back for a moment. This close, Suri could see that his fingers were trembling on the surface of the table, nails bitten and ragged. He shut his eyes. "I cannot say."

"You cannot?" the king said softly, a condemnation. "Or you will not?"

Kiran inhaled sharply, pulling his hands back from the table. His wrap was hastily done, the robes ill-fitting and crooked on his shoulders. There was camphor soot on his bare shoulders, streaking up toward his hairline. "Death, somewhere. To someone. I cannot tell you. I do not know."

"Did you come here thinking that would be enough?" he said disdainfully. "Did you truly expect me to decide the future of the kingdom on a baseless outline of a prophecy?"

The other boy opened his eyes slowly. They were fully black now, but Suri could not forget that gleam of gold, the shine of divinity. It held him up even now, as if his bones were simply fire poured into a skeletal mold. "Perhaps I should not have. Your father did not."

The room had already been quiet, but now the quiet came alive, turned to something suffocating and thick.

"Leave." The word was so low, so strangled, that for a moment, Suri thought she had imagined it—that it had been some phantasm of what she'd expected the king to say rather than what he actually had. And yet, his lips were still faintly parted in the echo of the word, head tilted up in a malicious ghost of anger.

Kiran did not insist on staying. He had never sat down, and so he simply stepped away from the table, walked back to the door. He cracked it open, and then glanced back. But the king was not looking at him—he was not looking at anything, his eyes shut and mouth spread in a thin, uneven grimace.

"I will not beg you," Kiran said, the wind outside tousling his hair, pulling him out and toward it. And then he shut the door behind him and the silence cracked, broke into shards.

In the midst of the chaos, the boy king was strangely still, paralyzed by his own anger. Tarak was the exact opposite, trembling faintly, shaking the king and attempting to tug him to his feet to no avail. Finally, he gave up, letting his hands fall on the upholstered chair. His mouth moved in a question, in a plea, but still the king did not answer. He simply rose from the table and left, eerily quiet.

The people did not notice his exit. It was mostly chiefs and nobles, the former discussing how to adjust for the shift in troops and the latter fretting over how they could avoid the death Kiran had spoken of—*Perhaps we should leave for Chaaka? They say it's beautiful this time of year.* The handful of scattered servants, priests, and handmaidens were the only ones silent, having come to an inevitable conclusion—they could not escape. The soldiers would fight, and the rich would flee, but they would die.

Tarak's hands hung in the air, stretched out to call the boy king back. He glanced up as Suri approached him, bewilderment dulling the fear in his eyes. He looked nearly cadaverous in his shock. He didn't even try to hide it—he simply stared back, as if there was nothing to say.

Suri had heard, distantly, of the attacks on Marai. She had been in Dauri when it had occurred, sent to assassinate a state official who had been funding a rebellion. To that small, hardened child, it had seemed insignificant—another battle in a war, another sea of dead in an ocean of blood. And yet the aftershocks of it still hung in the air, written into the cracks of this broken city. The war was over, but it still lived on in all of them—in Tarak's odd, trembling shock, in Kiran's flame-soaked terror, in the king's barbed, bloody fury.

Suri lifted a hand, meaning to put it on his shoulder. But this was no time for comfort. She jerked her head toward the door. "Go to him. I'll clear out the room."

Tarak blinked at her, a haze clearing in his expression. He shot her a small, grateful look before leaving, shutting the door hard behind him. Suri turned to survey the crowded, panicked room—it had been sympathy, bravado, that had pushed her to speak. She knew the people would not care what she had to say, not with her treason-stained hands and the enemy blood that coursed through her veins.

But when she rang the bell at the center of the table, the chatter began to fade, slow but true. And when she spoke, they listened.

The knock was neat, careful, but it fractured Viro's patience nonetheless. There was no reprieve—he hadn't expected one, of course, but a childish part of him had wished for it. *If I am to die, at least give me the time to prepare.*

Tarak stood, head ducked in a faraway, thoughtful gesture. His shoulders heaved—Viro realized he was panting. He had run, for him. To stop him, to save him.

Clouds gathered behind him in the spaces between the pillars of the open colonnade. The sky was black with thunder and rain, sunlight a distant, unreal thing in the face of this oncoming storm.

"Let me in," he said, and so Viro did, stepping aside for yet another storm. He shut the door behind him and turned to look at the other boy, who wandered around the room aimlessly, as if saying goodbye. Finally, he took a seat on the white bed, spreading his hands on the blankets. When he spoke, his voice was hoarse with old screams. "I don't suppose you would listen if I asked you to stay."

Viro tried to swallow past the lump in his throat, but gave up, offering a flat, humorless laugh. "I do appreciate the attempt."

Tarak looked up, eyes shining with an ancient fear, a soft, lasting sadness. He crossed the room and sat beside him on the plunging, too-soft bed, put his hands over his. Finally, he spoke, gaze still on their fingers, calloused with age and loss. "Kiran does not lie. You know he does not."

"If it were real, would he have stayed and tried to convince me?" he mused, too afraid to look up.

He shook his head. "He does not lie, and he does not beg. Think what it must be like, to see catastrophe twice before it happens, to be ignored both times."

"And by the same blood, too," Viro noted. He exhaled, pulled away from Tarak's hands. They were not soft—they had long since been weathered by life. But there was a certain warmth to them; it was difficult to forsake life when he knew he was forsaking this. He forced himself to meet Tarak's gaze, and the other boy was already looking back, mouth twisted with a shadow of fated grief. "Perhaps my father made a mistake. Perhaps I am repeating it. Perhaps that is what all humans are fated to do—fall into old, familiar outlines and prepared graves.

"But I cannot let them invade on the basis of protecting my own life," he said, looking down. "If I allow this, then I will die soon enough, at enemy hands, no less. And there is always the chance that Kiran is wrong."

Tarak made a choked-off, strangled noise of bitter, fearful humor. He raised his hands, as if to embrace him or to slap him, but finally rested them on Viro's shoulders. It seemed as though Tarak was always doing that—always tethering him, another, sweeter heartbeat around his own. "You *know* he is not, you know—" he cut off, exhausted by the effort of trying to convince him his own life was worth something.

Viro shook his head, chest tight with spite. "Kiran will never face the effects of his actions, of his prophecies. He can play the saint all he wants, die his unsullied death and raise his hands to the heavens, professing he did all he could to protect this nation, to love it. But he will leave behind those that still suffer—they will no longer be his responsibility. And when he does, I am the one who will have to protect them."

"Do you really think he does not care for them?"

"It does not matter whether he does or does not," he said, suddenly tired. "We can only see as far as the reach of our own lifetimes, toward the horizon of our deaths. And his has always been too close for him to see anything at all."

Tarak let out a ragged sigh, lost and despairing. Viro reached up and put a hand on his, traced the lines of his fingers. He watched him do it, entranced by the movement and saddened by it as well. Finally, he asked, "If I begged, would you stay?"

Viro's fingers stilled in their movement, suddenly hyper-aware of the way Tarak's hands shook upon the embroidered fabric of his tunic. As if he couldn't bear to hold him tighter, as if the mere action would wrench him away.

"Please don't," Viro whispered, shutting his eyes so he did not have to see his expression. In the darkness, this was a game, nothing but an elaborate nightmare. "I am too afraid of what I would try to do if you did."

He blew out a long, slow breath. Viro opened his eyes, still faintly afraid, and found the other boy shifting forward, pulling his hands from his shoulders. They fell to the blankets, and he held them palm up, studying their lifelines. The way they tangled, the way they broke.

"Then let me stay here," he said, without looking up. "For now, let me stay."

And though Viro's breath caught, heart stuttering from one beat to the next, he let him. It was a quiet, wordless farewell—but that was all they had ever had, and so it should not have surprised him that it was how they would part.

20
LYNE

"It's your birthday," Kiran said abruptly. Suri turned to look at him from where he was stretched across the couch, head tilted against the arm. He wiggled his feet in her lap.

"Just about," she said warily, checking the time on the television. A few minutes after midnight. "Is this one of your fancy omniscient god things?"

He held up her phone; in the darkness, she could make out a blinking gray message box. "Dai just texted."

Suri leaned forward and grabbed it from him, and he let her take it with a faint, sharp smile. He stretched out his arms out behind him, and asked, "Why didn't you say?"

"Didn't think it mattered?" she said helplessly, hiding her expression in the shadows. In truth, she had spent the last few days since the sweet fiasco hiding out in her room, emerging only for food and quick trips over to Aza and Dai's apartment.

But tonight was the season finale of one of the shows they always watched together, and so she had to stay, for the sake of holy routine, and already she felt overwhelmed. It had been so much easier to ignore her feelings when she'd thought she was alone in feeling them.

"Why wouldn't it?" he returned, sounding genuinely baffled.

Suri had no lies left, and the truth wasn't an option. She shrugged and played with the edge of the folded blanket draped over the side of the couch. On the screen, someone pushed their friend into a pool, and it moved to a clip of them trash-talking one another.

"Come on," he said suddenly, taking her hand. She arched an eyebrow, useless in the darkness, but let him tug her to her feet and through the shadowed room. Kiran opened the pantry door, her hand still intertwined with his.

She didn't pull it away. "What are you looking for?"

"Candles," he replied cheerfully. He slid out two separate containers, one the size of his palm and then a larger plastic one with a red cover. "And sweets."

He led her back to the nook and heaved himself up, taking a seat on the edge of the table. Carefully, he pulled off the lid and drew out a golden sweet, soft with butter and heat in his hands. Then he stuck a candle in it, blue as swimming pools, as saltwater taffy.

Suri took it from his outstretched hands. "I thought you could only make one wish? There's going to be a party at my grandmother's shop, and she won't be happy if she learns you stole mine."

"Who told you that?" He looked at her, aghast, as he leaned forward to light the candle. His pinky finger burned with flame, swirling around the thin white wick and splitting as he pulled back. "You can make as many wishes as you want on your birthday. They are an inexhaustible resource."

"Really?" she asked, amused despite herself. There was something charming about the phrase. "So I could blow this out, and you could relight it, and I could wish again, and we could repeat it all day?"

"There is a certain refractory period," he conceded, lips twitching in a smile. "A few minutes, usually. But yes, technically. Do you want to?"

Suri pretended to think about it briefly, but she had already made her mind up. There were only two wishes she wanted to see come true. She shook her head, and cupped the sweet in her laced fingers, regarding the flame. Then she leaned in and blew out the candle, plunging them back into the darkness. Her lips tasted like smoke and sugar.

In the illuminated, contoured shadows of the nook, Kiran reached forward and broke the sweet in half, soft and pliant in their gathered hands. He took one for himself and then lifted it to her lips. She stared at it, faintly bemused, and then took a hesitant, dainty bite.

He raised his eyebrows. "I would've thought you'd eat it all in one bite."

She glared at him, shoving her half of the sweet toward his mouth. He bit into it easily, lips brushing her fingers even as he laughed around the sweet, a muffled, dampened sound in the late night. He chewed and swallowed, eyes fixed on hers, bright as hot coals. They were still holding hands, impossibly.

In the living room, the end credits to the show played. A small window popped up in the corner displaying a preview of the next program—a cooking show where meals had to be made from ingredients all the same color. Today, it was blue.

Suri ate the rest of her sweet, and then he slid off the table, the action bringing him slightly closer. The candle had been blown out, the wish sent off to be granted or forgotten, the sweet eaten. But still, they lingered.

She tilted her head back in a yawn, rocking back on her heels with the force of it. He held out a hand, steadying, mouth quirked to the side in a smile. "You should sleep."

"I should," she agreed, unable to think of anything other than her own fatigue and his fingers loosely grasping her shoulder. With great effort, she stepped back toward the living room, toward the dip of space that led into the hallway. She pressed her lips together, unsure, then asked, "Do gods get wishes?"

"We grant them," he said, moving to stand by the couch. The light of the television shone through him, glassy and pale. "But we don't get to wish. I suppose we could grant our own, if we desired it enough. Why?"

"No reason," she said, too quickly. Torn with embarrassment, she slipped down the corridor and shut the door behind her. She exhaled, counting her breaths as she listened to the sirens in the distance, the swell and dip of the traffic. But he never came, and even when she lay down on her bed and turned off her lamp, she didn't sleep.

The next morning, she rolled out of bed, weary and dry eyed, and shoved herself through the motions robotically. After showering, she shuffled back out to the living room, stretching her arms out as she yawned.

The living room was not as empty as she had assumed it would be. Everyone was in their usual spots, chatting amiably and pausing only when she came in. She stared through them for half a minute, then asked, "Why are you all here so early?"

"It's eleven," Aza said, jerking her head at Kiran. "That one didn't want to wake you."

The words pierced through her half-asleep haze, and she rubbed at her face self-consciously to avoid looking at him. "You should've woken me up."

"Maybe," he said, shrugging. "You're awake now. Your friends have plans for the day."

She raised her eyebrows, glancing at them. "Do I want to know what that means?"

"We won't tell you, anyway," Miya said cheerfully. "It's a surprise."

It didn't end up being as much of a surprise as advertised—they took her out to brunch at the same restaurant they always went to, and she ordered a stack of pancakes that she didn't quite finish. They were soaked through with sugar syrup and cream, and she'd already saturated her body with sweets all through the past week. Dai and Miya split her leftovers between them, and Kiran poked at other people's plates, stealing scraps of omelets and stray blueberries.

After, while the others went shopping at an antiques store on Holloway, Ellis went with her to a new action movie they'd been anticipating. She and Ellis had bonded over their mutual enjoyment of the senseless, unrealistic chaos that defined the films when they'd met, doing an icebreaker in Junior Lit. The rest of their friends thought they were coarse and meaningless, so they had a habit of watching late-night screenings alone.

On screen, cars exploded. Fire swung outward, consuming and thoughtless, and drowned people in the blaze. Debris fell from the sky, scattering the ground and killing more people. It was a remarkably morbid movie, but most were.

Without looking away from the screen, Ellis said, "So—"

"If you mention my roommate," she warned. "If you *allude* to him, I will crush you like a soda can."

He grinned, teeth bright against his skin in the darkness of the theater. He didn't smile often anymore, not since that inexplicable incident in October, and the sight was startling. "That's all the proof I needed."

Suri leaned back in her seat and let out a low groan. "How did you even hear?"

"Anybody who's spent more than five minutes with you two together would be able to figure it out," he told her, faintly amused. "It's not exactly rocket science. But Miya does keep me updated."

"Can we not talk about this right now? I'm actively avoiding thinking about it too closely. And it's my birthday."

"It is," he agreed, and magnanimously changed the subject. "Nineteen, huh?"

Unsurprisingly, she also didn't want to think about her age. The main character jumped out of an exploding building and onto a nearby rooftop, and her eyes tracked the movement, listless. *Nineteen.* Nineteen years of her life had gone by, and she didn't feel like she had achieved anything substantial. She felt a little like she was a bed bug on the surface of the earth, a speck of human that would become a speck of dust.

There was nothing particularly noteworthy about her life, and it didn't bother her, not usually. But sometimes, she would lie awake at night, wracked with guilt—she had been given all this time, and still she was no closer to avenging her family, and truthfully, she didn't know if she ever would. She loved Kiran's stories, but she wasn't the protagonist of a fairy tale, a rigid path to victory or tragedy set out for her from the very beginning. She was a side character, an extra that left set as soon as possible and spent the rest of the night at home, soaking in the stable mediocrity of her life. Her problems were not meant to be solved—they were an insignificant plot hole, a detail included only to fill pages, if included at all.

She wondered, briefly, fantastically, what it would be like to matter.

Dangerous, probably, she thought, watching a series of oceanside condos topple headfirst into the sea. Aloud, she asked, "Do you ever wish you were a kid again?"

Ellis considered the question, tilting his head. Then he said, "Not really. I didn't know what I was doing at any given moment."

She raised her eyebrows. "And that's changed how?"

"Fuck off," he said, but his voice was soft in the near-silence of the theater, and the incongruity nearly made her laugh. "Would you go back?"

Would she? She thought about it for a bit, then shook her head as the villain threatened to blow up the entire city. "I like my life, for the most part."

"I'm sure you do," he said slyly, and she shoved him, and he fell onto the shoulder of the young mother sitting beside them, and she glared at them, weary, and a few minutes later, they were sitting outside the theater doors, struggling to keep themselves upright.

Slush soaked through her jeans, and her teeth were chattering through the laughs, but still she couldn't calm herself down. Tears were warm against her cheeks, and she thought they might freeze in the cold winter air. Ellis, almost gasping from laughter, wasn't much better off. When their friends returned after another fifteen minutes, they found them leaned against the brick façade of the theater, incomprehensible and wet-faced.

Eventually, they pulled themselves into silence, wiping at their faces; they held each other's gaze for a second before lapsing into raucous, ugly laughter all over again, and the others had to steady them.

"Where are we going?" Suri inquired as they crossed the street, leaned against one of them, tucking her head into the crook of their neck.

Kiran glanced down at her, mouth curved in a distant, unfamiliar smile. Not quite unfamiliar—it had been, once, but she thought she was close to understanding it, felt as if she was on the precipice of a realization that painstakingly circled the borders of his heart. It was a nice heart, bloody and scarred and golden through and through, and she wanted to know it so badly she nearly did. Wishes were strange that way. "It's almost six. We're going over to your grandmother's shop. Are you okay?"

"I think," she said, wiping at her cheeks. They were cold and only slightly damp, but already she felt a little warmer. "Sorry for cry laughing on you."

"It's okay," he said graciously, and pulled her in closer with his other arm as a group of kids ran past them. She could hear his heartbeat through the searing warmth of his skin; she felt it like a drumbeat, like a song, and when they paused in front of the shop and she disentangled herself from his arms, she felt it still.

"What is it?" he asked, and she realized she was staring.

You have a song in your heart, she wanted to say, wanted to lean forward and press her ear to his chest so she could hear it again. *Do you know that?*

But she couldn't form the words. They were not meant for such raw, inelegant confessions. They were not meant for confessions at all.

Her grandmother unlocked the door and let them in, the others oohing and ahhing at all the correct times even though they'd all seen the shop on her birthday before and would likely see it again. Only Kiran took it in with some measure of wonder, reverent in his curiosity.

Every year, on her birthday, her grandmother decorated it with a near ridiculous level of effort. When she'd been younger, she had been embarrassed by the cut paper banners and painted signs. Everyone who stopped by would wish her a happy birthday while they chatted with her grandmother, but she would still pout, sullen, until they cut the cake in the evening and her puerile anger faded in the face of her hunger.

As she'd grown older and let go of that odd, self-conscious shame, she'd grown to enjoy the decorations. She wasn't above bragging good-naturedly, though sometimes she felt guilty that her grandmother never, ever let her help.

"It's *your* party," she would snap, all bark and no bite. "You can pay me back by doing your chores."

She was making no effort to hide her pride now, though, talking with Kiran as he gestured at the decorations. Her chest felt tight, looking at them together, looking at everyone. Miya was balancing carved trinkets on her head, Aza was competing with her, and Dai was trying to convince them to stop as Ellis recorded the entire incident on his phone. Her grandmother glanced over, scolding them as Kiran let out a soft, helpless laugh and pressed his fingers to his mouth to stifle it when she glared back at him. *Family,* she thought, and it felt true and too big to believe, a secret she had stumbled upon and now immediately wanted to bury again. She was afraid if she took it out and held it in her hands, coveted it properly, it would grow wings and learn to disappear.

It didn't matter if she didn't matter, not really. As long as she had them, as long as she had this.

When she returned to the present, dizzy and warmed from the inside out, they were all staring at her. Warily, she asked, "What is it?"

"You're crying," Aza said pointedly; she said it like an accusation, like an apology.

"What?" she reached up and wiped at damp cheeks, swallowing a sniff. "I'm not crying."

Ellis gave a soft snort. "You are."

Suri folded her arms, a last ditch-effort at saving her dignity. "And I said I'm *not*—"

"Cake?" Dai interrupted weakly, hands held up as if he meant to intervene.

"Yes," her grandmother said smoothly, like this was what she had planned all along. "Time for cake-cutting. Take a seat while I bring it downstairs."

They were all children under her watchful eye, and obediently, they sat in a ring around the wooden table.

Ellis held up his phone. "I still have the video."

Dai deflated visibly.

Suri's heart felt like it could hold a song in it, too. Like it could twist itself into something tangled and consonant and carry a melody like words carried stories. It was a heartening thought, and she held it close even as her grandmother descended the steps with the cake, unsteady with two bottles of soda tucked under her arm. Kiran immediately rose and went to help her—despite her irritated, insistent assurances that she was fine carrying them, he slipped the soda bottles out and placed them on the corner of the table, taking the other edge of the cake platter so they could guide it down slowly.

Her grandmother glared over at him, but it held little heat. She had never been good at staying angry with him. He smiled back, amiable, as she stuck nineteen candles into the smooth surface of the frosting. As she began to light the candles, the cream glistened, curving upward in small, accidental tufts.

She finished, gestured for the others to begin singing. Miya started loudly while the rest joined in, jostling her in an attempt at embarrassment. They finished, dramatic and glorious and hers, and she shut her eyes and wished with every beat, every string, of her discordant, uneven heart. And then she leaned forward, the heat against her skin more familiar than breath, and blew the candles out.

Like always, the conversation devolved into a discussion of birthday presents, where her grandmother resolutely declared that this was the best present she could possibly give, and Miya and Aza tried to outdo each other with increasingly ridiculous presents, jet skis and penguins and heated blankets, all the way up to quantified happiness, glowing in jars.

Suri sank into the comfort of it, the silence amidst the noise. Unwittingly, she wandered out of the shop front, ducking under the curtain of beads into the back room.

The 'back room' was a misnomer—the curtain led out to a narrow hallway that branched out into the rooms that made up the bulk of the shop. The meditation room—Suri's old bedroom when she had lived here—bordered the back entrance.

The floor was smooth and dustless; rolled-up prayer mats were leaned against the opposite wall, along with yellowed copies of hymn books. Even though Suri had given her grandmother full agency to scrap the room, there were a few things she hadn't changed.

Along the windows, shadowed against the dark of night, she'd pasted old crayon drawings. The hasty, uncaring lines brought a faint stab of embarrassment, but more than that, she felt strangely unmoored. As if standing in this room, she had been set adrift in time, and if she were to walk back out to the shop front and glance in a mirror, she would see a child staring back.

There was a photo album open on her grandmother's desk, flipped to a page halfway through; she had been looking at it before they had knocked.

On the page, Suri was celebrating her ninth birthday. She grinned up into the camera, missing one of her front teeth. Her black hair was pinned back with purple butterfly clips, and her face shone with this striking passion, a vigor she'd since lost. Perhaps it was youth, all-encompassing and impossible to quantify. Or perhaps it was something else—perhaps all she had now was fear adorned to resemble pragmatism, well-intentioned and paralyzing.

She was so tired of being afraid.

A knock jarred her out of her reverie. Suri glanced back, found Kiran leaned against the doorjamb. An unreadable, unknowable emotion slid through her, slow as syrup. He inclined his head in a greeting, then said, "They sent me to look for you. Said I'd likely have the most luck? Rana figured you'd be here."

Her mouth twitched upward in a faint smile. "It used to be my room. Some of my things are still here. It's… odd, seeing them again."

He ran his hands absentmindedly over the side of a bookshelf, scrutinizing the carefully alphabetized paperbacks that filled shelf after shelf. A swell of laughter rose, distantly, and he made a face. "I can imagine. Are you aware that Miya bought you a plot of land in a rainforest?"

"I am now," she said, surreptitiously shutting the photo album. His eyes tracked the movement, and he crossed the room, slipping it from the desk and retreating when she swung at him, soft, soundless steps on hardwood. They laughed without noise, without impact. It was as if they existed in a world of their own, harsh and barren and lovely in its emptiness, in its capacity to be sculpted into worth. A void strained and stained by love.

Kiran gently paged through the photo album, silent as he examined the pictures. It felt voyeuristic to watch him, and she began to clean up the desk, slipping pens back into drawers and uselessly fiddling with the edges of stacked papers. Her periphery burned.

He held up the photo album, open to a picture of her wearing bunny ears. She could not have been more than four years old in it, and Suri was startled by the roundness of her cheeks. His mouth was a tight line, trembling with the attempt to suppress laughter. "Why have neither of you ever showed me this?"

"Because of *that,*" she said distastefully, indicating his expression. "It's not like you've earned the privilege of making fun of tiny me. *You* didn't even get me a present."

There was a time, when they'd first met, when she would've been afraid saying something like that to him would get her incinerated. It jarred her that the words came so easily now, that he had slipped silently through glossy white ribs, a knife to the heart. He smiled at her, slight and mischievous. "I've gifted you with my company and sparkling wit."

She rolled her eyes. "That doesn't count."

"Do you want one, then?" he asked, continuing to peruse the photo album. The words were offhanded, but there was an odd inflection to them, an uncertain suggestion. "A present?"

"Anything?"

"Within reason," he conceded, but then his smile twisted, becoming crooked. "Or without. Anything that I can give you, I will."

The possibilities dazed her—the carrying, simple truth in his voice, the resolve. She glanced away and steadied her voice. "Like a wish?"

He shook his head. "Wishes are made indiscriminately, simple requests. Then they're sent to the most appropriate god, based on their domain, and it's decided whether or not they are granted. Prayers are made to individual gods, regardless of their domains."

"So a prayer," she said, tracing the curve of her grandmother's signature with her fingernail. It felt carved within her. "I don't pray a lot."

"Not a prayer," he said, with a ghost of amusement. "And that doesn't entirely surprise me, for some reason. Prayers require that you know a god's name, their divine one, and you haven't yet figured mine out."

"Did you make up your name?" she asked suddenly, turning to look at him. "*Kiran.* Is it a nickname?"

"Half of my mortal name," he supplied, a shadow passing over his face momentarily, as it always did when he mentioned that life. It wasn't difficult to intuit it had not ended particularly well. "I'm an outlier; I have two names, one my parents gave me and one humans did. Three, actually. The gods have their own little nickname for me, too. There are two others like me, but one's dead. You probably won't ever meet him."

A jagged, heedless energy animated him now as he fiddled with the pages of the book. He looked nearly nervous. "If you want, I'll tell you who I am. It can be your present."

The statement was colorless. She dropped her hands to her sides and held his gaze. "You don't want to tell me."

"No," he said quietly. "I don't. But I will, if you ask."

"I already know who you are," she said, lifting her shoulders in a shrug. "I don't need your name. I'll wait until you want to give it to me."

Kiran studied her for a moment, brows drawn together. For once, she didn't look away. "Then what would you like?"

"A kiss," she suggested coyly, a joke strained with the weight of hope. She regretted it immediately, but there was no way to turn back time—they would laugh awkwardly, and lapse into even more awkward silence, and careen precariously into a new conversation.

Impossibly, he had not yet laughed. He shut the book carefully and placed it on the edge of the desk, crossing the distance between them. It really was a very small room; he was close enough she could trace the details of his face with her eyes. Insignificant, common things held her attention now—the curve of his cupid's bow, the narrow slant of his nose, the smooth arc of each eye. Her heart felt trapped between beats, a paper-thin ghost of itself soaked in gasoline and left to rot beside a lit match.

"Are you sure?" he asked, nearly inaudible in his uncertainty. His eyes were shuttered, dark lashes fanned out like smoke. Corporeality seemed like a distant notion, just then.

"Yes," she said, surprised both at the fact that she had spoken—that she had not simply stood there, paralyzed with desire and fear—and that she had managed to say it with such force. It faltered, inevitable. "But it's all the same. If you don't want to—"

He reached out and took her hands in his own, and she cut off, the words petering off into charged silence. And then he bent toward her, and pressed a single, chaste kiss to her lips.

For a moment, neither moved—it was a little like they had fallen into a pocket in time. Insects in amber, oblivious and half-dead already. Then he pulled back, slowly, and leaned his weight against her, pressing their foreheads together. She felt lit from within.

"I shouldn't have done that," he whispered softly, ruefully. He was close enough that his breath smelled of sugar, of buttercream and diet cola.

"Why?" she rasped. Despite her best efforts, she felt a stab of hurt, sharp and throbbing. *It doesn't matter,* she told herself. *It doesn't matter if this doesn't work out. There will be other fish in the sea, and those fish will be entirely human, and this isn't the end, so don't get upset—*

"Because now I want to do it again," he said, exhaling a shaky laugh, and she knew, instinctually, that it did not matter to her in the slightest how many fish there were in the proverbial sea. She wanted this one.

His throat shifted in a swallow, the lines of his face tight with strain. She waited for him to speak; he carded a hand through his hair, composed himself, then said, "Do you want to go back? They're waiting for us."

"Okay," she said, toneless and emptied out by temptation, and followed him back out to the shop front.

Everyone had been waiting for them, in a sort of way—they glanced up, scrutinizing, when they reappeared, as if the two of them were the 'after' panel in a 'find the differences' puzzle. Suri had little interest in playing along, and deflected the sly, frequent questions.

The party lasted two more hours, stretching until it was nearly midnight, and then they began to fragment; Aza and Dai headed off first, citing early rehearsal the next morning, then Miya, then Ellis. Her grandmother regarded the pair of them silently after they spent another twenty minutes cleaning up. The candlelight behind her limned her face, aging her as she looked up at them.

Finally, she said, gruff, "Don't stay up too late."

The door slammed shut, and they glanced toward each other, amused, before reality set back in.

The walk home was silent, but not quite awkward. They parted easily, without words; he pulled his bookmark out of a paperback on the coffee table and she went to take a shower, stood under the spray, unfeeling and overwhelmed by the realization she was happy. As a child, joy had been a noun, and it'd defined her in broad, unforgettable strokes. A fundamental truth of the universe; the sky was blue, and she was happy.

She'd lost it in adolescence, thrown it off like an overly thick blanket on a balmy summer night and fallen deep into that pit of consuming, gritty cynicism that so easily came to those confronted with startling, upsetting truths about the world around them. It was only in adolescence that she understood she had nearly died—her parents would not come back, and her grandmother prayed for an hour and a half each night, sore, bruised knees on hardwood, for her safety. Joy was something like a verb, a fleeting sensation. It was there, and then it was not. If you had never held something, it was impossible to long for it, impossible to love it.

But now, she felt like joy was an adjective; it would not stay, but might linger, like a smile, a candle flame. Under the searing, cleansing stream of water, hope chained her.

She wrapped her damp hair in a towel—it had grown long recently, brushing against the tops of her collarbones—and knotted it at the top of her head, padding absently into the kitchen for a glass of water. Epiphany buzzed through her, and she felt distant with it, unreal. When she returned to the living room, Kiran was staring at her strangely, gaze fixed on her chest. His book was splayed against his own. "Is that new?"

"What?"

"The necklace," he asked. "Is it new? I've never noticed it."

It was not entirely his fault—Suri usually tucked the chain into shirts, hiding the pendant from view. But her night shirt was loose on her shoulders, baring the skin above her collarbones. She touched it, a learned gesture, before crossing to sit at the opposite side of the couch. He shifted to make room, pulling himself up into a sitting position.

He waited for her to speak, and she cupped the pendant carefully, the metal warm and damp from the shower. Then she tilted it forward so he could get a better look at the design. His gaze was inscrutable, colorless. Suri explained, "It's a symbol of—"

"Athrasakhi," he finished wryly, oddly cutting. "I'm familiar."

There was something unfamiliar about the timbre of his voice—sharp and bitter, coffee and blood-stained steel. He used the phrase the way her grandmother used it—*I'm familiar,* as though they knew someone and severely regretted ever meeting them. Tentatively, she ventured, "Do you two not get along?"

The corner of his mouth quirked up, dimpling his cheek. "Something like that, yes. Why are you carrying his pendant around?"

"It's a long story," she said, leaning back against the arm of the couch. He nodded, a silent request for her to go on, and she continued, "I don't know entirely how it works. But my grandmother said I was born a little after five, before the sunrise. And so when I first cried, the sky was red—red as blood, as garnets. That time—the inception of dawn, darkness bleeding into light—is his blessed time, apparently. There's an old myth about it and all. But it means he's supposed to protect me, so my parents bought the pendant, when they were alive."

She laughed a little, stilted and humorless, and added, "He hasn't been doing a very good job so far, considering everything that's happened. You'll have to scold him for me when you leave."

"I will," he said, eyes bright with something unfamiliar. His eyes fell shut, and he leaned his head back, exposing the long column of his throat. She watched him swallow, a brief, wracking movement that interrupted the stillness of the night. Like a ripple on the surface of an endless sea, a shift in the darkness that laid beyond stars. Finally, he said, "Do you resent the gods? For what they've done to you, and your family?"

"I'm within my limits to," she agreed, curling into the side of the couch. It didn't feel at all like winter. "But the gods didn't kill my family—or at least, I assume they didn't. I'm allowed to resent fate, I think. I resent the murderer; I resent the berries, though I don't know if it's fair to resent something that's born to kill. I don't resent the gods, though. At the very least, they tried—they sent you."

"The *sankhili* did that," he said, but he was smiling.

"Maybe," she conceded. Part of her wanted to tell him, wanted to let go of that meaningless, naive secret—*I wished for a sign, and you came.*

She had always been afraid of hope, in the same way she figured most people were afraid of black holes. Desire was something that consumed, she knew, and to desire impossibility was to let it consume you entirely. Hearts splintered with love and splintered with loss, and to fear one was to fear both—it was safer to resist them both, to draw thick, black demarcations in shining permanent marker, explicit, clear lines that gently reminded her of what could and could not be desired.

They'd slipped into some midnight land where they existed untouched by desire and recklessness—she had felt so, thought so. It was the way they had always been, after all; all nebulous, silent softness and deathless yearning. But even here, her desire threatened to split her, threatened to spill out of her and empty all the cracks in the earth.

She pulled herself off the couch, a sudden, jerky movement. Her skin felt overwarm, even though she hadn't touched him. He watched her wordlessly.

I want to wash myself clean of this love, she thought. But it was a lie, and it did not feel like it could be real, not even for a moment.

Suri shut her eyes. "Goodnight."

The darkness did not swallow his voice. It was quiet, but it carried in the silence, and she fisted her hands to keep from reaching out and holding it. "Goodnight."

Like the night before, she did not sleep until daybreak.

Kiran dreamt of the battlefield.

War was so often silent. Not to him; he had been created from the cacophony of it, from the shrill, cutting sound of metal rending flesh. He did not stay to tend to the dead in the ensuing quiet—that was Dhaasan's job, and he took even less pleasure in it. Yet he knew the silence lasted, agony stained and dragging. Humanity fell, and the silence lived on.

But now, he found himself standing on a soundless battlefield. It was a clear, quiet plain, uneven and gray with soil and pebbles. Wildflowers and weeds scattered across it, brief pockets of life in the arid, empty underworld. Anybody else would have considered it an arbitrary field, smooth and rolling and close enough to the sea that salt cut through the air. But he could smell the tang of iron, knew that war reverberated through the earth and changed it—this was a place meant for blood, and meant for death.

Kiran shifted as he glanced around. His calloused bare feet stung, pricked from ragged rocks, but did not bleed. He didn't often dream, these days. When he did, it was of violence. Of gore-streaked monsters, of viscera spilling out onto cold, hard stone. Of himself.

"How soft you've become." A familiar voice came from behind him, precise and disdainful. He turned to face it—in the distance, mountains rose up from the ground, gnarled claws ripping into the sky above.

A boy stood across from him, a few feet away. He wore blood on his cheeks and soot on the bare skin of his shoulders, and Kiran's face. His dark hair was tangled and dusted with ash and gunpowder, unbound and wild around his face. Blood tipped ragged fingernails, dripping crimson onto dry, packed dirt. He looked every bit the part, the feral, ruthless son of war.

This was not a dream he had ever had before.

It was disorienting, to see himself like a reflection in blood. They had the same fine-boned face, hollow-cheeked and haunted, the same air of a saint that had burnt away to nothing and held the ashes himself.

And yet, they were not the same. It was a twisted, imperfect projection—it was him, but not all of him. This was his savage divinity laid bare.

The boy sneered, a ripple in the mirror. "Look how you gawk. Do I repulse you? Are you that revolted by yourself?"

He inhaled slowly, but his chest was tight. This was an airless world, an empty one. The dead did not need to breathe. "Are you here to mock me?"

"Perhaps," he said, asperous. "Or perhaps I am here to mourn what I have become." The god took a step closer, stone shattering under his feet, and raised a hand. His fingers grasped Kiran's chin with a bruising tightness, leaving streaks of blood on his skin. "Look at you. Rotted with your own weakness."

His other hand crept over his chest, over the cotton of his robes. "I could cut your heart out, and you would let me. I doubt you would even notice until after it had stopped beating. Do you understand what I mean to tell you?"

"No," he whispered, and it came out a rasp. He hated the quaver in his voice, how he loathed and feared himself in equal amounts. And yet, this was the truest version of himself. This was his divine essence, what had burst alive in the flames after his mortal heart had burned away to ashes. He had not been born soft—he had learned, pieced together old memories and tried to recreate it in stuttering, distorted forgeries. But gentleness had never come easily to him, despite his lingering mortal hope. It was not as if the boy was wrong—it made him weak, and he had always known it.

The god rocked back on his heels, scraping his gaze across his face. "Go native if you wish. Let their mortal love—stained by ignorance, as you well know—wash away your clarity of mind. Indulge in the illusion that they are capable of caring for you. I will not stop you—I doubt I could, even if I tried."

"But," he said softly, leaning in so his voice was overwarm against the shell of his ear, "Do not forget yourself. That world is not for you. And if you remain like this, soft and frail as an infant, you risk the lives of those around you far more than you risk your own." His mouth twisted sharply. "In their world, kindness is repaid. In ours, it exposes vulnerability. Do not forget which one you belong to. They will not wait for you to learn."

The words rolled through him, acrid and true. They felt like poison, felt like ancient secrets and hidden, suppressed vitriol. Ink swirling through clear, still waters. "Who?"

The line of his mouth was a knife. "Even if I were to say their name, the *sankhili* would distort the sound. It is unlikely you will even remember this conversation when you wake. I can only hope my warning will linger, that you will act with some measure of caution. But I am not optimistic."

He watched him for a moment, that acerbic silence souring the air, before Kiran realized he meant for him to speak. He exhaled, and asked, as evenly as he could, "Why do you hate me?"

The god's eyes glittered with fire. But when he spoke, there was a cold amusement to the words. "I don't. I am afraid, just as you are afraid. It is simply that we fear separate things."

Kiran knew what he feared, the knowledge of it intimate and hollowing. And, looking into his own eyes, smooth with primeval wrath, he thought he might understand his other fear.

Before he could voice it, the boy stepped backward, a deliberate, graceful gesture that held faint unease. "Heed my words, *naiyin*. Before it is too late."

He felt empty, unsteady. It had been a long time since someone had called him that.

The god waved his hand in a practiced gesture and disappeared into smoke. In its wake, the air smelled faintly of iron.

Seconds later, another presence replaced him.

He had thought he knew true fear. The notion of it seemed unbearably naive now, a child presuming to know the depths of the universe after seeing the moon rise once.

It came like his memories had when they had first begun to return—sensation emptied of meaning, a throbbing, wordless sense of dread.

Kiran turned to face the other end of the battlefield. Someone stood in front of him, a cruel, ugly piece of power sculpted to resemble something person-shaped. In the distance, the sea crashed against the rocks, ceaseless and violent.

He couldn't breathe—his chest was filled with blood, with bile. It dripped down his skin. It coated his heart, oily and black. He was not flesh at all, only a suggestion of it, only a vessel for poison. Terror carved him into tepals, and scattered them on dry, cracking soil.

The figure smiled—they existed without a face, and yet he knew, instinctually, that they were smiling. They smiled, and it cut into the world, split the soft flesh of reality and let it bleed.

"Wake," they said.

Kiran opened his eyes. The room was dark and empty; the glow of the waning gibbous moon cast everything in stark relief. There was no spectrum of soft grays—the world existed entirely in light and the absence of it.

He sat up fluidly, unthinking, and leaned forward so his hands laid flat on the cold wood of the coffee table.

Divinity was a ghost in his bones. He curled one hand into a fist and then extended the other, drawing symbols on the wood gracelessly. He did not need to tell his body what to do—it knew, just as it knew fear, as it knew wrath. And he sat there for hours, hunched in a smooth arc, until dawn broke and he slumped, exhausted; index finger crooked as it continued to trace a circle, and a line that cut through it.

21
ENESMAT

Viro left the next morning with little pageantry, but pageantry nonetheless. He was dressed in full uniform, though he'd opted out of the more flamboyant decorations the more ostentatious military leaders were fond of. That taste for flair had long since left him, and in any case, Kiran felt like riding off to the battlefield, possibly toward death, wasn't the best occasion to celebrate.

The king shook hands with the palace officials, ministers and diplomats and envoys, holding a brief, polite conversation with Galen as Lucius tried not to ogle him. The other boy had always had a morbid fascination with Viro, as though he were a scientific specimen. *The Rage of the Lost Youth,* labeled with ink on cleanly cut parchment.

Surprisingly, he acknowledged Suri, taking the time to shake her hand. Odd that they would become equals this close to the end, he thought, and then chided himself for the bitterness of it. Was it a victory, if he had succeeded in averting one vision of death and destruction only for them all to be doomed by another? Perhaps this was the gods' sense of humor.

In the vision of that dawn on the hill, he had been given something frustratingly detailed with absolutely no context. Here, he was given even less; simply the sensation of metal piercing skin and carving through flesh, the suggestion of blood, ragged breaths in the distance. He could not know where it took place, who died, only that odd, pervasive sense of *wrongness* he had felt all those years before, and the sinking knowledge it would result from the king's departure.

Viro paused by Tarak. The captain refused to look him in the face, keeping his gaze on his shoulders. They did not speak, but for a moment, Kiran thought the king might've smiled faintly.

Then he moved past the captain and lingered by him. Kiran held his gaze, did not look away even as the other boy examined him, as if looking for a some specific emotion, a hidden message.

But there was nothing more to say; Kiran wanted him to stay, and he would not, and they both knew this. And yet, driven by a sudden macabre, he leaned forward and pitched his voice low. "At least *try* to stay alive."

Viro smiled, a thin, sharp thing directed outward. "I will."

He smiled back, or tried to—it was frail, sadder than it was amused.

And then he was gone, the gates of the city shut behind him. There were troops with him, guards and reinforcements and extra supplies, but he could not help but suspect that none of them would be of any help when Viro truly needed it.

Even before the crowd had fully dispersed, Kiran found himself turning away, walking back to the palace. He felt sick to his stomach—a part of him wished he had swallowed his pride, had bound Viro in manacles or simply yelled at him until the words had gotten through his thick, impenetrable skull.

He let that strained, self-deprecating regret guide him, and he wandered through the palace aimlessly before finally ascending the north tower and pausing in front of the aviary. He rooted around for the key beneath the loose brick, but it was not there, and the door was cracked open slightly—someone had already entered. Gently, he opened it further, shutting it softly behind him.

Suri was leaned against the bars lining the platform leading out to the aviary windows. She had opened them slightly, just enough that the room wasn't quite as stuffy as usual, airy with petrichor and ozone. She jerked her head toward the dark, cloudy sky, slouched against the metal. "A storm is coming."

"Hopefully, Viro avoids the worst of it," he said lightly, but her gaze was heavy, uncharacteristically soft, as if she could see his worry as clearly as if he'd painted it on his face. He forced himself to look away. "What brought you here?"

She lifted her shoulders in a shrug and descended the stairs, crossing the column in the middle of the room so she stood by him. "It is… peaceful up here. Quiet. And the view is beautiful. As I am sure you know."

"I do," he said, rueful, and the words brought back years of memories, of stolen moments beside the aviary windows. The silence of this world at night, the lovely, dark chill of it, the knowledge that there was life around him—that the world was not just blood and steel and funeral pyres.

A shrill caw interrupted them, cutting through the silence that always seemed to blanket the aviary when Kiran entered. The windows nudged open further at the insistence of an occupied kagha, who slipped through the gap and arced over them, landing, surprisingly, on Suri's wrist, half outstretched as if she had subconsciously expected this.

Though he could not believe that she had. She was bloodless and trembling, the fingers of her other hand raised to pet the kagha and yet still in the air, unwilling to go through with the act. There was a folded piece of cloth tied to the bird's left foot, a scar right below it.

"It's for me," she whispered. And then, stricken, she raised her gaze to Kiran's. "But I did not send them anything—this is—this is…" she trailed off, frowning down at the kagha. "This is not related to my… my assignment."

"If they are invading," he said, the words sour and burning even as he spoke them, "They may want you to leave beforehand. To avoid getting caught in the massacre."

A small, bitter smile flickered on her face. "I doubt they would care. And yet…" still frowning, she reached down and untied the small piece of folded cloth from the bird's foot. She nudged the bird and it flew upward, returning to its place among the rows of nearly identical kaghas.

Suri made a strange, choked noise and he glanced away from the birds. He had not thought it possible, but she looked even more pale, the thin piece of cloth shaking in her hands. She backed away from him until her back hit the column at the center of the room, and she slid down it, eyes wide and empty.

He crouched down beside her, tentatively placing his hand on hers. It was cold—most were to Kiran, yet he could tell that there was something unnatural about this clammy, fear-wrought cold.

She looked up at him, lips parted as if to speak. Instead, she handed him the silk missive. He squinted at it in the storm-dimmed light of the aviary. From what he could see, it was a stream of written Najan, yet, effectively, it was all gibberish. He had read enough Najan literature to recognize the structure of the sentences, the syllables, but every single word was meaningless.

"It is a code," Suri said, oddly remote. "My… My brother and I made it when I was younger, when I went on my first assignment that required us to communicate long distance."

He stared at the not-quite words, then glanced back at her. "What does it say?"

She heaved a single, shuddering breath. Her mouth twitched to the side, faintly amused. "He says my parents plan to kill me."

For a moment, Kiran did not breathe. "How does he know?"

"He overheard them talking with another brother of mine, one who, in their words, apparently, 'had not deigned to form as close a relationship with me'," she said. That self-deprecating, resigned smile had not left her. "The plan, it seems, had always been for me to kill the king and for them to invade—and then depose me and place one of my brothers on the throne. Anyu—the one who has sent the message—had been their first choice, but I suppose they ascertained he wouldn't… support it."

Kiran's blood felt like ice in his veins. "And now that you have stopped communications…"

She let out a harsh, humorless laugh. "Once they reach the capital, I am as good as dead." Her mouth twisted in a ghost of anger. "Even after all I have done for them, I am little more than a loose thread that must be tied up. An issue to resolve."

When he spoke, he tried his best to keep his voice steady, even though it felt as though the world was slowly beginning to crumble around him. "You must run, then."

"What?" she blinked, shock washing over her face. "Run?"

He forced a faint smile. "You have to leave the country. So they cannot find you. So they cannot kill you." Kiran rubbed his thumbs against the backs of her hands. "It may not be ideal, but at least you will not have to bend to their demands. You can live out your life the way you care to."

Suri's expression shifted, darkening. Taking in all the possibilities that now lay in front of her, there was nothing hopeful about the furrow between her eyebrows. "Leave?"

"Yes," he said, trying his best to sound encouraging. He tried to imagine how Suri would navigate the cities of the rest of the kingdoms on her own, and immediately knew she would take to it like a fish in water. "Leave Athri. It is not as if you ever meant to marry Viro, anyway."

Kiran had said it partially because he had thought it might bring back a spark of humor to her face, vanquish that dark, pensive apprehension. But she only frowned, lifting her gaze to his face. "And what about you?"

Frost was a disease, a thin, creeping layer over his own heart. In his bemusement, he let go of her hands. "What about me?"

Suri's hands dipped down and grasped his own again, holding them tight. They were still cold, but not as much as before. "What will you do?"

"You know what I will do," he said gently, but the words came out soft, wavering. "In five days, remember? I will die."

His voice broke on the last word, and he hated himself for it—hated his own weakness. The gods had given him nearly eighteen years, and still he yearned for more, still he could not help but wish he was meant for something more than fire-kissed blood on stone and the promise of prosperity. But if this was the role he was given, the fate he'd been handed, then he had no choice but to go along with their wishes. If there was one thing prophecy had taught him, it was that fate did not care who you were, did not care what you loved and how you loved it. The intensity of your love, of your existence, were of no use to anyone—except perhaps those who would one day tell your story.

Suri pulled a hand from his and held it against his face, pulling him out of his reverie. For a moment, he stared back at her. Her copper eyes were alive with anger and defiance. "Come with me."

Now he was the one unsteadied. He could feel himself being slowly unmoored, set adrift in this endless ocean. "What?"

"Come with me," she repeated. The words seemed to buoy her, animate her. She leaned forward, hand still chilled against his cheek. "I know—I know you do not want to die. Come with me."

There was a rhythm to the way she spoke, a lovely, intoxicating cadence to it. And more than that, the promise of the words themselves allured him. The thought of leaving this death—bought and paid for in his blood, long before today—far behind, where the gods could not reach him.

And for what? a contemptuous voice in his head asked. *Athri will die, for your remaining decade of peace? The people will starve and suffer and live on in stuttering misery, just so you can escape a death you have already cheated once?*

If he left now, he would be dooming them to a fate worse than death, to an unstable, fortune-drained life that would only grow worse and worse until the fire in his blood finally consumed him. They didn't deserve that, and he knew it as well as he knew his own heart.

But do you? What have you ever done to deserve death?

"Kiran," Suri said, curling her fingers into his cheek, the touch unbearably gentle. The hope had faded from her expression, but the defiance and anger remained. But it was a touch sad now, as if she knew what he would say.

"I cannot," he whispered, turning away. Even now, he could not bring himself to move her hand from his cheek, and so he reached up with his own and placed it over hers. "You know I cannot leave. I cannot condemn them."

Her mouth twisted downward, bitter but unsurprised. "I thought you would say that. I knew you would. Yet it still hurts to hear it." She dropped the hand from his cheek, but his skin stung with the memory of it. She picked up the letter from where it had fallen to the ground and examined it with a long, weary exhale. "If I am to leave, I must do it soon. Before the week is up. And we must get rid of this."

Kiran smiled, sharp but not without humor. "I think I know a place where we could do that."

He allowed himself a single indulgence, taking her hand in his own and holding it tight as they descended the north tower. They did not acknowledge the touch, for to do that was to acknowledge it was forbidden—to acknowledge it was something they could not truly have.

And so he led her up toward the temple, to the brazier that had burned all night in the midst of his unanswered, desperate prayers, and he took the letter from her hands and laid it in the fire. Carefully, so they could see the ink swirl and burn. So that they could see the cloth crumble into ash.

Suri burst into the war room. She had not been able to sleep all through the night. Anyu's careful print felt seared into her brain—*I wish I had more stories left to give you, but I don't, so you must go find one of your own.* Exhilaration and terror warred in her chest; she had dreamt of this freedom, hungered for it, and yet she could not help but think of whether she too doomed Athri by leaving it—she was only one person, a single soldier, and she would die if she stayed, whether on the front lines or by Rohit's hands. But to simply leave without a second thought—she couldn't fathom it. An assassin's work had always been, in a kind of way, a coward's work. But she did not feel like an assassin anymore.

And then, sometime in the early morning, she thought of something. Part of her dismissed it as sleep deprivation-induced insanity, an illogical notion. But the more she considered it, the more she realized that perhaps it might work.

Kiran was not in the cottage, or in the garden, or in either of the temples—he had conspicuously avoided the city since Viro's departure, as if he knew how it would end, and could not bear to be confronted with buildings he had seen crumble once before. So Suri had taken to checking every single room in the palace—earning her mild irritation under the guise of politeness from the officials and servants already in said rooms.

In hindsight, perhaps she should've suspected he would've gone to the war room. He had lived through the first war standing beside the captain and the boy king. Even if he was fated to die before it began, it was not truly surprising that he meant to stand beside them before the second.

Tarak's head was bent over a stack of correspondence, his dark hair falling into his face. When he glanced up at the sound of her entrance, it cut his gaze into shards, obscuring the whole of his expression. His eyes were dark and bloodshot, and he looked strangely gaunt in the candlelight. He smiled at her, but it didn't quite meet his eyes; there was an intense, strained fatigue in the lines of his face. "Your Highness."

Kiran sat beside him at the expansive desk at the back of the room, studying the parchment with jagged focus. His eyes narrowed as they met hers, black eyes flashing with a pensive suspicion. Like he knew why she was here. He likely did.

"I need to speak with you," she said, breathless. "Now."

He shot Tarak a sharp, concerned glance, but the other boy waved him off. "You have been fussing over me all day and night. Go help the princess."

Suri avoided his questioning gaze as he reluctantly followed her out past the corridor, into the sodden courtyard. The packed soil of the land surrounding the palace was damp and soft to the touch, from days of incessant, tumultuous storms. She frowned at the crowd and noise, a result of impending war. "Is it possible we could meet somewhere quieter?"

Kiran inclined his head. "The aviary?"

She shook her head. "Quieter than that. Somewhere no one would think to find you."

He held her gaze, thoughtful. Then he led her out of the palace up to the cottage. Shutting the door behind him, he nodded toward the empty room. "Only a handful of people know of its existence, and they would not interrupt." He folded his arms. "Suri, if you are here to persuade me to leave again, I told you the first time—"

Suri spread her hands in a placating gesture. "But what if you ask Avya?"

He drew back, as if struck. Warily, he said, "Ask him? For what?"

"You said your death will restore the balance in Athri," she said, trying to keep her voice steady. In reality, the memory of that night still held her tight with longing and dread. "That if you sacrifice yourself as the living proof of his wrath, Avya will bless the nation again."

"Yes," he said slowly, "But what does that have to do with any of this?"

She leaned forward. Hope was a destructive, uncaring burn in her chest, a hollow warmth. "Can you not simply ask him to bless them without your death? If his blessing—his approval—is what the nation needs, then can it not be just as powerful as your blood?"

Kiran's expression wavered faintly. "He would not agree."

"How do you know?" she demanded. "Have you ever asked?"

His complexion was ashen, the color of dusted soil. "It is not just his blessing. My existence is imbalanced, unstable. Chaos begets chaos. And even if—even if you are right, and the nation could survive without my blood, there is no reason for him to agree. To save a single, mortal life—to extend it for a decade more. He gains nothing."

Suri heard none of it. "So you have not asked. For seventeen years—you have not asked."

There was a spark of true, lasting terror in his gaze. Perhaps, she thought, he had been too afraid of what the god would say. Perhaps it was easier to live in resignation than to die broken from hope.

Finally, he exhaled, looking away. "It could backfire, Suri. It could end up harming them instead of healing. And that is only if he agrees. I will die soon enough, anyway. There is no value in doing this."

He was still leaned against the door, fingers crooked as if he meant to leave at any moment. She rose and crossed the room, tilted his face down forcibly to meet her gaze.

"Tell me you want to die," she said, steely. "Tell me you care nothing for life. If you do, I will not force you into anything."

Everything about his gaze spoke of mourning, of stained yearning. A desire for everything he could not have, a hundred wishes spoken without sound and discarded in the dark of night. Softly, he said, "I cannot."

She made a frustrated, strangled sound. "Then ask him. *Please.*"

"I cannot," he repeated, trying to look away. But Suri turned his head toward hers, his skin overwarm under her fingers. They were close enough that they could have kissed and no one would have known. Another meaningless secret they had kept close.

"You cannot?" she asked. "Or you will not?"

His expression hardened at the king's words. But fury—fear, and hope, and something that resembled a faded, burnt-out suggestion of love—had blazed to life in her chest, and she would not let go of this simply because he was too afraid to face the possibility of wonders. She thought she had some understanding now, of the boy king's contemptuous anger toward Kiran's tendency toward overwork, his simple acceptance of his own death.

"You live as though you are already dead," she whispered. Each word sunk into him, cut through his heart with clean, sharp blades. "You live as though your life is nothing but a prerequisite for death, for true purpose. Have you ever fought to stay alive? Have you ever allowed yourself to think of life as something to love?"

He swayed under her grasp, shaken visibly, but his dark eyes were inscrutable. After a moment, he raised his hands and pulled hers from his face, lowering them between them. Without meeting her gaze, he said, strangely bitter, "He has not spoken with me for the better part of two moons. But let us go, and see if he cares to keep me alive."

Kiran turned, letting go of her hands, and held open the door for her. She shivered—somehow, in the time they had spent inside, the weather had become even worse; thunder rumbled in the distance and lightning limned the city below in intermittent flashes of bright white.

The braziers of the temple had been lit, but in the damp, electric morning, the fires burned low, sputtering and flickering. Kiran ran a hand through them, checking the temperature, and made a face before turning back. "I do not know how he will react to me…" he paused, looking for the words. "Bringing a friend. For your own safety, I suggest you stand a good distance away."

Suri tilted her head in a question, but he didn't elaborate. She backed away until she stood at the very entrance to the temple.

Kiran turned his back on her, but she could still see his hands trembling as he lit a match and dropped it into a golden bowl at the center of the altar, covering the carved icon. He reached into the bowl and lifted the fire out, slowly lowering himself so he was kneeling before the altar.

For a few moments, he was still; his hands, wreathed in the amber flames, hovered over the bowl, his head bowed over the stone. And then, too quickly for her to intervene, the fire fell from his fingers and his head tilted back at an unnatural angle, the muscles of his neck taut as he slumped against the altar.

Kiran was too shocked to feel pleased or afraid.

The world, at the very least, was familiar—he was in the cottage, perched on the edge of that old wicker chair the captain had made for him as a child. Avya was stretched out on the settee, his feet pressed against the opposite arm.

He looked as he always had—a broad, dark-haired young man with eyes like faded embers. But there was something strange, different, about him now, and after a moment, he realized the god was unsmiling.

He registered, distantly, that his mouth was hanging open, and made a formidable effort to shut it. There were so many things he wanted to say, so many things he *needed* to say. And yet, he found himself asking, "Why were you silent until now?"

Even he could not help a small, inward wince at the plaintiveness of his tone, as if he were still a child looking for guidance and validation. But Avya simply looked away, a certain sadness coloring his expression. "There are things even I cannot meddle in. These past few moons hinged on your decisions, independent of any advice I could have given you."

Something about his timbre chilled Kiran. "What does that mean? Why is now any different?"

"It isn't, not truly," he said, pulling himself up against the arm of the settee. "But I know this decision is one you will not allow yourself to make without my counsel. So I am temporarily ignoring my responsibilities."

"Your responsibilities to ignore me," he said, mouth dry.

"Precisely," he said, lips quirking in a half-smile. At Kiran's clean lack of expression, he sighed, looking away. "I know what you mean to ask, even if you are too afraid to put it into words. You want to know if I will bless Athri without your death—if I will allow you to escape with that princess of yours."

Though he spoke with a kind of teasing amusement, the phrasing of it embarrassed him, and he looked away, ears burning. Avya laughed warmly, but when he spoke, his voice had lost all trace of its previous humor. "How do you feel about humans?"

Kiran met his gaze, faintly shocked, but the other looked to be serious. "About humans?"

Avya nodded, leaning back against the upholstery. "There is this running joke among the gods, you see, about the cruelty of humanity. Their capacity for self-destruction. And you're torn between both worlds, with enough god for them to see you as something to be set apart, and yet human enough to feel the constraints of your own existence. But you want to stay among them for a few years longer. Why is that?"

There was no easy way to respond, but Avya stared at him, fully expectant that he could and would. Kiran shifted on the chair, pulling up his knees. "I suppose… I would like to die on my own terms. I would like the freedom to live among them as something more than a bridge, a tool."

"Are you not afraid?" he prompted, as if he could see Kiran's deepest, darkest fears, and had no qualms with spreading them upon the table beside them like playing cards. "Perhaps I should not, but I fear for you. I do not deny you should be given the opportunity to die on your own terms, but I cannot understand why you would want to stay there longer than you truly must. Are you not afraid that, in the end, they will disappoint you?"

"A little, perhaps," he said, frowning. "But I believe in their inherent good. I wouldn't have survived as long as I have without the kindness of those around me."

"After all you have lost at their hands?"

"I lost my parents at yours," he returned. For a moment, he was afraid the words would anger the god, but the skin around his eyes only crinkled in consideration.

"True enough," he conceded. "It may be simply that I worry too much for you. The other gods certainly think so." He gazed over at him, thoughtful, then continued, "I do not think this is a good idea. I have known humanity for far longer than you have, and though I care for them, I can't trust them. But I trust you, and if you truly think the chance to live out your remaining years beside them will free you, somehow, then I will allow it."

Kiran's chest tightened suddenly, and he realized it was the sharp pain of suffocation—he had forgotten to breathe. "Why?"

The god smiled, and there was a fond, rueful edge to it. "I can't see the future like you, but I would like you to have the option of a happy ending, if fate will allow it. Even if it is hard-won."

And then Avya waved his hand abruptly and the scene dissipated, the cottage turning to smoke around them.

Suri was shaking him, her mouth caught in the middle of his name. When she saw that he had regained consciousness, she leaned back, mouth set in a grim line. She inclined her head in astonishment. "What was that?"

He swallowed hard and looked away, unable to meet her gaze. *Are you not afraid that, in the end, they will disappoint you?* He took a moment to steady his voice, and then said, "An audience."

There was a beat of silence, and then she asked, "What did he say?"

"He said—" his voice broke and he cleared his throat. It had been so warm, so comfortable in that strange, dream-like land of divinity. But here—there was no playing at softness, at the notion of peace. The rain splashed against the temple floor in fat, heavy drops and dripped from his skin, chilling him. Kiran forced himself to look up at Suri, to hold her concerned, faintly hopeful gaze. "He said I may go. That I… I may live."

Beside him, the enduring fire in the brazier flickered once, twice, and then gave out.

Viro knew something was wrong even before the messenger arrived.

It was the same rolling, consuming nausea, the same barbed sense of wrongness he had felt nine years ago. As if his blood had turned to broken glass in his veins.

Yet, as much as it was intuition, it was also a logical sense of discomfort. They had arrived in Karur the previous night, and yet none of the villagers had reported any signs of a Najan invasion, not yet. Apart from occasional attacks by bandits, they had spent the past few moons relatively untouched. None of which fit at all with the message they had been given days before, from a chief Viro knew well—that he trusted, but couldn't find in the encampment.

What if the message had not come from the chief at all? a small, insidious voice in his head whispered. *What if this was all an elaborate trick, hinging on your bullish impudence?*

The idea was not without merit; he was not known for his patience, for his ability to coldly, savagely execute his own plans. He had always acted with his heart, even when it scarred him. But something about this felt different, crueler than a trick. It felt, he thought, like a death; a supernova held in the hollows of a heart.

And so, when the messenger did burst into the encampment, eyes fearful and shocked, Viro did not feel surprise as much as he did a sharp, bitter kind of amusement.

Of course Kiran was right, he thought. *Of course there is an attack on some other part of the kingdom and I cannot help, stuck here in the borderlands.*

Then the messenger spoke, and reality fractured into meaningless shards.

The words did not set in the first time, nor the second. They could've repeated them a hundred times, shouted them from the rooftops, written them into the fabric of the earth itself, and Viro knew he would not have understood them.

Distantly, he knew the messenger was still speaking—people were asking him for orders, for a plan of action. A plan of retribution. *Something.*

But there was nothing he had to say, nothing he could give. The words—the sharp, hollowing truth of them—had emptied him completely. He had not felt anything similar to this in nine years, had sworn never to allow himself to feel like this again. Had founded his entire life on ensuring that. And yet here he was, on the edge of the fucking nation, his heart cracked and swollen.

"Your Majesty?" someone was saying, an edge of unease to their voice. "Should we return?"

Return? To where? To his body?

"No," he said, his voice unrecognizable to his own ears. It was something rough and emotionless, sandpaper against skin. "I will return alone. The rest of you continue watching the border."

And then another clamor began as they argued over who would accompany him to the palace, because there was no chance he could possibly return *completely* alone, and then who would stay? Where would they go? How would they divide up the troops?

Viro heard all of it and none of it. On the edge of this endless plain of nothingness, this sea of smooth, pale apathy, there was an imperceptible spark of emotion.

Time slowed to a crawl; the journey back was nearly unbearable, every second stretched into entire years, entire lifetimes. It fell short of being excruciating only because he felt none of it—there was absolute coldness in him, an odd, consuming frost. As though he watched from the eyes of another, still hidden in a cocoon of dyed cotton and stardust. Metamorphosis in reverse.

The city was silent when they returned; vaguely, he knew this was due to the fact that it was too late to be night, too early to be morning. But there was something sinister about it, a soft, whispering knowledge. The sound of shared grief, of old pity, the city's familiar rites of mourning.

Kiran met him beside the gates. His shoulders were bare, but he wasn't shivering. As if he had known when Viro would arrive—as if he had waited.

There was nothing warm in his gaze. No semblance of pity, no sign of kindness. It was anguish turned to steel and turned inward—the simple, clean break of bone into the soft flesh of a heart. Viro knew it, because he knew he looked the same way.

"Tell me they are wrong," he said, the words nothing but a thin, high rasp in the airless night. There was still some small, piteous part of him that held out hope—against all odds, it wished. With such raging, terrifying intensity, it wished.

Kiran's expression cracked visibly. He did not have to speak—there was nothing he could've said that would have conveyed the truth more effectively than that inability to continue.

"Where…" he could not finish the sentence. Kiran held out a hand toward the palace, and silently they returned. His pace was brisk but uneven, as if he had been on his feet for the greater part of the day. He paused in front of the room, glancing over at Viro with a reluctance, a pensive concern. And then he opened the door, and the world washed out into strange, arid silence.

It was not white noise; it was a complete lack of sound. As if he had entered another world, identical to their own save for the fact that sensation had long since disappeared. He could not feel his hands; he could not feel his own heart.

Viro walked up to the bed where they had lain his body. It was sparsely decorated, as he had always had it, with a single blanket and pillow. Stretched out upon the mattress, eyes fluttered shut as if he were only asleep, only unconscious, was Tarak.

He held out a hand to touch him—it was trembling so much it hurt to hold it up, hurt to move it, hurt to *think*—and brushed it against his cheek. Thinking back on it, he would wonder why he did that. He was so clearly dead—his skin held an odd, unnatural pallor, lips parted in a rigid facsimile of his familiar, strained smile. And yet, he reached out and held him.

His skin was cold to the touch, stiff under his fingers. The tactile knowledge of it was something stronger than words, stronger than logic. It found that tiny, insignificant drop of hope, and set it aflame.

22
LYNE

A wish, and nothing but a wish. That was the way her birthday began to seem as time flew past them, cracking open to reveal the hoarfrost of early winter. It felt like a dream, an old memory Suri recalled every now and then.

Kiran had changed again. Was it even possible to know someone like him, secrets tilted inward like the petals to some infinite, half-bloomed rose? There was no way to know. She dreamt of what lay at the pistil sometimes, and it was too saccharine for her to understand that they were nightmares until after, heaving on the bathroom tile. The stigma was always empty bullets and lullabies, always.

There was a jagged intensity to him now, but it held none of the blithe cheer that had laced his actions when he had first appeared. Languor was a distant, foreign notion—she hadn't seen him still in weeks. If he wasn't gardening, then he was in the kitchen, dicing vegetables and eating them raw. He had developed an alarming habit of cracking his knuckles incessantly, either for the sensation or the sound of it. It was the uneven, precipitous vigilance of a prey animal, deer in headlights, roadkill in motion.

When he toyed with the hilt of the kitchen knife, point up, eyes dull with familiarity, and she held out a hand to tentatively brush his shoulder, he might look at her with a measure of bemusement before glancing down at himself with surprise. She had always suspected that there was a kind of dissonance in his heart, but she hadn't thought he'd stick around long enough that she would have to watch it split him apart.

At night, he disappeared. Not for long, not forever. But she noticed regardless, the strain in her chest loosening and tightening like a cord between them. The innermost seal had been thread-thin for days now; this was something entirely separate, and she didn't dare put it to words.

Part of her—a small, foolish part that asked gods to tell her stories so they did not have to play at sleep—was convinced this was something that would pass, even as the rest warned her to stand back. Candle fire was always warm when first lit, after all. It never burned at first.

And so she decided to rope him into a holiday movie marathon the weekend after exams finished. Usually, she spent the first days of the winter break hanging out with the others or helping her grandmother restock the shop and deliver packages. But her grandmother had assured her she was fine on her own, Ellis had gone off the grid, Miya was at the beach with her aunt, Aza and Dai were at a family reunion, and even if any of them *had* asked, she wasn't sure if she would've agreed to leave the apartment.

If she was being entirely honest with herself, she was more concerned by Kiran's unease than she felt comfortable letting on. On more than one occasion, he had hopped over the wrought-iron edge of the balcony and stood on the inch-wide cement ledge, shoulders tense, staring down at streets silver and flashing with life with a distant scrutiny, a watery disdain.

When she proposed the movie marathon idea to him, stretched across the couch and toying with the television remote, he simply arched his eyebrows. He was standing on the back of the armchair, a lightbulb tucked into the crook of his elbow. His toes were loosely curled into the upholstery, unimpressed by the fall.

"Why?" he asked, terse, twisting in the lightbulb and jumping down soundlessly. Crossing the room in two steps, he threw open the curtains, saturating the room in sunlight. It seared and seared and Suri looked away, flipping through channels on the television.

She lingered on the movie marathon, contemplating the beginning of the first movie; three young sisters spoke to their parents in frustrated tones as they explained why their vacation had been canceled last minute. "Why not? I thought you liked human movies."

He stared through her, still for just a moment—a glitch, nothing more. Then he moved to pull a dog-eared copy of an old paperback off the top of the bookshelf, brushing off dust with his index finger. It gathered and puffed into the stagnant, dead air of the apartment. "How long is it?"

Flicking through the television guide, she made a show of checking until the next normal program—a rerun of an old gameshow at three in the morning. "Eighteen hours?"

"Eighteen hours," he repeated, dry. He shrugged, a jagged, violent movement, blowing on bruised knuckles. "Why not?"

Why not? Their friendship was ridiculously incidental. Suri wondered how her autumn would've turned out if she had slept through the knock on her door that night, and he slotted himself into the gaps on the couch, leaning back against the opposite arm. She watched as he made an admirable effort to keep himself still. She figured it was half out of an attempt at respect and half out of pride, a puerile challenge with himself.

He lasted all the way through the first movie, gaze glassy and disinterested as the children danced through a winter wonderland, peppermint staining their tongues. The second began, and he exhaled slowly before taking out a thick silver coin and passing it over his knuckles, soundless and flickering.

She shifted, and it slipped out of his fingers, brushing her ankle on the way down. On screen, the family's holiday dinner had been ruined by their golden retriever. Chastened, the dog pouted at them over spilled mashed potatoes.

"Sorry," he said abruptly, retrieving the coin. "I just—"

"Can't sit still?" she cut in wryly without looking away from the screen.

Kiran watched her for a second, as if trying to discern whether it was a joke or not. She wasn't entirely sure herself. Finally, he frowned—it cut across his face. "Is it that obvious?"

Laughter burst out of her, unbidden. She couldn't tell him the truth—that he dripped tension like gasoline, that he moved as if he meant to rend—so instead, she said, "You need to unwind."

He gazed at her, faintly disdainful and unappreciative of having his own words thrown back at him. "And this—" he gestured toward the screen; the golden retriever was on a journey to find himself, paws deep in gray snow— "Is going to help me?"

"What will?" she pressed, and there was a note of true curiosity in it. It felt too much like desperation for her taste. "Are you demeaning Dusky and his quest?"

His dark hair was bound with a Dai hand-me-down—a banana clip with a smile drawn on it. A piece came loose and hung in his face, a thin stream of smoke. He did not smile, but his expression was shaped like he meant to. "I would never. I just don't know that the sugar and spice collection is going to help all that much."

"Exactly," Suri said, reaching forward and taking the coin from his fingers as he poised it to fly upward. He made a noise of irritation, anger without appetite, but did not take it back. "You don't know. It might. Try."

It was an imperative; resigned, he leaned back, and they watched the rest of the movie in near silence. She laughed enough for the both of them, suppressed, embarrassing giggles she only allowed him to hear because they'd already slipped out accidentally in the past. There was no salvaging her reputation, not with him.

Dinner time came and went. His stare drilled into the side of her head, insistent and pleading. She relented, and he pulled himself off the couch to go fiddle with things in the kitchen. Moments later, there was the distinctive sound of metal whistling amiably through the air.

A little over half an hour later—on screen, a teenage girl, splotchy faced with the weight of her own emotions, confessed to her crush as the first snow fell—he reappeared with two plates of some stir-fried dish with sliced poultry and vegetables. The first bite burned her tongue, but she kept eating. It tasted like cloves and winter.

Despite his initial protests, Kiran had grudgingly relaxed. She doubted he would've admitted to it if she had asked, but she knew him as well as a heart could know a knife without bleeding out, savage and bacchanalian. There were small things—his shoulders were not so sharp; sometimes he might exhale and it would not rattle unevenly. Contentment still flickered on the horizon, a mirage of an oasis in a suffocating desert. At the very least, he didn't look like he was being held at gunpoint anymore. Small victories.

She played with the idea of asking what had made him so agitated in the first place, but she doubted he would give a straight answer. Even when he was feeling cheerful, even when the question was an impersonal one, it was rare that he tossed out explicit, clear information. Even now.

Suri asked anyway. Impulse control was not her strong suit. He regarded her over his empty plate—bluish light from the television turned the streaks of oil and spice greasy and murky looking. "I don't know."

"You don't *know?*" she repeated, raising her eyebrows.

"I don't remember," he clarified, leaning to the side to place his plate on the coffee table. He rubbed at his eyes, distorting the shape of them momentarily. "I couldn't explain it if I tried. It's—" he broke off, snapping his fingers as if he'd reached an epiphany. "Have you seen the dark?"

"Yes?" she said, cautious and bemused. "When I turn off the lights?"

Kiran shook his head. "Not that kind—real darkness. I would've thought you might've seen it. It's in caves, sometimes."

She had—her grandmother had taken her to Enesmat when she was five, for some kind of religious rite she had little knowledge of and even less interest in performing. On the way to the temple, they had passed by a chasm. It had looked like a god had clawed through the soil and stone and emptied it out. She still remembered the pure, ink-deep blackness. The darkness, yawning.

"I've seen it," she amended abruptly. He didn't question the validity of her knowledge.

"Imagine stepping into it," he said, his voice going low and smooth as it did when he told stories. His hands rose and took hers, overwarm to the touch. There was a ritualism to this, an intimate, unspoken sanctity. "Passing over your skin, feeling you, *knowing* you. Malice given form and talons."

Suri shivered, the low, hollow timbre of his voice scraping over her skin. "And?"

"I remember it," he whispered, and it was a little like a confession. "It is all I can remember, and you will ask what I remember it *from,* and the truth of it is that I don't know. It's all the sensation of it, only the sensation of it. I can't feel anything else."

I can't feel anything else. Shadows crawled over her heart, but her hands felt safe, tethered. She said, "That sounds terrifying."

The corners of his mouth turned up, too quick for it to be practiced, in the first smile of the day. The first smile of the week—the first smile in gods knew how long. Surprise and pride warred in her, edged by a chastising cynicism. As if it had to be said, he affirmed, "It isn't pleasant. But you were right. This is helping a little, I think."

The words made her happier than they had any right to. "I told you. Movie magic."

He tilted his head in a question before blinking. "Oh, yes. The movies are helpful, too."

She didn't know what he meant by that, but before she could ask, he took her plate and reached for his and went to wash them. The end credits continued, ceaseless, and the introduction to the next movie played. Carols echoed in her head; she'd hear them for weeks.

By the time he'd returned, the movie was well underway. It reminded her a little of that corny classic they'd watched with the others months ago, the couple who'd met as children and died as adults and loved each other the entire time. This one took the idea a little further—it spoke of a pair of soulmates, destined for one another from birth, who didn't meet until they were in their twenties. There were a hundred near-misses, of course, brief non-meetings where they slid past each other, unaware. But once they did, it was love at first sight, bittersweet and syrupy with the heft of fate.

Kiran watched it with the same mild interest as he did all the others, cheek pushed into his fist. She nearly couldn't bear his apathy, his clean lack of scorn. She couldn't, actually. "Doesn't it amuse you?"

"What?" he glanced over at her, caught off guard. "Why would it?"

She gestured toward the screen—the characters gazed into each other's eyes, rain soaking cloth to their skins. Reality bent around them, sheltering them from obstacles and from what she assumed could only be hypothermia. "True love. Soulmates. The entire franchise of marketable romance. I thought gods would find it stupid, or… I don't know. Hopeless? Since there's no such thing."

He held her gaze for a few beats, the line of his mouth curving downward, thoughtful. Then he plucked the remote control from where it rested between her thigh and the back of the couch and paused the movie, sliding off wordlessly and disappearing into the hallway.

After a few minutes, he returned with two skeins of red yarn and a knife. The knife made sense—she thought he might want to get buried with a knife, if gods ever got buried. The yarn was something of a mystery. He sat down in his old spot, pulling his knees up and folding his legs and gesturing for her to do the same. She shunted her legs to the side and leaned forward, interested despite herself.

His gaze was sharp, assessing. "Why do you think there's no such thing? As soulmates, true love. Whatever you want to call it."

It wasn't what she expected him to ask, and she drew back. Tilting her head in consideration, she said, "Intuitively, I think it's silly. Looking at it this way, though—you said that reincarnation's a thing, right?"

"I said that a long time ago," he replied, faintly surprised.

"I know." The words came slowly, as if she were pulling them into life through amber. They flopped around in her mouth, damp from the trip and waiting. "If it's a thing—if none of us are ever really dead for that long—"

"You can be," he supplied, expression oddly shadowed. "You can choose not to reincarnate. It happens; souls tire."

Suri held his gaze, and it felt a little like an act of violence. "When they do, though. How can true love be real if everything depends on who you meet and when you meet them and if you happen to reincarnate at the same time as someone you think you might be able to love? How can *soulmates* be a real thing? It seems a little ridiculous."

"It does seem that way," he agreed, and she knew he was about to disprove her, but he wasn't sly and terrible about it. A smile flickered on and off his face. "The real answer is a little hard to believe, if I'm being honest. Oddly, fate is a romantic."

He leaned forward and unwound the skeins, gently teasing out two strands the length of his forearm. Kiran held them up, one after another. "This is person A, and this is person B. Do you want to name them?"

"Jane," she said, after a pause. "And Richard."

"Okay, Jane and Richard," he worried his bottom lip absently, drawing out more thread. "The yarn represents their lifelines in the river of rebirth. Souls are black, reflective like glass, but this is as close as I can get."

Kiran pulled the threads close to one another so that they touched at a single, tangential point. There was a precision to his movements, a careful rhythm. "So, Jane and Richard are soulmates. I'm going to borrow your terminology, because I don't have a better word for it in a language you're familiar with. They're soulmates, which isn't always romantic, but in their case, it is. And they fall deeply in love, it's all very beautiful and film-worthy. Following along?"

She nodded, and he glanced up and smiled at her, quick as a blink, before twisting the threads around each other so they were intertwined. He handed one of the ends to her, took the other and pulled, gesturing for her to do the same. The connection only tightened. When he spoke, he was markedly closer than he'd been before. "If you try to split them, it doesn't work—they're bound by heart, by soul. And it begins here—" he took the other end from her now, and braided them around one another, a rope of red yarn, "And it does not end, not ever. Death has no bearing on the soul."

He removed his knife and soundlessly cut through the rope, slashing through the intertwined threads in the middle of the braid. He held them up, angling the twisted threads so she could see them. Red wool fuzz drifted down his wrist. "A single death is just that one cut. The threads keep touching, their souls are still twined—that is fate's business, something different entirely."

He spoke of those lofty notions—death, fate—as if he knew them intimately, close friends he had gone to tea with. Suri wondered absently if he resented either of them.

"So," he continued, a smile coloring his voice, "Soulmates are a thing. And they work around the issue you mentioned—of meeting someone in the right lifetime, at the right time—because of it. Their souls are intertwined, which means they more often than not reincarnate into the same lifetime, with similar ages—or age gaps—from when they first met." Kiran dropped the threads, running a hand through his hair. "I've heard it said that this means they inherit the same issues from their past selves. But I don't know the validity of it; I've never seen it happen, not up close."

"Really?" she asked, picking up the threads and running a thumb over where they still twisted together. "Even after seventeen hundred years?"

"Even now," he said, wry. "My job doesn't lend itself to romantic escapades, or observing those on them."

Suri dropped the threads, and he picked them up, untangling them and wrapping them back into their respective skeins. She toyed with the ends of the cut pieces of yarn, still twisted around one another, and tied one around her wrist on a whim. His eyes tracked the movement, but he didn't say anything.

When he returned, she meant to ask him where the remote had gone. Instead, she said, "What's the word?"

He blinked. "What?"

"The word," she repeated; he took a seat beside her and procured the remote from the cushions, resuming the movie. The characters continued to stare into each other's eyes lovingly, confessing their undying affection as the world washed itself away. "You said there was a word for how it all works, in a language I don't know."

The tips of his ears flushed gold. "There's no practical use for it anymore. It's a dead language."

"I don't want to use it," she said, and it felt a little like an admission. Against her will, she could feel her cheeks pinking. "I just want to know, for the sake of knowing."

It was the truth, but not all of it. She wanted to know something that only he knew, some small, wondrous secret long forgotten by the dead and long forgotten by death. The mere thought of voicing this made the flush creep over her face. She could only hope he wasn't paying a great deal of attention.

Kiran had not looked away from her since she had first spoken—his gaze swept over her expression, scrutinizing and a little self-conscious. Eventually, he mumbled something, too quietly to properly hear.

"What?" she asked, leaning in closer. On screen, the rain stopped, and the clouds parted—the sky was glorious with color.

"*Uttriyasi*," he repeated, so softly she could barely hear him. He'd looked up; if she tilted to the right, their noses would touch. Realization rolled through them at the exact same moment and they drew back, too quickly for it to look smooth.

Suri rubbed the back of her neck awkwardly and forced herself to look over at the screen. She tasted the word in her mouth, tried to wrap her lips around it. It stumbled through her unevenly. *"Uttriyasi?"*

"Yeah," he said, smiling a little too much for it to be the truth. She glared, and he corrected, "A little heavier on the vowels. *Uttriyasi.*"

"Uttriyasi," she said again, and it came easier this time, and she said it twice more. It felt like the word held a kind of power in it, a power separate from its identity as a secret, love-stained and deathless. It tasted euphoric and rain-sweet. "What does it mean?"

Kiran made a face like he'd tasted something sour, but said, "There are multiple translations. The direct translation is *forever love.* But my favorite, personally, is *eternal heart.*"

She laughed a little, and he glared at her, nearly hurt. She reached forward and took his hand in hers; it seared her, but she couldn't find it in herself to care. Suri spoke without looking up, making a game out of playing with his fingers. She traced every individual scar with the pad of her thumb, trying her very best to be gentle. "It's just fitting. It feels like the sort of thing you would like." She paused, passing her thumb over one that arced across the palm of his hand, and then added, "I like it too. It's pretty."

He smiled in her periphery, and her chest tightened once; she dropped his hand, turning back to the still playing movie. But they were still close enough that they kept their meaningless connections, their ruinous touches. His toe brushed against her knee and it was all she thought of for the rest of the movie.

The next movie took them to the edge of midnight, and she managed to follow the plot a little more. After that, she wrapped herself in the dull blanket of her mild interest in the next movie, used it to fend off thoughts about using the boy like a pillow. Eighty percent of her was strongly in favor of the idea. Ninety percent.

Halfway through, he beat her to it. She didn't notice for a few moments, even though she'd registered the physical sensation of his head on her shoulder—strange, overwarm, but not unpleasant. She just stared at him, unthinking. Her head felt like someone had smashed it open with a sledgehammer and mucked around in the red gooey parts.

She could feel her heartbeat in her bones, could feel his, too. She wasn't even sure which one was which—neither of them sounded like a song anymore. Or maybe they both did. Maybe they'd twined, and now it was the same song, a melody that carried in the soft, sweet night air. There was no way to know.

Wake him, she thought, and immediately felt cruel for thinking it. Of course she couldn't wake him. It was a sobering realization, if only because it meant the inverse was true—she couldn't wake him, so for a little bit, they would have to stay like this. Already, it was unbearable—already, she was consumed by the knowledge that this was something she could not hold onto.

He twisted to the side in his sleep, curling into her. A tremor ran through him, once, twice, and then faded. A hundred silent earthquakes, unsteadying him momentarily. But none of them would break him, she knew. None would crack, and none would shatter. He was solid as stone.

We can stay like this for a little bit, she thought, the words sleepy and untrustworthy even as they floated through her mind. But she was too tired to move. *After a few minutes, I'll get up. After this scene, after this movie.*

The remaining two movies slid past. She stared at the screen, scraping her gaze across the characters as they lived and loved and lost. It blew over her, just like dust. Just like ash. Sensation was a grain of sand, infinite. She did not move her shoulders, not once.

Uttriyasi, he'd said. Suri watched the end credits of the last movie play, watched fluorescent light blur and sing right in front of her, and hoped helplessly, stubbornly, that he had one of his own.

The next day, Ellis called her on the landline, and the entire world listed to the side.

23
ENESMAT

Viro did not cry. He made no sound—in fact, he did not turn back at all. From the moment he had entered the room, it was as if his world had narrowed to himself and to the body on the bed. Further even, simply to that body, as it consumed him and hollowed him.

Hours passed, and still he stood there. Kiran watched him sway on his feet, from fatigue and strain and perhaps, a distant grief. After an hour more, he sank to his knees, and then remained there, expression shadowed by the bent angle of his head and the paralyzing weight of loss.

When he finally spoke, Kiran nearly didn't register the sound of it. It was too low, too coarse. "I wish to be alone."

Alarm bells went off in his head. "I do not think that is a good idea—"

"Kiran," he whispered. It was an exhale more than it was a word, a thought formed into reality. "Please."

And so he left.

It had all fallen into place perfectly, a sickening execution of the vision from days ago. He had been at the temple when it happened, helping Kita clean up in the wake of Avyakanth. They had been talking, laughing, lost in their own thoughts. Death had not seemed like something real then. How quickly things had changed—how cruelly fate worked.

There was frustratingly little information about it, too—the murder had been executed within the confines of the captain's rooms, a clean knife to the heart. He had been found crumpled, with a piece of cloth on his chest that held only the Najan crest—that taunting, familiar symbol of braided flowers and a crown.

The general consensus was that it had been the handiwork of the Najan spy—the same one who had leaked information to the Najan Army, and the same one, Kiran now suspected, who had fabricated the message of an invasion from the west. It would have been impossible to execute the murder if Viro had been within the span of the mountains—from peak to peak, he would've felt it. Kiran did not doubt he had felt it in the borderlands. He would've felt it at the bottom of the ocean.

Kiran had learned loss young, but that changed nothing of what it felt like—grief was something sharp-toothed and vitriolic under his skin, and it clung to him with the intensity of rage, of fear.

He found Suri in her rooms, gazing out at the night. She was dressed in a thin nightgown and robe, and folded on the bed, she looked surprisingly young, oddly small. And then she turned to face him, and the weariness, the familiar anger, in her expression aged her.

"Do you know who it is?" he asked.

The corners of her mouth twisted down in a self-deprecating, pained smirk. "No. I have my suspicions, but none seem likely. Those that have the means do not have the motives, and those that have the motives do not have the means, and those that have both have firm, true alibis that place them far away from the murder. And yet—" she broke off, frowning. "I cannot help but feel as though I know who it is. There is something… strange about the crime, but I cannot place it, not fully."

Her jaw was set, that rebellious determination hardening her expression. But Kiran saw further, to the bruises under her eyes and the gaunt, bony angles of her face. She was working herself to death, and gods knew what lengths she'd had to go to gather information when she was a prime suspect.

He opened his mouth to tell her so—she wouldn't listen, but perhaps if he reasoned that she needed the energy to continue investigating, she might—but she spoke first. "I know why you are here."

Kiran tilted his head, nausea emptying him. "You do?"

The princess turned from her post at the window, fiddling with the thin fabric of her nightgown before looking up to meet his gaze. There was something sad, but faintly resigned about it. "You came to tell me you cannot leave."

He leaned back against the door, curling his fingers into the engraved wood. "I cannot leave Viro, not now. On top of this—it would break him. Even if it is only for a few more days, for the semblance of prosperity more than the reality of it, I must stay behind. And besides," he said, a crooked, humorless smile flickering to life, "Someone must convince him you are innocent after you leave. It would be far too easy for him to come to the wrong conclusion if you flee without context."

"Will you tell him the truth?" Suri asked, an odd, curious light in her eyes.

He shook his head. "It's too convoluted. He will assume it's fiction. No, I will simply…" he lifted his shoulders in a shrug, spreading his hands. "Misdirect his attention. Bring up the more likely candidates. I will speak to Kita about it as well, so she can take over once I am… gone." He shot a glance at the adjoined rooms. "Have you spoken to your handmaiden about your… trip?"

Suri frowned, looking away. "I don't think I will. I think she has found something here, in this city—with your friend. A kind of home she never could have had in Naja. I would not want to take her from that. It is better for her to think me dead and a traitor than to let go of this."

He hesitated, then wrapped his arms around himself. "Promise me you won't come back."

She narrowed her eyes, but there was an edge of tension to her voice when she spoke. "What is that supposed to mean?"

"If you know me, then I know you," he said, pushing off from the door. "You will leave, and then you will return and fight for the city. Regardless of whether you die, of how you die, you will return. And I understand why—even with Avya's blessing, even if Viro did not need counsel, I think I would struggle to leave as well. And I know it is selfish to ask this, but I must. Promise me you will leave, and that you will never return to Marai. Promise me you will save yourself."

Suri did not answer for a long moment; a muscle jumped in her jaw, strained from displeasure. He had hit at the heart of the matter, he knew. She had only planned to leave the city as long as she could return after his death.

If she returned, Viro would not care why she'd left. His capacity for such insignificant affairs had been exhausted. There would be nothing he could do for her.

Finally, she swallowed hard. "Okay. I promise."

"On Idhrishti's grave," he pressed, the name of the foreign saint sour in his mouth. *To die for love, to die for a star*— "Promise me."

"I swear a holy oath on Idhrishti's grave," she gritted out, defiant. She glared up at him. "Are you sated?"

She cannot die if she is not here. He tried his best not to let any of his relief into his expression, though it was a close thing. "Yes. Thank you."

Her brows drew together as she examined him. *Don't ask, don't ask, don't ask*— "How is Viro?"

It was the first time she had called him by name, and yet Kiran could not feel surprise at that—only chilling, honey-sweet relief that she had not asked why he was so insistent. He had an inkling she already held a measure of suspicion regarding his desperation, but still, he knew if she asked, he would not be able to lie.

He scrubbed a hand over his face. "I have only ever seen him like this once, nine years ago. And even then, it was not quite as bad—he had allowed Tarak to stay beside him, even after he cast me out. Now, he is alone. He refuses to let anyone in to examine the—the body. He simply sits there beside him, serving some kind of silent vigil."

Suri pursed her lips, almost as if she was concerned. "How will he fight a war? My parents will not wait for him to finish mourning."

But Kiran could recall how quickly the numbness of the first war had sharpened into that jagged, indiscriminate fury, that caustic determination. "I do not doubt he will fight the war. But I cannot help but fear that he will not care about surviving it."

It was startling how quickly that spark of flame grew.

The simple act of physical touch—of cold, emptying sensation—had extinguished the hope and ignited something sharper, darker in the same instant.

Kiran had not returned to the room, but Viro could feel his presence like a tether, a hook in his chest where a heart had once hung. He wanted to return, and yet he did not want to push too far. There was a time where he would have felt grateful for that kindness. Now, he was not wholly sure whether he still held the capacity to be grateful.

More than anything, he felt unmoored. Tarak had always been a pillar in the endless tempest of his anger, a north star he had followed thoughtlessly. The world could have died, and still he would've stood waiting, and all Viro would have cared for was that he continued to stand—that he continued to live. And now he was gone, and the world was still alive—what was the purpose of it? What meaning could he possibly find in the light of the early morning, in birdsong, in that distant, nebulously shaped knife that they called love?

There was nothing left. Nothing of meaning, nothing of matter. Only the emptiness, and that single flame, an arrow of flickering retribution.

But there was a war on the horizon, and he would confront it alone. *What would Tarak do?* he thought before glancing up, gaze alighting on the flat, cold angles of the boy's lifeless face. Despair was something corrosive, wrath given form and intent and turned inward toward the numbness that remained. A slow burn spread outward, warming him. It took the cold away, slow but sure, and left something dark and oily in its place.

Tarak is dead, he thought, over and over. He had sunk into the River Asakhi, the realm of ghosts, of gods. His counsel was an illusion. All he had left was a body and the suggestion of warmth. But that warmth was no longer there.

His chest felt tight—with tears, with wracking, trembling sobs that could not come. He was swollen with them, the hollows in his chest glutted with sorrow that could not leave, could only scream into something nascent and vitriolic.

Blood could only fall for so long—vengeance was an imperfect, dissatisfying desire, and yet it was all he had left.

Nine years prior, Viro had learned agony, and it had swallowed him, and so he had awoken in a desert of rage, a thorn sharpened by loss. And in that oily, infinite night sky, there had always been a single star, the last remnant of light in a world of ink and shadow. And he had followed that star to the edges of the desert, to the ragged depths of his heart. He had followed that star, and he had learned it, and he had loved it.

But the star was dead. The sky, hollow and desolate, threatened to swallow him again, shatter all that remained of his soul into bone ash and shadows. The star was dead, and he was lost.

Since Tarak's death, sleep had eluded Suri entirely, a blank ecstasy that never quite panned out into something tangible. And truly, she did not mind it—it gave her more time to look for the true culprit. But it had been three days and nearly three nights since his death—she was running out of time. She had held off on Isa's kind offers of comfort for long enough—eventually, the mourning period would end. She would have to leave—Kiran would have to die.

The most frustrating part of it all was that she knew who had done it. There was no clear, concise evidence trail, no suggestion of reasoning. It was simply this intuitive knowledge, this raw, searing truth that held no identity. Like a name on the tip of her tongue, fates held in two trembling hands.

Kiran nagged for her to rest like a cranky grandmother. It would have been irritating if she did not find it so endearing. But there was a kernel of truth in his insistent demands for her to get some sleep. Perhaps she would wake up more refreshed for once.

She laid down gingerly on the mattress, and could not help but wonder if Tarak had died like this—whether it had been swift, kind. Or whether he had died on his feet, the twist of the knife cruel and heedless.

Suri shut her eyes, and the world fell away around her.

A riverbank replaced the darkness, the one from her nightmare so many weeks ago. From the story of Nila, long before she had ever heard it.

But her hands were clean—she was dressed not in that unfamiliar chemise, but in the maroon wrap she had worn on the night of Avyakanth. The fabric stuck to her skin, damp from river water. And yet she was not shivering.

Further down the river, someone knelt by the water. Their hands were bloody, but the figure of their body was shadowed, blurred by the dream. Suri rose without conscious thought, following the line of the ink-black water until she stood by them. Once again, she was struck by that suffocating sense of recognition—the feeling that she knew this person, but could not form their identity in words.

The figure swayed back and forth by the water, leaning into the river to dip their hands in and pulling back without rhythm. When they spoke, it was not the voice of a single person, but the voice of hundreds condensed into a quiet thrum. "I really wish I hadn't had to kill him. He was so kind."

Suri's heart had gone fully silent in her chest. There was no sound in this silent, dead world, apart from the splash of blood against water—against tears. "So you admit you killed him."

The figure laughed, tilting their head back in an odd, youthful gesture. The moonlight shone on their face but did not illuminate it—simply suggested the existence of facial features, the notion of cruelty in that thin, sharp mouth. "I have never hid it, my lady. It was only that you searched in the wrong places, looking for… what? Resentment? Malice? Tarak was not a hated man. He was simply an avenue to someone who was."

That, at least, did not surprise her. Suri had long suspected that the motive of the murder had not been to destabilize the guard—it had been to destabilize Viro. It was only that she could not understand who would know enough of them to cut so deep so swiftly. It spoke of a thorough understanding of the palace, an unfathomable capacity for cruelty.

"Why Viro?" she asked. "Why war?"

The figure glanced up at her, still wreathed in shadow. They pulled their hands from the water, wringing them meaninglessly—they still dripped with blood. After they were satisfied, they leaned back, sitting cross-legged on the dry grass.

"Why war?" they echoed. They held her gaze, the planes of their features resolving from shadow into skin and bone.

There was a ghost of a grin on the figure's face, something ferocious and ruthless. "Why not?"

It was the knife—sweet, cold metal pressing against the skin at the hollow of her throat—that awoke her, strangely enough.

Suri inhaled sharply, so loudly the knife bit into her flesh, a silent warning. She could sense the blood on her throat—the warmth of it, the thickness of it, the nauseating smell of metal and death. It took all she had not to retch then and there. Then again, she had little chance to.

Mohini angled the knife downward, an iron-tipped promise. Her expression was unreadable in the faint shards of moonlight that filtered through the windows.

"I really hoped it would not have to end like this," she said softly, but her gaze was hard. This close, she smelled of blood and roses.

"No," Suri whispered. "This is what you desired all along, is it not?"

Her smile was equal parts rueful and merciless. Suri nearly could not recognize her as the sweet, demure maid that had served her for the past few months. And yet, there had always been this edge to her, an unknowable bitterness. Too late, she saw it. Too late, she understood.

She swallowed hard, which was difficult enough with the knife against her throat. But this game of bravado, of survival—Suri knew it well. She had grown up dancing through it, knocking over pawns and steering kings of stone and queens of marble. Carefully, she asked, "Why? Why do *you* want war with Naja? You're Athrian."

"'You're Athrian', she says," Mohini repeated, mocking. "I am not doing this for Naja, my lady. I lost all of my family in the war, did you know? A clean massacre. They lay under unmarked graves even now, lost to time. No one will ever remember their names. And after? I was thrown into servitude like a dog, sent to pamper and care for the remnants of a family that failed to protect my own."

"Then why do you want another war?" she managed, slowly wriggling her hand out from under the blankets. When she had first arrived, she had slipped a dagger into the rip in the mattress. Hopefully, Mohini had never noticed—had never thought to disarm her. "Athri has been at peace for nine years."

The young woman sneered at her, the expression unfamiliar and biting on her face. "At peace? As long as Athri is alive, as long as it holds land for your family to conquer, we will never be at peace. The war will never end." She shifted in position inadvertently, placing weight on Suri's wrist. Inches away, the dagger waited. "And truly, I do not care for Athrian victory or Najan victory. I care only that your people fight—that you die. That king of mine, the *nakshi*—I trust that he will do his level best to destroy all of you. He has that anger hidden within him. But I knew he would not act on it without the proper circumstances."

"You have been manipulating him this entire time." Suri felt ill. "And—Lucius?"

Her expression hardened, slightly. "He was endearing, I will give him that. So willing to let me look at the missives to be sent and written, so willing to let me participate. I convinced him to leave the city earlier tonight, under the guise of a present. Hopefully, he will find someone kinder to love."

Unfathomable cruelty, she had thought. And yet, this was somehow harder to bear. It was the blade-sharp rancor of someone who had nothing left to lose.

There was a hint of a cruel pride in her smile. "I saw you fail to do your duties, as well. The unsent letters in your dresser. Your moonlight romance with the god-spawn. It was almost amusing to watch you fall further and further from a possible threat." She shifted the knife against her throat, observing the trickle of blood. Fortunately, it freed her grasp from Suri's wrist. "That is why I find this so sad, I think. Part of me wonders whether I cannot simply let you run away and savor your newfound freedom for a few days. You will die either way."

Suri leveled a steady gaze at her, even though her heart was battering against her ribcage. "Then let me. Your plan will succeed with or without my interference. You know it is so—otherwise you wouldn't have come here."

Mohini smiled humorlessly. "It is too late for you to run now, my lady. I have already left the letter—by morning, the *nakshi* will be asking for your head, and the *thyvaayan*'s." Her eyes twinkled cruelly. "I do have a sense of compassion, after all. If you two are fated to die, is it not fitting that you die side by side?"

Suri had worked to control her fear response to the blood—slowed and steadied her breathing, rationalized the situation, broken it down into its component parts. And yet, at those words, mindless terror washed over her. *She implicated him in Tarak's death, somehow. In the betrayal.* Despite her best efforts, her voice wavered. "Viro would not believe it. Viro would never believe Kiran helped kill Tarak."

"Are you confident, my lady?" she leered, a jagged grin stretching across her face. "Would you bet your life on it? Would you bet his?"

Could she?

Before she could respond, Mohini drew back. The eerie, uneven light of the moon and the darkness of the room rendered the girl a dangerous ghost, one of wrath or war. She ran her finger along the length of the blade, inspecting the blood on the pad of her index finger before slowly moving off the bed.

"That was an admirable attempt," she said, nodding at the mattress. "To get the knife while restrained." Her smile turned cold, derisive. "We are more alike than you think, my lady. It is just that I have always enjoyed my work, and you have always seen yours as a curse, a prison instead of a birthright. Though I suppose the details are meaningless now. Enjoy your last night alive."

The door clicked shut behind her. Suri touched her throat with one hand, fingering the shallow cut. Her chest was tight, as if she were still trapped under the blade, suffocating.

She still had time—the sun had not risen. It was possible Viro hadn't yet seen the letter. If she ran, perhaps they could make it.

She didn't bother packing anything. There was nothing here of purpose, of consequence that mattered more than her own life. Her knives would have to stay behind—if he caught her with them, there would be no trial, no time for explanation. She would have to find new ones, carve them out of metal and bone.

Then she remembered the last letter in the drawer—which Mohini might well have used as proof for her betrayal. She lit the letter on fire, white ash dusting the floor and her wrists like snow and bone dust.

Suri left as quietly as she could, shutting the door gently behind her even though her hands were still trembling so hard she could not push the hair from her face. It hung around her face, obscuring her sight for brief moments as she ran down the west tower. The corridors were empty, but there was something twisted about the silence, something *wrong*. A cosmic joke, a tragedy on the brink of collapse.

Her footsteps were inaudible on the damp, packed earth of the north gardens. The air was filled with the scent of blossoms, but it was nauseating, sickly-sweet and spoiled. Above, the endless darkness of the sky had begun to lighten, the eternal night coming to a close.

Her bare feet bled on the uneven, jagged rocks that littered the path up the mountain. But she did not slow, did not acknowledge the pain. She could bandage those wounds later, when they were both alive and safe and *away*. She sprinted past the temple, the brazier unsettlingly empty, and toward the cottage.

The garden was in full bloom, luminous under the slowly fading moonlight. From here, Suri could see the darkness within the cottage—he was asleep for the first time in months. The irony of it burned all the way down. She banged on the door, erratic and desperate. When it finally swung open, her knuckles were an angry red, the skin splintered and peeling.

Kiran squinted at her, eyes sleep-narrowed and hazy. Dark curls swung into his face, fragmenting his gaze. "Suri?"

"We have to go," she said. Her voice was nearly unrecognizable to her own ears, high and guttural and imperative. "Now."

He scrubbed a hand over his face. "I have to stay, for Viro, we talked about this—"

"Viro is going to kill us both," she managed, the words falling out in a long, meaningless rush. "It's—it's Mohini, my maid, she killed Tarak, and now he's going to kill us, and we have to leave *now*—"

Kiran reached over and put a hand over her heart, searing in the cold of night. His gaze was black as pitch, uselessly steady. "Calm down, Suri. Explain what happened."

Suri pulled away with a strangled sound of frustration. "I cannot. We are on borrowed time, even now. I will explain everything later." She wrapped her hands around his free wrist, and tugged him out, dragging him away from the cottage.

As they ran, Suri tried her best to condense her understanding of the events into a few jagged statements. Kiran sucked in a breath as they exited the thin, narrow path hugging the cliffs. The grass of the clearing surrounding the temple was soft beneath their feet, but Suri could not help but think of how it was damp with dew, just like the dry grass of that dreamland had been drenched, softened with blood. "The letter implicates me, as well. And now you are afraid he will believe it in his fury—that he will kill both of us. So we must escape."

"Yes," she said, breathless. "There is no time to explain the truth to him. The evidence lies in her favor."

He looked unconvinced—perhaps a shard of him held out hope that Viro would not believe the letter, as Suri had. But she was long past hopes and wishes. If there was any chance Viro would believe them, it paled in comparison to the possibility that he would not think to.

Kiran gestured toward the entrance to the temple. "We must stop here for a moment. Avya has no other shrines for miles, not ones he will listen to. If I do not explain what has happened, he may fear the worst."

Suri frowned, but followed him up the stone steps. Kiran lit a match and dropped it into the brazier, his movements quick and edged with a terror-soaked disbelief. The blood-red glow of the early morning, still too dark to shed much light on the temple beyond the suggestion of stone and fire, cast him in sharp, unfamiliar relief. As if he was nothing more than a limb of the god he served.

Cold wrapped around her, slow but sure.

Without looking up, he said, "Where do you suggest we go? I have rarely left the city, apart from brief diplomatic escorts. You know this world far better than I do."

She didn't answer, couldn't. It was fitting that the night had begun with a knife pressed to her throat, that that was how it would end.

"I cannot understand why the princess's suggestions would be of any use," Viro said softly. He glanced down at her, one hand binding her arms together behind her back and the other digging a thin dagger into the hollow of her throat. His eyes were the color of dried blood. "As neither of you will be leaving the temple."

Kiran's hands flinched in the flames. He looked up, stricken. As if he had not quite believed it, not until this moment.

"At first," Viro began, voice rough with cold, hard fury, "I could not believe it. And yet, the letter did not lie. The words made sense, in a harsh, mocking kind of way. Of course the princess would have orchestrated this—I always suspected, I think, but I never acted on it. Because Tarak trusted you. He thought you were worth it." His eyes flashed with an oily, tempestuous malice, a weaponized volatility. And then he glanced up at Kiran and his expression twisted into something nearly pained. "And you. I cannot understand you. In a way, I never have. After all Tarak did for us—for you—you, what? Did the princess trick you into killing him? Or was that your decision entirely?"

Kiran drew his hands out of the fire and held them up in a futile attempt at placating him. "Viro—"

"Do not call me that," he snapped with a violent intensity. "I always thought you might abandon your post—your only true duty to this nation—given the opportunity. And look—look at how ready you are to turn your back on the people you claim to love. Is loyalty such a meaningless thing to gods? Is that why murder came so easily—why *escape* comes so easily to you?"

Kiran took a step forward toward where they stood at the top step of the temple. She nearly let out a bitter laugh at the whims of the gods—her knives were in her room, and if she moved to disarm him now, he would assume the worst. Viro's dagger dug into Suri's artery, and her chest wheezed in protest. "Run," she whispered. "Kiran, run."

He ignored her and took another step closer. "Viro, the letter was a lie, a diversion. Suri did not kill Tarak. *I* did not kill Tarak. You know this. Put down the knife."

"I cannot," he said softly. In the glow of the fire, the light of the slowly paling sky, he looked like a child—like a ghost. And yet there was a mad glint in his eyes, an anger that agony had fractured completely. As if he could split open, and all she would find was broken glass. "An example must be made. His death must be atoned for, Kiran. Even if it is by your blood."

Viro twisted the knife—but not across her neck. Too quickly for her to track, too strong for her to block the attack, he slid the knife down the surface of her blouse and drove it between her ribs.

24
LYNE

"Ellis," she repeated, the name gone stale in her mouth. "Take me through it one more time. Slowly."

His eyes were wide, wild with panic. "I came home, and they said she was gone, and she hasn't come back, and—"

Miya nudged a steaming cup of tea toward him. They'd all dropped everything and returned to help him out, and fortunately enough, timing had worked in their favor. Most of the vacations had been set to finish soon, so travel plans weren't as much of an issue.

The boy, hunched over in his fatigue, stared at the mug listlessly, eyes tracking the swirling streams of mist. In all the time she'd known him, Suri had never seen him like this. Emptied out, brittle with terror. He didn't take the tea, but after a few more moments of silence, he repeated what he knew of the situation.

Months ago, in early autumn, he'd had an inkling that something was wrong—his younger sister Annabel, barely fourteen at the time, had begun acting strangely. Not strangely enough for anyone else to notice—their brothers were out of the country, their parents were usually too busy to notice tiny shifts, and the others were too young to realize. They were the kind of changes that built up over time—staring open mouthed into a mirror for hours on end, overflowing the bathtub after forgetting to turn off the tap, waking early and sleeping late and losing chunks of time in the middle of the day with no explanation. At first, he'd waited patiently for her to explain—they had a relatively healthy relationship, and he had always thought she trusted him.

But she hadn't. Not at first, not ever, and as the days passed, he wasn't sure who to turn to. She had been losing more time, appearing at odd hours of the night for a change of clothes or a muffin. If he did press her for details, she'd always default to the excuse that she was staying at a friend's house, but never let him know which friend.

It was her gaze that had scared him the most, he said, back in the early days. The way she'd stare straight through him, straight through the plaster of the walls. As if the world was a wasteland, miles upon miles of emptiness, and she was the only one privy to the truth.

But things had gotten better for a while, or at least he figured they had. In November and early December, she returned to the house for longer than brief stints. She ate food—occasionally, she would make conversation. And he had felt grateful for every bit of it, uncertain but optimistic, at the very least, that this meant whatever had happened earlier had been an accident. And that soon enough, she might explain the truth of it. Everything, he said, had been going perfectly fine. Until the day before winter break came, and he returned from university to find the house ransacked, her room a mess, and the family in disarray.

They had thought she'd run away. He'd known better.

"That was four days ago," he finished, exhaling. "We've been out since then—at the police department, putting up posters, searching around the city. I only remembered—" he waved his hand in a dismissive, fatigued gesture— "To call you guys just recently. And before you say anything, I know. I know it's unlikely we'll find anything, and even less likely that we'll find her. I just—it's not like we can do nothing. It's not like I can just pretend everything's okay."

There was a beat of silence. Surprisingly enough, Kiran was the one who spoke first. "You don't have to."

Ellis glanced up, wary and intrigued, and they all followed, looking toward him expectantly. Back-tracking a little, he simplified, "Nobody expects you to be okay with this. It's a horrible thing that's happened to you and your family, and I wouldn't wish it on my worst enemies. But all you can do for now is continue searching."

The boy forced a smile, pale but appreciative. It was a nice enough sentiment, sympathetic and encouraging, and there was a certain measure of genuine warmth in Kiran's voice. But he had reacted to the entire situation—to Ellis showing up in tears, to him confessing the situation, to the rest of their friends showing up and effectively occupying the apartment—with a startling lack of surprise, a faint dispassion.

It wasn't the sort of thing she could confront him about—she was running on little sleep herself and she was prone to overthinking, fixating on small details and creating webs and webs of theories from them, and there was no time to ask even if she mustered the courage. But he picked up a stack of posters and straightened them, a nervous tick, and her gaze caught on the movement unintentionally.

"How about we go out and put up posters?" Aza suggested in the midst of a new, pervasive silence. Four cups of tea sat untouched on the table. "Ellis can stay here and rest."

He narrowed his eyes. "I don't need to *rest*—"

"Yeah, you do," Suri cut in, relieved to be of some use. "I'll get out a spare blanket and some pillows. You can take the couch while we're out." Holding his gaze stubbornly, she added, "Refusing to take care of yourself isn't going to bring her back."

Ellis flinched, setting his gaze on the wall behind the television stand. "Later. I'll rest after we finish putting up posters."

"Later?"

"As long as you sleep afterward," Dai interrupted, shooting a nervous glance at Suri. Ever the pacifist. "Promise to sleep afterward."

"I promise," he gritted out, toneless and inflamed with helplessness. "Happy?"

The question went unanswered; Kiran passed out stacks of posters and they readied themselves wordlessly. Then they went out into the city, pouring onto the streets single-file, like ducklings or small children.

Bound by a lack of a proper plan, they wandered uncertainly toward the center of the city. Eventually, Miya spoke up, told them all firmly to meet back in an hour. Her eyes shifted from side to side, waiting for someone to come up with a better plan. They didn't; the group fragmented and dissipated, and Suri clutched her sheaf of posters like a lifeline.

More often than not, she lost herself down familiar streets. She would continue down a path stubbornly and find that she'd been walking in a circle. It was as if the city had turned its back on her, as if she was lost in a phantasmagoria of the world she had known. The wrong side of a mirror, all rippling, reflective darkness.

The city swarmed. There was a method to the madness, sure, a rhythm Suri knew well. But this new, strange city, the uneven, malicious reflection of it, spun to a harder, coarser beat, and it swallowed her whole.

I'm losing my mind, she thought, nearly walking straight into a streetlight. She held up a hand just to see that it existed, afraid it would flicker and disappear. It touched the pole, felt cold, frosted steel, and the sensation rocked through her. A reminder of her own mortality. *This is real. I'm real.*

Suri thought of Ellis's stories of Annabel then, as the city twisted around her, amorphous and chaotic. *She was losing time—to something. Somehow. She would look at me and I swear, there was no recognition. Of me, of anything. Bruises,* he'd burst out, shocked by the fact that he'd forgotten and horrified by the memory of it. *She would show up, middle of the night, with bruised wrists and cuts on her collarbones. No explanation, no words. I tried to keep her from leaving once, and she just snuck out ten minutes later. No one listened, and she never—never answered any questions. Not ever.*

She dropped her hand from the pole, rolling up her sleeve to examine her wrists. No bruises. At least she wasn't entirely gone.

Fear thudded through her. *Tell* anda, she thought, begged. *Tell the others. Tell Kiran. Tell somebody.*

But she couldn't. It wasn't as if she could prove there was any connection between what she was feeling—faint shivers and strange thoughts—and Annabel's disappearance. It was all pure conjecture, like everything had become these days. Smoke and mirrors, dreams and nightmares and the darkness that pooled in the absence of both.

A teenager sprinted down the sidewalk, pushing people from side to side—a mother with a child in her arms listed to the side, an accidental shift that knocked a burly man carrying crates of produce into her—Suri reached out, desperate and unsteady, fingers slipping against damp brick, and tripped over a crack on the sidewalk, tumbling into a side street that led out to a crowded avenue that usually cut across the northern side of the city. It wasn't her area to patrol, and she took a seat on the asphalt. The faint burn of pain and exertion and the cold of the winter air negated one another. She inhaled and exhaled slowly and let the feeling come back into her limbs.

Distantly, she registered warmth.

It was familiar, not in the way of small flames and stovetops and hearths. Familiar like her heart was familiar, familiar like sensation itself.

She had been wrong—the side street didn't lead out into the avenue she had thought it did. It led out onto a smaller back road that looped around a park, enclosed with a tall, imposing fence that kids liked to practice jumping over. A ripped down jacket was hooked on a prong, feathers falling like snow.

The error didn't surprise her in the slightest. She knew the city, but this wasn't her city.

A voice cut through the air, low and familiar, and Suri flattened herself against the brick at the edge of the alleyway. Carefully, she turned to peek into the street, ducking her head so the shadows removed her from vision. She was shaking so hard she could feel it in her bones, nails cutting into the meat of her palms, the pain of it extraneous. *Was this what fear felt like?* She couldn't remember. It was a nightmare she had lived through so many times it had disappeared from her heart entirely, leaving behind only ghosts and muscle memory.

"...you hurt?" the whisper came again, rising enough to be audible. But it was only from the natural lilt of the voice; she couldn't understand the conversation from where she stood. Suri shifted closer.

Kiran, she thought, and it was shaped like relief. How dangerous solace was. Thoughtlessly, she moved to step into the light, holding herself back with some combination of anxiety and innate self-preservation.

The street was empty save for them—Kiran stood with his back to her, wrapped in the heavy black coat. It hung on his shoulders, overlarge and fluttering in the faint winter breeze, rendering him little more than a warp in reality.

A girl stood across from him, in leggings and a T-shirt so faded she couldn't make out the logo stained on the grayish fabric. Her shoulders were hunched, frame curled inward and strained with the pensive fear of a child and the empty daze of senility. Her complexion was the same as Ellis's—dark as wood, as soil—but her eyes were a faded blue, like rainwater. There was a cloudiness in them Suri could detect even from far away, a puddle frozen over.

The girl, Annabel, did not respond to Kiran's first question, simply stared up at him for a moment. Then, she lunged forward and tried to cut his throat.

Suri's breath caught, but it was buried by the crisp, precise sound of metal cutting through the fog. Kiran regarded her, expression hidden by the angle, arms loose at his sides. He had only taken a single step back.

The knife sagged in Annabel's hand, arm crooked at a strange, unnatural angle. She looked like a marionette, strings hung and ready. The winter sunlight made her skin look glossy and strange, waxy with pallor.

Still, she did not speak. Kiran moved forward and plucked the knife from her outstretched hand, tucking it into his coat pocket. He took her hand in his, examining it closely before letting go, pushing slightly so it fell back to her side. It was something of an interrogation, of an autopsy undone.

"Annabel," he said softly, the name strange and foreign-sounding in his mouth. "Where are you?"

Suri blinked in surprise at the question, at the remoteness with which it had been delivered. But the girl didn't reply, didn't even move. It was difficult to fathom that this was the same person who had tried to kill him earlier—she didn't look capable of conversation, much less murder.

Kiran exhaled, a deliberate, displeased sound. Grasping her chin loosely, he turned her face from side to side, a detached kind of scrutiny defining the movements. Her chest felt cold with the sight of it, with his strange disdain.

"Well," he murmured, "They've done quite the number on you. I wonder if the phrase 'permanent damage' ever occurred to whoever did this." He sighed then, saturated with pity and an eerie regret. "I suppose you won't tell me, even if I ask who."

Annabel was silent. Then, her face moved—jaw crackling in motion, eyes blinking slowly. An automaton given direction and intention.

She said, "You have to die."

The god laughed unpleasantly. "Would that it were so easy. Did they ruin you to kill me? That's a terrible waste. I would expect this is something separate."

The words rolled over the girl. There was something vague and lifeless about her gaze, milky with disregard. Finally, she repeated, "You have to die."

This time, he didn't make an attempt at conversation. He brought up his free hand to her temple, tapping it lightly with the pad of his index finger.

Day after day, Suri found herself mystified by the simplest displays of magic. And yet, all Kiran's thoughtless fires and strange charms paled in comparison to this. They were circus tricks—bunnies and hats, flaming hoops and aerial dances. This was power, and it didn't care to play at pretenses. It was brutal and wild and even from a distance, she could feel the cruel intensity of it. There was no malice in it, but that didn't matter. Natural disasters didn't care to kill—it didn't mean that they were benevolent.

Threads of ink danced under the surface of the girl's skin, swirling madly. He pulled his fingers away, and the threads came away. They glittered in the harsh, too-bright sunlight, and he touched each one, considering.

Clucking softly, he drew one out, glittering silver and blue, and blew on it. It caught fire and shattered. *Dark magic, bad magic.* "That's the worst of it, I think. You won't be at risk for further deterioration, at the very least."

There was a beat of silence as the air shone with the shards of mortality. He touched a few other strands of energy, altering them slightly. Black to white, black to gold, but they always returned to the smooth, opalescent sable. She still could not see his expression.

Eventually, he spoke, quiet and hard. "I wish I could do more for you. I really do." Kiran moved his index finger in a circle, counterclockwise, and the threads twisted around it, settling briefly. Then he pressed it back to her temple, and said calmly, "You've lost your memory of the past three months. Even if anyone asks, you cannot remember anything. Getting home safely is your only priority. Is that clear?"

Annabel nodded, and it was still the movement of a machine, slow and grinding, but there was a certain element of understanding to it. As if she were defrosting, slowly, ice cracking and melting under the surety of flame.

"Run along, now," he said, nudging her slightly. Her brow furrowed faintly, and then she turned and walked down the street carefully, as though every movement required conscious thought. She did not turn back, not once.

It was only after she had disappeared from view that Suri remembered to breathe. An exhale wracked her, and she thought Kiran might've flinched. But he did not move, did not waver.

Relief, she thought. The girl had tried to kill him, that was obvious enough. But she had never feared for him. She was relieved, because she had been afraid for Annabel. Afraid that he would hurt her, somehow, with that strange, coarse magic.

Suri felt hot with shame. He hadn't tried to hurt her—he'd helped her, broken whatever was binding her, wiped her memory of horrors unspoken. But still, she could not forget the impassive evenness of his voice. He had pitied her, perhaps, but whatever he had seen in her soul had not shaken him. It was little more than an unfortunate development.

She was being unfair to him, and she knew it. But she could not help but feel as though the figure in the street, still swallowed by dark fabric and the faint smell of smoke, was someone she did not know very well. Someone who did not want to be known. And as much as she was afraid, she was carved from curiosity just then. It felt far more dangerous than power.

By the time Kiran finally turned to leave the side street, she was already gone.

Suri wandered aimlessly throughout the city, wasting time until the hour was up. The intense malice of before had disappeared somewhat, and the streets remained familiar, her heartbeat steady. As steady as it could be, considering the circumstances.

She bought a candied apple, speckled with pecans and powdered sugar, and ate it at the edge of the shopping center. Children laughed and ran by, bound with colorful, knitted garments and bright smiles. She felt distant from it all, the uneven bite of sweet, cooked sugar and sour apple dulling on her tongue. It all tasted like ashes, overwrought and surreal.

Once all that was left was the core, she tossed it into a nearby waste bin, licking her fingers before they froze over.

She was the first person to show up at the agreed-upon meeting place. It was an old-fashioned stone fountain, still running smoothly in the cold. Coins sparkled and shifted under the weight of rippling water. Suri considered making a wish, but figured she'd likely used all hers up for the time being.

Quickly enough, the rest of her friends trickled in, empty with suppressed disappointment. Kiran perched on a low pillar, expression smooth and inscrutable. Ellis showed up last, mouth sharp with hopelessness.

They all went around, sharing what they'd found—nothing, for the most part. When it came to her, Suri lifted her shoulders in a shrug. The lie tasted sour in her mouth even as she spoke. "I put up the posters, but I didn't—didn't see her."

He would explain, she was sure. She didn't have to say what she'd seen, because it was inexplicable and terrifying and he would cut it into easily digestible chunks the others would fully understand, and everything would be okay.

Dai finished speaking and nodded at Kiran, the next person in the circle. He shook his head lightly, eyes hooded and distant. "I didn't find anything."

Ellis deflated visibly. His phone buzzed—he fished it out of his pocket, slow with dread, and nearly dropped it. He shut his eyes, speechless. "They said she just came home. She's not talking that much, but—she *is* talking. A little. And—" he cut off, disoriented and hopeful. "I'm going to go home. Sorry for—" he waved a hand.

"Don't apologize," Miya replied, savage, and the corners of his eyes crinkled with something akin to fondness.

After he was gone, there were a few moments of awkward silence—there was no easy way to navigate the aftermath of a tragedy like this, so easily shattered and so strangely put back together. Eventually, they all said goodbye and returned home, promising to meet up soon. To hang out, to talk, to pretend at a state of security.

Once they'd passed the corner, Suri turned to Kiran. She knew what she wanted to ask—*why didn't you tell him?* She knew it, and she opened her mouth, expectant. Nothing came out.

He glanced over at her, sharp-eyed and waiting. But she couldn't ask the question, no matter how much the curiosity ate her. Anger bit through her—*and why should she?* Why did she have to ask? Why couldn't he explain of his own volition?

Because she could justify his silence with Ellis; there was no way to explain what he had done without explaining who he was, and that had never been an option.

But it was more than that—his expression was impenetrable, that old, empty venom coloring his eyes. Questions threatened to burn through her, jagged with desire. They had always been like this, in a way. One unattainable, unknowable in distinct, dangerous ways, the other consumed by questions shaped like bullets, like graves. They only existed by way of spilt secrets.

She couldn't know whether he had noticed her presence in the alley. She couldn't know whether he resented her for it, whether he scorned her curiosity or disregarded it. She couldn't know anything, not unless he told her.

Suri waited for him to explain. But he never did, and she could never bring herself to ask.

Kiran wanted to tell Suri things, and it terrified him.

He pondered on this while he waited for the tub to fill, sitting cross-legged in the slowly rising water. The bathtub, ironically, was the only place he felt safe.

There was something soothing about the knowledge that he could not hurt anybody under the weight of the water. He didn't have to worry about his traitorous heart, about bones carved from malice and ash. The cold water rendered him powerless, mortal.

While waiting, he ran his fingers through the water, tracking the smooth ripples, the way the liquid resisted and broke against his touch. And he thought of his fear, disassembled it and examined all the operative parts.

The girl, Annabel, had saddened him, which surprised him for entirely different reasons. It had been a long time since he had felt pity; he had long since hardened himself to the cruelty of humanity—to pity one was to pity all of them. But it had been clear enough that whoever had hurt Annabel had not been human, not entirely. Her memories had been mangled and broken, her sense of self dipped into graceless malice and frozen solid. And it had been done artlessly—it was the work of an impostor or a sadist, someone who only knew enough divinity to hurt.

She had said she had been sent to kill him, which discomfited him further. The notion that there was an entity out there happily willing to wreck entire minds, entire lives, in order to get a rise out of him was unsettling. Already, he was an inconvenience and a danger to Suri and Rana and all close to them. Already, he had stayed for too long.

How soft you've become, he thought, a memory and a presage. The words were someone else's, but he heard them in his own voice.

So, he had healed her—not entirely, as he suspected that was impossible. But to the extent of his own ability.

And after the revulsion, the whispering dread—*who will you hurt next, simply by existing?*—had passed, he had thought immediately, impossibly, of Suri. Of how she might hate him for such an act, so clearly inhuman, of how she might ask her questions, pressed together with sharp, dark-eyed curiosity, and seek guilelessly to understand it. He had thought of her, and unbidden, he had wanted to tell her of what he had done. Because it was important—because they told each other things when they were important.

Except that was not entirely true. Because they told each other things even when they were not so important, even when there was no good reason for the other person to know. She told him about her classes and her friends and her hopes for the future, the latter offered with self-conscious gruffness and ducked, bright eyes. And he told her useless trifles about his past, memories twisted so far into fiction they bore little resemblance to anything that he had lived.

Before, the thoughtless need to tell her would not have struck him as odd. It was true enough that he had been wary of staying in a single place for more than a night, of speaking to another and having them respond. These were things he did not indulge in, and even without his memory, he had felt the strangeness of it. But now, he *knew.* And the cutting, bitter knowledge—that he had not bared himself the way that he had with her in millennia—terrified him. He hadn't thought he had the capacity for softness, for trust, and it had made him foolish and prideful.

How he wanted to tell her. Not with the rushed, expectant desperation of a sinner, not as a confession. It was a desire borne by habit, a careless kind of trust. He wanted to tell her just to hear what she would say, just because he felt like he had to. As if they were capable of reciprocation, instead of chasms laid edge to edge.

The water had risen over his shoulders, and he twisted the tap shut, disrupting it with his movement. The world felt liquid and liminal around him, as though he could lean his head back and melt straight into the water, following it down the drain to a different life.

It had been a long time since he had been human, and yet he was still the same coward. Weaned on idealism and yearning, a martyr through and through.

Kiran shifted in the water, and his shoulder ached from the burn. He lifted his hand and gently traced the lines of the new *sankhili.* It had come with the darkness, with the nightmare that he had not been able to recall the next day, slumped and crooked on the coffee table. He hadn't noticed the new mark until he had undressed for the shower, bleary with fatigue.

As far as he could tell, it was meant to bind his power. Not as the old one had—that had blocked it entirely, rendered it useless. Now that it had disappeared fully, this new one—jagged and small, hooked under his collarbone—tempted him to use it, only to rain down pain if he did. Healing Annabel had inflamed it, rendering him speechless with agony for a few moments. The cold water slid over it, soothing the burn for only a few seconds, a temporary balm.

Tell her, a tiny, traitorous voice whispered. *Tell her of the chains, and of what you did to Annabel.*

Kiran tipped forward, submerging himself in the water. It was beginning to warm from his skin, but it was still cold enough that it shocked him out of the syrup-sweet reverie he'd fallen into, that airy, ethereal dreamland where telling her was a foregone conclusion, a *need.*

And yet, again and again, he saw the world burning around him. It was a nightmare borne from the past—sprung from battlefields and dead cities and ash-stained burial grounds—but all souls returned, and their stories returned with them. Time was a tapestry woven from old threads. The world had burned once, and so it would burn again.

I can't, he thought again, repeating the words until they lost meaning under the glassy emptiness of the water. If she knew, she would want to help—she would *try* to help, no matter the cost. And maybe, just maybe, she might ask him to stay.

He feared that most of all, of course. Because he knew if she asked him to stay, he would. Wordlessly, senselessly, he would stay. The world would burn, as it was always meant to do, only this time he had lit the match and flung it, uncaring—and he would stay.

25
ENESMAT

Kiran felt the knife just as painfully as if it had struck his own heart. It was a sharp, burning twinge in his chest, a flame that did not, could not, die. It consumed him until all that remained was ashes and the suggestion of smoke.

The cruelty of humanity. Their capacity for self-destruction.

He stepped closer to Viro. The knife was still buried between her ribs—she was still alive. Her eyes were sharp and wide with pain, but her chest was heaving slowly, her mouth twisted in a facsimile of a smile. Viro was staring down at her as if the matter of her death was something distasteful, but necessary. An objective on a list, a means to an end.

He stepped closer. Viro released her body, and she crumpled to the stone, caught between the two columns of the temple. Her hands lingered over the knife in her chest, grasping it loosely, but she didn't pull. Her mouth twitched upward bitterly—she knew what would happen if she tried.

Kiran stepped forward, and knelt beside her body, taking her in his arms. In death, her skin was too warm, searing with heat. Her eyelids fluttered as she turned to look at him, gaze molten and impossibly fond. "You were not listening the first time," she chided, as if he were a child. Blood dotted her bottom lip. "I told you to run, Kiran. As fast as you can, as far as you can make it. Run."

"Not without you," he said, voice strangely steady.

She grimaced, but her eyes were bright. "So stubborn. You are a fool. And perhaps I am a fool for loving you. I wonder…" she cut off, voice hoarse and faded. The color was draining from her skin, but she managed to finish, gaze fixed on his, "I wonder where that leaves us now."

And then she was gone.

He had spent seventeen years walking beside death. And yet, strangely, this was the first time someone had ever died in his arms. This was the first time he had watched the light leave someone's eyes, watched it hollow them completely. A second before, he had been holding Suri in his arms—now, he was embracing a corpse.

He laid her gently beside the edge of the altar and drew himself up. He felt as though he were a corpse himself, nothing more than a set of bones and a flame formed into the shape of a beating human heart.

When he spoke, his voice was nearly inaudible even in the silence of the early morning. The sky continued to lighten, that oily, empty blackness fading into a dark, expansive red. Not the color of fire, but of blood. "Have you ever wondered what would happen if I gave myself to the earth before the auspicious time?"

He would have died in eight hours, if this had not happened. But eight hours was enough—to die now was something wholly different than dying then.

Viro still stood on the top step of the temple. His gaze sharpened from that mercurial anger to something guarded, wary. Afraid.

Good, he thought. *Be afraid.*

His fear meant nothing, now. It would change nothing. The king of Athri was just as powerless as Suri had been seconds before, trapped by the promise of a knife.

Kiran had always thought of power as something to hold carefully, to wield with reason and kindness. Something to be shared—something to drive peace. But now, he thought it resembled the knife in his hands, the ceremonial dagger that had always laid beside the stone idol, meant to be used once—only once.

Power would only ever consume, would only ever kill. It seared through humanity, uncaring, and left a trail of corpses in its wake. And yet it was so fragile. It was so easy to misuse, so ephemeral. Without a strong grip, it would slip away.

But if you held it carefully, angled the blade properly, it could cut through anything.

"I have," he said, his voice still touched with that odd, remote quiet. He examined the ceremonial dagger in his scarred hands—the holy daggers were all jeweled and lovely, but this one was different, he knew. The *kita*-studded hilt had been carved from the heartwood of the kino trees below, the iron first cut and sharpened when they had begun to build this temple. This was a knife as old as his fire, and it had been made for him.

"I have dreamt of it, of death, countless times. I have considered all the possible outcomes, all the possible results. And sometimes, I wonder what will happen if I sacrifice myself early."

"Kiran," the boy said, holding his gaze. It was unreadable; perhaps it was not, and he was simply too distant from his own body to read it. Everything about the world around him seemed foreign—even the cold stone under his feet felt peculiar. All he could depend on was the feeling of fire in his hands, in his lungs.

"I cannot know, of course, what will happen before I do it," he continued. "Sometimes I wonder if it will backfire—if it will double the curse for another eighteen years. And other times, I think perhaps it will cure the blessing just as well as if I sacrificed myself properly. But do you know what I suspect will happen?"

He did not say anything. Kiran had not truly expected him to, and yet the silence chafed at him. He held up the ceremonial dagger, shifting it so the metal shone in the firelight. Without looking up, he said, "I think it will have no effect at all. My blood will spill, and the world will continue, untouched by the hands of the gods."

The king seemed to find his voice, gravelly with anger and tinged with an odd, sharp fear. "You would ruin this nation. You would destroy these people, for the sake of your divine wrath, your lost love." His eyes narrowed in a faint, revolted challenge. "Are you even capable of that?"

"Am I?" he echoed, tracing the lifelines of his empty, spread palm with the tip of the knife. Kiran turned and held the boy's gaze steadily. There was so much emotion in those eyes, a tempest of raw *feeling.* And he could not feel any of it—just the echoes of that old fire, that first flame. "There is no divine wrath, Viro, just as there is no divine virtue. I am not a tool for you to wield as you would a scythe, reaping souls as payment. And if this country falls, it will be you who tore it down."

Are you not afraid that, in the end, they will disappoint you?

"Do not disappoint me," he said, and then cut his palm open, and placed it on the carved icon at the center of the altar.

The sacrifice was differentiated from past rituals by one simple aspect—intent. The act of bloodletting was common enough; it was his intent, his flame-bound heart, that determined the purpose of the blood, and the effect of it.

He turned the blade inward, slid it between his ribs—there was a reciprocation in the act, a physical death as well as a spiritual one. But even if he had not split his heart, he would have died simply from the wish, the decision to give up his blood.

It was a wish that rose and found the thrones of the gods and waited to be judged, and that was why he was not entirely surprised when that warm, hollowing fire in his chest grew into something spiteful and blistering.

I told you, Avya whispered, flames wrapped around his heart. *I should not have let them hurt you.*

The god's anger was alive, a dark, destructive flame that held a certain measure of malevolence—of true wrath. Kiran welcomed it, even as it burned through his mortal body, through his brittle bones. A small, logical part of his mind tried to push it away, tried to cleanse his mind of the relentless fire of that sharp, jagged anger. Yet the greater portion of him turned its back on it. *There is no point,* it said, lost in old, broken grief. *Let it in. Let it burn you away.*

And so he did, and as the flames grew into a dissonant, shattering throb of fury and of loss, they consumed him entirely. His hands slipped from the altar and he fell to his knees beside it, trembling with fire. And that caustic, nearly pleasant burn was the last thing he registered before he slipped from consciousness, and the city caught flame.

He opened his eyes, and found himself in the meadow of *kantal.* This time, he was standing, hands clasped in one another, skin smelling of smoke and amber.

The endless day had passed, and now it was night. The blackness of the sky above stained him as though it was ink, the tepals of the flame lilies gleaming though there was no glint of warmth to reflect against. They shone in the darkness, individual flames borne from bone and flint.

Kiran reached out a hand to touch one, brushing his fingers against the shell of the flower, and it curled against his skin as if it sensed a kinship in his divinity-riven heart. The ribbon of the tepal wreathed his wrist, vicious and lovely. The tip grazed the edge of his lifeline, and then melted into blood.

His skin was wet, rich with scarlet—he broke away, staggering back from the broken blossom and into darkness. But it was not enough. The flower dissolved entirely, the deep green tendrils and leaves falling away into salted hot liquid that soaked into the dark soil of the meadows and gave way to the birth of something dark and terrible.

When he wrenched away frantically, he touched another set of flowers, golden stamens pressed flush against the point of his elbow. Heat spattered the back of his arm as the *kantal* flowers disappeared into blood. The night swallowed him, depthless and absolute, and unsteadily, he stumbled from flower to flower sightlessly, ruinous. Poisoned dirt stained his feet, and yet he could not stop, twisted by some power beyond his control, a rhythm that wound through the field of flowers and swept them into iron-sweet death.

The darkness was everything; it was bitter, blistering light and he had seared himself into blackness, empty sockets drenched with blood and crushed tepals. He was a blind man in a world of colchicine and turned soil. He was a gelid dream inverted and shattered.

Madness devoured the meadow until the last blossom had fallen to his touch, until the ink of the night had sunk into the soil. His skin was vermilion-soaked, ready to ignite. He could taste all the blood he had wrought, sour iron coating the back of his mouth, and he curled his toes into the dirt to keep himself from falling to his knees.

The sea of crimson receded as the earth swallowed it whole, tremors running through the haunted, airless darkness until the soil thrust forth a nascent nightmare of its own, already streaked with blood and venom.

The nightmare smiled, lightless, and danced across the drowned dirt toward him, kicking up ashes and broken tepals with every movement. He twirled and ran and set flame-spun hands on his shoulders, grasping them so tightly that the ragged nails split skin. And then he leaned in, so close the blood on his lips wet the shell of his ear.

"Die," he whispered, voice sweetened with cruelty, and so he did.

The first few times the story was told, there were differing accounts of how precisely the fire had begun. There were no survivors—the fire burned the city in its entirety, sparing not a single house, not a single heart. It swept through the streets relentlessly, its only focus to burn.

Some speculated that the fires of Avyakanth reignited spontaneously, and untouched and unmediated by the hands of man, burned all in their path. Others were convinced that it was the work of that Najan spy—the one who had killed their captain, who had broken their king. They had set strategic fires throughout the city, choking out escape routes and dooming the people to a single, inescapable fate.

But the version of the story that spread like wildfire spoke of the cause as not something borne of the city proper, but of the kingdom's reclusive, divinity-touched prophet. The young messiah, driven mad with lost love.

And in this story, it was his wrath that had burned the city—he had always been imbalanced, not fully settled in his own body. In his bitter fury, he had blamed the whole of humanity for his pain, had cursed them all to burn the same way he had. And so the fire had spread, not driven by the physical hunger for air, but by a more ruthless desire, an appetite for death.

The story, as it went, said this anger lived on even after his death—that it became a deity in and of itself, something cold and remote from the warmth of humanity; a god named for a razed nation, for ashes and ashes. But the story, as close as it was to the truth, was not wholly accurate.

And yet it held a kernel of old fear, of god-struck awe, and so it survived regardless. In that temple, high above the dying city, a tale was spun from dust and ash into something that held flame—something that held power. And it cut through the truth, through the remnants of those that were below, even as they cried out; even as they burned.

In the palace, entire rooms were abandoned to the fires. Screams layered over one another in a cacophony of pain as people struggled to escape the flames, trapped underneath the weight of others.

In the aviary, a girl stood beside the windows and watched the city burn. And when the flames reached her, she smiled.

In the temples of Marai, priests clutched each other in terror as flaming braziers turned to liquid and seized them; the ceilings crumbled from melting supports, paintings on carved stone blurred by smoke and flame. Two girls clung to one another, watching as the north tower listed precariously to the side. And as it fell, threatening to crush them and then following through, one did not tear their gaze away from that shadowed echo in the distance, from another burning temple.

And in the soft paddy fields on the outskirts of the shattered city, one watched the flames and mourned the death of a thousand hearts.

26
LYNE

At night, Kiran left. Suri knew this—she felt it in her chest. Sometimes, after he left, she would ghost her fingers over her heart and trace the outline of that old burn.

He had never explained, and she had never asked. It was one of those things they left to rot outside in the winter cold, secrets choking them from within. But he had never told her why he had helped Annabel, and it had unsteadied that careful, tenuous balance between them.

It wasn't his fault that she laid awake at night, consumed by unspoken questions. But she was tired of bleeding and bleeding, and so, a few days after Annabel returned to her family, she waited to feel him leave—a faint strain in her chest like a thread pulling taut—and then she rose and dressed.

It was foolish, and it was dangerous, to play games like these with gods—to dance on slender, uneven ropes threading chasms, deluded by bravado and a refusal to fall. Even if she wished it away, she was still mortal; she could still fall.

He wouldn't let her, though. She didn't know him, not the way she desired to, late at night with her fingers curled into fists and heart aflame with the dream of it. But she knew he would not let her fall, even if she slipped. Even if she jumped.

Kiran paused near the meadows that wrapped around the city limits. The darkness of him—black hair, black coat, dark skin and bright eyes—stood out in stark relief against the desaturated wildflowers, the bouquet stiff and pale against him. He looked like some god of oblivion, of mourning, a reaper in the dead of night.

Suri followed him out of the meadow, onto the slender footpath that wound around the hills. Sparse, distant trees cast delicate, tangled shadows onto the cement and dirt. She traced them carefully and followed him through the narrow opening and out into the rolling emptiness of the country beyond.

From here, they could easily see the towns and suburbs that dotted the countryside; the city's overflow sprawled across knotted ground, covered with asphalt as though it was hard candy. This was a world that had fallen asleep, soaked with darkness and the whistling melody of the breeze. If she strained her ears, she could hear the dissonant song of the city, but it was already beginning to fade.

It was a world asleep, but Suri still startled at the emptiness of the parking lot, the eerie cast of the moonlight against the shining stone of the temple. Kiran ran his fingers over the wrought-iron gates, gentle and reverent, before slipping in. The faucet creaked in protest but obediently began to spill out water, and he washed his feet quickly, twisting the tap off just carelessly enough that it still trickled to the stone below. A joke, perhaps, a kind of wordless acknowledgement of her presence. But it was not enough—Suri wanted words, wanted answers.

A truth pierced through her, raw and unsurprising. She had spent weeks ignoring it only to be confronted with it now, standing at the steps of some old, loved temple, a temple that had belonged to her family but would never belong to her.

She wanted his heart; the desire devoured her. Even if it was made of fire and to know it was to fall into ash, she wanted the entirety of it, with the passion of maenads, the madness of gods. It did not matter to her that she had none of their magic, none of their clever golden blood. She was mortal, so she would return; Kiran's river of death would release her, and she would live again. Fate tangled threads and cut them in patterns that were so cruel and so lovely, and yet it allowed mortals to love. And in the end, love made immortals of them all.

Following the god's steps, she brushed her hands against the pillars to guide herself in the near-darkness. This close, the air smelled like aged blossoms and honeyed milk and incense, and she felt saturated in it.

What little moonlight illuminated the angles of the temple from outside disappeared entirely the moment the door fell softly shut behind her. She could only navigate the temple by the shifts in the darkness as her eyes slowly adjusted to the black.

Light blazed through the shadows; Suri watched, entranced, before ducking behind a nearby shrine. Kiran's index finger was held up, a small ball of flame burning steadily above it. He used it to light a bronze candelabra discarded at the edge of one of the larger shrines, carrying it with him to the back of the temple.

Suri counted her breaths as she traced his steps on uneven, glittering marble. He lingered in front of a smaller shrine, near the back exit. It still held a few elements of the grandeur of the main shrines—the same carved pillars, stories written into the stone that hung overhead. Unlike those, it didn't have an inner and outer sanctum, only an iron lattice pulled tight over the idol within. Kiran tinkered with it before slowly dragging it upward, the shrill screech of it cutting into the night.

From here, she could not know which god he was honoring. A golden plaque hung on the far pillar, but the candlelight fell short of its edges.

Tucked behind another shrine—Makai's, or Ashri's, she wasn't sure—she watched him work through the steps of his old routine. He moved with the ease of practice and the tremulous hesitation of mourning. *Atonement,* he had said, when he had carried a hundred flames in his soul and let them flicker for her. She wondered, distantly, whether this was another method of atonement, self-flagellation sustained by centuries of careful repetition.

After, he removed the bouquet from his coat, drawing stems out one by one. He pinched fingers around petals before pulling them all off in a single movement, scattering them over the statue. Suri felt the cadence of it, the rhythm of the strewn blossoms and whispered prayers. He performed the service as if he was a priest, not a god.

His fingers were stained with ash and holy water by the time he finished. The waning moonlight caught him when he turned, the planes of his face streaked black and silver. "You can come out now, Suri."

Suri felt cold with knowledge. She had wanted his heart, and in his own wordless way, he had given her parts of it. It did not change the consuming, uncaring nature of the desire, the need to have *everything* instead of perfumed, fragile pieces. But it warmed her. "Who is this?"

It was a question he had prepared for; his expression dipped under the weight of it and smoothed out accordingly. "A friend of mine. He's dead."

"I thought gods didn't stay dead."

Kiran shook his head lightly. "He will return, eventually. But his death was sacrilegious—it extends the period of death. I don't think you will be alive to see him. He is as good as dead, in your mortal definition of it."

In the uneven firelight of the candelabra and the distant moonlight, he looked almost sorrowful. Then he looked up, and his eyes shone. "I assume you have more questions. Otherwise, you wouldn't have followed me."

It was such a useless, cruel phrase, and she nearly resented him for it. *More questions.* He could not know how, more often than not, they were urgent, formless, incomprehensible. She felt as if she might split from the force of them, crack and shatter into shards as the dark parts of her heart grew and swallowed the earth.

He ducked his head, and it resembled apology. Suri stepped forward until she was close enough to feel the heat of the candelabra. And him, always him. The god was so much warmer than camphor and flame could ever hope to be.

Instead of asking a question, she found her lips shaping a confession. "I feel like I'll never know you. Like you could stay for decades and centuries and millennia, and my bones could strip themselves clean with the effort of it, and I still wouldn't know you entirely."

Instead of frowning, he laughed, and it was such a surprisingly sweet sound that she startled, leaning back. Temple bells and chilled, sweet water, bright and lovely. Even when it faded, his face was still shaped like it. "You know me so well it terrifies me, Suri. You know me better than gods and mortals, better than anyone who has lived for centuries." He tilted his head, the line of his mouth sharp and fraught with incredulity. "That kind of knowledge is dangerous, you know. You could rip me apart without a blade."

Suri lifted her chin. "I wouldn't. You know that."

"I do," he said, unsmiling. His eyes were chips of ore, glittering and hard. "Would you want to know me?"

Her lips soured with unspoken words. *I would want to know you entirely, in this life and in every one that follows.* "If you'll let me."

The corners of his eyes crinkled. "I would give you anything, if you wished for it."

"Except for another kiss," she said wryly. They were close enough now that she could steal one, if she dipped in quickly.

But she didn't want to; they had never been the kind to take from one another.

"Except for another kiss," he agreed. He took a seat on the stone floor in front of the sanctum and leaned forward into the grate, putting out the flame of the candelabra with his thumb. She sat beside him, cold marble chilling her bare shins.

"Tell me a secret," she whispered, tipping her weight onto his shoulder. She felt warmed from within. "One you've never told anyone."

He was silent a moment, shoulders rising and falling under her cheek. Then he said, "I used to have a brother."

"What happened to him?"

"I lost him," he said eventually, so softly the words disappeared into the air seconds after he let go of them. So softly that when he turned his head, exhaling a laugh against her forehead, she had to strain to discern them from the viscous quiet. "It was my fault, of course. But I lost him."

By dawn, the shrine was cleaned and closed, and they had already begun to return home. When light began to spill across the sky, washing it in shades of red, Suri tilted her face up and watched the world come awake. Wordlessly, Kiran mirrored the action and watched the sunlight turn the darkness ruddy and soft, and thought of the old myths of dawn, of the beauty and the artifice of them.

In all the old stories, gods and devils were infallible and invincible, carved out of spells and stone. When the heroes sought to kill them or to know them—so often the same thing—they quested to the deepest, darkest cracks of the world, splitting the earth and looking for items so lost, so abstruse they assured the impossibility of deicide. The wishbone of a firebird, the burial ground of the first person they had ever blessed, the sacred, rusted weapon they had lost in battle. Beautiful, unattainable things presented on the cusp of victory.

Kiran had always loved those tales, the sharp, effervescent wonder of them, bubbles popping on his tongue every time he spoke them into life. And when he had been taken aside, gently and fearfully, and told the secret of their existence and their deaths, he had nearly laughed from disbelief, from jagged scorn. *It cannot be that easy,* he thought, and yet it was—there was no other word for oblivion in the language of gods, but he had only just begun to learn it.

It had not taken him long to understand that their sugar-sweet poison was impossible in itself. What seemed inevitable to humans was unfathomable to them. There was a perfect, fate-kissed balance to it.

Because gods could never be human, and humans were defined in broad, beautiful strokes of terror and love and ephemerality—immortals couldn't understand such things, couldn't understand how emotions struck paper-thin skin and set it aflame.

He could, of course. And that was the humor of it, the cosmic punch line, kismet leaning forward and tenderly sliding one of his own knives between his ribs. He could, and the knowledge had been burned from him for years and years, but it still lingered, soul-deep. Gods couldn't love because they had never been taught how to, had never traced the vessels of a beating heart so gently and so fearfully, afraid of cracking it open and shattered with the need to swallow it whole.

Kiran had been taught, and even if the knowledge was faded, Suri had taught him again and again.

It wasn't as convoluted as the myths, not so grand or timeless, but he thought the secret of their deaths was lovely in its own way. No one would ever die from it, none but him, but he had grown himself into something golden and wrapped for death once before, and so it did not bother him, the notion of dying again for the sake of some old, inexorable rule.

No, what bothered him was the simplicity of it, the knowledge that all those heroes had traveled to the Asakhi and sifted through its waters, and fought demons and lovers and themselves. All for the sake of holding out a relic on an engraved, shining platter, so they could defeat evil or love it. They never failed, he knew, but he also knew that those lost treasures were not why they won.

Killing a god seemed simple enough; heroes leaned close and ran them through, dressed in new, jeweled blood. But golden hearts were born strong—they split not from blade or stone, but from trembling fingers wrapped around hilts, still shaped in love and prayer.

The night at the temple had been a mistake. Suri had confessed once, and her heart was still bold and greedy with the memory of it, as though she could confess again and again, and ask him easily for things she knew he could not give her.

She woke one morning to see him on the balcony, leaned against the wrought-iron bars. The glass doors were frosted with cold—his expression was obscured, his posture loose and inscrutable. For a moment, her head murky with sleep, she remembered that old nightmare of hers. The figure of him, silhouetted against a red dawn, before he disappeared into ash and tepals streaked with blood and gold.

But the sky was thick with clouds, and though his shirt hung oddly off his frame, wavering in the faint wind, she didn't see him break apart and fragment into dust. He was still real.

Suri slid open the glass doors and stepped out into the winter air. Absently, she traced the whorl of a jasmine bud as she passed the garden to stand by him. Her fingers were damp and perfumed, and when she brought her hand up to prop up her chin, she could smell the sweet, heady scent of the flower.

Kiran was looking out over the city, pensive. Heat wicked off him, and the frost around them melted endlessly. Then he turned to look at her, and she held his gaze and thought, without pretense and without fear, of the raw beauty of his eyes. They looked like nectar, saccharine and strong, like the molten warmth of them could fill her entirely, like it could drown her.

This was not daybreak, dangerous and infinite. The world around them was ash-gray, damp with snow and salt. It was not made for confessions. But Suri tired of these silent exchanges, strained with yearning and the desire to speak aloud what seared them from inside. She tired of this wordless, vagabond love that had no birthplace and would have no grave, not unless they gave it one.

She opened her mouth, and spoke.

Her lips parted, but he cut in before she could speak. "Are you afraid of death?"

It was not entirely desperate misdirection—he was curious to hear her answer—but her mouth puckered as she took in the question. "Yeah."

She didn't explain herself, but he hadn't expected her to. Kiran leaned away from her, cutting a jasmine blossom off the plant with his nail. He cupped it in his hands so she could see the smooth, velvet curve of the flower. They were so close that the air was fragrant, heavy with the night-sharp sweetness of the jasmine and the sugar citrus smell of her shampoo.

The bud was soft against his curled palm. Flame wound through it, and turned it to ash.

She held his gaze, unaffected by such small wonders. A smile threatened to touch his lips, but he held it back and curled his fingers in. The bud reformed and bloomed, a blossom made of ash and smoke. Her lips parted for a moment, with suppressed awe.

Delicately, she stroked the blossom, flinching when the pads of her fingers touched the ash petals. "It's real."

"Real as hearts," he said, and pinched the flower between his index finger and thumb, watched the breeze disrupt the dust. Then he leaned forward, and tucked the stem behind the shell of her ear. Her skin was cold to the touch, chilled by the air and thick human blood. His fingers burned where they'd brushed against it.

He let his mouth curve into a smile, faint and faded. "From death to life. You should not be afraid."

Suri echoed him, but it was brittle. "Shouldn't I?" Her fingers brushed against the curl of her ear absently, burnt-sugar eyes fixed on his. "Tell me, do wishes die when we speak them aloud?"

The line of her mouth was dangerous—still, he shook his head. She dropped her hand from the flower and turned away, glancing out over the city. There was nothing of interest to see, not for a girl who had loved it her entire life—she had turned for the sake of it, for the smooth nature of the movement and the way it would carry her away from him. "You said gods can't wish. So, on my birthday, I made two—one for you, and one for me."

Something like a plea tore through him; it came out the other side blood-soaked and empty. Suri turned back and took his hands in hers, smaller and softer and colder.

"I wished," she said, bitten nails leaving half-moons in his palms, "That we could both have happy endings."

Kiran was alive with the memory of burnt cities and a past composed entirely of dead flowers and bleeding steel. And it formed words and warnings inside him, whispering to him in that ragged, sorrow-sweet voice he'd never forgotten, telling him to *run, run, run.*

His hand pulled out of hers; he placed it on the iron railing and wrapped his fingers around the cold metal.

"You'll have a happy ending," he said, quieter than he'd intended to. But in the silent winter morning, his voice carried. "You will."

"And you?" she asked, tipping her face up so it held the thin sunlight. A muscle jumped in her jaw, tense with every word and every question that lived inside her. "Who will give you your happy ending?"

He tried to smile, but it came out strained and ugly with old pain. He could've lied—he could feel it on his tongue, the artifice he could've spun out into humor and purposeful ignorance. *I'll find one someday.* But she would've seen it, and the untruth of it would've hurt her. "Some of us don't get happy endings, Suri. Not all tragedies mend themselves in time."

Her eyes narrowed, defiant. "I don't care about the rest of the tragedies."

There was an implicit statement in it—*I care about yours*—and it seared all the way down; he didn't dare hold onto it for fear it would fall into ashes in his hands, the kind that did not put themselves back together and breathe alive into something more beautiful. Lightly, he said, "Fate loves all its tragedies. I don't think it will let go of me that easily."

"I'll bend fate," she replied, graceless and lovely, "And I'll break it, and I'll empty that river of yours until the world's drowned with old tragedies and happy endings."

Despite everything, he laughed a little, unconscious and too soft for it to be anything but strange. It surprised her—the stubborn set to her features softened momentarily and she watched him wordlessly, the ash flower trembling in the breeze.

"Would you believe me," he asked, soft as petals, soft as palms, "If I told you I'd be bad for you?"

"Like old films, then," she said, after a moment had passed. Her voice was careful, gaze clear and scrutinizing. He wondered what she meant to find in him, what latent secret or hidden horror she found so interesting. "Love stories."

What were love stories but dreams of worlds where the sun and moon could linger beside one another long enough to learn the language of the other's heart? "Yes."

"Do you want to know a secret?" She didn't mean the words as a question; she held his gaze, teeth gritted, eyes bright, hair dancing around her face like black flame. She was every bit of fire he held inside his heart. "I've never believed in fairy tales. Nor in love stories."

"You believe in happy endings," he said, and her mouth split in a jagged smile.

"I believe in happy endings," she agreed, "And I believe in the gods who grant them. But I don't believe in their silence damning us. If the gods never answer, then we learn to make happy endings of our own."

She was not speaking of her own—Kiran felt unsteady, like he could tear into ash and disappear into the flower behind her ear and stay there forever. He was broken with the weight of this love, a bird that had forgotten how to fly.

His lips lifted in a humorless smile. "But fate—"

"Fuck fate," she said savagely. "And I swear, Kiran, I swear to all your dead saints, if this is why you're going to leave—because you think you're *bad* for me—"

She cut off abruptly. They didn't talk about him leaving—it wasn't something they did, because they were both afraid of losing things they loved, and they were both in love. But the air was ripe with confessions and secrets now, and the sharp iron tang of regret disappeared in the mist of it.

Kiran leaned back, and her eyes tracked the movement. They didn't speak.

Don't ask me to stay, he pleaded. *Please, don't ask me to stay.*

"Has the inner seal broken yet?" she asked, as though she could not feel it in her own chest as he felt it in his.

"Not yet," he said tonelessly, and the last word hung between them, a promise and an answer, and he pretended not to notice the way it sliced through her, straight through flesh and sinew to shining white bone.

She would not speak, so he made himself spit out the words, clumsy and useless. "I can't stay. You know I can't."

But they were speaking of different things entirely, and he knew it. They both knew he would have to leave, after his 'sick leave' ended and he returned to his jobs. Suri meant *stay* the way humans did—to stay in a heart, to learn the lines of it and never give it up. She meant it in the way of *uttriyasi—live and die and live again, and dance across the threads of the world, through darkness and light, and always come back, always.* She meant it like two whispered, wondrous words—*find me.*

Kiran knew this without her having to say it, because he knew her heart how children knew stars in the sky, taught before embarking on journeys. He used the pieces of her heart—the traceries of vessels, the bloody heartstrings, the warm, ceaseless rhythm—as constellations, a bright, infallible sea of light that would always lead him home.

A long time ago, she had told him to run. He had not obeyed her then, but he had spent the rest of his eternity running. And now she was asking him to stay, asking him to *stop,* and he was afraid of telling her the truth because he thought it might make it real: he wasn't sure he knew how to.

Snowflakes fell, and dusted her cheekbones like war paint. Carefully, he cupped her face and drew his thumbs across her cheeks, wiping away the flakes.

Her skin was so cold under his fingers; they were so close that moving closer was far easier than moving apart, and the realization of it startled him. He began to draw his hands away, but she pulled hers up and held him in place. Ash petals fell away and twirled alongside the snowflakes.

"Why do you touch me like that?"

"Like what?" he asked, gently testing her grip. It tightened, and he gave up, returning to stroking the tops of her cheekbones with his thumbs. Her eyes were dark with unspoken emotion, sorrow without all the sharp parts.

"Like you're afraid of burning me," she said, unsteady under his hands. "You touch me like you're afraid of hurting me."

The smile came to his lips unbidden, small and bitter. "I'm good at things like that, burning and hurting. The closer you get, the worse your chances get. If you fear death the way you say you do, you should stake me through the heart and feed me to the carrion birds."

She made a face at the wording, leaning back unintentionally. His fingers slipped, and her grip tightened, nails digging into the backs of his hands. In the suffocating cold, the pain tethered him.

"You wouldn't hurt me," she said, so firmly it held no warmth. She said it the same way that others would say the sky was blue, the way they would say their heart knew how to beat.

"I could," he returned, but she caught his gaze, too sharp for the limp, weak words to have any real sway. *Could he? Or would his fire bounce off the surface of her skin, tempered by tenderness?* He would not have been surprised to learn that she was immune to him.

"You wouldn't," she repeated, turning his face to meet hers. The words came slowly, sharply, as if they stung and bit on the way out. "Tell me why you can't stay."

Her palm was too cold against his cheek, and he wanted to warm her until the chill left them both. "I was never supposed to stay."

Suri's eyes shuttered, dark lashes feathering the tops of her cheeks. There was something strained and knotted in the uneven line of her mouth. "Tell me why you *can't*."

But he couldn't, not in words. *I can't stay, because*—because what? Because he had been born from blood, and he would return to it, knives scissoring through the membranes of his heart the moment he'd opened his eyes. Because he'd burned the world down once, and he'd do it again if she asked him to. Because he had lost so many from the simple, cutting sin of staying beside them, and he couldn't bear to lose her, not again. Because his was a myth with no happy ending, a tragedy that swallowed its tail, infinite. *I can't stay, because I think I'm in love with you.*

"I'm an inconvenience," he began, and the words came easily; they were not lies, after all. "I live in your apartment and earn money given by your grandmother and irritate you both endlessly. Your lives would be much easier without me, you—" his breath caught, and he took a moment to steady it. "You deserve someone good and whole, and I'm neither. I'm not even a person—I'm person-shaped. There's nothing in me worth the effort of caring for."

Suri dropped her hands back to her sides, and took a step back. She looked as if he'd struck her.

"You're an idiot," she said, wondrous with anger. "You're a fucking idiot."

She gave a sharp, incredulous laugh. "I don't even know where to begin. *There is nothing in me worth the effort of caring for?* Do you not know how much the others care for you, how much my grandmother cares for you? Who are you to decide the ease and cadence of our lives? I—" she paused, exhaling slowly. She fixed her gaze on the ground below. "Are all your reasons to leave this stupid?"

Kiran didn't acknowledge the question. Perhaps she was right, and they thought they cared for him. But in the long run, they would be better off if he were gone. "Why do you think someone bound us together, Suri? Have you never wondered whether they might come back? The longer I stay here, the more danger you'll be in."

"I'll be in danger no matter what," she said simply. "I've been in danger since the moment I let you in. I've been in danger since the moment my parents died. There was no escaping it, not for me. If you leave, technically I'll be in more danger."

Still, she would not look up. He examined the ducked curl of her head, the tight fists at her sides. "You really, truly want me to stay, then."

"Yes," she said, unflinching. Her heart was the inception of diamond, glittering and adamantine. What a pair they made, a heart that held scars in place of vessels and a heart dipped in iron and filled with fire. Hers would never break, and his would never learn how to heal.

And it cut across every law of his soul, every bound memory and every mortal one, but he stepped back from her. There were seas between them, entire worlds and entire lives. His mouth tasted like ash.

Her gaze scraped across the snow-dusted stone below them, voice little more than a cold rasp. "You're not even going to try. You're not even going to give this a chance."

Kiran looked at her, and he saw the fractured, broken threads of Annabel's soul. He saw shattered pottery, and blood filling the clear water of a shallow pool like ink. He saw unmarked graves on the freshly broken ground of a battlefield, and red-flecked lips mouthing a single word, a single command. *Run.*

A laugh rolled through him, low and quiet. "I don't mind if you hate me for it. Spit on my shrine, or wish for another early death, or thank fate for my tragedy. Do whatever you need to do. But I will not stay and doom you."

Suri forced herself to look up, the movement so slow and cutting it could have drawn blood. "Don't."

But he was already gone, and the winter air had washed away the remnants of his presence, leaving behind only the faint scent of smoke and ash.

27
ENESMAT

Kiran could not understand why the city was burning.

He seized the bloody knife on the altar, holding it close to him as if it would explain—as if it would tell him the secrets of the flames. But it did not, and above, Avya did not answer him.

Viro was dead, slumped against a column and half melted—and yet, Kiran could not fathom having killed him. The city was dying, and yet the flames were not his. But there was no other fire, no other flame-spun heart that could have burned them, and so it must have been him—it must have.

His head ached, chest still pained with the echo of death. But death could not free him from this pervasive, sickening scene: the odor of burning flesh and blossoms, of blood turned to smoke, of gods turned human with ferocious love.

It is your fire, said that old, wry voice, mocking him. *It is your fire, and these are your ashes.*

He was wreathed in cold fire, knelt on the stone of the temple floor. It ripped him apart from inside, metal hooked into flesh and meant to rend. A hundred ashen heartstrings severed in a second, sweeping him into blissful oblivion.

This time, he did not dream of divinity. He knew there was nothing left in him that resembled the stars, nor the gods. There was only this strange, ceaseless fire, this sea of wrath and blistering *kantal* blossoms melted into blood, this nameless, aching regret.

Kiran shut his eyes and waited for the flames to take him. When he opened them, he was in an unfamiliar, empty cavern, twice the size of the palace in width and length, and yet empty throughout. The walls were the color of probed flesh, wound through with veins of black and red. Along the near side, a slender, rushing length of liquid ran from onc edge of the cavern to the other, uninterrupted and volatile. From darkness to darkness.

"Are you sure this is a good idea?" someone said, resolving from vague, faded static into a real voice. "He has the constitution of an infant. Mortals usually cannot stand the strain."

"I do not think he would agree with that assessment," another voice replied, familiar and faintly amused. Kiran blinked once, and the cavern was no longer empty. A man in dark mourner's robes stood beside the river, gripping a carved holly staff. He scrutinized him with piercing silver eyes, his ebony complexion glinting in the low light.

Beside him stood Avya. There was an odd, sad smile on his face. A smile of mourning, of pity.

Kiran's blood was ice in his veins. "Where am I?"

"Poor critical thinking skills," put in the man beside the river—a god, then. "The others will mock you for centuries if you go through with this. They will say you are far too soft for your position."

"Oh, hush," Avya said crossly. "They already know I am too soft."

Kiran glanced around the empty, beating cavern. Distant, overlapping voices twined with one another and sang in the background. "Dhaasthur."

Neither of them replied, but the man beside the river glanced back in appraisal. Whatever he saw, he did not feel the need to make a comment upon it—he snorted and focused on the river once more. Once in a while, he would tap the staff gently against the floor of the cavern, and strands of dark, shining liquid—almost reflective, like mercury—would leap into the air and dissipate.

Dhaasthur. The land of the dead. Which meant the man beside the liquid was Dhaasan, the god of the dead, and that was the River Asakhi. The river of souls, of death. Of rebirth.

Kiran could not help but think that it was rather small for the underworld. Dhaasan made a scornful noise. Without deigning to elaborate on how he knew his thoughts, he said, "This is only one of many places where the river touches the earth, boy. *Asakhi* is everywhere, just as death is. To think it confined by the constraints of mortal lands is disappointingly naive."

"Kiran," Avya broke in gently. Impossibly gently. "Do you know why you are here?"

"I died," he said warily. "I sacrificed myself, and died."

Avya and Dhaasan exchanged glances. Frustration burned in his chest. "Where are they? You have to take me back—you have to save them. The city was burning. You have to go save them."

Avya's gaze softened slightly. "I cannot. You know why I cannot."

Kiran knew, but he could not force himself to face it. He already felt changed, unnatural. As though he knew intimately every single emotion he was meant to feel, and yet sensed none of them. There was something horribly distant about the entire ordeal, a crushing, impossible despair he could not access, a heart he no longer had.

He tasted bile on his tongue, acrid. "I killed them."

"No," Dhaasan cut in, throwing a glare in Avya's direction. "You did not. Blame yourself for whatever you want, boy, but you did not kill those people."

"Then—"

"I did," Avya said firmly. Even now, his gaze was steady. But there was a sharp resolution he had not noticed before. There was no softness there—the death of an entire city was little more than a simple punishment. Kiran heard Viro's voice, echoing: *An example must be made.* "I have given them many chances, for centuries and centuries before your birth. I told you they would hurt you, and you did not believe me. What did you invoke? 'Their inherent good?' How little that helped you in the end."

"You burned the city down," he whispered. "Because of me."

The god of death narrowed his eyes at him, as if in disbelief. "The boy's even more pigheaded than you are."

Kiran ignored him. Self-hatred was a welcome, jagged ache in his blood in the face of this newfound lack of sensation. "Intent. I must have sacrificed myself with a latent intent—to hurt. Otherwise, you would not have been able to burn the city and accept my sacrifice in the same breath."

His mouth thinned, and he knew he was right. The god held up a hand. "It was my decision. If you'd had any say, you would not have done it. I know that. The people would have known it. Dhaasan knows it—"

"Unfortunately," the god grumbled, tapping his staff once again.

"This is not your burden to carry," Avya finished, his gaze uncomfortably bright.

The words washed over him. He held the god's stare defiantly. "So why am I here? Why am I not—" he nodded toward the river of souls. "Dead, as I am supposed to be? Awaiting reincarnation?"

Dhaasan barked out a sharp, harsh laugh. "I do not envy you now, old friend."

Avya folded his arms. There was an edge of something resembling nervousness in his eyes—if gods even felt such things. "Kiran, as you know, you are part human and part god. An uneven, imprecise mixture."

Anxiety chafed against him. "And?"

"And," the god continued, "There has always been more god in you than mortal. More flame than flesh. And when you… died and invoked my blessing and I burned the city, you took in more of my fire in my wrath."

"What do you mean to say?" Kiran whispered. Distantly, he registered the crack of stone, the rumble of pressure.

Dhaasan paused beside the river, glancing up toward the ceiling of the cavern. Kiran could not—he felt as though if he moved his attention away from keeping himself still, he would crack, would split apart into flame and ash.

Avya's gaze had not left his. "You did not wholly die in the temple. There was enough divinity in you that you simply lingered, lost between two states. And so I… I allowed you to ascend. I gave you more of my power, enough to make you something near whole. And yet, it is not mine anymore." He glanced at the ceiling of the cavern, and then back. "You have made it your own. Despite what any of the other gods may say," he said, shooting a look at Dhaasan, "It is entirely yours now."

Kiran thought he might vomit. The ache of an old wound throbbed in his chest, six sharp points splintering flesh—flesh that was no longer mortal, that no longer bled red, that no longer beat with a proper heart. "I slaughtered an entire city, and—and as a present, I am given godhood?"

"Nearly every single word in that sentence was incorrect," Dhaasan said scornfully. "As I said previously, constitution of an infant."

The ceiling of the cavern rumbled. Stalactites of crimson crystal struck the ground beside Kiran at odd angles, pointing outward from him. As if he were a point of impact, a splatter of blood.

"Calm yourself," Avya said, holding up his hands in a placating gesture. There was something so terribly ironic about that, Kiran thought. He had gifted him this fire, this decorated wrath.

But when he spoke, his voice was so steady it amused him. As if this anger was something so easily controlled. "If I am not dead, then why am I here?"

"Oh, you're certainly dead," Dhaasan answered, tapping a soul. It shimmered and disappeared, sent to the world above. "Gods die too, though our deaths are few and far between, and we always return before long. But your soul is drained. If you returned to the mortal world in this form, you would be little more than a sentient wraith."

He *felt* like a sentient wraith, but kept silent. Avya said, "I wanted to let you know of what happened before you left for the river. I hope you do not resent me overmuch."

His blood felt caustic in his veins, corrosive with fury, and yet he could not resent the god. Only himself, for dooming the city. For condemning them with his last breath.

Kiran nodded at the river. "How long must I spend there?"

Dhaasan grinned, an eerie sliver of white against his cool, dark skin. "As long as you would like to spend, godling. A thousand years or a thousand seconds. It is up to you entirely." He lifted his shoulders in a faint shrug. "Though you may as well consider the chaos the human world will return to without your presence. They have offered you such beautiful titles, such broad domains."

An odd, jagged shard of anger cut through him, but he steadied himself, reaching out to press the palm of his hand to the closest stalactite. It seemed to pulse under his fingers, warm to the touch. Quietly, he asked, "What do you mean?"

The god of death ticked off names on the fingers of his free hand while using the other to mediate the souls of the river. "God of wrath, god of fire, god of war—"

The titles sickened him, and yet they fit. They fit the cold, insatiable hunger, the utter lack of *feeling* that roared through him even now. If this was how gods felt all the time, he thought, it was no wonder they looked to humans for entertainment.

Or perhaps that was just him, borne by flame and tempered by wrath.

"It is your choice," Avya finished. There had been a moment, when the stalactites had fallen, when his warmth had been subsumed by a kind of thoughtful wariness. But now it had dissipated—there was a sadness in his gaze, a deep sympathy. Yet still no regret. "You may spend as long as you want in the waters of the Asakhi. I will not come to retrieve you. Neither will Dhaasan, nor any of the other gods. My only request is that you return when you are ready. There is work yet to be done."

He slipped between the stalactites, sending a last wary glance toward the two gods. In his head, he struggled to grasp at the names of the dead. As he approached the waters, he strung them together, a hymn for those he had hurt. Perhaps immortality would give him the chance to atone; perhaps it would simply be a kind of eternal agony.

—Isa, Kita, Lucius, Viro, Suri.

Kiran stepped into the darkness and let it swallow him whole.

28
LYNE

The inner seal wasn't broken, not yet. Suri could still hear the words in his mouth, soft and sour, twisting his lips sharply. Not *yet.*

He left, but he returned late that night. Because he had to, because the seal would not let him disappear. He made no attempts at indulging in locks, in doors—she heard the quiet thud of footsteps against the cement of the balcony, and the glass doors screeched open. The footsteps continued down the hallway, lingering outside her door for a moment before returning back.

He had never planned to stay, not ever. And she had always known that, even if she'd sometimes hoped otherwise, but even if she couldn't change his mind, it didn't mean she had to keep close and hurt herself even more. She was a creature created by and damned by hope, but she wasn't self-destructive. She wouldn't let herself become self-destructive.

The rest of the year passed in a silent, awkward blur—she wasn't sure whether she was avoiding him or he was avoiding her, or whether they were tripping over themselves pressing their bodies into shadows the moment they realized the room wasn't empty. She only ever heard the soft thrum of his footsteps in the late night, before the moon fell.

Sometimes, her grandmother would drop by, or a few of her friends. She gave them all the same answer when they saw the empty living room, noticed the stale air. *Oh, he's sick, so he's sleeping in my bed, and I'm taking the floor. I'll tell him you dropped by. I'm... busy right now? Let's hang out another time.*

She wouldn't be able to sell it if she went out with them. Cabin fever was beginning to set in, so much so that she nearly missed *school*, but she knew it was a fragile sort of thing. It would only take the barest allusion to him for the anger to shine through on her face, and then it would all fall apart, a house of cards or petals.

Are you two fighting? Well. Nothing that can't be fixed with a good talk—

Suri didn't want to talk. Suri wanted to forget every kind thing he had ever done and every kind thing he had ever been, until she could let him go without it searing hard, caustic lines into her skin and bones. It was cowardice, but there were no gods left to judge her for it and deem her soul unworthy.

She threw herself into searching for the sigil. It was another kind of insanity—she hadn't ever been able to find it, and neither had Kiran—but it felt fitting that this was what she would return to, in the midst of all of this. To something that would never yield answers, slamming her body against a locked door just to feel the edge of blood.

Two days before the new year broke, she found something on one of the forums. A single post, with a photo of the symbol and a link. She clicked on it and waited, hollow.

This site can't be reached, her laptop told her. The server's IP address could not be found.

It didn't surprise her all that much, the clear white screen, the heavy black text politely informing her she was destroying herself looking for things that wouldn't exist and people that wouldn't stay.

Give it up, a voice whispered, low and quiet in the back of her head. Strangely, it was her own, if dispirited and desolate. It would not let her go. *Give it up.*

So she did. There was no point in living a life founded on crumbling, mossy gravestones. The mystery still allured her, even now, but she was tired of chasing it. She was tired of burning scarred flesh on prayer flames. She was *tired.*

She shut the laptop, and it felt a little like a betrayal, a rueful hesitation running through her. *This can't be the end.* It was. There had never been anything to find, after all. She was digging through dry, black soil to find smooth bedrock. No gold, no treasure, no magic underneath. Only stone and magma.

The next morning, her eyes snapped open suddenly, winter sunlight casting the entire room in shades of blue. Wariness threaded through her like dread—part of her felt like something would've changed, should've changed as a result of her decision. But nothing had. It was all the same life, the same silence. In the end, it didn't matter.

The realization washed the trepidation from her heart, but when she left her room to find breakfast, the living room was empty. He'd already left or he'd never returned; there was no way to know which one.

She felt shivery with fatigue. She poured a cup of orange juice, drained it, and went right back to bed. Maybe, all this time she had been the one who'd gotten sick, and she'd never noticed.

Suri awoke to the sound of someone breaking down her door. Choppy, coarse sounds, destruction in a single note. She was out of her bed before she had the chance to examine the possibility of who it was. Instinctually, she knew it wasn't Kiran—if he'd wanted to enter without a trace, he would have. This was either a thief or an unwanted visitor.

She opened the door to find Miya leaned against the edge of the stairwell, Aza perched on the rail with her collar up. *Give it up*—she could try all she wanted, but suspicion would always be carved into her bones.

"Get out of my house, Santana," she said, supporting herself against the doorjamb.

Miya's dark eyebrows flicked upward, scornful and concerned. She slipped past Suri into the apartment, taking a seat on the couch and crossing her legs. "Where the hell have *you* been? It's New Year's Eve and you look like a pigeon crapped on your will to live."

She was clad in a slippery, diaphanous dress that came down to the middle of her thighs, with tall black boots. It was a party outfit, and Suri, drenched as she was in pigeon shit and nihilism, felt her heart sink. "I'm—sick. I can't go out."

"Did he get you sick?" she asked, leaning forward. Her dark eyes shone. "You don't look feverish."

"What do I look like?"

"Like you need a drink," she said, lips twisting in a grin. Suri glared at her, but her smile was impenetrable, a mask of rouge and glitter.

Aza slid off the rail and followed her in, gently shutting the door behind her. She stared up at Suri for a moment, pinching her cheeks and stretching them outward before huffing and letting go. "You're not eating enough. Maybe you *are* sick."

"Not anymore," she assured her, the words tasting stale and strange in her mouth. "You sound like my grandmother."

"She's smart," Aza pointed out, leaning over the back of the armchair. "The party's across town—if we want to get there in time, we should leave soon."

Suri bit back a groan. "I told you, I'm not coming. I have plans."

"What plans?" Miya challenged, eyes narrowed. "Sleeping through the new year?"

"I'm allowed to rest."

"'Rest' ended several days ago," she said, sauntering toward the hallway. "Now, you're just moping."

"Over what?" She had never told them about her conversation with Kiran, and she didn't plan to. There was no way to simplify it without taking every single salient detail out of the issue.

Miya shrugged over her shoulder. "Hell if I know. I'd ask, but I know you'll just lie. Wouldn't want to scare you off."

Reluctantly, she followed her and Aza into the mess of her bedroom. Miya let out a melodramatic moan at the state of it—clothes hung over furniture, empty water bottles on the windowsill, rumpled covers—and pressed the back of her hand to her forehead. "How am I going to dress you from *this?* I can't even tell where your clothes are supposed to be."

"You've performed stranger miracles," Suri said, taking a seat on the edge of the mattress and curling her feet into the carpet. She felt threadbare, ephemeral. "Do I really have to come?"

Aza held her gaze. "Do you really not want to?"

Did she? Even now, she wasn't sure. At the very least, it was a change of scenery. She could feel the walls of the apartment beginning to press in around her, relentless and cruel. Suri inclined her head.

Miya's mouth curled in triumph, but she couldn't be sure about whether it was due to her acquiescence or the fact that she'd uncovered the closet door. *"Finally.* Now we're talking."

Casually, she updated her on what she'd missed while cooped up in the apartment. Rifling through the glittering, dark clothes, Miya explained how Ellis's moods had stabilized of late. Shyly, he'd let them know that Annabel was improving rapidly—even though she still spent the majority of the day sleeping, when she was awake, she was willing to talk to him, willing to eat and laugh. It was a startling transformation, according to him.

Suri couldn't hear it without remembering how it had come about. The memory burned through her, even now. Miya tossed something at her, and she startled, catching it late. It nearly slid through her hands as she held it up to the light, glancing over at herself in the mirror. A satin camisole, rose gold and shining in the low light. She couldn't remember when she'd bought it, but she suspected Miya had roped her into the decision.

"This, too," the girl added, handing her a black leather miniskirt and a matching jacket. Her smile was sharp and warm. "Don't look at me like that. It'll look good on you."

She didn't look away. "This feels like a trap. It's thirty degrees outside."

Aza snapped her gum, but didn't disagree. "Wear it with the jacket and spare yourself. It's better than arguing with her."

It was, and they both knew it. Arguing with Miya was like lighting a fire in a hurricane—maybe you'd keep it burning for a bit, but you'd always end up hurting yourself more than the rain and wind ever could. The girl in question beamed at them both in turn, and Suri reluctantly went to wash her face and change into the clothes.

The party was hosted on the far side of town, either by a senior or an alumnus. She suspected there would be people like her there, too—dragged there by friends, utterly unfamiliar with the host, disinterested in the societal institution of New Year's Eve but unwilling to spend the night on their couches alone.

Miya knocked at the door, and it opened moments later, revealing neon noise she could feel in her bones and the smell of sugar and alcohol. Suri's stomach turned, but she followed them inside reluctantly. Aza leaned in close and whispered, "Do you want a drink?"

She nodded, scanning the crowd for anybody she recognized. In the dim light, the faces were shadowed, slipping away from her like skin under oil. Her gaze caught, knotted on a group at the far wall, near the hallway. She could feel her mouth drop open, a visceral response. "Fuck—*you two planned this, didn't you?*"

"You never asked," Miya pointed out smugly, her voice nearly drowned out by the music. "If you'd asked where the boys had gone, *maybe* I would've told you."

"I'm leaving," she said, ignoring another shove from the crowd, using it as momentum and leaning back toward the door. Terror and sharp, avoidant displeasure felt hot in her veins. "I'm going home."

"Well," Aza said under her breath, audible only because she was so close. "That answers the question of whether you two are fighting."

Suri turned her cold gaze onto her, and the other girl shifted uncomfortably under it. "How did you even know? I never told you and he—" she waved a hand, dismissive and unwilling to talk about him, even in vague terms. "He wasn't around."

"Exactly," Miya cut in, leaning against the doorjamb. A couple came in, arms slung over one another, and walked around her. She barely registered their presence. "You two are best friends, attached at the hip. I've never seen you without one another for more than a couple of hours, classes barred. And suddenly, he's nowhere to be seen? *Sick?* Like disease could pull one over his eyes. The apartment doesn't even smell like incense smoke anymore, so I know he hasn't been with you."

Attached at the hip. The sentiment sent a low, warm throb through her before she realized the only reason they ever spent so much time around one another was because the *sankhili* wouldn't let him leave. In the early days, it had hurt if they were in separate rooms. The notion of them being *friends* was a casual lie of his to explain his presence. There was nothing maudlin about it—their relationship had always been something of reason, of needs before desires. *Either he stays with me, or we move back into the shop, so I guess I'll put up with him.*

"We're not fighting," she said reflexively.

Aza and Miya traded amused glances. "Really," the latter said. "Well then, why don't you go over there and say hi?"

She gave them the coldest, sharpest glare she could manage, but they didn't budge under the weight of it. She'd learned it from them, after all. "We're not fighting, it's just that—I don't want to talk about this right now. How did you even get him to come?"

Parties didn't seem like his scene, at least not these kinds of parties. The chaos of it seemed like something he might enjoy, but not the crude glamor, the artifice and shine. He was more likely to observe it from a rooftop a few blocks away, mocking it in that mild, faintly warm tone of his while she tuned his words out.

Rotted with desire. She felt the echo of it, again and again. How she wished she could let go of this love, scrape it off her heart with knives and acid.

Aza shrugged. "Honestly, I didn't even know if Ellis and Dai *could* convince him. Miya said it was above their pay grade. But they must've broken through, since he's here, and you're losing your shit. Careful, fish tank."

Suri glanced to the side, and removed her elbow from where it was leaned against the side of the tank, slowly applying pressure and pushing outwards. "Fine. Fine. You got us both here. So what? What's the big plan? Were you just going to shove us in an empty bedroom and lock it until we made up? He'd just climb out the window."

"Probably," Miya agreed, but her indomitable smile was beginning to fade. "Listen, we didn't think this through that much—"

"Do you ever?"

"And," she continued, frowning at her, "I don't really know what's going down between you two, so... Sorry for meddling. If you want to go home, you can. We won't stop you."

Aza held out a plastic cup and she grudgingly took it, making a face at the flavor. They both looked faintly apologetic, a novelty.

"I don't want to go home," she said firmly, and realized it was true. Their expressions brightened slightly, as if they were afraid to be obvious about it. "*But.* I don't want to talk to him, not now. And I'm still angry with all of you."

"Fair," Aza conceded. "I'll go over and talk to Dai—so we can try and keep you apart. Did—" she hesitated, then shook her head and continued, "Did he hurt you? Should we kick his ass?"

She tried to imagine it—Aza stepping on his chest and arms with spiked boots, Miya taking a stiletto to his insides—but she couldn't, not quite. There was nothing soft in him for them to hit. Her lips quirked in a small smile. "He didn't hurt me. We just..." she swallowed a laugh, glancing up toward the shadowed ceiling. "Had a disagreement. He might leave early." She tacked on the last part accidentally, the words slipping out as if they had a mind of her own. She heard Miya inhale sharply, but didn't meet her gaze.

"Does he have a reason?" she demanded, righteous fury sharpening her voice.

Suri couldn't bear everything inside her. She tipped the contents of the cup into her mouth and let it burn all the way down. "He has a lot of reasons. So many." She held out her cup, dragging her hand through her hair with the other hand. "I'm going to go get more. I'm sure you two have more important things to do than stick around and babysit me."

Distantly, she registered Aza's protests and then Miya's quiet suggestion that they leave her alone for a bit. *Yeah,* she thought, tipsy and bitter and too self-pitying to be worth much. *Leave me alone.*

The arch at the far side of the room led out into a hallway and the kitchen. By the time she reached it, fortunately, Aza had pulled Dai aside, and so the boys had found somewhere else to go.

Thankfully, the kitchen was empty enough that she could navigate it without too much trouble. A granite island stood in the center—*definitely an alumnus,* she thought vaguely—covered in empty cups, plastic straws, and liquor bottles. She made it to the other side with little issue, refilling her cup with a tall glass bottle with a colorful logo marking the neck. A little bit sloshed out, dousing her wrist and falling to the floor. She cut it with a half-empty bottle of lemon-lime soda.

Suri brought the cup to her mouth and the mixture seared, sweet and heady. After the novelty of the first drink and the second wore off, she pulled out her phone. She hadn't been lying when she'd spoken to Aza and Miya—they'd come to have fun, and she felt uncomfortable forcing them to keep an eye on her and her pity party.

And honestly, she'd rather plunge her head down a toilet bowl than go find Ellis and Dai. They would've stayed with him—gods help everyone if they hadn't—and she didn't want to see his expression once he realized how many drinks she'd had.

She got another drink and ducked out of the kitchen, threading through the crowd dispassionately until she made it to the balcony.

The sun had disappeared beneath the horizon, the sky clear and black and empty save for a few stars. *The fruits of light pollution,* she thought, leaning over the rail and tilting her cup from side to side so the liquid inside caught the faint moonlight.

She knew her friends had good intentions—they always did. They went out looking for Annabel because they had good intentions; they went to every single one of Cherry Headache's gigs because they had good intentions. Suri liked that about them, and about her grandmother, too—sometimes, she liked to fancy herself a kind person. But kindness didn't really work the same way languages did, the same way ink spread through water. The altruism could rub off, start to sand down her edges. But she had always had those jagged, barbed points inside, broken glass waiting patiently to turn outward and draw blood.

She nursed her drink and let the night air wash through her. It was cool and sweet on her skin, and though the memories it drew stung—another winter moment, sunlight casting shadows on them both—she welcomed the pain along with the cold.

She tipped her cup back only to be met with a thin drop. Her phone told her in bright, blinking script that it was thirty minutes to midnight. There were a few messages from Aza and Ellis shining up at her, asking where she'd gone.

She tossed the cup into a nearby waste bin and ducked back into the apartment, startled at how quickly the heavy smell of alcohol, perfume, and body odor assaulted her.

Miya and Ellis were speaking in hushed tones beside the edge of the couch. When they noticed her approaching, they flinched, silencing for a moment before beginning to speak again. It wasn't particularly subtle, but she couldn't really fault them for it.

"Sorry for disappearing," she said, slinging an arm over Miya's shoulder. She didn't really feel all that apologetic, but the effort was what counted. "Did I miss anything?"

Ellis exchanged a glance with Miya, and she felt a faint stab of annoyance. Maybe she deserved it, but she was tired of them coddling her. She wondered if he had it any better. Probably. She couldn't fathom him allowing someone to baby him without taking a few limbs off in the process.

Finally, he said, "Nothing much. Dai's been complaining since we got here. At least we can leave soon. It's nearly twelve, right?"

"Yep," she said, popping the p. The television was already on, playing a livestream of one of those New Year's Eve programs where people waited for the clocks to chime midnight with breathless, euphoric glee, even as the snow blanketed the ground and choked the warmth from their skin. She shot the screen a cursory glance, watched a few seconds of some flamboyant performance before turning back. "They don't have any champagne here."

"It's a travesty," Miya agreed, but she was uncharacteristically jumpy. Her mouth was quirked downward in an odd facsimile of her usual smile. Still a little self-conscious about the slip earlier, if Suri had to guess. "Are you having a good time?"

Define good time, she thought. She was having the time she'd expected to have—liquor, winter air, peaceful brooding space. Surprisingly, nothing had extraordinarily fucked up yet, which probably meant she was having an amazing time, even though her heart still felt like someone had run it through a paper shredder. "It's not bad." She hesitated, then figured she owed them an attempt at normal human emotion. "It's nice, getting out of the apartment. I'm having fun."

Miya and Ellis exchanged another glance, tinged with relief and excitement. And then, right on time, everything fell apart.

"What the *fuck?*" someone shouted. They traced the sound back to a boy, doubled over in pain. His face was shunted to the side, one hand pressed to it with excruciating force. A few feet away, hands still curled into careful fists, stood Kiran. Dai lingered by his shoulder, but he was leaning back a little, subconsciously. Suri didn't blame him—she'd never seen Kiran this angry, and it startled her a little. If she wasn't so sure of his control, she might've feared him burning the entire building down.

A crowd had built around them as the clumps of people littering the nook scattered outward, unwilling to be caught in the crossfire. Now, they stood on the edges, close enough that they could keep updated but far enough away that they were safe. *Joke's on them,* she thought bitterly. If he really cared enough, it didn't matter how far out of his line of vision they stood. But, judging from the hard, empty expression on his face, he didn't care enough.

"What the *fuck?*" the boy repeated, words muffled by his own fingers. In her mind's eye, Suri saw it all play out—a slap across the face or a punch to his left cheek, quick as venom. She'd seen him mimic the motions enough times she could've drawn it in her sleep. *"What is wrong with you?"*

Kiran didn't speak—his mouth twitched a little to the side, in something that could've been a smile, if it calmed enough for the iron muzzle to be removed.

Ellis and Miya were at her shoulders, looking out over the mess. The party hadn't even slowed—this was one pocket of hatred in a world of chaos that wouldn't, couldn't stop for them. On the television screen, the countdown to midnight continued.

"Why did he do it?" Ellis murmured to Miya. She whispered something back, but the buzzing in Suri's ears drowned it out, emptying the world of everything else. *Why did he do it?*

Aza weaved through the throng of people beginning to build up, breaking through the crowd to stand beside her brother. She pulled him down by the shoulder, whispering furiously in his ear. He shrugged helplessly, muttering back. Distantly, she registered the host beginning to notice, registered some of the guests helping the bruised boy up from where he laid, sprawled across the sticky linoleum, throwing a nasty glare back at Kiran. It was a useless gesture—the glare hit stone and bounced right off.

Until that moment, his gaze had been on the boy, a simple, empty wrath that had no need for other distractions. His knuckles were bruised and flushed beside him. He glanced up and caught her gaze.

The line of his mouth twisted sharply, but he said nothing. Suri heaved a breath and steadied herself, even though she didn't need to—whatever faint inebriation she'd felt earlier was entirely gone.

She stepped forward, ignoring the way it wrenched her away from Miya and Ellis's soft grasp of her shoulders, ignoring the smears of blood and alcohol and soda on the floor. She walked up to Kiran, twisted her fingers into the collar of his jacket, and dragged him down the dark hallway without another word.

People scattered, flattening themselves to the walls and clearing an aisle for them to walk. She suspected this was because of Kiran, but she refused to turn around and meet his gaze, so she couldn't be sure. Suri kicked open the doors—mostly occupied bedrooms—until she found an empty bathroom and shoved him in, locking the door behind her.

Leaning back against the carved wood, she could still feel the music in her bones, the distant drone of the television. But her blood sang with a melody entirely different, jagged and brighter than moonlight, than sunlight. It nearly felt like anger.

Her phone buzzed—Dai. *Andrew's pretty pissed. Where are you guys?*

Bathroom, she texted. *Buy us some time while I fix him up.*

K, he replied, with two frowny faces and a fist emoji. It was a nice gesture, but the warmth of it passed straight through her and came out colder on the other side. She slipped her phone back into her pocket and glanced up.

He had heaved himself up so that he sat on the edge of the fake marble sink, legs brushing the floor. His gaze wasn't on her—he was tilting his outstretched hands from side to side, examining the drying, deep red blood on his knuckles with a dispassionate, inured clarity. It was difficult to reconcile this version of him with the boy she'd seen staring back at her a few moments ago, true, real hatred in his bones, bright enough to burn.

She folded her arms, discomfited and annoyed by it. Artifice on artifice, but she couldn't yet tell what was lie and what was truth. Finally, she said, "Are you hurt?"

He lifted his gaze to meet hers, eyes dark as amber. In the orange light, they looked bloodred. "That's not the question you want to ask. Not really."

Suri gritted her teeth. The boy hadn't had time to get a hit on him, and she doubted he would've even if he'd tried. *Are you hurt?* Only if they counted injuries that went deeper than blood and bone. "Fine, I'll bite. Why did you hit him?

His lips spread in a cold, cruel smile, but even that was practiced, fake. Paint slathered onto the mouth of a mannequin, glistening and smooth to the touch. "Because I wanted to."

Anger flared up in her chest, all that broken glass pressing against the boundaries of her ribs. "Do not fuck with me right now. You didn't knock his teeth out for fun."

"I didn't," he said softly, sliding off the edge of the counter and leaning back against the marbled stone. He didn't look like a god, but he looked like he could've been one, all vengeance and warmth, obsidian wrapped in veins of gold. The smile sharpened, and he tilted his head. "I didn't knock his teeth out. I might've broken his nose. What if it was for fun? What would you do then?"

She knew he was goading her into disgust and fury, trying to cut off the conversation before it became anything worth worrying about. She knew he was trying to escape.

"I would drag you out there again so you could apologize to him—" she began, keeping her voice as indifferent as she could.

"Like a nanny," he cut in, tipping forward in a fluid sort of movement. He smelled like sugar and smoke, but not the perfumed incense smoke she was so used to. Like exhaust, cigarette smoke.

"If you need to be babied, then I'll fucking baby you," she snapped, glaring at him. *There goes the attempt at neutrality.* "But I don't need to. Because you didn't do it for fun, and I know it. I know you."

Do I? It was a gamble, a hasty, imperfect dance, but that was all they had ever had.

He was silent a moment, and then he said, wry, "So you do. You know me. And why do you think I did it?"

Suri pushed off from the door. It really was an incredibly cramped room—one step forward would place them dangerously close to each other.

Then again, just standing here was already dangerously close. *I want to wash myself clean of this love.* She wanted to burn it away, blow away the ashes so that the silver flakes rested at the corners of the world, one for every single star.

"I think," she said slowly, "I think he did something that pissed you off, so you acted without thinking. But you don't regret it." Amber eyes, black heart. She would see the flame of him in her sleep. "You never regret anything."

Slender red rivulets traced the skin to his fingertips. When he brought a hand up, to press the laughter from his lips, blood flaked off, falling through the air like petals.

The attempt at keeping himself silent was unsuccessful, the sound hard and sharp and a little sweet, a little lilting. It was everything she loved about him dipped in iron and set to cool.

"Half marks," he managed, carding one hand through his hair and leaving those thin, red flakes behind. "I regret many things. I don't regret this, though, so I suppose I must give you credit for that."

She curled her hands into fists so they wouldn't dart out to catch the flakes. "Why did you hit him?"

"I punched him in the face because I couldn't remove his accessory organs without getting you five in trouble," he said calmly.

"You had a reason," she bit out, attempting to school her features into a semblance of tranquility. It failed miserably—she could feel the sharp tilt of her eyes, the twist of her mouth. "Tell me what he did that made you hit him."

He held her gaze, stone against stone, and didn't look away. "No."

"And you don't care if everyone blames you for no reason?" Her anger was aimless and malicious and it echoed and burned through her. "You don't give a shit if they all think you hit him for fun?"

"No," he said again, shuttering his eyes and leaning back against the counter. "I really don't. I don't *give a shit.* Does that surprise you?"

"Tell me why you did it."

"I have anger management issues, and he was the closest thing with a heartbeat I could find," he replied, leaning in so close his nose brushed hers. "I hit him because I wanted to see him fall. I—"

"Kiran."

The sound of his name unsteadied them both a little; he was so close that she could see the tremor run through him, too quick to track. She drew back a little, just enough to hold his gaze. But his eyes were empty.

"I won't repeat those words," he whispered. "You can't make me."

Suri blinked, bemused. "What did he say?"

His eyes flicked up, hard but resigned. "Did you recognize him?"

"Vaguely," she admitted. They'd had a few classes together senior year. She remembered him being one of those class-clown types, the kind who irritated others far more frequently than they amused them. "Why?" His mouth was set in a thin line, and she exhaled, not bothering to hide her exasperation. "If you don't tell me, I'll ask Dai. Hell, I'll go find Andrew."

"I'd advise against it," he said, in a weak facsimile of his flippant, mild mien. He sighed, rubbing at his eyes. "He said something very—crude. About… you. He—" he cut off, nostrils flaring. She was reminded, vaguely, of when he'd tried to control all those candles. Restraint on the edge of chaos. When he opened his eyes, they were clear and gold. "I can't do it. I can't say it. I don't think Dai will say it either, he has a low tolerance for those kinds of comments. You'll just have to take our word for it."

She glared at him. "I don't want you fighting my battles for me."

"I would've stood aside if you wanted a chance," he said, a smile tugging at the corner of his mouth. "If you want, we can go find him now. I'm sure I can buy you a few minutes of peace and quiet with him. I'll throw in the clean-up for free."

Suri wanted to smile back at him. She wanted to make this into a joke, wanted to play this off as something insignificant, and wash off Kiran's hands and walk out and join the party again. She wanted to let go of whatever was between them, distorted with passion and rotted with desire, wanted to cure them both of this disease. She wanted it so badly, but she knew that even now, what she wanted most was to believe the lie of it.

"Why did you do it?" she asked, even though she already knew. Even though she'd always known.

"Because," he said, the end of the word lilting up as if in a question. His features were faintly strained with the weight of the words he couldn't say—she saw them, gentle dips carved into his expression. His lips twisted uselessly. "Because."

I won't stay. Suri took his hands in hers, and ran the edges of her nails against his knuckles and watched the blood flake away. The skin underneath was bruised gold, paler than his bark-brown complexion. She rubbed the pads of her thumbs against the backs of his hands, and he shivered. "Because what?"

His gaze was heavy. "Don't look at me like that."

"Like what?"

"Like—" he broke off, worrying his bottom lip. "Like you care about me."

Suri dropped his hands, dried blood under her fingernails. In the low light, the red yarn on her wrist looked dark as dawn. "I look at you like I care about you because I *do.*"

"Yes," he said, quiet and hard, resting his hands lightly on her shoulders. It felt like an act of tenderness they weren't allowed, and despite everything, she leaned into the touch. "I know. But you shouldn't."

Her eyes slitted. "Kiran—"

"You know," he interrupted, mouth curved in a too-sharp imitation of a smile, "One day, you're going to look back on all of this and it'll be like a bad dream. Like a nightmare."

"I won't forget you." Hands curved over the back of her jacket, thumbs on her collarbones. "Because you're going to come back."

His expression shuttered. "Are we still discussing this?"

"We are," she said. Her skin burned where he was touching it, but anger had already set her aflame everywhere else. *Selfish,* whispered a small voice in the back of her head, but she was past caring. "The symbol? A dead end. And if whoever bound us was so dead set on ruining your life, wouldn't they have returned by now?"

Kiran gave a choked sort of laugh. "That doesn't mean they're gone forever, Suri. It's too much of a risk."

She reached out, grasping his face in her hands and turning it toward her. It was not a soft kind of touch, and still she marveled at the fact that she was allowed it. His skin was feverish under her hands.

"If you give me one good reason," she said, so calmly it felt as though her voice belonged to someone else, "If you give me one good reason, I won't ask again. I promise."

He didn't meet her gaze. "Everyone I have ever stayed with has suffered for it. And I don't want that for you, and I don't want that for your friends. It is better that they all think I left early, so that you can all move on and live better lives."

Suri exhaled, an uneven sound that betrayed everything she'd meant to keep hidden. "Okay. Can I ask you something, though?"

"What?"

"How long has it been since you let someone stay beside you?" he stiffened under her hands, but she held him steady.

"You let me into your heart. Is it too much to ask to be allowed to stay there?"

He didn't answer, and she let out a breath. *I guess that's that.* The tension melted from his frame, hollowing him. "I don't know. You're terrifying and wonderful and I'm not selfish enough to want you so much that I would doom you for it."

"But *I* am," she said, and in that moment, she felt like a wildfire. Her grasp on his face was bruising; she pulled him toward her, knocked their foreheads together until they were close enough that she could see the clear shine of his eyes, smell sugar and smoke.

And when she spoke, it was little more than a whisper in a world that still spun with the distant sound of music and chaos, but it carried, and she knew he heard every word. "We make our own happy endings; I don't care if catastrophe lives in your shadow. Even if you set this world on fire, I will build you a new one out of the ashes. From death to life, Kiran."

"Suri," he said, just her name, only her name. The way he always had, dark soil and wood ash, but entirely different. As if he was saying it for the first time, holding it in hands seared by a prayer flame and born anew. "You're speaking of miracles."

"Rebirth was made for miracles," she said. "Gods were made for miracles, and humans are made of them. What's one more?"

Everything, she knew. But she felt like perhaps this love was a miracle worth dooming herself for.

"'What's one more?'" he repeated, soft and musing. In the distance, a countdown built. He bit his lip. "You'll regret this before long."

"Maybe," she murmured before leaning in. "But I don't think so."

It wasn't like their first kiss, faint and brief in a world she'd thought she'd left behind. This was harder, without kindness or softness. It was sour wine and bitten lips, and the desperate, futile attempt to leave behind an imprint on the heart of another, knotting threadbare strings so they would never unravel.

They pulled apart and he rested his forehead against hers, breathless. The countdown finished and exploded into noise. *Five, four, three, two, one!* There was a certain irony to this, she knew. They were celebrating the new year in a stranger's bathroom, dried blood on his knuckles and under her fingernails. But she couldn't bring herself to care.

"Happy New Year," she whispered, pressing a kiss to his cheek. She could feel him smile against her, and it felt like a miracle all on its own, the chance to have this and hold this and not have it disappear in her hands.

He kissed the crown of her forehead, and tucked her hair behind her ears. "Happy New Year."

Everyone agreed it was the worst New Year's Eve celebration ever—on account of Andrew's broken nose and subsequent tirades directed at Dai, and at Aza just because she had stood too close. After he'd exhausted himself, face swelling to truly astounding proportions, the time after the countdown had gone relatively smoothly, until someone had spilled their drink on the television, and it had sparked and caught fire. Then the host had kicked them all out and put out the flames with a sand pail.

Suri and Kiran listened to the others review the night's laundry list of faults the next day—sprawled across the floor, as they always were—and agreed, mindlessly, that it had been a horrible night, even though they'd left long before the television had caught fire. She had always wondered how exactly he'd managed to return to the balcony without wings, and had been pleasantly surprised to find out he was willing to show her the process.

In the glow of early afternoon, winter sunlight streaming through the open glass doors, it felt like the past few days had been a strange, elaborate nightmare. She couldn't remember what it felt like for the apartment to be so empty, hollow through to its bones.

That morning, after Kiran had fallen asleep—another kind of miracle, but one she was slowly beginning to acclimate herself to—she'd texted Aza and Miya, the way she'd promised, and explained everything. At least, she'd explained it to the extent she could, stopping short of magic and catastrophe. Miya, hooked on her every word, tired of replying in full sentences around fifteen minutes in, and began to speak exclusively in shocked emoji faces. Aza spoke only once, at the very end. *Ask him if he's willing to mess up Andrew's face again. It'll be more fun if there are two of us.*

Suri hadn't dignified that with a response, but Miya had sent a string of fist emojis.

"Let's have a redo," Dai said abruptly. He was leaned against the side of the armchair, his rough draft of the graphic novel open on his thighs. From where she laid curled up against the side of the couch, Suri could make out eraser marks and the outline of several planets.

"Of what?" Kiran said, ducking back into the living room. He took a seat beside her, handing her a mug of coffee before sipping from his tea. She moved her left hand a few centimeters to the side, so it just barely brushed his. A smile flickered over his face and disappeared. How greedy she was for these small indulgences.

Miya's gaze tracked their hands, and she arched a dark eyebrow, pulling her knees toward her and wrapping her arms around the fleecy pajamas. "New Year's, I'm guessing." At Dai's nod, she added, "I think it's a good idea. We could have it here, if you two are cool with it."

They'd all agreed it wasn't a half-bad idea, coming to a consensus on everything but the champagne itself, at which point Kiran called her grandmother on her cell phone when she wasn't paying attention and had her scold them all. In the end, she relented to bringing it for them, since she had some lying around and 'no good use for it'. Suri knew that was just grandmother speak for 'I'm going to go out and buy some, but if you see the price tag, ignore it or face the full force of my wrath'. But she'd had enough wrath to last her through the winter, so she was willing to submit to her grandmother's kindness. If she was going to preach to Kiran about letting others care for him, she might as well follow her own advice.

When the sun set early that night, darkness spilling out over the sky and swallowing all the stars, they were all back again, laughing and joyful and alive in a way that carved itself into her bones. This was the kind of memory that never left, the kind that pushed nightmares back into shadows, inch by excruciating inch, until all that remained was light.

There was still darkness now—she knew there always would be, knew the glow of peace was a far-off specter rather than a reality she could believe in. But the notion of it was overwhelming, sweeter than the night-crisp air and the saccharine sharpness of the champagne. It felt like every single star she couldn't see in the sky above, every single time she'd woken from a nightmare to see the sun beginning to rise against a bloodred sky.

The glass doors slid open, the shrill sound cutting through the soft noise of the traffic. Distantly, she could hear canned applause on the television, Ellis falling to the floor on a Twister mat, the sharp crack of laughter. Joy, as an adjective.

"Aren't you cold out here?" Kiran asked, handing her a plastic flute of champagne.

Suri took it, tilting it so the moonlight shone through the clear, golden liquid. She allowed herself a small sip before answering. "Not really. And anyway, you're here now, so it's not an issue."

His eyes crinkled, betraying that small bit of embarrassment she knew he always tried to hide. He emptied the champagne flute in one swallow; it would have no lasting effect on him. This was just his way of blending in, but there were worse masks to wear.

She tilted her head back and inhaled deeply. Here, the air always smelled of soil and warmth, even as the stale smell of the city weighed down on them. Tonight, it smelled sweet, from the sugar of the champagne and the open jasmine buds, cut through with the sharp, earthy smell of Kiran's tulasi plant.

She leaned against the wrought-iron rail, and he stood with her, and everything felt right. There were eternities in this moment, and every single one held a kind of impossible, divine magic. Time was something that bent and broke around them, allowing a taste of immortality.

After she'd finished the glass, she played with the stem, transferring it from hand to hand. When she glanced up at him, his gaze was resting carefully on the horizon, on the crest of the hills where the moon met the earth. There was a sadness in his honey-sweet eyes, but a kind of hope, too.

"You never told me how the story ended," she said abruptly, nudging him lightly. She'd only just remembered—he'd left off a couple weeks ago, before everything in their lives had gone downhill with such speed and intensity. The last time, the festival of the fire god had ended, and after speaking briefly, the princess and the priest had gone their separate ways early into the night. She still suspected he'd amended that part, since he'd refused to meet her eyes the entire way through.

Kiran looked at her askance. "I suppose I didn't. Do you still want to know?"

Did she? She'd always reached out to stories to conjure a world of magic she didn't think she was allowed, a kind of fantastical wonder she figured she would never find in real life. Now, those same wonders were close enough to touch. She reached up a hand and traced her finger across the arc of his cheekbone and considered it.

"Yes," she answered decisively, dropping her hand from his face. Even if these tales wouldn't buoy her the way she had once begged them to, she wanted to know how this one ended.

Kiran leaned back, bracing himself against the rail. He spoke without looking at her, eyes fixed on the darkness that laid beyond the moon. "It ends like all those stories end. The princess and the prince realized they were better than the worlds they came from, and put aside their differences. They fell in love, they united their kingdoms, and they lived happily ever after. And everyone in the lands knew prosperity for eons to come."

"What happened to you?" she asked, the words slipping out before she could catch them. Suri had had her suspicions, of course, but she'd never revealed them. It felt a little sacrilegious, to incorrectly guess at someone's entire past.

But he didn't glare at her, or even smoothly correct the mistake. He did something far stranger, and even after her memory of this conversation faded and all that remained was the peaceful silence and the smell of flowers and earth, she would remember this. Kiran tore his gaze away from the sky and glanced down at her, and after a few moments, he smiled. And it was a wound, so it bled. Even when the smile faded, she could see the shape of it curving his lips, could see how fate had taken a knife to his skin and slashed it open.

It was the first time he ever referred to that boy in the story as himself, and in all the days that passed after, he never repeated the mistake. But then, just then, with unseen bandages hanging from his lips and a champagne flute tucked between his fingers, he forgot to fear fear. "I did what I was born to do. I died."

Here she caught her breath, and he laughed a little, steadying her. Moments after the admission, he seemed to forget he'd made it—as if he'd never mentioned himself at all. It was a careful kind of secret, held between the shadow of knowledge and the reality of it, and Suri tucked it between her ribs for safekeeping.

"It's an old story," he said, shaking his head ruefully. "I thought you would like it in spite of that, though."

"I did," she said, and found it true. "It's just that—"

The glass doors slid open; Dai poked his head out. "It's almost midnight! We're going to pretend to mimic the countdown again."

"We'll be right in," she called, and he grinned, the doors slamming shut again. Kiran was watching her with a faint, warm amusement. "What is it?"

"We already had our New Year's celebration," he said mildly, and her cheeks burned with the memory of it. "Do you want to repeat it?"

Her face heated. In her periphery, she noticed the tulasi plant and slipped away from him, kneeling beside it to cut away two leaves. She handed one to him and took one for herself without looking up. Finally, he said, "Is this a gift?"

Suri glanced up at him. "New Year's wishes. Like resolutions, except these will actually work. If you light them on fire, we each get one shot. Or—I forgot gods can't wish. I'll wish for you."

He passed a hand over the back of his neck in chagrin. "I don't know actually. Whether gods can wish. Technically, they shouldn't be able to, but—I've never tried, myself."

She leveled a glare at him, and he ducked his head, chastised. Finally, she sighed. "Okay, so we both get one wish. Are we keeping it secret?"

Kiran tilted his head, and lifted his shoulders in a shrug. "Your choice."

"Secret, then," she said, faintly relieved. She held up her leaf, and he dutifully set the serrated tip ablaze before doing the same to his own. They gripped the stems of the leaves with both hands, like votive candles. "On three. One, two—"

The amazing thing about wishes was that anybody could make one. There was a simple balance there, an undeniable equality in the worth of all wishes and all souls. The color of one's skin and the color of one's heart were meaningless—what mattered was the wish itself, the way it carved out a hollow of its own in the vast desert where miracles were born.

And there was always the chance that a god might not grant it in that moment—it might pass out of their hands if the quota was done for the day, or if they found it useless and unimportant. But the next day, there would be another chance.

Impossibility was a limitation circumscribed around a small chunk of an endless, beautiful world. It was a human word, through and through—there was nothing truly impossible in a world built from the ashes of old miracles into the bones of new ones.

Even tragedies could learn happy endings, given enough light and enough love.

Three.

They closed their eyes and blew out the flames. And, from the smoke of the burning leaves, two new wishes were born and twisted into life.

EPILOGUE

Viro was in a good mood, which really wasn't that strange. It didn't take a lot to put him in a good mood—chocolate, sunshine, videos of small animals dancing to old pop songs. He considered himself agreeable; Tarak called him mercurial. He'd looked it up on the Internet once, drawn more by the warm knowledge that Tarak had his own word for him rather than curiosity. *Prone to sudden or unpredictable changes of mood or mind.* He decided to take it as a compliment.

This time, though, he had a reason. It was the first day of classes for the spring semester, and he was *ready.* He'd packed his laptop and his notebooks and his color-coded pencil pouch, and after he was nearly finished, he wound his lucky charm around the zipper. Tarak had bought it for him in the seventh grade, during a field trip to some amusement park. It wasn't a particularly fuzzy memory—he vaguely recalled getting nauseous on a rollercoaster made for third-graders and throwing up in the bushes. But the charm—three golden stars hanging from thin metal chains to a hook—had been the definite high point of the trip. He'd gotten him a shining yellow one of the sun, and he knew the other boy still used it as a keychain.

Really, the only thing missing from the first day of classes was Tarak himself. Viro was loitering beside the university gates waiting for him—usually, they walked to school together, but when he'd gone over this morning, his mother had told him Tarak was sleeping off a late night. He wouldn't be late, of course. He didn't think Tarak was capable of being anything but perfectly on time. But *Viro* was half an hour early and his latte was cooling in his hands even as he sipped from it.

He glanced longingly toward the nearest lecture hall. But no—he would be strong. Tarak would show up, and then they'd walk in together, and he could explain why he'd stayed up the previous night, and everything would be fine. Classes would begin, and then he would be in his element.

It was just this in-between area that felt a little awkward, he knew. Lingering between the different circles of comfort in his life, dancing in this gray, muddled cold.

I'm happy, he told himself firmly. *I'm happy, and everything's fine.*

Viro glanced up and down the street. He was starting to get a little anxious, just first-day jitters—nothing a walk wouldn't take care of. It wasn't as if Tarak would show up in the next three minutes. He pulled his headphones on and turned up the volume, balancing his latte in the crook of his elbow while he chose a song.

The walk calmed his nerves—surprisingly, the cold latte helped a little, too. By the time he rounded the curve of the intersection, the glitter of the gates in the distance, he felt a little closer to his initial excitement. He tossed the empty latte cup in a nearby bin and continued up the street.

Viro always listened to his music near maximum volume. It was a common side effect of spending the majority of his adolescence listening to music as loud as it could go—his ears had given up on anything remotely near low volume. A nice, quiet song was played at half volume. If he wanted to feel *anything,* he had it at max.

Right now, he wanted to feel everything.

He could hear the music in his bones, and it washed the remnants of his anxiety away. But it also made him vulnerable in a way he had never really thought to worry about. It wasn't that he was particularly gullible—though he had a tendency toward it, at times. It was more that the possibility of being kidnapped had never truly seemed like something worth considering. Kidnappings were something made for news broadcasts, for high-stakes thrillers and fiction.

The first thing he registered was the sickly-sweet smell; the second was the wet cloth. The third—that was the blackness, the sheer emptiness that came with loss of sensation.

That was what he remembered most, after everything happened. That simple, cutting lack of feeling. The knowledge that what he had once known had been ripped from him with vicious, uncaring fingers, stolen. In the blink of an eye, everything familiar disappeared.

The door on the van—entirely white, painted in broad, black strokes with some old sigil no one who noticed it recognized—slammed shut and drove off, leaving no sign they had stopped in the first place. But, on the asphalt beside the iron gates, there laid a severed metal charm, painted gold and silver. From a ring, two stars hung.

GLOSSARY

Athrian

angadi: central markets

arrack: distilled alcohol drink made from fermented sap of coconut flowers or sugarcane

atha: older sister

kagha: large black bird of prey

kantal: gloriosa superba / flame lily

kita: gemstone naturally found in Niravu mountains, bluish-purple and clear mineral

magizham: mimusops elengi / bullet wood

nakshi: war dog — from "nak" (war) and "shi" (dog)

olai chuvadi: dried palm leaves used to document information

sirai maravuri: wood fiber cloth

thyva: blessed/divine — from old Enesmati "thyva" (heaven, home of the gods)

thyvaayan: prophet, "voice of the gods" — from "thyva" (blessed) and "aayan" (voice)

unthi: vase traditionally used to clean idols in religious services

uttriyasi: soulmates, "eternal love" — from "uttri" (forever) and "asi" (love)

yavana: westerner, refers to Europeans

Najan

anda: grandmother, affectionate term for old lady

hehyava: reaper, "daughter of the blood spring — from "hehya" (blood spring) and "ava" (girl)

muru: granddaughter

St. Idhrishti: patron saint, prince of Naja who fell in love with a star and died tragically

Enesmati

Ashri: goddess of the heavens; sun and sky

Kazha: mother goddess, goddess of the earth, love, and family

Avya: god of fire

Makai: goddess of the sea and water

Nila: goddess of the moon

Athrasakhi: god of wrath and war (lesser god of fire)

Dhaasan: god of death and rebirth, servant of Asakhi

Dhaasthur: underworld, land of Asakhi

-kanth: refers to the festival of a god, most commonly the festival of their birth

Asakhi: death/rebirth — related: River Asakhi, river of souls

ACKNOWLEDGEMENTS

This novel first came to me when I was younger. Back then, it was little more than an idea, a suggestion of the way the story might end more than anything else. I knew I wanted it to be about love and about fate, and how, in truth, they are both antonyms of one another.

But it was only until recently that I realized that, more than anything else, I wanted to write a story about freedom, and how the freedom of human choice is a magic in and of itself, left solely for us.

This novel would have remained merely in my head if not for the support of those around me. Thank you to Tanya Mead for taking on my project and helping me polish my prose. Admittedly, I do have a bit of a comma problem.

Thank you to Alana Abesamis for bringing the story to life in the beautiful cover.

Thanks to A.K. Ramanujan for his translations of Classical Tamil poetry from Sangam Literature.

Thank you so, so much to all of the friends who had to put up with me talking about The Book, complaining about sleep deprivation as a result of writing The Book, and the discussions of numerous near-disasters that ensued while trying to juggle schoolwork, college applications, and the process of publishing The Book. All of you are troopers, and your advice was priceless.

And finally, thank you to my family, for always supporting my passion for writing and for pushing me to challenge myself.

ABOUT THE AUTHOR

Varsha Ravi is a senior at California High School. She was born and raised in Illinois, before moving to North Carolina. She is currently living in the Bay Area, California. *The Heartless Divine* is her first novel.

She can be reached at www.varsharavi.com.

Made in the USA
Lexington, KY
05 December 2019